Praise for Larissa Reinhart's Cherry Tucker Mysteries

STILL LIFE IN BRUNSWICK STEW

"Reinhart's country-fried mystery is as much fun as a ride on the Tilt-a-Whirl at a state fair. Her sleuth wields a paintbrush and unravels clues with equal skill and flair. Readers who like a little small-town charm with their mysteries will enjoy Reinhart's series."
— Denise Swanson,
New York Times Bestselling Author of the Scumble River and Devereaux's Dime Store Mysteries

"Still Life in Brunswick Stew proves beyond doubt that Larissa Reinhart and her delightful amateur sleuth Cherry Tucker will be around to entertain us for many books to come."
— Lois Winston,
Author of the Anastasia Pollack Crafting Mystery series

"Cherry Tucker finds trouble without even looking for it, and plenty of it finds her in Still Life in Brunswick Stew...this mystery keeps you laughing and guessing from the first page to the last. A wholehearted five stars."
— Denise Grover Swank,
New York Times and *USA Today* Bestselling Author

"Reinhart lined up suspects like a pinsetter in a bowling alley, and darned if I could figure out which ones to knock down... Loaded with Southern charm. Can't wait to see what Cherry paints herself into next."
— Donnell Ann Bell,
Bestselling Author of *The Past Came Hunting*

"The hilariously droll Larissa Reinhart cooks up a quirky and entertaining page-turner! This cha   ·   'outhern, surprisingly edgy, and de

Agatha, Anthony   Ryan,
                                                        uthor

D1533968

PORTRAIT OF A DEAD GUY

"*Portrait of a Dead Guy* is an entertaining mystery full of quirky characters and solid plotting...Highly recommended for anyone who likes their mysteries strong and their mint juleps stronger!"
— Jennie Bentley,
New York Times Bestselling Author of *Flipped Out*

"Reinhart is a truly talented author and this book was one of the best cozy mysteries we reviewed this year...We highly recommend this book to all lovers of mystery books. Our Rating: 4.5 Stars."
— *Mystery Tribune*

"The tone of this marvelously cracked book is not unlike Sophie Littlefield's brilliant *A Bad Day for Sorry*, as author Reinhart dishes out shovelfuls of ribald humor and mayhem."
— Betty Webb, *Mystery Scene Magazine*

"*Portrait of a Dead Guy* is pure enjoyment, a laugh out loud mystery with some Southern romance thrown in. Five stars."
— Lynn Farris,
National Mystery Review Examiner at Examiner.com

"Larissa Reinhart's masterfully crafted whodunit, *Portrait of a Dead Guy*, provides high-octane action with quirky, down-home characters and a trouble-magnet heroine who'll steal readers' hearts."
—Debby Giusti,
Author of *The Captain's Mission* and *The Colonel's Daughter*

"A fun, fast-paced read and a rollicking start to her Cherry Tucker Mystery Series. If you like your stories southern-fried with a side of romance, this book's for you!"
— Leslie Tentler,
Author of *Midnight Caller*

STILL LIFE IN BRUNSWICK STEW

The Cherry Tucker Mystery Series
by Larissa Reinhart

STILL LIFE IN BRUNSWICK STEW

A Cherry Tucker Mystery

LARISSA REINHART

HENERY PRESS

STILL LIFE IN BRUNSWICK STEW
A Cherry Tucker Mystery
Part of the Henery Press Mystery Collection

First Edition
Trade paperback edition | May 2013

Henery Press
www.henerypress.com

Copyright © 2012 by Larissa Hoffman
Cover illustration by Jessie Porter
Author photograph by Scott Asano

ISBN-13: 978-1-938383-40-3

Printed in the United States of America

To my sister, Gina, for putting up with me,
and to my sister-in-law, Chrys, for putting up with Crohn's.

ACKNOWLEDGMENTS

I would like to thank the following:

John Peterson for your expertise in poisonous farming substances.

Vicki Locey and Cheryl Crowder for your goat expertise.

Officer John Upole for giving me such great information about the life of a rookie officer in small town Georgia. And to Mayor Jim Sells of Grantville, Georgia for helping me find a police officer willing to listen to my odd questions.

Palmarin Merges, a real-life Cherry Tucker, for sharing your gallery knowledge.

D.P. Lyle, MD, for teaching such a wonderful class about toxins it made me wish to poison people in every story I write (but I won't).

Dan McIntosh for teaching me about insurance fraud.

The Hen House girls for all the laughs and hand holding. Special hugs to authors LynDee Walker and Gretchen Archer who make me giggle every day.

Terri L. Austin for keeping me sane and giving me opportunities to make you snort.

Denise Plumart for being such a supportive critique partner and to Jen Tanner for her wealth of information about everything.

My cheerleaders in Andover, Peachtree City, Highland, Orion, New

Bern, and Dallas, particularly the Funks, Niebrugges, Reinharts, Hoffmans, Walkers, Concepcion-Metzlers, Johnstons, and Wituckis.

Linda, Chris, Gina, and Mom for subjecting yourselves to my early drafts and for your support.

Art Molinares for all your support, willingness to help, and general marketing guruship.

Kendel Flaum, my extraordinary editor, for believing in me and Cherry. Thank you for teaching me how to be a better writer. You blow me away with your genius.

And to Trey and the girls. I cannot do this without you.

ONE

They should've kept the mud pit.

That was my first thought when I heard another brawl had ensued, the second or third of the day by my count. This happens when festival committees get all high-brow and replace four-wheeling with an arts and crafts display. What kind of crazy wants to walk around an old cotton field to shop for macramé pot holders and corn husk dolls? Or even quality art, like my Cherry Tucker still life oil paintings. Or exquisite Raku pottery from my buddy, Eloise Parker.

That's my opinion, anyway. Based on the fact that the Annual Sidewinder Brunswick Stew Cook-Off took place smack dab in the middle of a Georgia summer when you needed activities like mud pits to cool off the locals.

Bad enough the hundred year old argument over the origin of Brunswick Stew breaks out every time you get Virginians and Georgians together. And we all know there is only one town of Brunswick with a giant iron kettle for a landmark. Which would be in Georgia.

Sidewinder's also in Georgia, but a tenth of the size of the Golden Isle of Brunswick. Sidewinder's not even a town. More like a spit in the road farming village that once was a plantation burned down by Sherman. My hometown of Halo is bigger, and we aren't even big enough for a Walmart. Some might say Halo's not big enough for my art studio, but I'm not much on what folks say.

Unless they're customers, of course.

Eloise begged me to participate in this cook-off turned art festival, which is why I'm spending my weekend slumped in a camp chair, drinking tea by the jug, and sweating up a storm. And not selling any paintings. People come to taste stew, eat pulled pork, and watch the rednecks churn up the Georgia clay with their four-by-fours. So when the guy hawking koi ponds in the booth opposite leaned into our tent to report the newest altercation, I jumped at the chance to break my boredom. Actually, my jump was more of a sweat-soaked slide out of my seat.

"Eloise," I asked. "You want to come and see what the fuss is about?"

"And miss the possibility of a single customer? I'm not hauling my butt out of this chair except to get more stew." She stubbed out a cigarette. On the folding table sat her second or third bowl of the thick Brunswick Stew, brimming with shredded meat, tomatoes, butter beans, and corn. "One of my students gave me a bunch of free tickets to his family's booth, and I plan to use them all. My Crohn's isn't bothering me, so I'm eating to make up for the times my stomach doesn't let me."

Although the stew had a lovely cinnamon color, eating it in record-breaking heat held no appeal to me. Particularly the amount Eloise had already consumed. The concoction of veggies and meat once got poor folks through hard times by tossing in whatever you could salvage. I've had it made from chicken, beef, pork, venison, and even rabbit. Some like to add squirrel with their pork. However in college, after enjoying a bowl with a large side of tequila shots at a Savannah bar, I vowed never to touch the stuff again. Does not taste as pleasant the second time around.

Watching Eloise eat made sweat break on my neck. "On a scorcher like today, I would think you'd rather have a Sno-Cone than a hot bowl of stew."

"As a Sidewinder native, it is my duty to eat Brunswick Stew, particularly at our annual cook-off," said Eloise. "I love Brunswick Stew. You should know better. How long have we been friends?"

"Let me see," I pretended to think, not trying to hide my grin. "Seems I beat you in the Forks County Art Competition in third grade..."

"And I stole your drawing and you promptly announced it over the PA, getting me in all kinds of trouble. I still have the handprint on my behind."

"Serves you right, you art thief."

"I loved your drawing," Eloise's eyes grew misty. "I couldn't help it. I'd never seen such a beautiful unicorn."

"It was not a unicorn. I would never draw a unicorn."

"I'm pretty sure there were rainbows, too." Eloise laughed at my horrified look. "You were eight. Anyway, I recognized talent then and now. I'm lucky to have a friend like you."

"Are you kidding? You're the one that got me into the Reconstituting Classicism gallery show. If I can pull off something great, that crowd will pay big bucks. I'm down to my last twenty dollars and change." At that thought, I fished in the pockets of my cutoffs to look for Sno-Cone change, disappointed to find only thirty-five cents and a few gum wrappers.

"No one around here wants a portrait made, not even one of their pet," I moaned. "I had the hunting dog market cornered there for a while. The art well in Forks County has mysteriously run dry ever since I was snubbed by the Bransons after painting the portrait of Dustin. Then Shawna Branson became president of the Forks County Arts Council and suddenly I have paintbrush leprosy."

"How are those classical paintings coming?" Eloise dropped her eyes to her stew bowl. She knew me well enough to avoid conversation about Shawna Branson. "Aren't you supposed to send digital photos of the portfolio soon?"

"Week from Monday," I said. "Plenty of time. I'm doing famous Greek statues as paintings. Except to make it edgier I'm covering the model's body in tiny Greek letters. Head to toe."

Eloise swatted me with her spoon. "You haven't done them yet? Don't make me look bad, Cherry Tucker. The show is organized by my old drawing professor at UGA. He's still ticked I went into pottery. I'm hoping to get back in his good graces and get my own show out of the deal."

I held one hand over my heart, the other palm up in Pledge of Allegiance mode. "I swear I would never do anything to make you look bad, Eloise Parker. You have my word. I'm just having a little trouble convincing my model to pose nude as the *Dying Gaul*."

"Who are you using as a model?"

"Luke Harper."

It took a moment for Eloise to regain control over her laughter. I helped her right her chair when it threatened to tip.

"Luke is the perfect model for a Greek statue," I explained. "Tall, lean, with great muscle definition. Especially those indentations between his waist and hips." I paused a moment in delicious ecstasy, ruminating over Luke's V-cut. "He even has the dark curly hair and the straight nose of a classic Greek. And I don't think he's got a drop of Greek blood in him. Pretty sure Harper's not a Greek name."

"Nor Roman. You just want to paint Luke naked," Eloise cackled. "This doesn't have anything to do with art."

"Of course it does. I have an eye for beauty, that's all."

"You got a thing for beauty, all right. As long as it's got a—"

"You can stop right there, Eloise Parker. No need to get trashy."

"I'm not the one obsessed with painting Luke Harper nude."

"He never lets me paint him, nude or otherwise. I don't get it. What's the big deal?"

"Probably because he's worried the criminals in Forks County will laugh at him after seeing his bare ass in a painting," Eloise lifted her brows. "Hard to arrest somebody when they're laughing at you."

"The criminals of Forks County will never see his bare whatever. The paintings would go straight to a gallery in Athens. No one in these parts would ever see it," I said.

"But they'd hear about it. No way you can stop the biddies from clucking about something like that."

"You're an artist. You're supposed to encourage me." I pointed at her neat rows of Raku ware lining the table in our tent. The traditional Japanese pottery style used lead glazes and a quick firing and cooling process. Eloise favored black pots hand-molded into interesting shapes with a white glaze applied in sparing drips and splatters. Refined elegance. Neither of us was making money, though, unlike the Redneck Golf Club booth next door. Attaching a stick to a beer can is a lot easier than rendering shadow and depth on a bowl of peaches.

"I need this gig," I said. "I'm not selling any paintings at this cook-off, not even my peach still lifes. And you know how tourists love Georgia peach souvenirs."

"Do what you need to get the Greek paintings done." Eloise fixed me with a lethal stare while lighting a cigarette. "You better not let me down or I'll hear about it. I don't need ulcers on top of Crohn's Disease."

I sobered, knowing the pain Crohn's had caused Eloise to suffer over the years. At one point, she had been whittled to skin and bones by the intestinal disease. She was finally looking like her old self. "I'm sorry, hon'. I owe you a debt of gratitude."

"I don't need your gratitude," she said. "I just want the works submitted. That's all I ask. Now go check out what's going on at the cook-off. You can't sit still anyway and it's making me nervy."

"Yes, ma'am," I saluted her, walked out of our tent, and into the scorching rays of the mid-day sun.

The hollering drifting across the stubby field had abated. I slowed my amble. Eloise and I had been given a spot on the far side of the festival near the pony rides, a slight in my opinion. I had to thread through the craft tents before I reached the food area.

I owed Eloise more than gratitude for getting me into the Athens' gallery show. Getting noticed in the Athens art community meant news of my work might travel to well-financed Bulldog alumni living in Atlanta or farther reaches. I assumed the educational praises lauded on the esteemed University of Georgia meant their graduates made inroads to places like New York. And everyone knew New Yorkers loved art. More importantly, if folks didn't start shelling out some bucks for my paintings, I was going to have to get a real job. Even worse, a job that might involve slinging hash, as my art degree didn't come with a minor in brain surgery.

I halted in the open area before the festival stage and glanced wistfully toward the booths of fried pies, funnel cake, and barbecue. If I didn't sell a peach painting today, there would be no Sno-Cones in my future. Nor beer tonight at the Viper, the local Sidewinder bar that Eloise said has the best catfish in central Georgia. And I did love catfish. And beer.

Spying a fried Moon Pie booth, my gut cried in anguish at the misery my lack of money created. I had second thoughts about hanging near a contest that involved watching other people eat, even if it was Brunswick Stew. To prevent more gut-ache of want, I glanced away from the food stalls toward the information booth to my right.

The officials had abandoned the booth for the cook-off, but a gigantic source of distraction did stand in the empty tent. With hands on his hips, he surveyed the flyers scattered over a picnic table.

When you're five foot and a half inch, any guy over six foot is big, but this particular man would put a steroid-infused Soviet weight lifter to shame. A frown twisted his mouth and his glacier blue eyes appeared troubled.

I hesitated at offering help. Max Avtaikin might be a supporter of the arts, but he had a dubious criminal background. And I kind of accused him of murder a few months back. Which is just plain embarrassing.

Before I could skedaddle, Max turned and caught me gawking.

I skimmed a hand over my limp, blonde ponytail, flapped the sweat off my neon pink halter, and entered the booth. "Hey, Mr. Max. You need help?"

He leaned in for one of those European double kisses. "Cherry Tucker. A pleasure, as always. Do you have the artist stand?"

It took me a second to understand his meaning. Max grew up in one of those Eastern bloc countries when they were still more bloc than country. Using his wily business acumen, he got rich and then got the hell out of Dodge. He settled in small town Georgia because of his odd love for the War Between the States. His accent moved with him.

"I'm selling little oils," I said. "Still lifes mostly. And trying to advertise my portraiture business. I've got a booth with my friend, Eloise Parker. She does pottery. You should check it out."

"I am wanting to see this art works, but I was asked to judge a food competition," Max said.

"Really?"

"You sound surprised, Miss Tucker."

"I just thought, with your, uh, recent trouble, folks would kind of..."

"I am involving in the community services." He shifted his stance. "You disapprove?"

"Helping the community is a good start."

"But?"

"You're still playing cards in your basement?" I asked, referring to his illegal poker games busted a few months ago.

Men like Max would play it cool for a while, but find a stealthier way to restart their business. Some folks don't care about local vice if it's kept indoors. There's a history of juke joints and moonshining in rural Georgia that's transferred to other realms in the modern era. However, I grew up around a county sheriff and know for a fact that doings behind doors eventually seep outside and run havoc elsewhere.

"I'm not understanding your meaning," he said.

"Oh, I think you do. But it's none of my business."

"That didn't stop your interest a few months ago."

I fiddled with my sunglasses, wondering what good manners dictated in this situation. Grandma Jo never covered apologies for accusing criminals of the wrong crime. "Well, I hope you're not messing around with poker anymore."

"I like games," Max paused. "And you do, too."

We shared a long look.

I had an inkling Max had some tricks up his sleeve that might warrant closer scrutiny. And oddly enough, he seemed to enjoy baiting me. Maybe he missed the excitement of outsmarting the secret police in his old country. I couldn't help a small shiver of pleasure at the thought of Max finding me a worthy opponent. Although he probably just found my antics amusing.

I gave Max a half-hearted shrug to show this rabbit wasn't about to sniff around his traps. If he wanted to corrupt Halo with his shady dealings, well, he just better be careful. I was dating a deputy.

"I have noticed you no longer have use of my nickname," Max said, steering the conversation down a different current.

"You want me to call you Bear?" Max's shadier cohorts called him The Bear.

"You used to call me Bear." He stroked his chin. "Maybe there is significance to your more formal manner?"

A shriek cut off our conversation. "Dangit, I'm missing the fight." Thankful for the excuse, I fled the stuffy tent.

Max caught up with me in two strides. "What is this fight? A boxing match?"

"Maybe boxing if we're lucky. Probably just some smart mouthing and shoving."

"Is this usual at the American festival?"

"America, I'm not sure. But Sidewinder, you bet. Partly it's the weather. My Grandpa says Southerners used to handle the heat until everyone got air conditioning. You find a shady spot for fishing or sit on your porch and wait for the sun to go down. Now we're running around in the sun like stray dogs working up a lather."

Judging by that shriek, it sounded like a stray dog howling up a storm. And that stray dog sounded a lot like Shawna Branson.

TWO

We rounded the corner of the fried Moon Pie booth, and the aroma of simmering meat and vegetables overpowered the sweeter festival smells of cotton candy and kettle corn. Unlike our jimmy-rigged tents in the craft section, this area held matching white tents for the cooking stations. Some booths had professional signs and all were decorated with kitsch, mostly in a redneck theme. Fake hillbilly teeth, corncob pipes, and battered straw hats prevailed. Portable grills and camp stoves held massive pots in a variety of conditions from sparkling new aluminum to rusting cast iron. All twenty gallons or larger to meet the one pot cooking rule.

Under a long tent in a roped-off area, a stretch of people sat at folding tables, expectant looks on their faces and spoons at the ready. I guessed this was the judging area Max had difficulty locating.

However, all eyes were glued to the passel standing near the judges' tent. Two men stood on the edge of the crowd, doing their best imitation of gorilla alpha male dominance without actually beating their chests.

Behind them, two lanky women faced off. Their snarling expressions matched almost as well as their big hair and flashy nails. The brunette and blonde obviously shared the same Sidewinder beauty shop. And clothing boutique. Both wore tiny sundresses swaddled in aprons proclaiming their team names in adorable curlicue letters and polka dots.

I recognized the signature curlicue style belonging to the meanest woman in Forks County, Shawna Branson. It figured she had found a way to make money off the festival. Now I understood the reason for my tent's position next to the pony manure dump. Shawna had it in for me since we were kids and my scrawny, little self out dodged her wild throws to win a VBS dodge ball tournament. She got me back by almost garroting me with a well-placed arm in Red Rover. We have been enemies ever since.

I scanned the crowd looking for Shawna and caught a glimpse of her bubblegum pink visor stating OFFICIAL in curlicue letters. Wearing a white seersucker shorts ensemble and platform wedge sandals, she waved a clipboard. Evidently the eardrum-piercing scream came from Shawna. An unhappy Shawna will rupture any number of body parts.

"Get back to your booths," Shawna yelled. "How dare you ruin this festival with your backwoods country shenanigans. I've put a lot of effort in bringing culture to this hillbilly folk fest. The Brunswick Stew competition is making a name for itself and you're going to ruin everything. We've got real people here. Out of town folks. Even foreigners."

"What is she meaning, the tall woman in the pink hat?" asked Max.

"She's meaning they had better break up their fight. Shawna doesn't want anyone making a spectacle of themselves unless it's Shawna."

The blonde woman with an apron reading "Team Cotton Pickin' Good" stepped forward and snatched Shawna's clipboard.

The crowd sucked in a communal breath.

"This will all be over as soon as you disqualify them." The blonde pointed a long, French-tipped fingernail in the direction of the brunette. "Team High Cotton is messing with our stew recipe. I caught Bruce and Belinda Gable going through our bins."

"Give me back my clipboard." Shawna yanked the board out of the woman's hands and studied the other couple. "And y'all just need to simmer down. The missing judge will be here soon. I don't give a monkey's hoot about your recipe, but I do care about you upsetting the judges. Go back to your cooking station."

"What happened to Joe McGill?" asked the tall blonde. "He's been officiating this contest for years. He'll know what to do."

"I'm the official now, and that's all you need to know," said Shawna. "I'm presiding over the Forks County Arts Council, and I took it upon myself to shape up this festival. So get your behinds back to your tent."

"Maybe I can help." A diminutive woman, as delicate looking as a baby bird, strolled forward wearing a straw hat that dwarfed her tiny head. "I'm Marion Maynard of Cotton Pickin' Good. It's true the Gables of Team High Cotton were looking through our bins, but some of the boxes did get switched around during the unloading this morning. Perhaps they thought we had their bins."

"Well?" Shawna stared at the accused couple.

Bruce Gable took a moment too long to answer and received an elbow jab from his wife.

"That's what happened," said Belinda Gable, patting her glossy, brown hair.

"Bullshit," said the heavier of the gorillas. He folded his arms over his Team Cotton Pickin' Good apron. "They were rifling through our stuff. Marion, whose team are you on anyway?"

"Don't be ugly, Lewis." The tiny Marion smiled at Shawna. "That'll be all. Thank you."

Dismissing Shawna, Marion and her giant hat strolled back to the Team Cotton Pickin' tent. Shawna gaped after her, unused to an abrupt dismissal.

With a few mouthed obscenities tossed at each other, the men scurried toward their stations with the women following.

"Now that's class," I said. "That Marion with the hat has some good breeding. You can tell just by her posture. You can't learn to walk like that with a couple cotillion classes. That's good genes, is what that is."

Max didn't reply. He probably had trouble following the argument. Shawna shooed off the festival bystanders and spotted us.

"Mr. Avtaikin," the snarl in Shawna's voice slipped into a sugary drawl. "Yoo-hoo."

"Hey, Shawna," I said, always prepared for a detente in our girl feud. "Hot enough for you?"

"Mr. Maksim Avtaikin." She ignored me to give Max a full eyelash flutter. Nauseating stuff. "You have finally graced us with your presence. I've been waiting your arrival most anxiously."

I wrinkled my nose. When Shawna tried too hard, she sounded like she swallowed Gone with the Wind.

"Show Mr. Max his seat and tell him the rules," I said. "He doesn't need to be whitewashed."

"It's not whitewashing. It's called being polite," snapped Shawna. She turned to Max, smoothing the seersucker over her abundant curves. "You surely need to keep better company, Mr. Avtaikin. This is an old county with old families. Some raised better than others. Since you come from Europe, you are probably unaware."

"We have old bloodlines in my country, Miss," said Max.

Shawna fanned herself with the clipboard in long strokes, eyeing Max like a malnourished tiger let loose in a hog confinement. "I'm sure you do. So you understand, as a business man, the importance of the type of company you keep."

"Are you hinting I'm not good enough to hang around Mr. Max?" I snorted. However old Max's bloodlines, I was pretty sure he didn't come from the elite. His people likely led revolutions against the aristocracy. Or sold black market armaments to the coup leaders.

"I understand this perfectly," Max said. "I will take my place with the judges. Good day to you, Artist." He gave a short bow to me and strolled past Shawna to enter the judges' tent.

"Hey Bear," I called after him. "Enjoy the stew."

He looked over his shoulder and gave the slightest hint of a smile.

The crowd swelled around me, eager to watch the judging. I dug my heels in to keep my spot in front. Teenage girls in matching gold aprons sashayed into the tent bearing trays of numbered cups filled with stew. As contestants for the Stew Princess pageant, the poor girls also wore headbands adorned with a bobbing, golden stew pot. Another Shawna idea to class up Sidewinder's country festival.

"You've got one of those looks on your face like you're either thinking hard or doing something unladylike," said a familiar baritone. Then he goosed me.

I spun to the side and took a quick second to admire the dark, brown curls—raw umber with a tad of burnt sienna in his highlights—that had finally grown back from his Police Academy buzz. I had missed those curls, even though Luke had a finely sculpted head. But Luke had a finely sculpted everything.

Behind his kick-butt cop shades, cool gray eyes studied me. "I thought you were working a craft booth."

"Taking a break to watch the cook-off judging," I said. "They send the cops out to break up the fight?"

"What fight?" Luke swiveled his gaze from me to the crowd.

"Between two cook-off teams. Don't worry, Shawna took care of it."

"Good for Shawna." Luke smirked at my scowl. "We're taking shifts at the festival and a couple deputies got hired to direct traffic. I just kicked a guy out for handing out some health drink without a permit. Did you see a short, beefed-up dude hauling a cooler and passing out Dixie cups with green stuff in them?"

"That would be Griffin Ward," I said. "Eloise's musclehead boyfriend. He came by our booth earlier to drop off stew and hassle Eloise. He forced her to drink the green stuff."

"Forced her?"

"That's what I would call the emotional blackmail he uses on her. Claims his health drinks have healed her Crohn's Disease. And she won't admit it, but I think he's gotten physical with her a few times. How can she go out with a jerk like that? Eloise is smart and talented. What is it about women with weight issues falling for guys with No Fat Chicks stickers on their vehicles?"

Eloise's family and mine represented a common characteristic of the Georgia cracker: our body types ran to extremes. My Grandpa and I leaned toward the whippet-thin, rangy side of the Southern physique. My sister Casey, like my mother, took my Grandma Jo's genes.

Their curves could run to pounds if left unchecked. With Casey's love of Southern cooking, she fought to contain her weight. Eloise's family gave in to the inevitable, finding happiness in bacon, butter, and lard. God bless them, they were content in their obesity, but Eloise suffered from a poverty that had to do more with self-image than money.

I sometimes wondered if Eloise found her Crohn's Disease a mixed blessing as the disease sometimes starved her appetite. I also wondered if Griffin felt that way as well, with his love of "No Fat Chicks."

"Eloise is a smart gal, but I've seen it all. You can't even imagine some of the domestic calls I've been on," said Luke. "Not just in Forks County, but on the bases when I was an MP, too. It's sickening."

"He does it again, and I'm going to get Eloise to put a restraining order on him," I said.

Luke sighed. "Chances are she won't do it. I don't get it. Some women get the living daylights beat out of them and won't even press charges."

My shoulders slumped.

"I shouldn't have said that. Don't worry. By the way, I have to cancel tonight," he said and leaned down to kiss me before I could argue.

"Again? Eloise and I are going to the Viper for catfish. No way in hell do I want to be a third wheel if Griffin Ward shows up. Earlier today, I thought he was going to take a swing at me when I told him to lay off Eloise."

"Don't bait a guy like that. Do me a favor and take off if he shows up." Luke lifted his shades so I could get a glimpse of his serious intent.

"All right," I said. "I'll leave Griffin alone. I wish you'd come out, though."

"We're stretched thin with the festival." He shrugged. "You wanted me to work in Forks County. I got switched off nights. You should be happy."

"I could talk to Uncle Will," I said.

"Do not. I don't like people who play favorites, and I sure as hell don't want that reputation. Bad enough the crap I get for dating you."

"What kind of crap? Why?"

"Don't worry about it. I've got to get." He twitched my pony-tail. "My shift here is over. I'll try to catch you later."

I watched him amble away, too agitated to enjoy the view.

Another broken date. From the difficulty of his twelve-hour shifts and his disinterest in doing much more than snuggling in his free time, the honeymoon period on our renewed dating status had cooled. It seemed we hadn't quite worked out what we were doing romantically. Other than some real hot snuggling.

Cornering him on the state of our relationship was harder than lassoing a squirrel.

My irritation grew as I watched the judges take an outrageous amount of time to appraise their tiny cups of Brunswick Stew. What was so hard about swallowing stew and voting up or down? They raised the clear plastic cups of stew to eye level, exposing various shades of brown. Using the pressure of a spoon, one judge tested corn, potato, and okra slices for durability. Another loudly slurped each minuscule sip and pondered the taste like it was fine wine and not a side dish for barbecue. One woman picked out each piece of shredded meat and laid the insignificant threads on her tongue before swallowing.

Where the hell did Shawna get these judges? They certainly were not the local farmers, bankers, and shopkeepers who usually presided over this event. Sidewinder's stew fest did get the occasional politician or high school football star, but these jokers seemed to have stepped off a higher epicurean plane to fall into our county gastronomical challenge. Once the locals figured out the charade, Shawna would rue the decision to axe the mud pit.

I was all for raising the cultural bar in Forks County, but there was a time and place for everything. A local festival roasting in the mid-summer rays of a Georgia sun was not the place to put on airs. Shawna had one savior that prevented the stars and bars crew from tossing their Natty Light cans at the tent. Max Avtaikin. He tossed back each cup without use of a spoon, wrote a single comment on his top-secret judging sheet, and slid his eyes to half-mast to wait out the proceedings. Around me, a few men elbowed each other and pointed out his lack of social grace. Women tittered and whispered.

But even Max's shenanigans couldn't keep me there. Between the heat and the heavy scent of food I couldn't afford to eat, I decided to give up on the contest and traipse back to our portable art gallery.

Before entering the tent, I took a moment to admire our contribution to the culture of Forks County. My small oil paintings of beach scenes, bowls of peaches, and bulldogs. Typical Georgia themes that folks around here could appreciate. And Eloise had placed her Raku ware pots in pretty patterns that caught a lot of eyes. At the front display table, I adjusted a small, cobalt blue-crackled vase, turning it to better show off the glaze. That's when I noticed Eloise hunkered in her chair, holding her stomach.

I hurried to her chair. "Are you okay? You're looking kind of puny."

She moaned. "Maybe my Crohn's is acting up. Never had an attack so bad. My gut is on fire, like I ate glass." She struggled to stand and teetered on her feet.

I grabbed her elbow. "Let me help." I wrapped an arm around her shoulder when her legs wouldn't accept her weight.

She shook her head. "I'm gonna be sick," she whispered.

"I don't care," I said and dragged her toward the front of the tent. "Honey, you can't even walk. You should have told me you were feeling sick earlier. I never would have left you."

"I didn't feel like this earlier," she groaned.

"Hey, can you watch our stuff?" I hollered into the koi pond tent. "My friend's sick."

The Koi pond guy rushed past his gurgling fountains and stared. "I'm calling 911."

I felt rather than saw Eloise's head shake, but I agreed with him. "There should be a medical station for heat stroke somewhere. Go get a nurse, too."

Eloise's trembling body began to jerk. We weren't going to make it to the Port-a-Johns.

I turned us toward the back of the tent and pushed through a slit in the tarp. The stench of horse feces assaulted us, and I felt like puking myself. I sank with Eloise to the ground and held her wispy brown curls away from her face. Crimson blood spattered the ground along with the mess of stew. She shuddered and fell limply against me.

THREE

People filled all available space in the ER waiting room at Forks County Hospital, spilling into the entrance and hallway until a nurse began directing less serious patients to other hospitals. The ambulance bay flashed blue and white, noisy with the crash of collapsing gurneys, shouts, rumbling motors, and squealing brakes. I chewed my lip, waiting in line at the front desk for news about Eloise.

"Your friend is one of these Sidewinder festival patients, is that right?" said the ER receptionist.

My face puckered into a worried frown. "Do you mean all these people got sick at the cook-off?"

The blonde behind the booth sighed, returning her attention to the computer. "Looks that way. Food poisoning is common at festivals. They've taken Eloise Parker from the ER. Follow the arrows to the main desk in the hospital and they can help you there."

"What can food poisoning do to someone with Crohn's Disease?"

She scowled. "Do I look like a doctor? Next in line."

I took the upper hand and turned away before my mouth could shoot off something I'd regret. She was overwhelmed.

A hand snagged my shoulder, turning me toward a body swathed in brown polyester.

"What are you doing here?" said Luke. "Did your Grandpa or someone get sick?"

"No, it's Eloise. The ambulance brought her here. She vomited blood."

Luke's long fingers massaged my neck. "I'm sorry to hear that. A lot of Sidewinder folks got food poisoning. I was sent here to make sure things didn't get out of hand. We heard the ER was overwhelmed. Are you feeling okay?"

"I'm fine. Eloise is the one who ate six cups of Brunswick Stew. That would make anyone sick."

Luke frowned. "Maybe give you a bellyache, but Brunswick Stew isn't going to make you that sick. Does everyone have the same symptoms?"

"Actually, I don't know. I didn't even realize there was a mass epidemic." I shuddered. "I'll never eat festival food again. Not after seeing what happened to Eloise."

"I'll check into it." He kissed my forehead. "Don't you worry your pretty little head."

"What's that supposed to mean?"

"Nothing. Things have calmed down now that the nurses have triaged the new patients. I'll walk you to Eloise's room. How was the festival other than the food poisoning? Did you sell any of your stuff?"

"No," I scowled. "I hate working festivals. Next time I'm going to paint some rocks. I'll probably make more money."

We entered the hallway leading from the ER into the main part of the hospital. I wanted to reach for his hand, but knew he'd feel odd to hold hands in public while wearing his uniform.

"Do you need help watching the booth?" Luke asked. "I'm on call here, but I've got buddies near Sidewinder that would help you."

"Naw. Todd is doing it for me."

Luke halted, causing me to stumble. "Todd McIntosh?"

"Do we know another Todd? I called him before I left for the hospital." I had sort of, but not quite, married Todd McIntosh once. However, we remained good friends. As loyal as a Labrador, Todd could be called on for help in situations where my own siblings slacked. If I needed help drinking beer, Casey and Cody would be at my side. Rushing to an out of town festival to sit in record-breaking heat to sell my paintings? Not so much. Therefore, I had dialed Todd.

"Todd's not working?" said Luke.

"It's Saturday," I answered. Luke must be working too hard if he couldn't remember the day. "Todd drives a delivery truck for a living. He'll do a good job packing up my stuff and will bring it to my house."

"Right." Luke drew out the word and changed the subject. "Let's go see about your friend."

We continued our trudge toward the front desk. The receptionist then directed us to another waiting area on the third floor where Eloise's family had congregated.

June Parker, Eloise's mother, spotted me. She waved me over, pulled me into her soft, considerable body, and hugged the tears right out of my eyes.

"I know you were with Eloise when it happened," she cried. "Thank you for taking care of her. I'm glad she was with a friend in her final moments."

I froze within her arms.

"Oh, baby," Miss June's body shook as she squeezed me tighter. "She didn't make it."

"What? How can that be?" Miss June released me suddenly, and I backed into Luke. I felt his hands grip my shoulders, holding me steady.

Eloise's sister, Mary Jane, slipped in next to Miss June and circled an arm around her mother's shoulders. "She arrived unconscious and passed a little while ago. The doctors couldn't do anything."

"I'm so sorry." Tears spilled down my cheeks. "I can't believe this. She was having a good time earlier, except for the blasted heat."

"She never liked to tell us when her Crohn's was acting up," said Miss June sadly.

"But, I don't think it was bothering her earlier," I stopped my words at a pinch to my shoulders. I looked up at Luke. He twitched his head in a quick shake. His somber eyes held a warning.

"I'm so sorry for your loss," Luke said. "How can we help?"

"I don't know." Miss June stared at the floor. "I just don't know. Someone from the hospital is coming to talk to us."

Mr. Parker lumbered into the room. Breathing hard, the heavyset man took his place next to his wife, but fixed his bloodshot eyes on Luke. "Were you at the festival, Deputy?"

Luke slipped a hand off my shoulder to shake Mr. Parker's. "Earlier, but not when Eloise took ill. I arrived at the hospital when we heard about the backup in the ER. I found Cherry there."

"I heard a lot of people got sick at the cook-off, son." Mr. Parker's face reddened. "Is someone looking into that?"

"I've been assigned to other duties, so I can't tell you if we're investigating the festival. I'm sure the county health inspector has been notified, though."

"Son, my daughter is dead," Mr. Parker said.

Miss June moaned.

Mr. Parker took her hand. "The ER doctor says it must be a complication with her Crohn's. This may be a coincidence, but I find it highly strange all these people are sick, but my daughter dies. I'm asking for an autopsy."

"No, Dan." Fresh tears wetted June's cheeks.

"Hush, June. It's for the best."

I could feel Luke tensing.

"Yes, sir," Luke said. "I'll tell the sheriff."

"You do that, son." Mr. Parker pointed a finger at us. "I want justice served. If someone gave her food bad enough to kill her, they need to be punished."

I moved forward to hug Miss June again. "We'll leave you with your family. I'll come see you soon."

Luke and I shuffled out of the waiting room toward the elevators. Just as the door swooshed open, I heard Mary Jane call my name. I left Luke behind and hurried to meet her.

She darted a look down the hall at Luke before focusing on me. "You heard what my daddy said, Cherry?"

"About the autopsy?" I lowered my voice. "That sounds reasonable to me."

"Daddy wants to know what happened." Mary Jane's ample cheeks shook with anger. "It doesn't sound like your deputy is too interested in finding that out."

"Luke's just doing his job. He's got a better poker face than anyone I know. If the sheriff's office talked about investigating, he'd never reveal it until given word that he can."

"Eloise dying ain't right," she whispered. "You were about to say so yourself when your deputy stopped you."

I felt my cheeks grow hot. "What are you saying, Mary Jane?"

"You know how it is with people like us. We're not important, and we can't afford lawyers. If the sheriff's office says it's just a bad case of food poisoning, nobody will check into her death. I don't care if Eloise did have Crohn's. They're saying it was a complication of her disease. That's a lot of bull. We've seen her through some bad times and there's been no warning for an attack like this."

"The autopsy is a good place to start," I said. "I don't know what else you can do. You think the hospital messed up?"

"You know the sheriff. You're dating a deputy. You know how stuff works."

"That doesn't mean they listen to me," I said.

"You need to try." Heavy tears coursed down Mary Jane's face. "For Daddy's sake. I want him to know someone is looking into Eloise's death."

"I love your family. Of course I'll do what I can." My skin felt hot and a golf ball-sized knot lodged in my throat.

"I know you will. You talk to your Uncle Will and get your deputy to listen." Mary Jane wiped her face with her hands. "I better get back to Momma and Daddy."

I walked back down the hallway after she left. We stepped inside the elevator without a wait, and the heavy doors slid shut, giving us a moment of privacy.

"Are you going to tell Uncle Will what Mr. Parker said?" I peered at him through watery eyes.

"Of course," Luke said. "But it's more of a matter for the health inspector to start an investigation into bad festival food. An autopsy for a food poisoning case sounds like a waste of tax payer money to me."

"Mr. Parker's right." I gulped through a sob. "Mary Jane thinks so, too. She knew you guys wouldn't care."

"Hey," Luke drew an arm around me. "I'm sorry about your friend, but you're acting like someone deliberately killed her."

"I was with her all day." I pushed out of his embrace. "She was fine when the festival started. She ate a ton of Brunswick Stew and then got sick. I'm sure the autopsy will prove it wasn't her Crohn's."

"Maybe her disease couldn't allow her body to handle the food poisoning," Luke said. "I'll give you that. Just don't start making trouble about this. We'll have to wait for the autopsy anyway."

"You need to hightail it over to Sidewinder and confiscate that stew." Anger began licking away my sadness, making me feel better.

"I'm sure once word got out about all the people puking in the ER, the health inspector shut down the booths. You should go home and relax. It's been a rough day."

"I don't want to relax." I said, setting my jaw.

"You don't know how to relax. There's a difference. You're letting yourself get all worked up," Luke said.

"My friend just died. How am I supposed to relax?"

"Maybe relax isn't the right word. You need to calm down. I'll come over and sit with you tonight when I get off."

"Tonight I was going to go to the Viper with Eloise." I hiccupped and a fresh cascade of tears flowed down my cheeks. "I guess I'll go to the farm. Do you want to meet me there?"

"How about I come over after you get home?" He brushed his thumb across my wet cheeks. "There's no privacy at the farm with your Grandpa and siblings questioning me on police business."

"Of course not," I said, "If I want privacy, I stay at home. If I want to eat, I go to the farm."

His eye twitched. I noticed that particular tremor had been making repeat appearances.

"I'll be over later." He pulled me into a rough hug. "I'm really sorry about your friend. It's okay to feel sad, hon'. Let yourself have a good cry tonight. I'll be there with tissues. You don't have to be tough all the time."

I nestled into his chest, feeling the comforting strength of his embrace and thought about not acting tough all the time. Could a person just go home and cry? Would that make me feel better about losing Eloise?

The problem, as I saw it, was crying never did me any good. Our family had a lot of good reasons for crying which was maybe why none of us did it much. The Tuckers and Ballards (my Grandpa's name) were better at getting mad. It suited us even more to get even. Tissues were for colds.

And according to my Grandpa only sissies got colds.

"Don't forget to talk to Uncle Will about Eloise," I said after pushing out of Luke's arms.

"Go home and get some rest." Luke turned to leave, but stopped, swiveled back, and flicked me with a sharp look. "I'm sorry about Eloise, but don't interfere with my job."

I watched him stride away.

If he wasn't going to go down to Sidewinder to check into that stew, I would.

FOUR

The road back to Sidewinder took me to the southeast corner of Forks County, a meandering drive through Loblolly Pine forests and past many farms. Because Halo's in the northern part of the county, we're stuck in the hilly fingers stretching off the Blue Ridge Mountains. My Grandpa had dairy cattle, but in his later years he sold his herd for goats. I don't know if he planned on milking them, but they certainly don't earn their keep. They destroyed all Grandma Jo's decorative planting in the front yard and were lucky enough to live after munching on azaleas. Down in Sidewinder they've got enough flat areas to grow corn and cotton. They even named their high school mascot The Picker.

Of course, in Halo, we're the Fighting Angels. Nobody's perfect.

My old Datsun pickup shuddered into Sidewinder, blowing black smoke and rattling her loose exhaust to announce my arrival. She was not crazy about these trips through sunbaked fields and roasting blacktop, and I couldn't blame her. The drive to the hospital in Line Creek had been excruciating because of the backup of vehicles coming in and out of the festival. But now, at only five o'clock, there was hardly a car in sight. I guessed the festival was a bust.

As the organizer, Shawna would be pretty steamed. I could imagine her throwing a huge hissy when she found out which booth caused everyone to lose their lunch.

The eeriness of the empty streets of Sidewinder nagged me as I pulled through their one four-way stop at the town's park and Legion Hall.

The Iron Kettle restaurant had only one car parked before it. Even odder, the sign hanging on the front door of the Viper read closed. Bad news for Sidewinder if a bar had to close on a Saturday night.

The festival grounds were located on a fallow field to the west of town. I pulled up and parked before the chain link fence and flashed my vendor badge to the woman sitting at a card table at the entrance. I squinted into the sun, surveying the fairgrounds. Empty except for people closing down their booths and carrying equipment to the parking lot.

"What happened?" I asked.

"Whew, it's hot." The older woman mopped her face with a handkerchief and straightened her straw hat. She glanced behind her at the sorry festival remains. "A bunch of folks took sick. I've never seen anything like it in all my years working at this cook-off, but I guess it's not surprising in this heat. Maybe some potato salad went bad or something. Never eat anything with mayonnaise when the temperature's above eighty-five."

"So they don't know what caused the food poisoning? What about the stew?"

"Girl, don't say that. It would ruin our festival more than an off-potato salad. Sidewinder counts on the money this weekend brings in every year. We get folks from all over the South. Even saw some from Texas and Tennessee today. No one can make Brunswick Stew like a Georgian, but plenty of folks like to try their hand. Particularly those Virginians that think they invented the stuff. Then there are all the barbecue folks that come to try it. Can't have a pulled pork sandwich without coleslaw, Brunswick Stew, and banana pudding."

She pulled off her hat, revealing a wet mess of gray hair, and fanned herself. "Maybe it was the banana pudding. A good banana pudding is made with eggs."

"So, it's not the Brunswick Stew? My friend ate a lot of it and got sick."

"Honey, I don't know what did it. We've had inspectors swarming this place, testing everybody's food. Guess we'll find out." She slammed the hat on her head. "But I doubt it's the Brunswick Stew. That stuff cooks all day. No bacteria can survive. I bet she ate potato salad or banana pudding with her barbecue."

"She didn't eat barbecue. She ate Brunswick Stew."

The woman stood up. "You listen to me. Brunswick Stew is a delicious, beloved dish we've been eating forever. No one gets sick from Brunswick Stew. It puts hair on the chest of men and will put some curves on that stick of a body of yours."

She crossed her arms. "Go on and get you some."

Plunking my fists onto my stick of a body, I shot her a look back. "Looks like you've been enjoying enough of it. Ma'am," I added to not be rude.

She flushed and thrust her massive breasts in my direction. "My stew cooking got me my husband. Men like meat in their stew and on the bones of their women." She looked me up and down. "And I'm not seeing any ring on your finger. You probably can't even cook."

"I don't need to cook."

She harrumphed. "Like I said, I don't see a ring on your finger. Where you from anyway?"

"Halo."

"Figures," she said, settling into her plastic deck chair. "Go on now."

I stomped past her. "Country," I muttered.

"Redneck," she returned.

I sped past the inflatable jumping games, wandered through the craft section, and halted at my partially dismantled booth. With sweat darkening his golden blond hair, Todd leaned over the PVC pipe frame, yanking on two pieces fitted together. A pair of slot machine cherries tattooed one calf. Sweat glistened on his shirtless back as he tugged on a pipe.

"Todd," I called. "Thank you for taking down the stand. I know it's a pain."

He stood up slowly, giving me an ample view of the lean physique and tight muscles that came from lifting weights and hauling boxes. Unlike Eloise's boyfriend, Griffin, muscles suited his long body and weren't propagated by supplements. He turned, rubbing his brow with the back of his hand.

My breath caught as he offered me a view of his upraised bicep and the hard swells and angles of his chest and belly. A vision for a Rafael-styled fresco on my bedroom wall with Todd as the subject danced in my mind before I caught myself.

Damn this weakness for beautiful men, I thought. Eloise knew me too well. I shuffled back a step and shoved my hands in the pockets of my shorts.

"No problem," he smiled, offering two long dimples on each cheek. "I put it on my honey-do list."

I edged back another step. "I don't think it's appropriate for you to call a favor for a friend a honey-do list."

"I'm just joshing you." He winked again and ambled closer, closing the distance between us. "We're not married anymore. You sent me the papers."

"You shouldn't joke about it. Signing the annulment papers took longer than our Vegas wedding. That's sad, not funny."

"I wish I knew what happened to that ring. It sure was pretty. I looked for it in Caesar's Palace. The security guards sure got ticked. You know, even if you take your shoes off, they don't like people wading in that fountain."

I rolled my eyes. "Never mind. I'll help you load the stuff in the Civic."

We worked together unscrewing the pipes and yanking them apart. Todd had nestled Eloise's Raku pots in scraps of fabric and Styrofoam sheets within large boxes.

I hoisted the last box in the hatchback of Todd's Civic, keeping far from his pheromone-laden sweat. Since Todd had already packed most everything else away in boxes, I poked my head out the back of his car to make a comment on his diligence but didn't see him anywhere. The aroma of barbecue and Brunswick Stew floated past the truck in a sudden gust of wind, and a sound like a chainsaw cutting through a block of cement startled me. I clamped a hand over my stomach and felt the sharp knock of hunger. My middle reverberated with another deafening growl.

"Cherry." Todd popped around the side of the booth next door, startling me. "I could hear you three doors down. You're hungry. Let's get something to eat. That pulled pork smells incredible."

"I'm not hungry." The chainsaw in my stomach revved again.

Todd's eyebrows drew together. "If that's not your stomach, what is that sound?"

"I can't eat festival food, Todd. A bunch of people took sick. Eloise died."

"She died?"

I nodded, biting my lip.

Without hesitation, Todd stepped forward, wrapped an arm around me, and pulled me against his slick skin. "I'm so sorry, baby. I didn't know. When you said they were taking her to the hospital, I thought she got heat stroke. Figured you two were sitting in the sun. It was hotter than two cats fighting in a wool sock today."

"We were under the tent." I pressed my hands against his stomach to shove myself away, but the bumpy ridges of his abs felt so pleasant under my fingers, I let them rest. My head dropped against his chest, and Todd stroked my hair.

"You've been through a lot today. How did she die?"

"It looked like she was having a fit. I guess it had something to do with her disease. Her daddy wants an autopsy." I sucked the inside of my cheek to prevent tears from welling in my eyes again.

"That's strange." Todd kissed the top of my head and nestled me tighter. "Poor Eloise. I didn't think she had anything life threatening."

"I know. Food poisoning doesn't usually kill people. It doesn't sit right with me or with her family. They don't trust the authorities. They want me to look into it."

"Of course they want you to look into it. You like to stand up for people like the Parkers. You got a talent for telling the big folks how the cow eats the cabbage."

A trickle of sweat dripped off his chest and smeared my face. I rubbed the wetness from my cheeks and pulled my head away. Looking up, I saw Todd's eyes darken. A familiar feeling washed over me. A feeling I once had in Vegas. Just before Todd snookered me into marrying him for a couple of hours.

Hindsight has taught me it's wiser, as well as cheaper, to avoid those particular feelings.

I hopped back, but Todd's hands lingered on my shoulders before sliding down my arms.

"Are you all right, Cherry?"

I swallowed the tightness in my throat and folded my arms across my chest. "Of course I am." I scanned Todd before returning my gaze to the pony rides. "Since we're done here, would it suit you to walk around for a minute? I want to check out those cook-off booths, especially where Eloise ate."

"Sure." He made two long strides toward the food booths before glancing over his shoulder. "You coming?"

That's what I always liked about Todd. He's so agreeable. And loyal. Like I said, the Labrador of ex-boyfriends.

"You think you want to make yourself decent first?" I asked.

He glanced down at his bared chest. Leaning over into his favorite muscleman pose, he brought his fists together and flexed his shoulders and arms. He continued with a series of poses, ending with an upraised arm bicep flex. The evening sun streaked his glistening body in gold and amber. Stick Todd in the English countryside instead of rural Georgia, and John Constable would have loved to catch that light effect in one of his landscape paintings (if Constable had considered Guns of Steel at Sunset a worthy subject).

"You don't think the concessions want to see my pipes?" He grinned, striking another pose.

"I think," I swallowed and folded my arms over my thumping chest, "they've got enough distractions today."

FIVE

We wandered through the cook-off area, watching the contestants pack up their stations.

"I wish I could remember which booth gave Eloise all that stew," I said.

Todd pulled a slip of paper from his pocket and examined it. "Team Cotton Pickin' Good?" His eyes flicked over the signs hanging from the various competitors' canopies.

"How did you know?"

"There were a bunch of tickets laying in a chair," Todd said sheepishly. "I was fixing to get me something after I finished putting away your tent. They're all for Cotton Pickin' Good. I thought at a cook-off you got tickets to try all the booths."

"One of Eloise's students gave her free tickets to their stew stand," I swallowed the knot in my throat. "Poor Eloise. Brought low by her love for Brunswick Stew. Let's check out this Cotton Pickin' joint."

The Cotton Pickin' Good booth stood on the periphery of the stands, one of the few tents that didn't bustle with activity. A young man with a neck tattoo and gaping plug earrings stood behind the tent, slowly packing utensils into a box.

He looked up as we approached. "We're closed."

"Already? What happened?" I asked.

"Got shut down by some official dudes. But we would have closed anyway. Lewis, our cook, is in the hospital." His nose wrinkled. He tossed a dirty knife into the box. "I'm supposed to head over there after I clean up. Even when he gets sick, I'm stuck doing Lewis's dirty work."

I latched on to that bit of information like a terrier on a squirrel. "He caught food poisoning, too?"

"I don't know." The kid grabbed a roll of paper towels, jumped, and slam-dunked the towels into the box. "My mom is freaking out. I don't think she'd freak out over food poisoning. Probably tell him to take Pepto and quit whining."

I glanced at Todd, but he was examining the mess in the box. Probably looking for leftovers.

"Marion's sick, too," said the teen as he half-heartedly lobbed salt and pepper shakers in the box. A bag of Vidalia onions followed.

I flinched at the mess someone would have to unpack and tried to concentrate on the mysterious sickness inflicted on Team Cotton Pickin' Good. One that may or may not be food poisoning. "Who else is sick?"

"Marion. Lewis's wife." The kid swept a jar of pickle slices off the counter into the open box below. It hit a pot with a clang. I bit my lip imagining pickle juice soaking into the cardboard.

"I feel bad about that," the kid said. "Don't care about Lewis, but hope she's going to be okay."

The boy's mess unnerved me, and his chattiness had a surly edge I didn't like. But gossip seemed ripe for picking with this one. "Need some help?"

"Suit yourself," he said.

I walked around the makeshift counter. Spying an empty tub, I began stacking the condiment bottles and cans of stewed tomatoes, peas, and corn into a corner of the tub.

Todd leaned against the counter to watch me, tapping a marching rhythm with his fingertips.

The boy fell into a chair. Pulling off his Cotton Pickin' Good ball cap, he wiped his sweaty brow with his forearm and replaced the hat over a mop of dishwater blond hair.

"So what's your name?" I flicked a glance at the gangly kid, figuring his age hovered in the late teens. I assumed he was Eloise's student and felt surprised a kid with attitude, a neck tat, and giant holes in his earlobes would give her free tickets. Maybe he liked art.

"Hunter Adams." He reached in his pocket for a can of tobacco, spun off the lid, and pinched out a wad.

I waited for his "thank you, ma'am" for helping, which didn't come. I'd let it slide for a minute. But not too long. I did have my pride and didn't want some teenage hooligan to think I enjoyed playing maid.

"So," I said. "You mentioned a Marion, a Lewis, and your mom on the Cotton Pickin' Good Team. Was Lewis in charge of cooking your stew?"

"Yep." Hunter's tongue fished the chew off his teeth and settled it in his bottom lip. "Lewis's been working on perfecting his recipe all year. Makes a batch nearly every Sunday. He was fixing to win this competition and then hit bigger cook-offs next year."

"When did he get sick?"

"My mom took him and Marion to the immediate care clinic about an hour ago. She made me stay to help clean up. I was supposed to leave this afternoon." He grabbed a paper cup and spit. "Friggin' Lewis. Ruined another Saturday night for me."

I exchanged a glance with Todd. Where did Hunter and his mom fit in with Lewis and Marion? Was polygamy alive and well in Sidewinder?

Hunter smirked. "Aunt Belinda and Uncle Bruce will have a good laugh at Lewis if it is food poisoning. I heard Mom went after them for cheating."

"Wait, the two teams fighting today? That's your family?"

"Aunt Belinda is my momma's sister. They don't get along too well. Lewis hates my aunt and uncle, but Belinda's all right." He spat and pointed with the cup. "There's another bottle of Worcestershire you missed."

I glanced in the direction of his point and swiveled to fix him with a good, hard look. Hunter tipped back in his chair with his feet propped on a cooler, working on his chew. While I cleaned up his stuff. "Now just a minute…"

"I don't get it," said Todd.

Hunter and I looked at Todd. His cerulean blue eyes blinked with uncertainty, but he spoke with serious deliberation.

"Your mom competes against her sister in this Brunswick Stew cook-off?"

"Because of Lewis," said Hunter. "Bruce and Lewis have been competing for years. Stew competitions, golf, poker. Since high school."

"That's a long time," said Todd.

Hunter shrugged.

"But where does your mom figure in? Lewis is married to Marion, the little lady with the big hat?" I said. "That leaves you and your momma…?"

"Mom works for Lewis and Marion," Hunter spat in his cup and glared. "At the Cotton Pickin' Good plantation."

"Plantation? We don't do plantations anymore."

"It's a tourist thing."

"What does she do? I assume she's not picking cotton."

"It's not my mom's fault." Hunter's spit shot past his cup and landed near my feet. "She got us a nice place out of it. If he'd divorce Marion, she might marry Lewis. He'll never do it though. He'd lose the land. And I'd rather see him dead than as my new stepdad."

"Holy crap," I said, unable to find a better reply to the admission of his mother's dalliance. They were almost as good as my own momma's transgressions.

Todd slapped a quick staccato on the counter, his version of "holy crap."

"He deserves to get sick," continued the kid. "Lewis is an asshole. Everyone in Sidewinder knows what he's doing with my mom, but he doesn't care. I hope he doesn't recover."

"Okay." Obviously this kid was sucking on pretty serious sour grapes concerning this Lewis. But Cotton Pickin' Lewis's sins were not my problem. "Do you know anything about other people getting sick at the festival?"

"No, just Lewis and Marion. Lewis couldn't take getting his precious contest shut down. Probably caused him to have a heart attack."

"Did he have a heart attack?" The hairs on my neck quivered. Were Eloise's symptoms similar to a heart attack?

"Don't know. And don't care."

"Look, here's the thing. My friend ate a bunch of Brunswick Stew from your stand today. She died this afternoon. I think you gave her stew tickets. Miss Parker, the art teacher."

"No shit?" Hunter stared at me in surprise. "Miss Parker died? Will the cops think Lewis killed her? That'd be kind of awesome."

He could have punched me in the gut and gotten the same reaction. I took a deep breath and shoved my hands in my pockets to stop me from slapping the stupid out of the boy. "I'm going to pretend you didn't say that."

"I'm serious. If they think Lewis killed her, maybe he could go to jail and my mom would leave him."

"Hunter, pull your head out of your behind. Your teacher, my friend, is dead. I'm sure Miss Eloise didn't sacrifice her life just to get Lewis out of your mom's pants!" I kicked the tub, nearly dumping out all my carefully arranged jars and cans. "I'm sorry about your momma and this Lewis, but that doesn't give you the right to act like an idiot."

I should know. My momma didn't have the decency to stick around and parade a Lewis in my face. She probably left us for a Lewis, but that didn't mean we sat around hoping people would die to bring her back.

"Be a man and help out your momma." I lambasted him with my best older sister glare, perfected from years of practice on my brother Cody.

"Don't you worry. I'm helping her out." Hunter spat at my feet and stood. "I'm going to help her right away from Lewis."

"Let's go, Todd."

"You got any stew left?" Todd hung over the counter, rapping the underside with his palms.

"No, man." Hunter untwisted his can and shoved another plug into his lip.

"You don't want to eat their food anyway," I said. "You want to end up with food poisoning?"

"That's right." Hunter offered us a smeary brown smile. "I wouldn't want nobody eating Lewis's stew."

"You certainly served plenty to Eloise."

"You're a lot like Miss Parker, ain't you? Something about scrawny women that makes them bitchy." He glanced at Todd. "You like doing scarecrows, man?"

"I'm not doing her," Todd said.

"I don't blame you."

"That's it," I fixed Hunter with a steely gaze. "You watch your mouth or you're going to be sorry."

"Or what?" Hunter swished the tobacco around his mouth. "You're going to stab me with a bony elbow?"

I lunged at Hunter and elbowed him hard in the stomach.

He bent over, gagging and coughing while tobacco juice bled out of his mouth and splattered his shoes. He looked up, sputtering frothy brown liquid. "You dumb bitch. You made me swallow my chew!"

"Just showing you what a bony elbow can do." I marched past him, knowing Todd would follow. "I did you a favor. It'll be a while before you want the taste of tobacco in your mouth again."

As Todd and I tramped to my dissembled stall, I fumed over the boy's remarks, but felt more troubled over the soap opera brewing in Hunter's life than his nasty words. How angry was this kid? Vindictive enough to spike the stew with something that could kill his teacher? At the sight of Todd's vehicle, I halted while Todd stumbled past me.

Todd's snort of laughter showed his thoughts occupied a less morbid train.

"What's so funny?" I said.

"You elbowing that kid," Todd grinned, "and making him swallow his chew. That was a good one."

"That kid deserved it. But it's not funny."

"I just love it when you do that kind of stuff, baby." Picking me up, he spun me in a quick twirl that flung my flip-flops dangerously close to the pony toilet. "You're acting more like your old self."

"Put me down. You're going to make me motion sick," I said. "And what are you talking about? My old self?"

"You've been quieter, lately." Todd set me down and carefully retrieved my flip-flops.

"What? Since when?"

"Last couple months. It's not just me. Everyone says so."

"Everyone?" I snatched the flip-flops dangling from his hands. "Everyone's been talking about me?"

"Quiet's not a bad thing," Todd backed up a few steps, his fingers rapping a tempo on his thighs. "Just doesn't suit you."

I eyed him, wondering if this had something to do with Luke. Our relationship had been the only major change in the last couple months. Besides the whole debacle with the coffin painting and the kidnapping, but that was old news. "I'm not saying you're right, but I can do quiet. If I wanted."

"You can do whatever you want," Todd spoke with a suspiciously lively gait. More of a canter than his usual drawl. "You're normally pretty feisty, and you don't take crap from anyone. I like you that way. You stick up for people."

"Are you saying I've been letting people down?" I crossed my arms and chewed the inside of my lip. Had I let Eloise down somehow? "Maybe Mary Jane thought I hadn't been a good enough friend to Eloise and that's why she wants me to do my part now."

Todd's face constricted at my guilty outpouring. "That's not what I meant. You're not letting anyone down, baby. But it's good to see you acting like yourself again."

"By beating up eighteen-year-old boys?"

A grin washed across Todd's face, making his dimples glow in the shimmering heat. "Yeah."

"I haven't done that in years."

Todd stepped into his car and grabbed the open window with one hand. "So are we going to Red's? We'll have a toast to Eloise."

At the name "Red's," my stomach revved to life with a sound that would put a Harley Davidson to shame. "Eloise would like that. I'll meet you there."

"Good. You need to get out more." Todd pulled the door shut and leaned out the window. "I better follow you. You never know when the Datsun will give out."

I crossed the field toward the parking lot, keeping a sharp eye for pony pucks. The smell of barbecue still hung in the air, bringing my thoughts back to the kid. I felt my anger toward Hunter justified, what with him disrespecting Eloise and his momma like that. Seemed like someone should have given his backside a swat or two growing up and he'd have a better attitude. But his life also sounded like one hot mess of family dysfunction, something that could easily sour a kid.

Luke and Uncle Will should hear about the family saga between the two Cotton teams, I figured. However, Luke seemed prickly about the whole "job interference" thing, even though my love of gossip could help his career. Besides, checking into a few things for a friend didn't equal interfering with the law. He was too danged sensitive about that.

Todd's red Civic rumbled behind me. I looked over my shoulder and caught his smile. It took the death of my friend to show me that my world had recently shifted. I hadn't even started the Greek paintings, dangit. Another show of disappointing Eloise.

Todd was right. I was better at butt-kicking than introspection. It was time to put my boots back on. Eloise deserved one hundred percent feistiness. No more letting my friends down.

SIX

We sat around a table at Red's County Line Tap, sucking on beer and chatting about the festival. County Line was once a mangy tavern that sat a few feet over the town line. A couple years ago, the new proprietor, Red, had transformed the whiskey-infused roadhouse into a sports bar. He attired the narrow room with flat-screen TVs and softball trophies. The long, mirror backed wooden bar still remained near the entrance and a small stage now sat at the far end.

Todd's band, Sticks, did not play tonight. We were somber for a Saturday night, as the death of Eloise was still fresh in our minds. One of Eloise's pots, black with a crackled white glaze, sat in the center of the scarred wooden table. Red providing beer and hot wings on the house in honor of Eloise had been a particular blessing in my penniless state.

"I heard Cherry kicked a guy in the stomach," said my sister Casey, joining us at the end of her shift. She whipped off her waitress apron, revealing massive exposure between her itty-bitty Red's t-shirt and belly skimming jeans.

My brother, Cody, looked on with irritation, more perturbed that I would get to tell the Hunter story again than by his sister's man-bait attire.

"You kicked a guy in the stomach?" asked Sid McKenzie, lead guitarist in Sticks. He eyed me warily across the table. New in town, Sid's first impression of me had been at a Sticks' performance. I had been hauled out kicking and screaming at Todd for writing unflattering lyrics about me. Sometimes I rub people the wrong way.

And it doesn't help to have these stories of me beating up eighteen-year-old boys.

"I elbowed him, not kicked him," I said. "But he called me a scarecrow and implied very improper things about my love life."

"Then shouldn't have Todd kicked his can instead of you?" asked Cody. My brother raised his brows beneath his Braves cap and pointed his longneck at Todd. "That's not very gentlemanly, Todd."

"I was gonna, but it's more fun to watch Cherry do it."

"Besides, Todd's not her boyfriend anymore," said Casey. She ran a hand up Todd's well-muscled arm and pinched his chin.

Todd grinned at my eye roll.

"Speaking of boyfriends, I'm surprised you detached yourself from the house just in case your cop should show up," said Cody. His brown eyes mocked me. Cody was born ornery. Instead of outgrowing that particular trait, he embraced it.

"Luke's got odd hours as a crime fighter," I said. "The superhero stuff makes him tired so he doesn't want to go out."

"Good thing we aren't all deputies or Red would go broke," said Todd. "Although Cherry and I have done some pretty good investigating on our own. Haven't we, baby?"

"What have you and Cherry investigated other than a Vegas wedding chapel?" Cody said with a laugh. "Not that it worked out too well for you, Todd."

"My timing was off."

I quickly changed the subject. "We got a good bit of gossip from that kid at the festival today. I wonder how long that autopsy will take. I'd really like to know if their stew was bad."

Red's door opened, and we swung our gazes to assess the newcomer. Luke nodded as a greeting and strode to the bar to grab a beer. His jeans and t-shirt melded with his lean body into lines that made me salivate more than the smell of frying chicken, but the man could wear a gorilla suit and still look hot.

I pushed from the table and hopped up to give him a private greeting at the bar. "How'd it go tonight? Catch any bad guys?"

He leaned in for a quick kiss. At the corners of his eyes, small lines scored his flesh. Shadows deepened the hallows beneath his cheekbones. I traced the cut of his cheek with a finger. What I wouldn't give for a quick charcoal sketch of this somber face.

"You look exhausted. Baby, go have a seat," I said. "I'll bring your beer. Have y'all been down in Sidewinder collecting evidence?"

He shook his head, refusing to let his deputy duties slip past his lips.

I crossed my arms over my black and silver sequined cami. "You know I'll find out anyway. The Halo grapevine is planted deep and well fertilized, so you might as well spill. Particularly when it could help a victim's family."

He shook his head and snagged the beer Red offered him. Pulling me into the circle of his arm, he leaned into my ear. "I'm not really up for a party. You want to head to your house after I drink this? Let me comfort you in private?"

"It's not a party," I gave him a look to check his libido. "We're sharing memories about Eloise. I didn't want to be alone."

"I'm here now. You're not alone."

"You know what I mean. Come and say hey to everyone."

Luke grunted but allowed me to pull him toward the table.

"Look what the cat drug in," said Cody. "Or was it the squad car that drug you here?"

"I'm off duty," said Luke, "but I can give you a trip to the station if you like."

Cody smiled with his teeth. "I'm not doing anything illegal. Yet."

"Good to have you here," said Todd. "Seems like we don't see you or Cherry much anymore."

"I may have been busy lately," I said not particularly enjoying the guilt creeping into the conversation. "But I'm certainly not abandoning my friends. I'm here for y'all."

"I thought you had some kind of painting deadline," said Luke. "And I thought you were broke."

"That's true, but it doesn't mean I should ignore my friends. I'm going to start sketching when we get back to the house."

"I am not letting you use me in a painting," said Luke.

"It's kind of fun," said Todd. "We used to have a good time when Cherry would draw me. She'd let me do all these crazy poses and see how fast she could get them down on paper."

"Obviously we have different ideas of fun," said Luke.

"Obviously we should be talking about something else," said Casey. "What do you think, Sid?"

Sid nodded, his eyes ping-ponging between us. "I want to hear more about the Vegas wedding. Y'all lost me there."

"Let's talk about the poisoning instead," I said quickly. "How many people got sick? Any as bad as Eloise? Did the health inspectors find anything?"

Luke eyed me over his beer. "How about you talk and I'll listen."

"I'm not sharing if you're not," I said.

"She got some good information today, too," said Todd.

"What information?" Luke set his beer on the table. "I thought I told you not to get involved."

"The Parkers want some details and they knew they'd get it faster from me than from the authorities," I said. "So, if you let some facts slide toward me, I can give it to them without a press conference. And I can let you know what I found out."

"So that's how it works? You expect me to corrupt an investigation in exchange for gossip?"

"Pretty much," I grinned and fluttered my eyelashes, giving him a flash of my Silver Sashay eye shadow.

"Something wrong with your eyes?" he asked.

I stopped fluttering and peered over his head at the bar. Shawna had walked in with a troop of well-dressed folks. Not a single Bass-Pro or Wrangler insignia among them. They looked just a tad out of place at Red's.

"Those look like the cook-off judges. I'll be right back," I said, hopping up, then dropped into my seat.

"Leave those judges and Shawna be," Luke said, pinning my arm to the table. "They've been through enough today without you interrogating them. Shawna brought them to Halo where it's quiet. The reporters are hunting for them in Line Creek."

"Did any of the judges get food poisoning?" Casey asked.

"They look fine to me," said Luke.

I noticed he didn't answer her question. "Eloise sure ate a lot. I wanted to see if any had tried the Cotton Pickin' Good stew. The chef and his wife both got sick. They went to the hospital, too."

"I don't see how this helps the Parkers," said Luke. "You're going to get them all roiled up about nothing."

"That's exactly why they want my help. Y'all think her death is just an accident. The Parkers want to make sure whoever made the bad food gets punished."

"Why would they ask you for help?" Sid said. "You're an artist, not a cop."

"Cherry's good at figuring stuff out," said Todd. "She uses that creative thinking. And she'll talk to anyone. Even teenage boys with switchblades in their pocket."

"Hunter had a switchblade?" I said.

"Switchblade?" Luke's eyebrows hit his scalp and fell to a glower.

"I'd say her thinking is more crazy than creative," said Cody. "The Parkers are like us and probably don't trust cops."

"The man you call uncle is sheriff," said Luke.

"He don't always trust cops neither." Cody pushed his cap up with his beer bottle. "Sometimes you got to look into stuff yourself. I'm actually working on some investigating myself."

"What are you investigating?" I glanced at Casey to see if she knew, but she shrugged.

"Something I don't want to talk about just yet," said Cody.

I snorted. Cody's investigations ran to pistons, carburetors, and dual exhaust. He likely found another muscle car to overhaul.

"Not letting trained officials doing their job?" Luke set his stormy gray eyes on me. "Do you hear how ridiculous that sounds?"

"We were raised to be self-sufficient."

"That's a joke. Cody and Casey still live with your Grandpa. None of you have full time jobs. How is that self-sufficient?"

With coordination not better seen by the Olympic synchronized swimming team, the Tucker crew delivered Luke our best stone-cold glare worthy of any redneck gold medal competition.

"I'm going to get another beer," Luke said and shoved out of his seat to stalk to the bar.

Cody's chair fell forward with a thud. "Actually there's something I need to check. I'll see y'all later."

"What's he up to?" I asked Casey.

"Dunno. He's been acting like that ever since he got home from the garage." Casey leaned toward me, nodding her head toward the bar. "What's up with His Crime Fighting Highness?"

"Dunno that either." But I had a sudden realization. Although Luke was also raised in Halo, we still faced each other from different sides of the tracks.

SEVEN

At Luke's approach to the bar, Shawna swiveled from her animated conversation with a vertically challenged man wearing khakis and a button down. She abandoned the businessman to sidle close to Luke. With a hair toss and a well-placed hand, Shawna captured Luke's attention.

"Probably asking her about the cook-off," said Casey sympathetically.

"Which is exactly what I wanted to do," I said. "I can't see the harm in asking a few questions for a friend."

"Luke's got a point," said Sid. "What can you do for the Parkers that the police can't? It's just food poisoning. Tragic, but that's it."

"What if it wasn't an accident? Who gets that sick from regular old food poisoning? Eloise pretty much died in my arms. What if it was meant for one of them?" I pointed at the cluster of Casual-Friday attired folks at the bar.

We turned in our chairs to study the judges. None of them looked worth poisoning, but then, my wild guesses didn't always pan out. At least, not right away.

"Damn," said Casey. "I never thought of that."

"If I wanted to poison somebody, that's how I'd do it," I said.

Sid scooted his chair further away from the table.

"What if it was meant for Mr. Max?" I said. "He was a judge, and he's probably got enemies. And I don't see him here tonight."

"Maybe he doesn't like beer and hot wings," said Casey.

"Then there's Eloise's boyfriend, Griffin. He was at the cook-off today. He's been known to get rough with her. Or maybe he's not cautious enough with his Genuine Juice formula and gave everyone botulism."

"Did this Griffin get food poisoning, too?" asked Sid. "Or are you just narrowing down the possible victims of bad potato salad to the hundreds of people who attended the festival?"

"Why does everyone think it was potato salad? Eloise didn't eat potato salad."

"Probably because of the mayonnaise," said Todd. "Bad mayo—"

"I know what the effects of bad mayo are like. Eloise didn't have spoiled mayo. You don't vomit blood with off potato salad."

"Eww," said Casey. "TMI."

"It's not that the police can't figure this stuff out," I said. "They're just slow. They've got to follow procedures. Wait on health inspector reports."

"So the Parkers have to wait, so what?" said Sid.

"Sometimes the victim's family wants swifter justice. Or at least answers. The Parkers have been through a lot with Eloise's sickness. She had new meds which seemed to be helping. To lose her so suddenly and in such an odd way, they can't grieve properly. And I know exactly how they feel," I grabbed Eloise's pot from the table. "I'm going home. I need to work on the classical paintings. I can't let Eloise down."

"Did you walk here?" said Todd. "Want a ride?"

I glanced at the bar. Luke and Shawna had their heads bowed together in conversation. Like a couple of chatty swans.

"I don't get that man," I said. "But if I'm leaving without him, he better notice it. Particularly considering the Amazon with which he's currently consorting."

I marched to the bar and tapped Luke on the shoulder.

A sneer unfurled from Shawna's glossy Ruby Lake lips. "I know what you're up to. You-know-what is still missing, and I have a good guess what happened to them. So just remember what I can do to you if you plan on using them."

I blinked. "What in the hell are you talking about?"

She curled in her middle fingers to point from her eyes to mine with her index and pinky. I assumed she was giving me the "I'm watching you sign." Or perhaps Shawna was a Longhorns fan and wanted me to note it.

"Just so you know, I'm leaving without you," I said to Luke. "But if you want to make it up to me, you can model for me tonight."

"No, ma'am."

"Then I'll see you at the farm for dinner tomorrow."

"If I want to make it up to you?" Luke said. "What about you?"

"What about me?"

"You questioned a kid with a switchblade. How do you think that makes me feel?"

"I also elbowed him in the stomach and made him swallow his chew after he insulted me. I hope you'd be proud."

Shawna snorted. Which is not a pretty response for an ex-Brunswick Stew Queen.

Luke's lips clenched together. His eyebrow nerve pulsed. "I sure hope you're joking," he said through gritted teeth.

"Luke, you wanted to speak to some of the cook-off judges," said Shawna, placing a hand on his bicep. "Let me introduce you to these fine people before I drive them back to the hotel in Line Creek."

Luke cut his eyes to Shawna and back at me. "All right."

"Dinner's at two tomorrow." I clutched the Raku pot to my chest and spun on my heel, hoping he got a good view of my huff as it walked toward the door.

Todd caught up with me outside. We slid into his Civic and tore out of the parking lot. It took us approximately one hundred and four seconds to reach my house. When Halo's population shifted away from the old whistle stop center, the town rezoned many of the early twentieth century homes off the square for businesses. A few old families still occupied the original avenues of Loblolly and Magnolia. My Great-Gam's ninety-year old cottage sat on the tail end of Loblolly, once the outskirts of town. Since we believe in keeping property in the family, the cottage was now my studio and house. Its proximity to Red's was a bonus.

"I had fun watching you question that kid," said Todd, sliding out of the Civic to open my door. "Just like old times."

"It's not like I used to spend my leisure time beating up teenagers," I said, then reflected on that statement as we threaded through the junk in my carport. "At least now that I'm not a teenager."

He hung back, leaning against the wall while I unlocked my kitchen door. I held the door open with my hip and turned to give him a quick goodbye hug.

Todd grasped my shoulder, stopping my hug. "You're being a good friend to Eloise. I'm sorry about her death."

"I wish I had been a better friend when she was alive. I should have stood up to her asshole boyfriend more. And I should have hustled on the classical paintings, knowing how important the respect of her professor was to her." I took a deep breath to keep my eyes from watering. "But thanks, hon. I'll get this all figured out."

"I'm sure you will." Todd released my shoulder to lean in for the hug. He snuck a kiss on my cheek and then hovered at the spot for a long second.

"You'll do the right thing. But you can't make everybody happy." His breath smelled faintly of beer and mint.

I wanted to pull back with a smart-ass comment, but for some reason I didn't move.

"Although you are good at making people happy," he continued. His lips were so close they brushed my cheek as he talked.

"How funny," I mumbled. "Your eyes look more azure than cerulean at this distance." I closed my lashes to save myself from the blue brilliance.

He turned his face fractionally and his soft lips followed, skimming my cheek to the outer corner of my lips. "You're like walking sunshine. Usually."

"Usually?" My bottom lip bumped his.

I wanted to shove him and laugh at the stupid "walking sunshine" line. It was so unlike Todd, my Labrador-like friend who liked everyone to think he was dumb and easygoing.

The door slammed behind me. Todd's hands were on my waist and in my hair, and I realized Todd must have kicked the door shut. And his lips seemed to be moving over mine while I was still processing the whole "walking sunshine" line.

Just like when he kissed me in Vegas, I thought. Right before he asked me to marry him.

His soft lips kept running over mine, pressing and nibbling until I gave in. My hands were already stroking the firm muscles of his back and running down those broad shoulders to the biceps he liked to show off.

I felt I should blame my mother for this ridiculousness because I was not the type to kiss one man when seeing another. She did hand me that genetic defect at birth. Beautiful men made us stupid. Even stupid for someone as stupid as Todd.

Wait a minute.

He "liked everyone to think he was dumb and easygoing?"

What if Todd was not really dumb? Or easygoing?

No way, I thought. This is Todd. Loyal Todd. Low maintenance Todd, who didn't want an annulment, but gave in because I was so angry.

And hung around me ever since. Because he's so dumb.

Or really, really clever. Cody calls him the idiot savant of poker, but isn't that what helps him win? His poker face?

Almost a better poker face than Luke's usual unflappable mug.

Luke? Dammit! What in the hell was I doing?

I jerked out of Todd's arms and tumbled to the ground. Looking around, I realized we had moved into my kitchen, and he was about to lift me onto my counter for easier access to my lips and other parts. I stared at the glazed eyes looking down at me and tried to identify any calculation in their blue depths.

Todd blinked, bent over, and held out his hand. "Sorry, Cherry. Are you okay?"

With my lips pressed firmly shut, I continued to stare and willed my heart to slow down and the rest of my body to cool off. Scuttling backwards, I moved away from the man I thought to be one of my best friends.

Now I wasn't so sure I knew Todd at all.

"Cherry? I'm really sorry." His face pinched in confusion, and he rubbed his hands through his hair. "I don't know what came over me."

"Don't you?" I grabbed a drawer handle and hauled myself up.

"Old habits are hard to break," he said shakily. His fingers began strumming the sides of his pants. "You're looking awfully cute tonight in that get up anyway."

I glanced down at my black tank top embellished in a sequined silver rose. The pocket lining of my shorts hung below the ragged threads of my cutoffs. Not like I was wearing a slinky dress or something.

"You better go," I said. "I don't know what's going on, but it's not good. I'm with Luke."

"I know." Did a frown just flash across his face or was I imagining things now? "I'm sorry."

My eyes traveled to his calf where the double cherry slot machine motif had been permanently inscribed. I had never asked him about the tattoo, never even mentioned it. He had it inked after we broke up.

Suddenly my head felt too heavy for my neck.

"Baby," Todd took a step toward me. "Are you okay?"

I shook my head and pointed at the door. Todd, thankfully, took the hint and left. Then I sank onto a chair and cried. After allowing myself a few minutes of boohooing, I forced myself to walk to the bathroom, splash water on my puffy face, and get ready for bed. I had no model for my Greek paintings, but had lost my gumption to work on it anyway.

I wasn't myself. I don't cry over a boy dumb enough to tattoo a symbol for an ex-girlfriend on his person. Why hadn't I just smacked him or yelled at him or thrown something at him?

Maybe I was more upset about Eloise than I thought. I had better settle these feelings before I did something really stupid.

Not that kissing Todd didn't top the idiot-of-the-week list.

EIGHT

Waking up alone on a Sunday morning has its benefits. No wrestling over who gets to read the funnies in the paper first. No arguing over whose turn it was to make the coffee and Krispy Kreme run. I had the whole morning to paint. Or sketch. Or embellish my clothes. However, I wasn't feeling artsy or craftsy. I didn't even feel hungry. I took my temperature, but it clocked in at ninety-six, so I knew I wasn't sick.

It'd been a while since I attended a Sunday service. What Halo lacked in drinking establishments we made up in churches, so I had quite a few to choose from. Since my buddy Leah directed the choir at New Order Fellowship, I figured that was as good as anywhere. Grandma Jo always said to look your best at church. I didn't need her additional guilt lumped in with all the rest of my feelings, so I dressed in a white sundress with large, black polka dots I had trimmed with crimson flower heads. A quick hot glue job of more flowers onto black flip-flops ensured extra pizzazz. I figured God was good with pizzazz at church.

Not that I was attending from feelings of guilt or conflict over Todd's kiss. I'd been meaning to get to church for quite a while now and just never got around to it. And it was the perfect place to hear about the fallout from Sidewinder, if there was any news to hear in this part of the county.

I found it odd that the very cook-off team who served Eloise her stew had more family disorder than a Jerry Springer rerun. I hoped something would turn up in the autopsy. But that could take weeks. Uncle Will would have to work with a lab in the city. Seeing as we're lowly Forks County with no reason to rush the results, the lab would get to Eloise after their own backlog. And even lowlier people like the Parkers would wait and wonder if they could have done something to prevent their daughter's death.

A short time later, the Datsun wobbled into the full parking lot of New Order Fellowship, gratefully halting under the scant shade of a crepe myrtle. One of her hubcaps rolled down a long line of cars to spin under a shiny yellow Mustang convertible. Even without the GAPCH vanity plates and Mardi Gras beads hanging from the rear view, I would have known that Mustang anywhere. Shawna Branson's college graduation present. I retrieved the hubcap and hurried into church, wondering why Shawna attended morning services in Halo instead of her hometown of Line Creek.

Entering the modern barn-like structure, I stood in the rear and scanned for an extra seat in the packed church. Three rows from the back, the imposing body of Max Avtaikin slouched in a pew. That sight brought me up short. I never took the Bear for a Christian. I scooted up the aisle and shoehorned myself between him and the end of the pew.

His eyelids flickered open at my wriggling. "Artist, what are you doing here?"

"I might ask you the same question," I whispered.

"You're an hour late."

"The way I figure it, God is a better late than never kind of guy."

"I take it you do not often attend the service," he replied.

"Are you pointing fingers?"

Behind us, a shushing commenced. I swiveled in my seat and took in a long row of older women pulling stern faces. I mouthed an apology. Turning around, I realized grandmotherly women surrounded Max. Not a surprise at church, but the absence of husbands made me wonder if there had been a collective fishing expedition I hadn't heard about.

I elbowed him. "What's with the blue-haired entourage?"

He shrugged and pretended to listen to the sermon.

In the front, Pastor Earlie gave a rousing amen and left his podium. Pride prickled my neck as I watched my buddy Leah rise and lift her arms, bringing the rest of the choir to their feet. Leah's braided extensions had been wrapped into a twist, leaving her long neck exposed. A body as sultry as her singing voice hid underneath the bulky choir robe, which she and her mother preferred to hide. However, I spied smoking hot heels underneath the robe that would put my decorative flip-flops to shame. I'd have to catch her after the service to hand out compliments.

Among the white robed singers, Miss Wanda, Luke's mother, swayed and sung praises. What with Luke just graduating from the Academy and his odd hours, we hadn't spent any time with his parents. Which was fine with me since my last dealings with them had been a fiasco. I hadn't pushed the subject of Sunday dinners at the Bransons with Luke, but today might be a good day to extend an olive branch. Surprising Luke with a good relationship with his parents might help me make reparations.

Craning my neck, I spied JB, Luke's stepfather, sitting in the front row with Shawna, his niece. I couldn't seem to shake her these days. Seems that Max couldn't either, except for Shawna's little mixer at Red's the night before.

I poked Max with my finger and leaned in. "Did you get sick at the festival?"

"Sick at the festival?" He frowned. "Is this an expression?"

"No, I mean literally. Did you take sick from eating at the cook-off? You tried all the stews, right?"

He raised an imperious eyebrow. "I am the Bear, no? It takes more than a sample of bad food to damage this beast."

"If you say so. My friend died yesterday." I felt a tremor in my bottom lip and bit down hard. "It may have been bad stew."

"I am very sorry for your friend, Miss Tucker." To my surprise, Max picked my hand off my lap and kissed it before laying it gently back in my lap. "My condolences."

"Thanks," I mumbled, then silently told my eyes to quit their watering.

Another round of shushing commenced. I darted angry looks at the post-menopausal set until I remembered my current venue. Before settling back in my seat, I caught sight of a brunette bouffant perched on a twiggy body who looked a lot like Hunter's aunt, Belinda.

I nudged Max and pointed. "What's she doing here? That's Belinda Gable from Team High Cotton. You probably tasted her stew yesterday, too. I would think she'd have a church in Sidewinder to attend."

Max peered over the rolled-and-set hairstyles toward the end of the pew where Belinda Gable sat. "She came with the other ladies. I know nothing."

I folded my arms over my chest carefully as not to squash my flowers. Max knowing nothing meant he knew something. I was ready to toss him a few more questions when Leah finished the gospel set with a crescendoing flourish of the Hallelujah chorus. I clapped.

Max looked at me askance. "Your enthusiasm, although unbridled, is noted."

"You have to admit, Leah is amazing. You should hear her sing in Sticks." At the thought of Todd's band, my voice seized.

"You were saying?"

But Max's reply was also cut short, this time by the final benediction and a mob of elderly women. They flooded the pew with the powdery scents of lilac and rose, shoving baggies of cookies and foil-wrapped plates at the man.

"Mr. Max, will we see you today?" Using her cane to wedge herself between us, a woman shoved herself into the pew.

I scrambled over the armrest before she crushed my toe with the rubber tipped impaler and almost stepped into a straw shoulder bag someone had left in the aisle. My flip-flop caught on the upright strap. I performed an aerial forward roll and landed flat on my back. My sundress flared out around me, scattering silk flower heads into the aisle. Quickly, I sat up and pushed my dress down. JB, Wanda, and Shawna stood before me. I scampered to my feet and held out a hand.

"Mr. and Mrs. Branson. Sir. Ma'am. Shawna," I babbled. "So good to see you again."

JB's eyebrows dropped, and he shoved his hands into the pockets of his Sunday suit pants. Open-mouthed, Wanda gave my outstretched hand a timid shake while Shawna ripped off a hearty snort.

"Good Lord, Cherry," Shawna said. "If you're going to flash everyone your panties, you'd think you'd pick a better place to do it."

I smiled wide, reminding myself that good girlfriends did not get into cat fights at church in front of her boyfriend's parents. And after last night's spat and Todd's kiss, I had some serious girlfriend karma to rework. "Good morning to you, Shawna. What brings you to Halo?"

"If you actually went to this church, you'd know I attend with JB and Aunt Wanda every Sunday."

"I'm glad to see you didn't suffer the same symptoms as the rest of the Brunswick Stew cook-off folks," I said.

She stiffened at the mention of the incident.

I couldn't help an incidental potshot. "Sorry to hear your hard work was ruined by food poisoning."

Shawna cocked a leopard-printed hip and folded her arms over her chest. Rings glittered from her fingers, chunky bangles cluttered her wrists, and a heavy necklace settled into her bronzer-dusted cleavage.

I always felt when wearing a strong print, like leopard, you should tone down the accessories. And cleavage. But that's speaking as a woman without cleavage.

"You wouldn't know anything about the food poisoning, Cherry?" Shawna's voice dropped just shy of acidic.

JB shot her an irritated look, probably for continuing the conversation with me.

"Did you hear I was looking into it?" I asked. Word got around fast, but I didn't think I had advertised my interest into Eloise's death.

"Why would you look into it?" Shawna spat. "I'm talking about your need to ruin every venture I commence to partake."

Wanda gasped and fluttered a hand to JB's arm. Shawna wasn't helping me improve my image with Luke's parents.

"Ruin your ventures? What about mine? In the past, you tried to destroy my portrait business by spreading unkind rumors about me. Do you know I've barely had a job since..." I stopped myself with a look to JB and Wanda's shocked faces. They had been one of my last patrons. I had a lot of bad girlfriend damage to overcome. "I had nothing to do with the food poisoning, Shawna. My friend, Eloise, died yesterday."

"Mercy," said Wanda. "I am so sorry, Cherry." She immediately wrapped me into a hug, my bad manners forgiven through the odd bond of death.

I wallowed in her soft arms for a minute then gently disentangled myself. "Thank you, Miss Wanda. I appreciate your concern. You'll be happy to know Luke has been a great comfort to me during this time."

"Why would Luke be a comfort to you?" JB said.

"Is there some kind of police investigation into her death or something?" asked Wanda. She patted my arm. "What's her family's name, honey? I'll send over food."

"The Parkers in Sidewinder," I said, momentarily confused. "There's not an investigation into her death. Yet. She had a chronic condition, which might have been exasperated by the bad stew."

"There's been no proof the stew was off," said Shawna. "I made sure the cook-off teams followed proper food storage procedures. You're trying to make me look bad."

"I'm stating the facts, Shawna. Eloise had a condition. She ate a bunch of stew. She died."

Shawna pointed a finger in my face. "You better watch your mouth, Cherry Tucker. The festival committee job is important to me. The cook-off has national exposure, at least in the South. If I hear anyone tampered with those stews, I'll know who did it."

"Why would I tamper with the stews?"

"To make me look bad," she screeched, then checked herself. "Just remember what I can do to you if you plan on using the you-know-what."

"As usual, I am still confounded by your vague references. You want to spell it out for me?"

"Now, now, Shawna," said Wanda. "I'm sure if Cherry did anything, it was just a prank, and she didn't mean any harm. You girls have always been so competitive and sometimes you take it too far. After all, why would she want to poison her friend?"

Shawna grabbed Wanda by the arm and swept her up the aisle. JB stalked behind them with an exasperated glance at me.

"Now what happened?" asked Leah, sauntering up the aisle. She had disrobed and her curvy figure now hid behind a black shift swaddled in an enormous multi-colored jacket. Scarlet toenail paint peeked from her open-toed red stilettos.

"I don't think those shoes match the burqa." I shook my head. "Never mind. I have new problems."

"What else is new?" Leah smiled and waved to a few parishioners still wandering up the aisles.

I followed her gaze and noticed Max had slipped away. I had to put that strange encounter on the back burner in my list of odd behaviors of Forks County. But it definitely warranted checking into.

"I just had a chat with the Bransons. I got the feeling they didn't know I'm dating Luke. And Shawna is ticked at me again. She thinks I tried to give everyone in Sidewinder food poisoning to make her look bad."

"Maybe you need to talk to Luke," said Leah. "And I keep telling you to ignore Shawna."

"That's like ignoring a python in your bed."

"True. I'd hate to tangle with her. What else is wrong? You look sad, not irritated." She studied my face for a minute. "Girl, did

you even put on makeup this morning? You've created a new definition for white."

"Eloise Parker died."

Her dark eyes widened, and she covered her mouth with her
hands. "No. I didn't hear that. I knew she was sick, but I didn't
think it was life-threatening."

"It wasn't. And I'm going to find out what happened."

Leah placed a hand on her hip. "And how are you going to do
that?"

"I'm starting with a visit to the bereaved and you're coming
with me."

"I'd be happy to visit the Parkers."

"We're not visiting the Parkers. We're going to visit Eloise's
boyfriend, Griffin Ward. He was kicked out of the festival after has-
sling Eloise. I want to find out just what he knows about Eloise's
death."

NINE

"I can't be late for dinner, Cherry," said Leah, fanning herself with a folded church bulletin. We had the windows cranked down, but it was still hotter than blue blazes in the Datsun. "Momma is probably already wondering where I am."

"I've got to be back for dinner, too. Don't you worry." I flashed Leah a quick smile as we sped down the country road. Although in the Datsun, sped is a bit of a misnomer. More like jerked forward with the occasional wheeze and shimmy.

"How do you talk me into these activities? I'm going to die from heat stroke in this truck."

"Take your jacket off. It's not my fault you dress like an Eskimo in July." I turned past the Viper onto a short street at the edge of Sidewinder. "We're visiting the grieving. A perfectly acceptable activity for a Sunday morning."

"If I had known, I would have brought a casserole."

"I picked up donuts." I jerked the gearshift into park. "That's plenty gracious enough for Griffin Ward."

I'd rather bring Griffin some Chinese water torture after the misery he put Eloise through, but an unexpected visit required an air of respectability. Which is why I brought Leah and a box of donuts. Generic donuts. I wasn't going to waste Krispy Kreme dollars.

"I should warn you. Griffin's been popping steroids since high school wrestling and they've done a number on his etiquette skills," I said. "Not to mention his anger management skills."

"What have you gotten me into?"

We examined the small white ranch with black shutters Griffin rented. The ceramic pot filled with dying petunias was Eloise's touch. "Looks like nobody is home," said Leah.

"Let's check anyway." I hopped out of the truck. "Come on."

Leah followed me up the cracked sidewalk, holding the white donut box before her. The slap of my flip-flops and the tip-tap of Leah's sexy heels broke the stillness. I hammered on the door before I lost my nerve. A long minute passed. I tried the knob, found it unlocked, and poked my head in.

"Griffin?" I called and stepped into his living room. "We're melting out here. Mind if we come in?"

"Cherry, we can't just walk in." Leah tugged on my dress from the porch.

"His door is unlocked. Maybe he's in the back." Gym equipment, a large screen TV, and a collapsing pastel floral couch packed the small living room. "We're bringing you donuts and our condolences, Griffin," I hollered.

A squeal of tires caused Leah and I to spin around and peek out the door. An older, red Pontiac Grand Prix bumped up the drive and parked next to my Datsun.

"What the hell do you want?" Griffin popped out of his vehicle. He wiped a towel across his bare chest, tossed it in the car, and slammed the door. He strode up the walk clad in a pair of purple training shorts, socks, and gym shoes. Without a shirt or doo-rag, his shiny head matched the glow of his shaved, bulbous chest.

"Glad to see you aren't sick from food poisoning." I almost asked him about his topless condition, but thought better. "I'm sorry about Eloise. I was with her when it happened."

He pushed past us and walked through the living room. Circumnavigating a bench press, Leah and I followed into the kitchen. With a polite frown, Leah turned a circle with the donuts. All available counter space in the kitchen was covered in vegetables, fruits, and large plastic containers. The kitchen table held plastic bottles, an industrial blender, and a large juicer.

"Where should I put your donuts?" she asked Griffin.

"I don't eat that shit," he said. "Toss it or take it with you."

"Okay," she pulled the word out slowly and began edging toward the doorway.

I wandered to the long counter and picked up a bunch of limp celery. "You're a health food nut, huh?"

"I don't eat the crap you do, if that's what you mean." He tried to cross his bulging arms over his bulky chest, gave up, and placed his hands on his hips. "My body is a temple, and I'm not going to fill it with a lot of shit. Like those donuts."

"That's funny. To me, most health food tastes like sh—"

"We're so sorry about Eloise," said Leah quickly. "You must be heartbroken. Is there anything we can do? Would you like a visit from my pastor?"

He shot Leah a look of disgust. "How's that going to help?"

I examined a giant jar of protein powder and moved to the next plastic jug. Sniffing the green-black sludge, I wrinkled my nose and backed away. "What is this? Compost?"

"Get out of there." Griffin swept the jug off the counter. "You're going to contaminate it. I've got to finish up this batch for the Green Gourmet."

"You're selling this stuff to the health food store? People buy this gunk?"

"Hell, yeah. At least people who are interested in being healthy, unlike you and Eloise. I tried to tell her the food y'all eat would kill her and she wouldn't listen to me. I could have saved her life if she had switched over to my diet."

"I'm so sorry, Griffin," said Leah.

"Yeah, sorry does nothing for me." He thumped the jug onto the counter. "It's too late for sorry. I finally convinced her to try a new blend and look what happened. I might have cured her of her Crohn's."

"You really think you would have cured her?"

"Obviously. Look at me. I'm never sick. The picture of health." He spun in a slow circle with upraised arms, allowing us to admire his shiny, perfect temple. Which reminded me of a Rubik's cube what with his short stature. "Eloise should have listened to me."

"Maybe she didn't like the taste," I offered. "She told me veggies bothered her stomach. And that's why she smoked all the time. The nicotine actually made her feel better."

"That's a load of crap. Veggies are good for you. Everyone knows that."

Leah flinched. "Maybe we should go," she said. "It's getting late, and I've got to get back for dinner."

"Yeah, go eat your Sunday dinner. Eat your lard and bacon soaked greens and macaroni made out of fat and bleached carbs. Fry your way to an early grave, just like Eloise."

"Come on, Cherry," said Leah.

I held up a hand. "Just a minute. You made Eloise drink something yesterday. Was it your special blend?"

"Why?" His eyes narrowed.

"I'm just wondering. Maybe she had an allergic reaction or something. Her parents would want to know. They think it's food poisoning from the Brunswick Stew cook-off. You could help the doctors if they knew exactly what she and the folks from the festival ate."

"I'm not helping those quacks. And I don't give a shit about the festival."

"What was in the special blend? Did anyone else try it?"

"It was specifically made for Eloise. You trying to say my Genuine Juice made Eloise sick?" Griffin flexed a beefy arm and paced forward.

"Cherry," Leah clutched my arm. "Let's go."

"She vomited blood in my arms," I hissed. "I held her while her body spasmed and shook. Her eyes rolled back in her head. In my friggin' arms! I want to know what killed her."

"Bad living killed Eloise." Griffin raised his chin. "She sucked in those lead pottery fumes, smoked cigarettes, drank, and ate bacon. She's lucky she lived as long as she did. I tried to warn her."

"She was doing alright until yesterday afternoon. All I want to know is what she had to eat and drink."

"And now I'm warning you. You best leave me alone. I loved Eloise despite her faults, but I don't even like you. I know you were trying to break us up all along. I tolerated you for Eloise's sake, but not anymore. You mess with me and somebody will be visiting your boyfriend with a box of donuts."

"Again, sorry for your loss." Leah dropped the donuts, yanked my arm, and pulled me through the kitchen doorway.

We hopped over the weight bench and banged through the front door. From the truck, we watched Griffin peer out the front window.

I turned to Leah before maneuvering around his Grand Prix. "Does he seem like a man mourning the loss of his girlfriend? Didn't I tell you Griffin had a screw loose?"

"I tell you one thing." Leah whipped out her homemade fan and dabbed at her perspiring face. "I am never going on a sympathy call with you again."

TEN

I left Leah at New Order Fellowship and tried to put Griffin out of my mind on the trip to my Grandpa's farm for the obligatory Sunday dinner. With my brain full of Genuine Juice and muscle-bound threats, I cranked the Datsun's wheel at the corner of the farm lane and almost forgot myself.

A massive, white billy goat popped out of the ditch. I pounded the brakes, avoiding slamming my truck into the cud-chewing hellion by a matter of inches. Tater the goat, more favored by my Grandpa than his own grandchildren, had a dysfunctional relationship with me and the Datsun. In particular, a sick love of playing chicken with my truck. Tater needed serious therapy. Which eventually might involve a close and personal encounter with tire tread.

My motor revved and Tater pawed the dirt. The bed of my truck still hung past the ditch and stuck into the road. The goat lowered his horns. His amber eyes gleamed. The tip of his beard dragged in the dirt and gravel while he waited for me to make my move. I revved. Tater pawed. I inched forward. He slammed his thick skull into my grill.

"Dammit, Tater!" I jammed the gearshift into park and hopped out of the truck.

Tater pranced around me, celebrating his victory.

"I can't just leave my truck here."

The neighbor's horses drifted to the fence adjoining our lane to watch the show. Tater bleated, and they bobbed their heads in agreement. I shook my fist and slipped into the Datsun while Tater danced along the fence line, trying to agitate the horses. I floored the little truck. Tater hung a sharp left from the fence and galloped alongside me, clearly enjoying the race. I made it to the split in the lane before Tater careened to the left, taunting me into T-boning him. I pumped the brakes, body slammed the steering wheel, and thrust the gear into park.

Hugging my sore stomach, I curled up into a fetal position on the bench of my truck. I could hear Tater butting the truck door, waiting for me to clamber out and yell at him, but for some reason, I just didn't have it in me. The thought of walking up the lane in the blasting heat with Tater snuffling my armpits and getting his slobbering cud all over my dress made me tired. A scrabbling sound accompanied Tater's head poking through my open window. He bleated and cocked his head, wondering what in the hell was wrong with me.

"I don't know," I muttered. "Go away."

I heard the scuttle of tires plowing through loose gravel and flattened on the seat, hoping the driver would go around me and follow the lane to park at the house. It wouldn't be the first time I had abandoned my truck in the middle of the farm drive, thanks to Tater. Hopefully, my siblings or Uncle Will drove the vehicle to the house for Sunday dinner. Chances were they wouldn't give the Datsun much thought.

Unfortunately, the vehicle slowed and stopped behind my truck. I heard the creak of a door and the shuffle of steps in the dirt. I gusted a long held sigh and flipped over on my back. A moment later, Luke peered through my window.

"Taking a nap?"

I shot up in my seat. "No. I was waiting for Tater to give up and leave."

"He's gone." Luke reached through the window and popped the door handle. "Took off when I pulled up."

"Figures," I said, sliding over as Luke climbed into the cab. "He only does this to me."

"I wonder why?" Luke drew an arm along the back of the seat. "Maybe he's got a thing for you."

A half-dimple popped in his cheek.

I averted my eyes.

"Yeah, well I've got a thing for him if he keeps ramming my truck." I scowled. "It's called a shotgun."

Luke laughed. "You want to tell me the real reason why you're lying in your truck?"

"Not really."

His long fingers played in my hair, rubbing the thin, blonde filament between his thumb and forefinger. I shifted in my seat to face him but couldn't bring my gaze up to watch his dimple disappear.

I should tell him. Get it over with. Be honest. Do the right thing.

But it was just a kiss. One I ended before it went too far, and I didn't want to see Luke and Todd get into a fight.

I looked up. Luke watched me with expectant eyes. Sweat beaded his forehead and his t-shirt was damp at the collar and under his arms. Even with the windows rolled down, the air in the truck was stifling, and I wondered how I could stand it a few minutes ago. The scent of Luke's sweat and maleness overpowered my senses. I needed to get out.

"It's hot in here," I said. "Let's go inside and cool off."

"What's wrong?" He drew his arms in, folding them, and gave me the look that said, "What drama am I going to have to deal with now?"

That's the kind of look that doesn't set well with women. Particularly when we know there's something wrong but aren't too sure how to put it into words or ideas that would make sense to a person of the XY chromosome. Because there's something about that XY combination that makes their listening skills turn off when an XX girl says, "I feel like..." That combination of words makes XY's eyes glaze over or roll back in their heads, and we're left just as frustrated as we were when they asked "What's wrong?"

And feeling hot and uncomfortable, I decided to toss Todd's remark at Luke. "Do you think I haven't been acting like myself lately?" I frowned. "Like I've been quieter?"

"Quieter?" A dimple popped into view again. "I've never associated you with that particular word."

"Todd thinks I haven't been acting like myself."

Luke's brows fell and lips puckered into a frown. The sweat had crept into his hair, making the roots darker. "Maybe it's all the meals you cook that are softening you. Or the fact that you want to stay home on Friday and Saturday nights and snuggle."

"Are you making fun of me?" I said. "I'm serious. I've been letting my friends down. What is it about you and cooking?"

"Forget cooking. Maybe we should test out your snuggling skills."

Before I could protest, he pulled me into a kiss. His full lips seared my mouth while I fumbled under the pressure. My lips slackened despite the rest of my body urging them to continue. I tried to push them into another go, but they felt dry as toast despite the rain of sweat dripping off both of us.

"What was that?"

I massaged my lips with my fingertips. "I don't know," I said, although I feared Todd had somehow poisoned my lips. "There's something wrong with me."

"Sugar, there is nothing wrong with you. Todd McIntosh is putting ideas in your head, ironic as that might sound. A bigger problem is the amount of time you spend with that idiot," Luke continued. "He gets his kicks from seeing you get in trouble. Todd likes seeing you riled up. I've been watching him. You better be careful."

The blood rushed from my head and I felt dizzy. "Careful?"

"I forgot you don't know the meaning of the word careful." The taut skin of Luke's cheeks stretched into a half-smile. "It means think before you act. Like questioning kids with switchblades. You don't need to feel like you've got to save the world. Or Halo. That's my job. You relax and let me do that for you."

I narrowed my eyes. "What are you saying?"

"That Todd McIntosh feeds your ego. You do the dumbest stuff when you're with him." Luke pushed his hand through his wet hair. "This truck is hotter than a witch's hat. Let's go in and eat."

I was about to argue that I could do plenty of dumb stuff without Todd when my stomach gunned to life. Tater materialized at my door.

"Maybe it's your stomach that draws Tater," said Luke. "He hears that god-awful sound and thinks you're calling him over."

I glared at the amber eyes staring at me through the window and decided to follow Luke out his side of the truck. How could Luke blame Todd for getting me riled up? Todd wasn't smart enough to plant ideas in my brain.

Or was he?

eleven

The smell of frying chicken filled the sunny yellow kitchen, causing me to wilt at the door. Grandpa and Uncle Will looked up from their conversation over tall tea glasses and Cody straightened from his kitchen chair slump at our entrance. At the counter, Casey mixed yellow batter in a glass bowl. Next to her stood an older woman with gray roots emerging from short, frosted hair. A blue tattoo on her left breast peeked from the neck of a white tank top, while shapely legs clad in denim Capri pants supported her top-heavy frame. The chicken momentarily forgotten, I examined the rough looking woman while the kitchen crowd stared at us.

"Y'all fall in a pool on the way over?" Cody asked, snickering.

I glanced at Luke's drenched t-shirt and wet, curling hair. Then my eyes fell upon my slick skin and the soggy V between my breasts where a single flower hung. Even my flip-flops appeared wet. I didn't want to see the kind of mess that lay on top of my head. My hair sure wouldn't curl prettily like Luke's. Probably looked more like a wet Collie. I needed a shower. But my curiosity about the tattooed woman in our kitchen kept me rooted in the doorway.

"You must be Cherry," she said. "I'm Pearl."

All eyes but Grandpa's flew from Pearl to me.

"Yes, ma'am. This here is Luke." I reached to give him a gentle shove into the kitchen, but he had already walked forward to shake her hand.

"Nice to meet you. Deputy Luke Harper."

Cody's mouth twitched, which should have given me a clue as to what was to come. Luke ambled to the table to give his regards to Uncle Will and Grandpa before sinking into a chair next to Cody.

"You got some tea for this boy?" Grandpa called over his shoulder. "Luke looks like he needs a drink. Y'all walk here from town? It's hotter than the hinges of hell outside."

"I'll get it, honey." Pearl walked toward the refrigerator while I picked my jaw up from the floor.

Pearl's getting the tea? My gaze flew to Casey. She stared daggers at the woman's back.

I remained stuck at the door, gaping at the scene before me. Pearl retrieved the glass pitcher of sweet tea from the fridge and scooted to the counter.

"Where do you keep your glasses, honey?" she asked Casey.

Casey narrowed her eyes into slits, barely opening her thin lips to answer. "I've got it." She flicked her brown ponytail like an irritated mare. It may be Grandpa's house, but we were standing in Casey's kitchen. "Ma'am."

"No bother, baby." Pearl began investigating our cupboards, hunting for a glass.

Casey popped open a door and snatched a glass, slamming it on the counter. "No problem."

A movement caught my attention. I glanced at the table where Grandpa and Uncle Will had resumed their conversation. Luke signaled me over, but I couldn't move. His eyes widened and he nodded at the two women bickering over who would serve him tea.

"I'll get it," I said, marching to the counter to retrieve the glass. "If Luke's too lazy to get his own tea, I guess I can catch his slack. I'm the one who invited him here."

"Wasn't me," muttered Cody. His brown eyes flickered to Luke, who caught the look and held it. Luke's shaming still burned Cody. Walking to the table, I kicked Cody's chair and handed Luke his tea. "So Pearl, are you a friend of Cody's?"

"No, honey." Pearl hopped to the stove to peek under the lid of a steaming pot. "I'm a friend of your Grandpa Ed. We met at a goat owners' coop meeting."

A curl of steam rose and the smell of pork fat and simmering beans filled the warm kitchen. My stomach gurgled, and I forgot about the goats.

Casey looked up from a muffin tin splattered with yellow globs. Her spoon slapped cornbread batter into an empty hole with a hearty thwack. I grimaced at the abuse.

"Them beans are just fine," Casey hollered.

Grandpa and Uncle Will exchanged a wary glance. I sucked in my breath. Pearl replaced the lid and turned away from the stove. She stuck her hands on her hips and gave Casey a knowing look. My sister tossed her spoon on the counter and shot one back.

We had walked into the shootout at the O.K. Corral. Grandpa ignored the women. Uncle Will grabbed his tea glass and turned toward Luke. Luke's eyes stayed fixed on me. The temperature of the kitchen rose about thirty degrees.

I pulled at my sticky dress and tried to jostle my mind into something distracting. I looked at Uncle Will. "Did you authorize the autopsy on my friend, Eloise Parker?"

I felt Luke prod my ankle with his boot, but the tension in the kitchen dipped. Casey turned back to her cornbread mess, and Pearl slipped onto a chair eager for news.

Uncle Will's chocolate brown eyes regarded me. He pulled his large hands off the wet tea glass to settle on his round belly, leaving damp imprints on the stretched t-shirt. "How do you know about the autopsy?"

I glanced at Luke, but his face had hardened into his deputy mask of blank indifference.

"Eloise's daddy said he was going to demand it," I said. "I agree with him. The whole thing is very odd."

"Eloise was sickly, Cher." Uncle Will eased back his large frame in the rattan chair, making it creak. "I'm very sorry about your friend, though."

"She was fine earlier even with her Crohn's. It's suspicious. That's no ordinary food poisoning."

"You think everything is suspicious," muttered Luke.

"An outbreak of that type has not gone by without notice, Cherry," said Uncle Will. "However, the hospital said her symptoms were not unlike a bad attack of that disease."

"I visited her boyfriend Griffin Ward today. He makes a kind of health drink called Genuine Juice, and he was trying to use Eloise as his guinea pig. I don't think she was going for it. He also brought Eloise stew. And he didn't get sick."

"Isn't he the meathead I kicked out of the festival yesterday?" said Luke. The tic above his eye spasmed. "You visited his house?"

"What's all this?" said Grandpa. "Who's Eloise?"

"Eloise Parker. My friend from Sidewinder. She makes pottery." Grief welled in my throat, but a sharp jab of anger helped me recover. "She made pottery. Made it until she was poisoned by bad Brunswick Stew or something else."

"Bad Brunswick Stew? How is that possible?" Grandpa glanced at Pearl. "You know how to make Brunswick Stew?"

"Of course," she scoffed. "My daddy always used squirrel or possum, but I make it with chicken."

Casey slammed the oven door, rattling the pot of beans. "Dinner will be ready in fifteen minutes," she announced and marched out of the room.

"She better pull those muffins out before fifteen minutes is up." Pearl shook her head. "I always make cornbread in a cast iron skillet. With bacon grease."

Something like a smile flickered on Grandpa's face.

"Pearl, you got family around here?" asked Luke, rubbing the nerve above his eye.

"My daughter, Amy, lives in Halo," she said. "But I've got a farm outside Line Creek. We raised corn and cattle until my husband died. Now I've just got the goats. I met your Grandpa because I'm looking to sell my herd. I'm probably going to sell the farm and move closer to Amy, too."

She smiled at Grandpa. "I'm finding I like Halo."

Cody and I exchanged a look of befuddlement. Why would someone be interested in an old curmudgeon like Grandpa? We don't have money and he's not even good looking. More like a stringy piece of jerky than a hot, hunk of beef.

"Pearl, how's that Sable doe?" Grandpa scratched his whiskers. "What was her name? Muffin?"

"Snickerdoodle," she corrected. "You know her name, Ed. I'm going to sire her with a Sable buck with good papers. Them babies are going to be beautiful and great milkers."

I noticed the gleam in Grandpa's eye and passed the thought that he might just be after this poor woman's goats. Terrible, I know, but the idea of Grandpa and Pearl having romantic liaisons gave me the heebie jeebies.

"Is that so?" said Luke. "And what is it about Halo that you like so much?"

I rolled my eyes and leaned into Luke, Master Subject Changer.

"Well, you've got a nice, little town here. People who appreciate goats like your Grandpa. Amy and my grandkids, of course. And I'm enjoying the bingo, too."

"Which church is doing bingo?" asked Uncle Will. "Methodist?"

"No, it's through the Ladies Auxiliary, but they don't meet at the VFW hall. Some man offered to have it in his house."

"Really? I hadn't heard that." Uncle Will rubbed his chin. "You heard about the bingo, Harper?"

"I don't pay much attention to the Ladies Auxiliary, Sheriff," said Luke.

"You should," Uncle Will winked. "You never know what those girls are up to. If you want to be sheriff someday, you've got to pay attention to the little things."

Sheriff someday? I glanced at Luke's face, but it remained shuttered. Was Uncle Will grooming Luke to become sheriff? I thought Luke was hoping to transfer to a city detective position.

Pearl hopped up and peeked in the oven. The sweet smell of cornbread mixed with the comforting aroma of chicken and beans and permeated the kitchen.

"These will be done in a minute," she said. "You should see this house where we play bingo. Looks like Tara Plantation. Even has a cannon in the front yard."

I stiffened. The only house that looked like a wedding cake with a cannon in the front yard belonged to Max Avtaikin.

A quiet, but unmistakable groan rose from Luke.

"You don't say." I circled the table to the oven. "This house has a game room for y'all to play poker, I mean bingo, in?"

"How did you know?" Pearl slipped the cornbread out of the oven. "A big, beautiful room in his basement with a chandelier and a cashier's booth just like on the casino boats. I went on a girl's weekend to Mississippi once."

"Got a bar with a reclining nude painted on the wall?" I stepped back as she maneuvered the muffins to the opposite counter.

"You've been to Mr. Max's house? I don't like naked pictures myself, but I guess some folks think it's art." She shook the muffins onto a sheet of newspaper.

I allowed the crack about art in the interest of busting gangsters. "I've been there once. And I know the man who owns the house. He's been in trouble for gambling before. Y'all better find another place to play your bingo."

"What?" Pearl stuck her hands on her hips. "Mr. Max is a gentleman. He says hosting bingo is a community service and even serves us tea and cookies. Calls the cookies biscuits. Isn't that cute? We adore Mr. Max."

I blinked back my shock. There was nothing cute about the Bear. Maybe ruggedly handsome in a scary, linebacker sort of way. We had made our peace, but I didn't trust him. He operated with ulterior motives for his ulterior motives. Serving little old ladies tea and biscuits had to be an underhanded way of filling his coffers.

"I saw Mr. Max at church today, actually," I said.

"Church?" Cody said. "Is it Christmas already?"

"You should talk, you heathen. You know Mr. Max was a judge at the cook-off, Uncle Will?"

"I am aware," said Will. "Thankfully, the judges were fine. Which makes it kind of doubtful all those folks got sick from Brunswick Stew."

Casey reentered the kitchen, her toenails gleaming with a fresh coat of metallic blue. Her eyes zeroed in on the muffins steaming on the counter. "You took my muffins out of the oven?"

"You don't want them to burn, sugar," said Pearl.

"I've been making muffins since I was six, and I haven't burned them once."

"I've been cooking a bit longer than you, hon'." Pearl shrugged. "You weren't here, so I took them out. No big deal."

Casey's lips disappeared inside her mouth. She marched to the counter and began pulling plates from the cupboard. I backed away from the scene and bumped into Luke.

"Let's go wash up." He snagged my hand, dragging me through the kitchen doorway and into the living room. We turned down a pine-paneled hall leading to the bedrooms and bathroom. Grabbing my other hand, he backed me into the wall, and pinned my lower body with his legs.

"I guess your definition of washing up is different than mine," I said.

He lowered his head, his breath caressed my face. "What are you doing? I told you how I felt about you talking to that kid and then you go to the musclehead's house? And you've taken to stalking Max Avtaikin at church?"

"It wasn't stalking. Just coincidence. I saw your mom and JB there, too. And Shawna."

"Did you now?" His eyes shifted. "Isn't that nice."

"They seemed a tad confused by our relationship."

"I don't pay much attention to my stepdad. And you know my momma. She's got her hands in so many organizations she doesn't know if she's coming or going."

"Oh, they just forgot we're seeing each other?"

"Well, sugar, I do work long hours. And although I'm temporarily living in their house, it doesn't mean they keep tabs on me."

"So what is it we're doing here, Luke? Whatever it is, it doesn't seem to be public. Unless you call Sunday dinners at the farm public. Which oddly enough involves your boss." I gave him my best what-do-you-say-to-that look.

He raised my arms to wrap around his neck and skimmed his hands down my sides to rest at my hips. "Let's not ruin the day by fussing," he whispered. "We can talk about this another time."

"I'll give up my fussing if you give up yours." Considering the mess I got myself into the night before, I didn't need any pot and kettle accusations.

Besides, between the distraction of his stroking hands and sultry lips, I was having trouble concentrating on much else. When Luke turned on the heat, I melted faster than a Daytona Beach soft serve. And dangit, he knew it.

"Agreed," he said, tipping my chin up with one finger. "You owe me a better kiss than the one I got in the truck."

His lips descended, crushing mine. I snuggled into his body, eager to redeem myself. However, as willing as I was, my lips refused to perform.

Like the dexterity of a two year old, my lips pursed and opened, sliding willy-nilly around Luke's tender skin.

"Did you have a shot of Novocain or something when I wasn't looking?" Luke gave me a strange look, wiping his face on his arm.

"I keep telling you something is wrong with me."

"The only thing wrong with you is your imagination. You need something to occupy your mind. You better figure out a new project. One that doesn't involve painting me naked, by the way. That Greek body paint whatever is not going to happen."

I wiped the drool off on the back of my hand.

"I'm going to clean myself up." Shoving open the bathroom door, he shot a look at me over his shoulder. "Get those lips working. I'm becoming a very frustrated man."

I slumped against the wall as the bathroom door swung shut. Maybe he was right. I just needed a new project. I wanted to start the classical paintings, but it looked like Luke would need more convincing. And I found it difficult to concentrate on drawing with this funk hanging over me. I wished I could do more to help Eloise's family. Uncle Will didn't confirm he was ordering an autopsy.

But he didn't deny it either.

I wondered if anyone else from the festival had died. I made a mental note to check the Halo Herald when it came out the following week. Or better yet, I could visit the newspaper office tomorrow and ask.

And while I was at it, I might as well inquire about this new bingo meeting. It couldn't hurt to check on the Bear's newest service. Maybe he had turned a new leaf and enjoyed providing cookies and coffee to the Ladies Auxiliary. Judging by his popularity at church, he was benefitting in baked goods. Strange he would allow himself to be mobbed. Unless he was encouraging these women for some other nefarious purpose.

A smile uncurled my tight lips. It felt good to have a plan.

TWELVE

The Halo Herald newspaper office needed a coat of paint following a massive attack against clutter, debris, and dirt. Grime on the plate glass window kept the inside mess hidden from passersby. But those who entered the office soon realized the twenty-four seven world of newspaper work didn't include much cleaning. Dust mites crawled in my nose, drawing out a giant sneeze that sprayed the piled folders, fliers, and newspapers on the yellowing Formica counter.

"Goodness me," replied a voice behind a stack of binders. "Bless you."

A woman popped up from a desk and approached the counter. Her short, russet hair, khaki pants, and fawn top gave her the appearance of a bright-eyed wren. Which I guess would make me a parrot in my chartreuse and violet tank with royal blue shorts.

"Can I help you?" Her voice had a pleasant lilt, like she'd been in Georgia some but had lived north of the sweet tea line as well.

"Yes, ma'am. I'm Cherry Tucker," I began.

"You're the artist who painted Dustin Branson's coffin portrait?" She hopped closer to where I stood.

"Yes, ma'am. I guess that probably caught the paper's attention."

"Anything related to a murder case catches my attention," she replied. "I'm Dorothy Cooper. August Cooper's daughter," she added as part of a small town member's automatic clarification system. August Cooper owned Cooper's Funeral Home. "You can call me Dot."

"Thanks, Dot. I'm inquiring about two things." Before she started a spiel about ad or editorial pieces, I continued. "Both are concerning investigations you might be looking into."

"Investigations?"

I guessed that word wasn't used much at the Halo Herald.

"One is the Sidewinder Brunswick Stew Cook-Off," I said.

"Sure. The food poisoning scare?"

"Yes, ma'am. My friend from Sidewinder, Eloise Parker, died after eating Brunswick Stew at the festival."

"What?" Dot's brown eyes gleamed. "The stew killed her?"

"I'm not sure. That might need investigating."

"Sidewinder doesn't have a police department. Is the sheriff's office checking into it?"

"Her father wants an autopsy." I drew a circle in the dust on the counter. "She had Crohn's disease, but I was with her all day and she didn't appear sick until she ate about six cups of stew."

Dot grabbed a notebook from her desk and began scribbling. "I'll check to see if anyone else got that sick."

"Check into one of the teams, Cotton Pickin' Good. The cook, Lewis Maynard, and his wife, Marion, also fell sick pretty bad. According to Lewis's girlfriend's son. And that's where Eloise got all her stew."

"Really? According to Lewis's girlfriend's son?" Dot's eyebrows drew together, and she cocked her head. "It's likely a coincidence, but I'll check into it. Lewis Maynard should be easy to track down."

"One more thing. Eloise had a boyfriend, Griffin Ward, who hassled her some. I don't know if it's related to the food poisoning, but it can't hurt to add him into the mix. He was selling his health food smoothie, Genuine Juice, at the festival."

"Okay." Her voice sounded doubtful, but she added his name to the list.

"Thanks. If you need any help, I'd be willing to go along." Reaching over the counter, I jotted my cell phone number on her legal pad.

"I'll think about it," she said. "What's your other investigation?"

I could feel my eyes sparking with excitement. "What do you know about the Ladies Auxiliary bingo meetings at Mr. Avtaikin's house?"

"Mr. Max's house?"

"You know him?"

"He's getting well known in the community."

"Is he now? I thought he was doing community service."

"I know about the gambling allegations, but they were never proven. Is there more to the story?"

"Well," I hedged, caught between suspicion and guilt. "I just wondered about this bingo deal. With the Ladies Auxiliary."

"As far as I know it's just bingo." Dot gave me a look that spoke crackpot. "I'll look into the Sidewinder food poisoning. And you know Max has been donating a lot of money to various causes. He wants to clear his name from any scandal."

"Why? Is he going to run for office?"

"Ooh, that would be interesting," Dot giggled. "We could use some fresh blood on the town council. At least he'd give me something nice to look at instead of the usual crowd."

Max nice to look at? The Bear looked like his name. A brute with cyan blue eyes. He used his size and namesake for intimidation, not for impressing the ladies. At least I didn't think so.

"He was one of the cook-off judges, you know. Mr. Max didn't get sick, none of the judges did, but I saw someone from the cook-off following him at church. Actually he was followed by a lot of women, come to think of it." I tapped my chin. "Don't you find that odd?"

"Were you also following Mr. Max, too?" asked Dot.

I gave her my best I'm-dead-serious stare. "As a citizen of Halo, I'm interested in making sure he cleans up his act. This town could use some revitalizing, particularly by folks who are interested in the arts. However, I don't take kindly to gangsters moving in."

Dot smirked. "It'd be helpful to have rich art patrons in Halo, though. From what I understand, Shawna Branson has been thinking the same as you."

"I also don't take kindly to Amazons," I sniffed. "Good day, Dot Cooper. Let me know if you hear anything and I'll do the same."

Dot watched me from the window as I stepped out the door of the crumbling newspaper office and crossed the street. I hoped the death of Eloise Parker would now receive the attention it deserved. I supposed I was the only one serious about buffing the rough out of Max Avtaikin. Shawna would encourage his unlawful activities as long as they brought in dollars for her causes.

A visit to the Bear's lair seemed appropriate.

THIRTEEN

I had visited Max's Antebellum-style mansion once before, and I will admit to feeling considerably intimidated by the lavish architecture and furnishings. The guy could give Graceland a run for its money. My last visit included Todd, but I figured it best to keep myself and my traitorous lips away from him for the moment. Luckily, he worked his delivery route on Mondays, so I felt no guilt in avoiding him.

The Datsun and I chugged east of town, where the hills and Loblolly pines drew heaven and earth closer. The tall timber crowding the road cooled my hot truck. I hung my arm out the window, enjoying the breeze snapping against my fingers and the damp scent of the forest. The road dipped into a slight hollow, and I sucked in my breath. The monstrous, white mansion gleamed against the azure sky. Columned and porticoed with a big-ass canon in the front flower bed, the house was a Southern gentleman's wet dream. And, it seemed, also an Eastern European miscreant's.

I parked in front of the veranda aware of the dripping mess of oil and rust I'd leave on his immaculate blacktop. Hopefully Max wouldn't care. He wasn't snobbish, and he didn't suffer snobbery in others. He came from humble roots, something he was proud to claim. However, he had the amazing ability to conjure cash from thin air. Much of which I suspect came from other people's pockets.

I rang the bell and tapped my flip-flops on the varnished wood floor of the veranda. A moment later, the great door swung open and Max ushered me into the multi-storied foyer. Despite the high ceilings, the house felt stuffy and warm.

"Artist," Max bowed and gave me the quick double-cheek kiss of his native land, "to what do I owe this pleasure?"

"Hey there, Bear," I said, attempting nonchalance amid the fluster of his European greeting. "What's with the internal temperature? You one of those guys who has something against a/c? Or did you forget to pay the electric?"

He gave me a puzzled look, one I had seen before.

"Why is it so hot in your house?"

"Ah. There is mechanical problem. Let us speak on the back deck where we can escape this insufferable heat. I am partaking of the lemonade if you would care to join me."

"Sounds good."

We trooped through the stuffy foyer into a formal living room decorated in gilt and deep reds. I stopped before a grouping of small, beautiful oils crafted in the Romantic style of the early nineteenth century. One tiny masterpiece featured a woman wearing a peasant dress standing in the midst of a modern, ruined building.

Despite her tragic contemporary setting, she maintained the fierce expression and proud bearing of the heroic Romantic subjects, much like one of my favorite Delacroix works. I squinted at the signature, but couldn't make out the scribble. Although I questioned his velvet and gold decorating style, Max had fine taste in art. I turned to compliment him, but he had disappeared through another doorway.

I hustled through a small hallway into a large kitchen. Max lifted a tray with a cut crystal pitcher of lemonade and glasses from the island's granite countertop. He paused before a set of French doors, and I hurried to open the door for him.

"You've got a nice art collection," I said.

"Another time perhaps we can explore the works. When it is not so warm. Today you have other business, I am guessing." The hint of a smirk made a brief appearance. "It seems your visits always coincide with business. I hope this one ends more pleasantly than the last."

I waved away his insinuation with attempted nonchalance.

I pushed Todd out of my thoughts and followed Max outside. The shaded deck overlooked a kidney shaped pool and a beautiful pool house, surrounded by palm trees and other tropical plants. The scene was so blissful, I almost hated to put the screws to Max. He handed me a goblet of lemonade and a thin lemon slice bobbed in the golden liquid. I almost cried at the beauty.

He eyed me and took a draw from his crystal glass. I smiled demurely, smoothed my parroty tank, and sipped from the glass.

"Holy crap, this is amazing lemonade." I gulped the rest of the drink and wiped my mouth with a dainty napkin. My Grandma Jo would have smacked my behind for my lack of manners. "I have never tasted lemonade like this before. What did you put in it? Fairy wings? Diamond dust?"

Max laughed. "Lemons, sugar, and the water. I also add the vodka sometimes."

"You better leave the vodka out of mine or I might not make it home."

"An interesting fact to remember. Try the biscuits."

We settled into the plump cushions of two deck chairs. I grabbed a cookie from the tray, took a bite, and moaned. I ate two more and forced myself to get to business.

"Bear, your popularity with a certain group of church women did not get by my notice. I also know Shawna Branson is interested in you."

"I commend you on your powers of the perception."

"Thank you. Besides the granny brigade, I saw Belinda Gable at New Order Church, too. She's not from Halo. I think she's stalking you."

"I don't know this Belinda Gable."

"She was on a cook-off team at the festival. Team High Cotton. We watched her and her husband fight with the other cotton team just before you participated in the judging."

He took a slow sip of lemonade, mimicking thoughtfulness. "What do I know of these people? I barely remember this argument. I was too distracted by you and Miss Shawna Branson fighting over me."

"I wasn't fighting over you," I gasped. "But what does Shawna want with you anyway?"

"She's interested in promoting the arts in the county. It's a good thing for you, no?"

"You tell me. I've heard she hopes it's not a good thing."

"I do not listen to women like this Miss Shawna Branson. She's better for the eyes than the ears, don't you think?"

I didn't like the direction of this conversation. I decided to pump the brakes and turn off onto a side street. "I also heard you have your hand in another gaming scheme."

"Gaming scheme?" An eyebrow rose, elevating the small scar. "What is this gaming scheme?"

"Bingo. I heard you're treating the old ladies to bingo."

"Always with your suspicions, Miss Tucker. I am offering a service to the community."

My eyes took a quick roll in their sockets while Max poured more lemonade. I ate another cookie.

"Why do you find the difficulty to believing me?" he asked.

"Because I know you. I know you wouldn't do anything without ensuring it could make a fast buck."

He watched me lick the crumbs from my fingers before commenting. "You find capitalism vulgar, perhaps? It offends your artistic sensibilities? Maybe you are a secret Marxist."

"I wasn't one for social studies in school," I waved my glass. "I've got no beef with making money. I am in financial straits at the moment and could use some cash myself. I've taken to selling paintings of dolphins and peaches at craft fairs. I've got a couple art professors who'd call that selling out."

"Your objection is not the way I live?"

"Hell, no. I wouldn't mind living in Lifestyles of the Rich and Southern, especially if it included these particular cookies and lemonade. Seriously, what is in this stuff? Heroin? Dried unicorn horns?"

"Perhaps you are jealous of the attention I receive from these women."

I almost fell off my chair, laughing at the idea of Max hooking up with the Crochet Club.

Or Shawna Branson. That thought sobered me up fast.

A gong chimed within the house and Max stood. "Excuse me for the moment." He gave a short bow and disappeared through the French doors.

I snatched another cookie and took a vicious bite. Once again, Max had deflected my questions. I promised myself to stay on the subject of bingo when he returned. To ensure that decision, I ate the remaining cookies. No sense getting distracted by a little butter, flour and sugar. With a hint of vanilla. As I pondered the ingredients, I strolled through the kitchen to the cozy sitting room hung with art.

I found a nice pen and ink sketch near the doorway leading to the foyer. It just so happened, my admiration of the sketch made Max and his visitor accessible for a quick looky loo. I peered around the door. A cluster of older women stood on the porch arguing with Max about the state of his air conditioning unit.

"I have the repairman coming today," he said. "The company said I must remain home between nine and four. It is frustrating."

"They always say that," said a sharp looking woman with tightly permed hair and glasses. "The minute you slip out, they'll show up. Guaranteed, Mr. Max."

Three other women nodded in agreement. I recognized one in a floral blouse and polyester stretch pants from the New Order service. With her cane, she pointed at glasses and permed hair.

"That's beside the point. Your young man can read the numbers while you wait for the a/c man."

"My dear," Max spoke gently, causing a small flutter of cooing from the crowd. "The house is stifling. I couldn't possibly let you in today."

"Your basement is cold as a witch's you-know-what. I keep my own thermostat on eighty-one. We're not going to melt."

"Sugar dissolves in heat."

This line from Max caused a titter to burst from the group. Two ladies turned an unbecoming shade of magenta.

I narrowed my eyes.

"In the meantime," Max strolled to the door and opened it, "tell your friends. I met so many lovely ladies at the church. Thank you for the recommendation."

"Mr. Max," said a shriveled woman wearing pearls and a baseball hat. She pressed a package into his hand. "I made this especially for you."

"Thank you, my dear. I will be sure to serve it at the next social hour." He leaned over to drop a kiss on her hand.

I turned from the doorway and hustled through the kitchen. If I hadn't known about the bingo, I would have thought Max was pimping himself out for shortbread and divinity candy. Maybe he had turned a leaf and actually performed a community service.

But Max Avtaikin was also the Bear. And the Bear didn't do anything for free.

I strolled onto the deck and refilled our glasses with the heavenly lemonade. Goblet in hand, I leaned on the deck rail and gazed out. A door swung open on the pool house. I did a double-take as Todd McIntosh strolled out of the small house to the pool. In a tiny Speedo. Very tiny.

Miniscule.

He dove into the pool and his body skimmed the surface in a slow crawl. Water sluiced across his broad shoulders as his powerful arms drew from the water. His lazy kick barely marred the surface, causing ripples to accentuate his long legs and tight bottom. I suddenly realized Max stood beside me, watching me gawk. I averted my eyes and took a deep pull from the lemonade.

"I apologize for my long absence," he said. His cool blue gaze swept off me to the pool. "I see you have found something to amuse yourself while I attended to my visitors."

"What is Todd doing here?"

"Swimming. Perhaps for exercise? It is a hot day. How long shall we suffer from this heat?"

"I mean what is Todd doing at your house, Mr. Obvious?"

"Cherry!"

I swung around to face the pool.

Todd stood in the shallow end, waving. "Cherry! Just a minute." He pulled himself out of the pool and stood in the itty-bitty suit, hopping up and down.

"Good Lord, stop that jumping," I yelled. "You're going to hurt yourself."

"Cherry, I'll be up in a minute. Or come down here! I want to talk to you."

I slapped a hand over my eyes. "I have to get out of here."

"So soon?" Max lifted the crystal goblet from my hand and placed it on the glass table. "Does my guest offend you? I thought Todd McIntosh was a friend of yours."

"I have to go."

I sped through the open doors with Max on my heels. In the foyer, Max pushed buttons on the security monitor next to the door. His past robbery must have taught him to be more careful.

"Is Todd working for you?" I questioned. "Are you running poker games again? I'll kill you both if Todd is involved in poker. He has a gambling problem."

A banging sounded from below, and I glanced toward the basement door at the far side of the foyer. I bounced on my toes, eager to get out of the house before Todd popped through the door in his all-but-nothing.

Max turned from the small security screen. "Why don't you ask him yourself? He sounds eager to speak with you."

I tossed Max a look of frustration. "I don't want to speak with Todd. I want to speak with you. You don't answer any of my questions."

Max leaned against the door, crossing his ankles. "So we speak now. What is the question I didn't answer?"

Below us, another door banged. Feet pounded up the basement stairs.

"Open the door," I said and tugged on the handle. Max eased off the door and ushered me onto the porch. "I'll get to the bottom of this bingo thing with or without your help."

Behind us, I heard the basement door swing open and smack against the wall. I ran down the porch stairs, glancing over my shoulder at Max.

"I want nothing more than to be of assistance to you, Artist," he called.

"I have a feeling you want to assist me as much as I want to assist you." I popped the door of the Datsun.

"Then my heart is gladdened," Max called, watching me slide into the truck. "We have the mutual concern for each other."

"Touché," I muttered and turned the key with a small prayer she'd crank on the first turn. The Lord answered my distress and the motor rumbled to life.

"Cherry, wait! Where are you going?" Todd rushed down the stairs onto the drive. He immediately hot-footed it back to the steps, dancing off the searing heat of the blacktop. "I need to talk to you."

I gave a last glance at the sculpted body of perfection, dripping water and dazzling the sun with his beauty.

"For the sake of all that is decent, put some drawers on!" I called through the open window and pulled away.

FØURTEEN

When Casey arrived at my house, she found me sitting on the kitchen floor in an old wife-beater and cut offs. With my legs spread on the linoleum before me, I poised a paintbrush above my knee. As soon as I had returned from Max's house, I threw myself into the Greek painting project to save my brain from turning into soggy grits.

Something needed to occupy my thoughts that didn't include Todd dressed in a Speedo. I decided to use myself as a guinea pig with the body paint portion of my painting. Although I had no model yet, I thought it best to be prepared when Luke finally caved.

Casey tossed her purse on the formica counter and stuck her hands on hips clad in black biker shorts and a matching racer-back tank. I hadn't seen Casey on a bicycle since she was ten, so I assumed this was some new look. Sparkly cobalt blue shadowed her eyes and Rose Madder pouted her lips.

Kind of rough for a Monday night. Which made me wonder where she planned to go after my house.

"What in the hell are you doing?" she asked. "I thought you were going to cook."

Although used to strange bouts in my creativity, it still shocked her to see the columns of tiny Greek letters running down my face.

"I know the Mu, Nu, and Xi under my chin are smudged and runny. It's really hard to see what you're painting when your head is tipped up," I said. "That's why my neck is so messy. I didn't even try to do my ears."

She covered her mouth in her hands. "Will that stuff come off?"

"Of course." I stood up carefully, holding my wet arms away from my body. "I tried the face paint stuff they have at the Crafty Corner, but it's too thick. I want the letters to look almost transparent so I switched to watercolors. I can thin them out to the opacity I want."

I held out my arms to Casey. "Which shade do you like better? I've got raw umber to burnt ocher on my left arm and blues on the other."

"I can't believe you're doing this." She shook her head. "I don't know. They look the same to me."

"I'm thinking burnt sienna, although I'm partial to the earthy reds. However this indigo is nice and will make the shadows interesting." I pointed to a Sigma painted in the crook of my right elbow.

"I don't have time for your craziness." Casey rubbed her forehead. "What's the cooking emergency?"

I bit my lip. "Will you cook a supper for me?"

"I cook dinner for y'all almost every day." She folded her arms over her chest. "And I'm getting tired of it."

I flapped my hand in the air, passing off her constant complaint.

"But at least you appreciate my cooking, unlike some people."

I got the feeling she was talking about Grandpa and Pearl, but I wasn't going to open that can of worms. Casey might start a "moving in with you" discussion.

"I know, I know," I said. "I want you to cook me a dinner here so I can serve it to Luke."

She arched a manicured brow. "Luke knows you can't cook." The brow dropped. "Doesn't he?"

"Yes." I leaned over, gathering paints and brushes off the floor. "But I feel like I've got to up my game."

"Why?"

The red beating into my cheeks matched the vermillion Omega drawn on my left shoulder. I took my time swirling the brushes in a little jar of water, remaining bent over until the blush passed. When I came up, Casey leaned against the counter, examining me.

"Trouble in paradise?"

"Nope, everything is fine." I hurried to the sink and began washing my brushes.

"Really?" Casey twirled a long lock of hair in her fingers. "I noticed after dinner on Sunday when Luke put his hands on you, you fidgeted and jumped around like he's got the plague. I call that trouble in paradise."

"I don't like public displays of affection."

Casey snorted. "Don't you want him anymore?"

"Don't be ridiculous. Luke is perfect. He's funny, smart, and brave."

"He's drop-dead gorgeous."

"Yeah," I smiled and rubbed the smeary paint on the back of my hand. "He's got those dimples that drive me crazy. And those beautiful gray eyes. I've tried mixing ultramarine blue, transparent blue oxide, and even Williamsburg's German Earth all with different amounts of white and still can't come close to his color. I think he can darken and lighten his eyes at will."

"And a superfine body," she said, ignoring my pontification on eye color.

"Yep."

"He looks like the kind of guy who'll keep you up for hours." She stared at the dingy kitchen cabinets without really seeing them. "You know, just keeping you happy in all sorts of ways."

I stared at her tight bike racer outfit, wondering for whom she dressed. This was getting a little uncomfortable. Turning to the sink, I began scrubbing the paint off my arms. When I glanced over my shoulder, Casey had lost the misty look in her eyes, but still retained a pink tinge to her cheeks.

"You been watching the women's channel again," I said.

"Never mind. Are you cheating on Luke?"

I gasped and spun around, slopping water onto the floor. "What?"

"You heard me. You're acting like a guy." She eyed me. "That man salivates over you, God knows why. Todd did, too. How do you do it?"

"Do what?"

"You keep these guys at arms-length, but they still want you. And it's not like you look like a Playboy Bunny or something."

"Gee, thanks," I said, my cheeks burning.

"It's not fair." Her brown eyes sliced through me. "I hope you're not cheating on Luke. You've got a chance for happiness."

Her face crumpled. I stood stock-still, dripping with water.

"This is not entirely your fault," she continued.

I knew she meant our mother, but I wasn't a big believer in playing the victim card.

Casey slipped across the kitchen for a hug and after a quick appraisal of my wet, painted self, patted me on the head instead. "It's going to be okay, sister," she said. "I'll help you get back together with Luke."

"We haven't broken up. I'm not cheating on him. It was an accidental kiss. And I stopped it. By falling down."

"Whoa." She stepped back. "Who'd you kiss?"

"Todd," I hung my head in shame.

"What did you go and do that for?"

"It just happened. I thought he was going to hug me and all of the sudden he was kissing me."

"Huh. I'm not surprised. But you stopped him?"

"Yes," I kept my eyes on my feet. "It just took me a minute to figure out what was going on."

"He must be a pretty good kisser."

I nodded, rubbing a tiny chi symbol off my shin with my big toe. A phenomenal kisser. The kind of kisses where you suddenly find yourself standing in a Vegas chapel, saying "I do."

"Sounds innocent enough. That kind of thing happens and it's not like you're married." Her foot tapped the ground. "Just don't tell Luke. It'll hurt him more to know than to not."

A huge sigh escaped my chest. "But now my lips don't work right with Luke."

"Sure," she said, like it was the most natural thing in the world to have your lips refuse to work. Maybe it was. Although Casey was currently in a dry spell, she had a lot of experience in the man department. I doubted she ever had problems making her lips work, though. And judging by her outfit, her dry spell would soon be over.

"So you'll distract him with food until this kissing thing passes." She began opening cabinet doors. "What are we making for dinner?"

An hour later, Luke entered my kitchen, sniffed the air, and walked back into the carport. I stared at the closed door for half a second and then yanked it open to glare at the man standing there.

"What are you doing?"

"I thought I had the wrong house. It smells like food in there. And by food, I don't mean wings from Red's." His simmering smile promised emerging dimples. He popped the top button on his shirt. "What's wrong with your face?"

"Nothing." The paint had scrubbed off, but my fair skin felt raw. I still hoped to entice Luke into modeling. I sketched faster than most artists.

My hope was getting him to pose tonight and hold out for the body painting later when I was ready for the detail work. In the meantime, he didn't need to know scrubbing with a bar of Lifeboy was in his future. "Come in."

I avoided a kiss by slipping through the door and heading to the stove. Luke trailed behind me and pressed his body against my back. He peered over my head as I pulled a lid off a frying pan.

"Darlin', is that chicken-fried steak?"

His hands slid to my hips and he leaned over to nibble my neck. I smiled and stirred brown gravy in a small saucepan, feeling like a tarted-up Betty Crocker. I had replaced my tank and shorts with a little spaghetti strap number I had shortened and edged in purple fringe. And covered in a ruffly apron. Getting gravy out of fringe could be tricky.

"Who made all this?" he asked.

I hesitated. "Casey."

"Thank the Lord," he said, abandoning my neck to grab a plate off the counter. "Let's eat."

I tossed the spoon into the gravy pot. "What do you mean?"

"Sugar, your heart is in the right place, and I thank you for the food." He nodded toward the sink. "But judging by all the tubes of paint and brushes lying around, I'm guessing your mind wasn't on dinner. I'm glad you took my advice, though, and started on a new project."

A buzz from his cell phone distracted me from answering. Luke strode to the other side of the kitchen where the phone vibrated across the counter.

"Sorry. Probably work." He turned away from me to answer the call.

As Luke talked, my phone rang. I hesitated, hoping I could glean some inside information into the criminal world of Halo from Luke's curt remarks, but turned toward the living room where my cell phone rested on my desk.

"Cherry?" said the breathless voice on the phone. "It's Dot from the Halo Herald. You got a minute to talk?"

"Yes, ma'am." I leaned around the archway to the kitchen. Luke scribbled in a small notebook while he listened. I zipped out of his hearing range toward the other side of the living room and stood in front of my large picture window overlooking Loblolly Avenue. "What's going on?"

"You were right about the Sidewinder poisonings."

"What?" I almost choked on the word. People rarely admitted I was right about anything. "Eloise was poisoned?"

"Everyone that was sick from the festival was poisoned. The owner of Cotton Pickin' Good place, Lewis Maynard, is in a coma. His wife, Marion, is hospitalized, too, although not as serious."

"No kidding. Poisoned with what?"

"Because of the number of people sickened at the festival, the sheriff pushed Eloise Parker's autopsy to the top of the lab's queue and had a battery of tests done, including a toxin screening. Are you ready for this? The medical examiner found trace amounts of arsenic. Right now they say the tests are inconclusive whether arsenic was the cause of death, but you bet the officials perked up after that."

My eyes widened until I had to blink away the dryness. "Arsenic?" A chill ran through me.

"Yes, ma'am. And thanks to you, I was at the hospital talking to the staff when they found out. You got me a great scoop, Cherry."

I nodded. The news devastated me. Someone had murdered my good friend. I would have been happy to have eaten crow on my hunch Eloise had been poisoned.

"Cherry? Are you still there? They are running tests on Lewis now, using hair samples to check for heavy metals. Tomorrow the hospital will start treating those sick for arsenic poisoning. Good thing Eloise's father pushed for that autopsy. Sheriff is rounding up his posse and is putting them on the trail now."

That statement woke me up. I scooted toward the kitchen and found Luke buttoning his shirt. He spied me and motioned he was leaving.

"I'm with a deputy right now," I said. "Let me call you back."

"You usually keep a deputy on hand?" laughed Dot. "We need to start hanging out more."

I dropped the phone on my desk and strolled into the kitchen. "Taking off?"

"Sorry, sugar. I've got to go."

"Is this anything to do with Eloise's death?"

He kept his look mild, but I could see a glint of consternation in his eyes.

"From arsenic poisoning?"

"How did you know that?" He folded his arms over his chest. "Was that your phone call? Listen, I know Eloise was your friend, but you need to stay out of this."

"I can help you, Luke."

"No, ma'am. This is an official investigation now. So you keep out of trouble."

"Luke, I already talked to Hunter Adams, the son of Lewis Maynard's girlfriend. Remember the kid with the switchblade? He's also Eloise's student. You know I also spoke to Griffin Ward. The meathead. Check into his Genuine Juice he was selling at the festival."

Luke studied me for a minute. Leaning forward, he kissed me on the cheek. "I'm sorry about dinner. Maybe you could make me a plate and stick it in your fridge?"

"Don't you want to hear about Lewis Maynard's girlfriend's son?"

"I'm sure Sheriff Thompson has a list of people to interview and it includes Lewis Maynard's girlfriend's son, dog, and mother, if need be." He opened my door. "This will probably keep me busy for a while, so I'll catch you later."

He paused. "Who called you?"

"I have my sources."

"Tell your sources to keep out of this investigation. It could get ugly." His eyes narrowed. "We're talking a mass poisoning. It could hit the news, and that'll slow everything down."

I hoped he meant bigger news than the Halo Herald. If Luke found out I had leaked the story to the press, I was really going to have trouble in paradise.

FIFTEEN

I had hoped to find Dot at the hospital, interviewing patients and tracking down arsenic results or at some such investigative work. Dot was nowhere to be seen. However, luck was on my side because I immediately recognized Hunter's aggrieved form schlepping through the hospital corridor. He wore a ripped t-shirt that played off his giant earlobe holes and the permanent imprint of his tobacco can made a neat circle on the seat of his jeans.

"Hey, it's Scarecrow," he said as a greeting.

I refrained from a similar retort, because I am a bigger person than that. And I wanted information.

"I heard Lewis was in a coma and Miss Marion is sick, too. I'm sorry. That must be rough on your..." I paused, searching for a polite term for dysfunctional family, "...situation."

"Yeah, it bites." He eyed me, finding my fringy sundress more interesting than Saturday's sweaty ensemble. Sometimes it takes a person a few minutes to adjust to my creative ingenuity. "You owe me for making me eat my chew."

"I'll buy you a coffee."

"Coffee? That stuff is disgusting."

This from the kid who swallowed chewing tobacco. "Fine, make it a Coke. Is your momma here?"

"Yeah, she's actually talking to the police." Hunter glanced over his shoulder and quickened his steps.

"Do you know what's going on?"

I spied a brown deputy uniform lounging at a nurses' station. He chatted with the pink smocked assistant on duty. It wasn't Luke, but I wasn't taking any chances. Keeping my head down, I scurried past. Hopefully, Deputy Wellington wouldn't recognize me and mention it to Luke. A side comment of "why was your girl in the hospital Monday night?" and Luke would be all over me like white on rice.

Hunter glanced at me, but waited until we were well past the nurses' stand to speak. "I know what's going on. Lewis must have poisoned his own stew. He's always looking for attention."

"A coma seems a rough way to get attention. And would he want to poison his wife and everybody else, too? Why do you think Lewis poisoned the stew?"

"Duh. He's the cook. Who else could have done it?"

"Anyone could have dumped something in while the stew was cooking. And maybe it wasn't the stew. Have the police said what was poisoned?"

"No." His face pulled into a scowl.

Jamming the elevator down button with his thumb, he uttered a few words that would have made my brother blush. I wondered if giving the kid a jolt of sugar and caffeine might be a bad idea. The doors slid open, we walked in, and Hunter paced the tiny box while we dropped to the basement. The arrival ding brought Hunter out of his brooding.

The doors opened, but he grabbed my arm before we could step out.

"I suppose you think I did it." His voice pitched higher and broke on the last word.

"I didn't say that." I shook off his hand. "I just meant it wasn't necessarily Lewis."

He seized my arm and backed me into the corner. The handlebar running the inside of the elevator pushed into my back. The doors slid shut.

"What are you doing here?" he growled. "And why are you asking so many questions?"

I jerked my arm and it slipped under his grip. He tightened his grasp and twisted it behind my back. Tears watered my eyes, and I bit my lip to keep from crying.

"You're hurting me. Stop it."

"You hit me in the stomach, and now you're going to buy me a Coke? I don't trust you." He yanked my arm, dragging me to my toes. "You're messing with the wrong guy, Scarecrow. I don't care about Lewis getting poisoned. In fact, I hope he doesn't make it."

"Why?" I gasped.

"I told you at the festival. I hate him."

"Hunter, you need to calm down," I panted. "I'm not judging you. I'm just curious."

The tension in my arm abated, but his grasp held tight. Spasms of pain rocketed through my shoulder.

The elevator door swished open. Hunter glanced behind him, and I jammed my knee into his crotch. He doubled over. My arm fell to my side, and I scurried around him. A tall, blonde woman wearing rhinestone-studded jeans and strappy heels strode into the elevator, blocking my exit.

Gaping, she pointed a finger at Hunter's doubled-over form. "There you are. What's going on here?" she asked.

As I tried to squirm around her, she grabbed my shoulder. I did my own wincing knee buckle.

"What did you do to my son?"

"I'm fine, Mom," Hunter groaned, attempting to stand.

"Your son just put me in an arm lock," I jerked my shoulder out of her grip. "So I kneed him where it counts. I'm thinking about reporting him to the deputy upstairs." Which of course I wasn't, since the last thing I needed was Luke to find out I let a suspect in a murder investigation pin me in an elevator.

"Shit," said Hunter. "Not the cops."

"I'm sorry. He's got a temper. When he sees red, he can't stop himself. I guess you don't know that yet. You've got to watch what you say to my sensitive boy." She glared at Hunter for a millisecond before turning to me. "Hunter, apologize to your girl."

I opened my mouth to explain I wasn't his girlfriend and noticed Hunter's look.

"I'm sorry," he said. "I get mad easy."

The woman hit the button for the second floor and the doors slipped shut before I could make my escape. She rubbed her son's back. The scratch of her long tipped fingernails against his t-shirt gave me the shivers.

"I'm Janine Adams," she said. "Hunter's probably upset about the news of his stepdad."

"He's not my stepdad."

Janine smiled tightly. "Of course not, you're too old for a stepdad." She leaned toward me and whispered, "I'm sorry. He gets his temper from his real dad."

I rubbed my shoulder and glared at the pair. "Who's his daddy?"

"He's gone," Janine said while Hunter delivered a death glare. "His stepdad owns Cotton Pickin' Good Plantation."

I glanced at her bare ring finger and wondered at the liberal use of stepdad. No wonder Hunter had anger issues.

"I've never heard of that farm," I said. "My grandpa's got a farm in Halo."

"It's agri-tourism, not a farm, although we do raise cotton," she said. "Lewis also has horses. And I'm helping him market the name. I have an Internet site where we sell Cotton Pickin' Good merchandise and we have a visitor's center for educational purposes. Once I got the rights to the name, you wouldn't believe how much the brand has taken off. Everybody thinks the name is sweet."

The elevator pinged and the doors swished open. Janine strode out, pulling Hunter along with her. Hunter slowed behind his mom. She didn't take notice. For all the talk about Hunter's "stepdad," Janine didn't seem concerned Lewis was in a coma.

My eyes widened as I watched Hunter retrace his steps back to me. Hospital staff and visitors mingled nearby, so I waited without much worry. However, my fists clenched and my right leg drew back, ready to do more damage to his testicles.

"I didn't poison Lewis and Marion," he hissed.

"I didn't say you did. But now you're acting suspicious. That was a dumb move." I folded my arms and delivered my own death glare. "You're lucky I don't scare easily."

"Are you going to tell the cop?" A look of fear skittered across his features. "It's your word against mine."

"Then you're in trouble," I pointed out with a voice patient enough for a kindergarten teacher, "because I'm not the one who is a suspect in a murder investigation."

"Murder?"

"Yeah, dillweed. Whoever poisoned everyone also killed my friend. And I want to know who did it."

Hunter's face paled. "I'm a suspect in a murder investigation?"

"If you're not now, you will be."

I squinted at the willowy figure with expensive hair and clothes. Janine either paid well to look young or wasn't much older than Hunter when she had him.

"You and your mom had better cooperate with the police."

"Will you help me?" said Hunter.

"Son, you just proved yourself a dangerous mess in that elevator. I'd have to be crazy to help you."

"What if I can help you figure out who poisoned the stew and killed your friend?"

I chewed on that for a minute, but Hunter seemed a little too unstable for my comfort level. "You should tell the police what you know, not me."

However, I was dying to find out more on this Lewis. What kind of man attracts a woman like Janine? I squinted past Hunter to see if I could tell which room the hospital assigned to Lewis.

Hunter glanced over his shoulder. His mom now argued with the nurse.

"I don't want to be a murder suspect. I've been in enough trouble that this could get me put away. The cops will have their suspect and won't even try to find anyone else."

"They can't put you away without evidence."

"Of course they can." His shoulders hunched. "I'm sorry for what happened in the elevator. I got scared and reacted bad. I have a real short fuse."

"That's more than a short fuse."

Janine marched down the hallway toward us. People shrank against the wall as she charged past.

"Bring your friend if you're worried. The one from the festival. He was cool." He spun around to meet his mother before she could yank him from the conversation. "I'll meet you at the Viper in Sidewinder tomorrow night. Seven o'clock."

"I thought you were coming with me. This is not the time or place for making dates," Janine said, grabbing Hunter's elbow as she flew past. "Visiting hours are almost over."

They disappeared into the elevator. I glanced back down the hallway, wondering if I could find Lewis and Marion's room before I left, when I noticed someone waving from the nurses' stand. Deputy Chris Wellington leaned an elbow against the counter, waggling his fingers at me.

I smiled sweetly, waggled back, and turned tail toward the elevator.

Dagnabbit. I'd been caught red-handed talking to a suspect.

There's one more mark on my bad-girlfriend card.

SIXTEEN

Since I don't ask for permission and asking for forgiveness wasn't likely, I decided to dodge Deputy Wellington and do a quick reconnaissance of my own. Hunter thought Lewis poisoned the stew, while I still had my eye on Griffin. His threats toward me and attitude toward Eloise's death needled me. I needed to determine if Griffin had been slipping Genuine Juice to anyone poisoned at the festival. Since I only knew of two other people who were sick, I thought the best plan was to find the one who was not in a coma. Marion Maynard.

One of the benefits of small town living is knowing many of the people you encounter in your day-to-day activities. This can also be a hassle if you're doing something you don't want the world to know, but the hospital was the perfect place to apply my small town networking skills. I knew a lot of night-shift nurses who swapped off child duties with their day-shift husbands. These women bore a strength of character I wish I had. During the day, they played mommy to their own brood and then caught the swing shift to play mommy with patients. One such angel of mercy, sparky Jess Chaney, walked a cart to the elevator. I pushed the button for her, and we began an informal catch-up waiting for the door to ding.

Then I hit her with the news about Eloise.

"That's terrible," Jess said, rocking the cart like a baby stroller. "I've been treating a lot of patients from the food poisoning epidemic, but that news hadn't made it around."

"I'm wondering if they know the source of the poisoning yet. If it was the stew, it could tear that festival clear apart."

"You think they'd shut it down for good?" Jess bit her lip. "Sidewinder doesn't have much more going on than the cook-off. Mike's parents work it every year. His daddy's got the garage and they sell more drinks that weekend than they do all year."

"That's a good point. I didn't think about someone trying to deliberately ruin the festival. I was worried Griffin Ward had done it accidentally with his veggie drinks."

Her eyes widened. "He was selling Dixie cups of that green stuff near the cook-off stands. And handing out business cards. You think it was off?"

The elevator door whooshed open and she rolled her cart inside. I followed, much to the satisfaction of Deputy Wellington. I gave him another wave as the doors closed.

"This is between you and me, Jess, but I heard arsenic tainted whatever everyone ingested."

"No. Get out of here." The cart rolled to and fro with her small shoves of disgust. "Arsenic? Like rat poison?"

"Dunno." I rocked back on my heels and considered the possibility. "Where do you get arsenic?"

"I have no idea. Poor Eloise. Do you think it was done on purpose?"

"I don't know that either," I said. "How do you treat arsenic poisoning?"

"It's a heavy metal, so if it's known immediately, they'd probably use charcoal therapy or pump their stomachs. Maybe a chelation IV. If it's only small amounts, your body will naturally get rid of it. It's the large doses that are fatal."

"You had a lot of people from the festival feeling sick. One died. One is in a coma. One is being treated, I guess. The rest were released? How can there be such a difference between the patients?"

"Depends on how much they ate, their body weight, if they already had any arsenic in their system. That sort of thing." She shrugged. "I'd have to see their charts to know for sure. If the officials know it's arsenic, they're going to bring all those patients back in to get that arsenic flushed out. Guess it'll be a busy week."

The door opened on the third floor. As Jess pushed her cart through the door, I scanned for cops and trailed behind her.

"Are you taking care of any poisoning patients tonight?" I kept the eagerness out of my voice. "Particularly Lewis and Marion Maynard?"

"You said one's in a coma? They'd be in ICU. That's not my department."

"How about Marion Maynard?"

She popped a hand on her hip and gave me a smirk. "Come on now, Cherry. You trying to mess with my rounds? You know I can't let you do that."

I crossed my fingers behind my back and stared at a smudge of paint I had neglected to clean off on my ankle. "No ma'am. You know I wouldn't want to interrupt your work. I'm just overcome with concern about Eloise and the good people of Sidewinder who might have a lunatic poisoner on their hands."

I looked up and caught her with a wink.

She laughed.

"You're as crazy as ever." She scanned her chart. "Miss Marion is in room 308. They're keeping her for observation and to run more tests, but she's much better today. You can sneak a peek while I start my rounds. Mrs. Maynard might like the company. She's a talker."

I gave Jess a quick hug and scooted in the direction of 308. "You're the best, Jess," I called over my shoulder, "even if you did marry a country bumpkin from Sidewinder."

As this was a local county hospital, it didn't take me long to find 308. I poked my head in the door.

The tiny Mrs. Maynard glared at the television screen parked high on the wall across the room. She jammed buttons on the remote with a stiff index finger and shook it like a maraca when it didn't mind her.

"You need help?" I sauntered into the room and held out my hand for the remote.

"The silly thing won't change the channel. I've been watching the news all day. They've run the same story three times about a gator crossing a highway and stopping traffic. You'd think they'd have something more important to pull out of their pocket than a gator."

"You'd think." I tried a few buttons with no luck and flipped the remote over to take out the batteries. I rolled them between my palms, reinserted them in the remote, and tried again. This time we got the switch to the Home Shopping Network.

"Thank you, you sweet young thing." She beamed. "I owe you a debt of gratitude."

"My pleasure, ma'am. I do the same thing at home. The batteries are almost done. Best find a channel you like now before they cut off again. Or better yet..." I stepped out the door and returned with the remote from the empty room next door. "I won't tell if you don't."

Her face puckered into a smile. "My hero. I was hoping they'd let me go home today, but everyone got flustered earlier and now I have to have more tests. My poor husband is very ill. I should be at his bedside instead of cooped up in here."

"I'm sorry to hear that," I said, wondering if I had the correct woman. If Lewis Maynard was my two-timing husband I don't think I'd be sitting by his bedside. "What's wrong?"

"We ate something which disagreed with us."

"Must have been pretty terrible cooking to lay you up like this." I gave her my best customer service smile and eased into the chair by her bed.

Marion looked the type who was not shy about sharing her illnesses. Although she took a minute to wilt back into the pillows she had just plumped, her face bore an expectant look. Like a child starved for attention.

"If it was a restaurant that made you sick," I hinted, "I would love to know which one so I can avoid it in the future."

"Much worse than that." She picked up a magazine and began fanning herself. "It was at the Brunswick Stew Cook-Off. I'm from Sidewinder, you see."

"I was at the festival myself. I had an art booth."

"Did you now? I didn't get a chance to see the craft fair. We were busy preparing the stew for the cook-off. Lewis, my husband, is very competitive. He just runs us ragged, but I like to do my best. Always give one hundred and ten percent my daddy used to say. Every year we try to win that contest. Our neighbors, the Gables, encourage Lewis's competitiveness which makes it all the worse."

"Do they also have a cook-off team?" I said, knowing the answer, but Marion was enjoying herself.

"They call themselves High Cotton, but I'm afraid they got that idea from my estate. Cotton Pickin' Good, we're called. The Gables are crass, I'm afraid."

"Sounds like it. Did they also get sick?"

"No." She frowned. "I'm a little worried someone might have tampered with our batch."

"Did the police confiscate the stew then?"

"By the time they arrived, we had sold out and I had cleaned the pot." She dusted her hands. "My daddy always said don't let the work pile up. Besides we needed the pot to make another batch for Sunday. Of course, by Sunday they had closed down all the booths. According to Miss Adams."

"Miss Adams? Janine Adams?"

"Do you know Janine?" Marion sniffed. "She's our office manager. Well, I guess we say marketing manager now. Daddy's little cotton farm has become quite popular."

"So I've heard. Don't you have an educational center? And sell Cotton Pickin' goods?"

"Yes." She shifted, tilting up her chin, "they call it agritourism these days."

"Did you try a drink called Genuine Juice at the festival?"

"That green stuff sold by Griffin Ward? I had a sip. He was passing out Dixie Cups, and it was so darned hot."

"Did your husband have one, too?"

"Just about everybody tried it. We humored the poor boy. He is entirely entrenched in fitness and health. Preaches worse than a Presbyterian. I told him it's not worth adding an extra year on my life if I had to drink that stuff."

I chuckled. Marion Maynard might turn a blind eye to her husband's obvious dalliances, but I liked her grit. "I wish I could have seen Griffin's face. I suppose you talked to the police already?"

She nodded.

"Did you tell him you tried the green stuff? I'm sure they'd want to know."

"You think it's important?"

"Well, yes, ma'am. If they don't yet know what poisoned everyone, Griffin's Genuine Juice needs to be accounted for."

"I didn't think about that." She tapped a manicured nail on her chin. "But I'm fairly certain it was our stew. I reckoned the Gables did it. On purpose or by accident, I'm not sure, but they were seen messing around in our cook-off area and have every reason to try and ruin our prize winning recipe."

"With arsenic? Isn't that a bit extreme?"

"How did you know it was arsenic?"

"I heard the nurse talking," I gestured to the door.

"The Gables are low-down, no-account backstabbing trash, my dear." She drew her nose up and stared down the length of it. "They swill beer, wear tacky clothing, and gossip terribly. I wouldn't put it past them."

Considering I also swill beer, wear tacky clothing, and gossip terribly, visiting the Gables sounded like my glass of tea. I wondered if the sheriff's office checked into the teams' rivalry.

Nurse Jess stuck her head in the door. "Sorry, ma'am, but Cherry needs to leave. Visiting hours are over and someone heard y'all talking."

I rose and shook her strong, thin hand. "It was a pleasure, Miss Marion. I might visit this High Cotton farm just to get a gander at this Gable couple."

"Well, don't say I didn't warn you. You come see me at Cotton Pickin' when I get out of here. I enjoyed our conversation."

"I'll do just that." I gave her a smile and sauntered out the door. I pretended not to notice the disapproving glare of the nurse at the station and strolled to the elevator. Possible poisoners seemed to be crawling out of the woodwork. I suspected Griffin. Hunter tried to pin it on Lewis Maynard. Marion Maynard thought the Gables had done it. I hoped Dot had more luck finding out what actually contained the arsenic.

The elevator doors glided open, and I stared at Deputy Wellington. He raised his brows and ran his eyes over my fringy dress. I shot him a fierce look, crossed my arms, and turned my back to stare at the floor numbers blinking over the door.

I had a feeling the sheriff's department wouldn't be too forthcoming with information. I'd have to dig around a bit myself.

seventeen

The next morning I ate Luke's chicken-fried steak and thought about my options for the day. Hunter expected me to show up at the Viper Bar with Todd later that night. But now that the medical examiner concluded Eloise's death as a poisoning, a duty call to the Parkers was in order. Eloise had attended the University of Georgia, so in her memory, I donned my Georgia Bulldogs tank embellished with tiny bulldog buttons, fixed a couple buttons onto my flip-flops for continuity, and headed out the door.

My Datsun heartily protested the trip back to Sidewinder. Her dash lights flashed and she cried at the crank, but the heat made me impatient to hurry our departure.

The morning sun beat through my windshield, turning my cab into an Easy Bake Oven. By the time I arrived in Sidewinder, I was a sopping mess. With my tank plastered to my scrawny form, the little bulldog buttons jiggled in wild abandon like they'd been set free in the dog park.

Eloise's parents lived in the center of Sidewinder in an early twentieth century Georgia bungalow like mine. The low-pitched roof needed new shingles and the pink clapboard siding could have used fresh paint.

A clutter of small statues and an overabundance of windmills populated the weedy lawn, evidence of a reckless love of home. Next to the front door, I recognized Eloise's work in three austere pots. Unfortunately, their simple elegance had been crammed with impatiens and an assortment of plastic pinwheels. At my knock, June Parker appeared and ushered me inside.

"Cherry, honey, how are you holding up?" She crushed me into her soft body.

As she was half a foot taller than me, I got a face full of chest. She released me and I tottered back. A wet imprint of my form remained on her cotton shift.

"I'm doing okay. How are you and Mr. Parker?"

"You know they determined she was poisoned?"

I nodded.

"Oh, mercy me. I guess everyone knows by now."

"Bad news always travels fast. But this puts the sheriff on the case quicker and we can figure out what happened. I'd say he's doing a good job. You have nothing to worry about."

"I guess." Her gaze stopped on the large clay pots glazed in a pretty cracked ultramarine blue. "Did Eloise sell many pots at the festival?"

It took me a second to catch up to her change of subject. "A few. Between the heat and the food poisoning, we weren't getting a lot of business." I thought for a second and remembered Todd had packed up our festival paraphernalia. "I'll get the ones she didn't sell to you, ma'am."

"Thank you, honey. Come have some coffee. I made a crumble cake. We've also got biscuits and I can whip you up some eggs."

We worked our way down the tight hallway to the kitchen in the back of the house. Bright paintings of flowers covered the walls. Cluttered but clean, the well-loved room smelled of coffee and bacon. Mary Jane and Mr. Parker sat at the kitchen table, leafing through a booklet. Miss June handed me a cup of coffee. I leaned between Mary Jane and her dad and remembered past meals spent with Eloise and her family at the same table.

Mr. Parker pointed at the booklet.

"We have to choose a casket."

Tears brightened my eyes. I nodded and patted his rough-knuckled hand.

"Food poisoning my ass," he exploded. "I told those fool doctors her Crohn's disease wouldn't have made her that sick. They wasted time. The police called it a 'tragic accident.' I've had it up to here with all of them."

"Sheriff Thompson did get her autopsy pushed to the head of the line," I said gently. "Has the report from the medical examiner come in yet?"

"Not that I know of. If you ask me, they're more concerned with covering behinds than investigating."

"Now, now," said Miss June. "They're doing their best."

"I want to know what happened. Arsenic doesn't accidentally wind up in your food. They want to look at her pottery stuff. Said there could be metals in the clay or glazes. I said it's called lead and she didn't die from lead poisoning."

"Do they think it was done on accident?" I asked. I knew Uncle Will wouldn't lay his cards out on the table for the victim's family. However, Mr. Parker made some grand accusations. "I thought it was a murder investigation."

"They're officially calling Eloise's death suspicious, however they think the poisoning was an accident. Someone's even testing the water. We've been drinking Sidewinder water for years and no one's died!"

"I talked to one deputy yesterday," said Mary Jane. "He said it could even be some kind of nutjob who poisoned the festival food for kicks. Get his name in the news, that sort of thing."

"And you think..."

"Someone killed my child and I want justice. She suffered too much with her disease to die like this." Mr. Parker's stony face crumpled. The beefy man dropped his elbows to the wooden table and covered his face in his hands.

My heart just about broke seeing this giant of a man crying like a baby. "I'll help you, sir," I said, rubbing his back. "I'm looking into Eloise's death."

Mary Jane leaned over her father's back and hugged him. "Cherry will help you. She's on personal terms with the sheriff."

"Unfortunately, Uncle Will isn't going to share with me any more than you," I said. "I'm just going to ask around and see what I can find out. The police have to follow certain steps in investigating which slows them down."

"Cherry, you be careful," said Miss June. "What if the police are right about nutjobs enjoying the notoriety of mass poisonings?"

"Thing is, I'm with Mr. Parker here. I don't think this is a psychopath case. There was too much strange behavior going on at that cook-off. I think this was a deliberate poisoning, and I'll be damned if I let that person get away with it, particularly if Eloise was the intended victim."

"At least one person understands." Mr. Parker straightened, his eyes red. "Excuse me." He pushed out of his chair and stalked from the room.

"He's embarrassed. I'll go see to him," Miss June said and hurried after him.

When we heard their bedroom door close, Mary Jane flicked me a sharp look. "Who do you think did it?"

"I don't know for sure. I've got several people on my list," I hemmed, unsure how the Parkers viewed Eloise's boyfriend. "Problem is there's only one suspect I can relate to Eloise. Can you think of anybody who would do her harm?"

"You mean like that sonofabitch Griffin Ward? I've always hated that douchebag."

"Exactly," I said and the doorbell rang.

"Hold that thought," said Mary Jane, rushing to the door. She reentered the kitchen with Shawna Branson.

I could not rid myself of this woman.

Dressed in a dark tank dress with sunglasses parked in her thick hair, Shawna carried a foil covered pan. Behind Mary Jane's back, her lip had curled, probably in disgust at the disorder of the Parkers and their home. People like Shawna found it a crime when folks didn't try to fit the ideal of gracious southern living.

Shawna stopped her saunter at the sight of me. "What are you doing here?"

"Visiting my friend's family. What are you doing here?"

"I am here to pay my condolences." She shoved the pan at Mary Jane. "I bet you're stirring up trouble."

Mary Jane slid the pan on the kitchen counter and turned to face Shawna. "Why would Cherry cause trouble?"

"Because that's what Cherry does. She's likely putting ideas in your head that Eloise sickened from eating at the cook-off. Which can't be true."

Mary Jane stuck her hand on her hip. "Why can't that be true? And who exactly are you?"

"Shawna Branson. You're probably too young to know me, although I'm sure my name rings a bell. And you're from Sidewinder. I live in Line Creek," she said, as if Line Creek wasn't twenty minutes away. "However, I am co-chair for the Sidewinder Arts Festival this year."

"You mean the Brunswick Stew Cook-Off," said Mary Jane.

I remained silent, enjoying the showdown. Mary Jane might not know Shawna, but she knew of Shawna's type and wouldn't put up with her bull. I liked this girl.

"It used to be just a Brunswick Stew competition, but I'm trying to elevate the little festival into something more worthy of Forks County. I'm also on the Forks County Arts Council. I thought we could use the fame of the cook-off to bring notice to local artists."

"Funny, nobody contacted me," I said.

"Important artists," said Shawna.

"Did you have a Paintograph exhibit at the festival?" I asked. Shawna thought blowing up a snapshot and coloring it in with glitter paint counted as high art. And would make her rich and famous. As my Grandpa Ed says, rich doesn't buy class. However, rich can make you greedy. And lazy.

"As a matter of fact, I did." Shawna turned to Mary Jane. "It's the latest technology in art. Just in case you want a final portrait of Eloise, I brought you my card."

Mary Jane took the card with a grimace. "Why on earth would we want a final portrait of Eloise?"

"All the families are doing it now," Shawna said, edging in front of me.

"One family did it," I said. "And I don't recommend it. Didn't turn out so well."

Shawna pivoted on her wedge slingback to face me. "Stop trying to steal all my potential clients."

"Is that why you think I'm here, to drum up art business?"

"Well, yes, and trying to defame my festival. Aren't you?"

"I'll defame the festival if it means the stew was poisoned."

"You better not." She fixed me in a narrowed, blue-green gaze. "Or I'll make you wish you hadn't."

"What are you going to do? Paintograph a crappy picture of me?" I turned to Mary Jane. "Are you ready for Shawna to leave?"

Mary Jane folded her arms and nodded.

I grabbed Shawna by the arm and pulled her down the hallway. "Leave these poor folks alone. Just because the Branson's wanted a portrait of their dead son, doesn't mean anyone else is crazy enough to do it. I don't encourage that kind of thinking."

"Don't think you can corner that market."

"You are a piece of work, Shawna. Your mind goes places a sane person wouldn't dream of."

"It's called creativity." She stalked off the porch toward her convertible.

I watched her tear down the street and wondered how badly Shawna wanted notoriety for her Paintograph business. Maybe she was exactly the kind of nutjob mentioned by the deputy. Did she want to "elevate" the local art scene—and thereby herself—enough to sicken folks, bring attention to the festival, and accidentally kill somebody in the process? Hurrying back to the kitchen, I snatched the foil pan off the counter. A pink, polka-dotted card with "Homemade by Shawna B" written in curlicue letters floated to the floor. I sniffed the familiar looking food in the pan.

"I do believe this fried chicken is from Chikn-D-Lite," I looked up at Mary Jane. "But you might not want to eat this. With a psychotic poisoner on the loose, you can't be too careful."

EIGHTEEN

After promising the Parkers I'd locate Eloise's pottery from the festival, I left them to their funeral arrangements. Perhaps her death was nothing more than a horrible accident, but dammit, I wanted to know for sure. And so did the Parkers.

I decided on a visit to High Cotton Farm on my way out of town. However, I didn't want to peruse the tangle of country roads leading out of Sidewinder in my hunt for the farm, so I stopped at Chaney's Garage for a Coke and directions. I figured this had to be Nurse Jess's in-law's garage. It was the only garage in the dinky town.

Kids buying candy and locals playing video poker packed the tight aisles of the small convenience store connected to the garage. I eyed the poker games and wondered if they had come from Max Avtaikin's business.

I had heard through the grapevine that selling video poker machines was one of his legitimate enterprises. Video gambling was legal as long as the machines didn't cash out over a certain amount. However, some places cheated and the sheriff's department made the occasional bust. Mr. Max made money either way.

I wandered past the shelves of junk food to the cashier's booth. The gray haired woman sitting before the racks of cigarette cases looked familiar.

She leaned back and stretched, straining the blue smock she wore. I immediately recognized her massive chest. This was the pushy gal working the gate at the festival who gave me a hard time. I forced a smile and decided to give her a second chance.

"Hey there, I'm looking for High Cotton Farm. Can you give me directions?"

Her eyes fell on my decorative Bulldog tank and her lip twitched. Maybe she was a Georgia Tech fan. "What you want with the Gables? You look familiar. You ain't a salesman are you? We got laws against door-to-door peddling in Sidewinder."

"Do I look like a salesman? I just want directions."

"Where you from?"

"What does that matter? Are you going to give me directions or not?"

"I remember who you are. You're that girl from Halo who talked ugly about Brunswick Stew."

Heads turned from the poker machines. I shoved my fists on my hips and raised my chin.

"Yes, I'm that woman from Halo. And I'm not talking ugly about Brunswick Stew. I'm investigating the possibility that it killed my friend, though."

"What you got against Brunswick Stew?" asked a poker patron missing a few teeth and a fair amount of hair.

"She's probably one of them food snobs," sniffed the cashier. "She's pretty uppity."

"I'm not uppity. I just won't eat anything from a festival that near killed half the patrons."

"Now you're exaggerating," said the cashier.

"Halo's full of snobs and fibbers," said toothless Joe. "Everyone knows that."

"You're thinking of Line Creek. And you're not doing much to impress me on Sidewinder as one of the great wonders of the world."

The cashier heaved herself from the chair and leaned over the counter, thrusting her gigantic breasts in my direction. Again. "Halo's the one giving Forks County a bad name. Your town's the one getting all the news about murders a few months back."

"Well, now it's Sidewinder's turn. Are you giving me those damn directions or not?"

"Not." She plopped back into her chair and crossed her arms over her chest. "Uppity."

"I am not uppity," I muttered and stalked away. A barrel of iced drinks in plastic jugs sat next to the door. I spun around. "You're selling Griffin's Genuine Juice?"

"I'm not selling you diddly." She arched a brow.

"Great customer service. You better hope those poker machines are legit." I slammed out the door. Next time I saw Luke I'd have him check into Chaney's store. Maybe the sheriff's department could do a raid. I'd ask for a ride-along.

Except it was owned by Jess's in-laws. I couldn't rat out a friend's in-laws. That would be a breach of small town diplomacy.

I walked back to my truck cursing the cashier and her ignorant country ways. I would have to find another way to locate High Cotton Farm. I felt the insufferable woman watching me through the plate glass window. Cranking my key, I let loose a string of expletives. My truck refused to start.

"Not now," I pumped the gas pedal and turned the key again. "Not here."

Nothing. Didn't even give me the ol' rrr-rrr.

"Dammit!" I hopped out of the truck to pop the hood. Flecks of yellow paint and powdery rust blew into the grungy looking cavern. Why hadn't I taken up Cody's offer of lessons on basic mechanics?

I glanced over my shoulder. The patrons of Chaney's store and the miserable clerk peered through the window, anxious for entertainment. Hitching my thumb in my pocket, I strode with relaxed ambivalence toward the garage. The smell of old oil and rubber assailed my nostrils. I stepped into the open bay, blinking to adjust to the darkness after the blinding sunshine. A mechanic in gray coveralls stood next to a younger guy in jeans and a Chaney's Garage t-shirt. I waved and strode over.

"Hey, my truck won't start. I might need a jump."

"Let's take a look," said the older man in the coveralls.

The younger guy followed him out of the garage. We traipsed across the parking lot with the store crew watching.

"Are you Mr. Chaney?" I asked the older man. "I know your daughter-in-law, Jess."

"Yep, and this is Jay."

"What year is this pickup?" Jay scratched his head. "That's a seriously run down truck. You should just put it out of its misery."

I sucked in my breath. "Don't talk about my Datsun like that. She's very sensitive."

"What did it do when you cut her on?" Chaney asked.

"Nothing. No clicks. No cranks. But the dash lights did flash."

Chaney tapped his nose while Jay peered under the hood.

"While I got you here," I said. "I went in your store and noticed you're selling Griffin's Genuine Juice."

"Yep, he's a local boy. Not selling too well, but I thought we'd help him out."

"Anybody complain of taking sick after drinking that stuff?"

"Sick? What you mean by sick?"

"Stomach ache. Vomiting. You know, sick."

"Nobody's complained to me, but to tell you the truth, nobody's buying the stuff. Looks like pond scum." Chaney held his hand over the engine. "Maybe I ought to pull the Genuine Juice if it's going to make folks sick. What'd you say your name was?"

"Cherry Tucker, sir."

"Where you know Jess from?"

"I grew up with her in Halo. Went to high school together."

"Halo?" He frowned. "What're you doing around here?"

Sidewinderers must think Halo was on the other side of Georgia instead of Forks County. "Visiting my friend Eloise Parker's folks. She died last weekend. Poisoned at the festival."

"You think it's this Genuine Juice?" Chaney looked stricken.

"Could have been. Could have been the Brunswick Stew, too."

"No way it was the stew," said Jay. "The Sidewinder Cook-Off is famous for Brunswick Stew all over the state."

I shrugged. I wasn't getting into another argument over Brunswick Stew.

"Must have been the Genuine Juice," said Jay. "You better dump that junk."

"Hell, Griffin can dump it himself," said Chaney. "I'm getting my money back. I don't care if he is local. I'm not supporting a poisoner."

"Um, I don't know for sure if the juice did poison people, sir," I said, feeling the weight of libel and slander fall to my shoulders. "At this point, it's just a possibility."

"It couldn't be the stew," Chaney shook his head. "We've been having that stew cook-off for years. Don't worry about Griffin. I'll take care of that nasty Genuine Juice. Thanks for letting me know. Why don't you cut the truck on now and see what happens?"

I climbed in the truck, turned the key, and the motor sputtered to a start. Leaning out the window, I shook Chaney's hand. "How did you do it? Magic?"

"Naw. Your truck don't like the heat. It just needed to cool down. You're going to need a new starter, though."

I exuded a lengthy sigh. "What's it gonna cost me?"

"Couple hundred, maybe."

"Shoot." Inside my purse, my wallet screamed. "Thanks for your help. Do you know where the Gables live? High Cotton farm?"

Chaney proved much more agreeable with directions than his clerk, and I told him so. For Chaney's sake, I hoped the police found the Brunswick Stew free of arsenic. He and the other small Sidewinder businesses needed that festival to continue. He might make poor choices in employees, but I hated to see a local business hurt because a sociopath wanted a bunch of folks to spew stew.

Or if some sociopath wanted somebody in particular dead.

Tightly packed rows of corn filled the fence line leading to High Cotton Farm's entrance. For half a mile I saw nothing but corn except for an occasional sign promising a fall corn maze and encouraging me to keep on moving forward. I wondered why they didn't name the estate High Corn Farm. If the place held cotton, it was hidden amongst the stalks.

Finally the lane opened onto a blacktopped drive big enough to hold Halo High's Fighting Angels football field, stands, and concessions. I idled the Datsun and studied the bright yellow parking lines covering the lot. Either the Gables put on a hell of a tailgate party or they expected an onslaught for their corn maze. On the far right end of the lot, a large brick house sat between a small grove of pecan trees. Closer to the lane, a traditional red barn rested next to a construction site. Behind the quaint barn, I could see the pitched metal roof of a machine shed.

Because the construction site was closer, I pulled up before the skeletal outline of a building and spied a small plot of cotton growing behind it. "Coming Soon! High Cotton Education Center" read a large sign. It seemed the Gables had ripped off another idea from the Maynards. This news would surely work Miss Marion into a tizzy.

My truck rumbled closer to the sign featuring a scale drawing and floor plan. While I leaned out my window and squinted at the drawing, Bruce Gable opened the barn door and poked his head out. Spotting me, he quickly pulled the heavy door shut.

In their love of competitions, maybe the Gables had also entered one for bizarre behavior. Although where I came from, we just call it rude.

I decided to leave Mr. Bruce to his barn and drove to the house. I left the truck running, hopped out, and slapped my flip-flops up the walk and onto the porch. Heavy curtains blocked all the windows of the two storied, brick home. I rang the bell. After a long minute, the metallic scraping of various locks tumbling sounded through the door. The heavy door swung open and an icy sheet of cold air poured out of the house and washed over me.

Belinda Gable stepped into the doorway, propping a hand on the frame to block my entrance. Lean and lanky like her younger sister, she towered above me with piled dark hair adding another few inches. Her black bermuda shorts and black silk golf shirt, tucked and belted with a gold chain, felt out of place in the heat of the Georgia countryside.

Frosty, blue rimmed eyes narrowed at my presence and gave my bulldog ensemble a brief, dismissive perusal.

"What do you want?" she said.

"My name is Cherry Tucker, ma'am, and ..." What did I want? I hadn't really come with a plan. I just wanted to meet the trashy Gables who Miss Marion seemed to think might have poisoned the Maynards' stew. I was also curious as to why Belinda showed up to church as part of Max's granny entourage. "I'm interested in your educational center. I heard about you at the Brunswick Stew cook-off."

"Just a minute." She slid the door halfway closed, blocking my view of the house, and turned away. A few seconds later, she reappeared with a brochure in her hand. "This should answer all your questions. What are you? A teacher or something?"

"No, ma'am. I'm an artist."

"Artist?" She propped the door a few inches wider and reexamined me. "What kind of artist?"

"Portraits mostly. That's my specialty. But I do all kinds."

"Portraits?" She frowned. "Do you have a card? Maybe we can do those funny sketches when the center gets up and running. We're still looking for additional funding."

"Not those kind of portraits." My stomach turned at the mention. I had spent my high school years working as a quick-draw artist at Six Flags. I'd have to be pretty desperate to return to that. In the distance I could hear my truck chugging away and realized desperate times might be near at hand. "Well, I can do quick sketches. Mostly I do studio portraits. Oils. Acrylics. I don't have a card on me. That's not why I came."

"Why did you come? Get to the point. I'm busy. Are you selling something?" She pointed to a sign next to the door that spoke of the evils of soliciting on their premises. Evidently, solicitors were not tolerated.

"No, ma'am. Actually, I've been talking to the Maynards and wondered why you both are building education centers."

I stopped as the door slammed shut in my face. I took that as the end to our conversation. Grasping the brochure, I hiked back to the Datsun. Some people sure were touchy.

Like they had something to hide.

NINETEEN

The Parkers set Eloise's visitation for Thursday. I had to do something to ease Mr. Parker's pain and let him grieve in peace.

That gave me two days. I had five days to pull together three modern renditions of Classical paintings for the gallery call. Considering I was much faster at drawing and painting than gathering information, I decided to continue my quest.

Besides, I couldn't really focus on sketching naked men with my friend's death hanging over me. I knew better than to air my grievances about Mr. Parker's frustrations with the law to Uncle Will. However, if I stopped at the Lickety Pig and picked up barbecue, I might catch him off-guard and learn a thing or two.

I wandered into the waiting area of the sheriff's office carrying two paper sacks smelling of heaven and smoked pig. Tamara, the receptionist, inhaled deeply and leaned forward. Her braided ponytail swept her shoulder. She pushed it back with red nails tipped in tiny black and jeweled G's.

"I like that tank you're wearing," she said. "The Dawgs is going to have a great season. We've got fresh recruits who look good."

"Glad to hear it." I set the sacks on the counter. "I am wearing it in homage for Eloise Parker. She went to UGA. Have you heard about her mysterious death?"

Tamara leaned back and crossed her arms. Her long nails tapped her biceps. "Now Cherry, you know what your Uncle Will said about giving you information on ongoing investigations."

"Oh him," I rolled my eyes and waved my hand, dismissing his little eccentricity. "Eloise Parker is a good friend of mine. I know all about the lab report showing arsenic in her system. I'm just wondering how arsenic could accidentally wind up in a person and kill her."

Tamara tightened her lips and shook her head.

I unrolled a paper bag. More essence of barbecue filled the waiting room. My stomach engaged in a sound that would challenge a jackhammer in intensity. However, I only had enough money for two sandwich meals and this was bribery barbecue. I could sacrifice for Eloise.

"Is that from Lickety Pig? I've been smelling it all morning and boy could I go for some pulled pork." Hunger sparked Tamara's eyes. "Are you sharing?"

"Well, I don't know. I thought I'd share with people who are sympathetic to Eloise's case."

"Cherry Tucker don't you tempt me with barbecue. I'll have the boys lock you up and we'll eat it in the property room."

"So you're not willing to give me the teensiest clue? Like maybe the source of the arsenic? Do they know if it came from the cook-off food or something else?"

"Do you think I want to lose my job?"

"Dangit," I sighed. "Then is Sheriff Will in?"

"He's back in his office. They've got a meeting in a few, but he's free now. I'll buzz you through."

"Thanks. Luke Harper isn't around, is he?"

"Funny, you're the third woman to ask today." She smiled. "You bringing him lunch, too? Don't blame you there."

My eyes narrowed. "What do you mean?"

"Word's gotten out about the newest deputy." She leaned closer, trying to whisper through the glass. "You know what the girls started calling him? Luquified. You know because he's so hot, he makes you..."

"I get it, Tamara. No need for the long description. Good Lord, don't you have anything better to do than drooling over one of your fellow officers? Aren't there bad guys to catch? People to ticket? Open this door. I haven't got all day."

One thing's for sure, Tamara wasn't getting any barbecue. At Tamara's buzz, I marched through the heavy metal door leading to the back offices.

The carpeted hallway and locked doors muffled any sounds, unfortunate for me. I had halfway hoped to overhear water cooler talk about the poisoning. Forks County didn't get a lot of poisoning cases. If I was a cop, I'd be chatting about the new case. Halfway down the corridor, a door cracked open and Luke peeked out. Spying me, he swung the door open and walked into the hallway.

"What are you doing here?" He ran a hand through his dark waves, then hooked it on his utility belt, a move reminding me of Uncle Will.

"Nice to see you, too." I held up the bags of barbecue. "Bringing lunch to you and Uncle Will, although I'm surprised to see you. Figured you be out on patrol."

He yawned. "Doing paperwork. Sorry about last night."

"I'm getting used to it. I'm just glad you're on days again. That seven p.m. to seven a.m. shift was ridiculous."

He nodded and gave an involuntary glance at the door he just left. "Thanks for bringing lunch by. I'll take it back with me." Leaning down, he smacked a quick kiss on my cheek.

I kept a tight grip on the paper bags. "I get the feeling you don't want me here."

"Exactly."

My face grew hot. I forced my words from tightened lips. "And why do you not want me showing up at the office?"

Luke took a half step back and glanced at the closed door again. "Now sugar, we don't need to get into this. It's been a long night and a long morning. I really appreciate you going to all the trouble to drive down here…"

"Who's in that room?"

"Nobody, just some of the other officers. We've got a meeting in thirty minutes. Why don't I walk you out to the parking lot?"

I stuck my nose in the air and whirled away. "No, thank you. I'm here to see my Uncle Will. I just thought I'd be NICE and bring you lunch, too. I was already in Sidewinder..."

He grabbed my shoulder and spun me around. "Why were you in Sidewinder?"

"Visiting Eloise's folks, of course. They are obviously torn up and needing comfort. The visitation is Thursday."

"Oh." Luke's stern looked relaxed and his shoulders sagged. "I'm sorry, hon'. Of course. I'll see if I can go to the viewing."

"Don't do me any favors."

He cupped my cheek and ran a thumb over my lips. "I almost forgot the victim was your friend. I got this funny idea you might be butting into the investigation. Chris Wellington saw you at the hospital last night, and...well, I know how you are."

I refused to be moved by his smoky eyes and soft voice. Or the face stroking thing. "And how am I?"

"You're a sweet, little thing for bringing me lunch and putting up with me biting your head off."

He always did have the best lines, although we both knew I wasn't a sweet, little thing. I snuggled closer, holding up a sack. "You can keep your lunch. I even bought banana pudding. I know how you love Lickety's banana pudding."

He glanced over his shoulder and backed me into the cinderblock wall. "How about a quick kiss?" he whispered. "Real quick, but real good. Since you're here and all."

My heart started thrumming, and I reminded myself to keep a firm grip on the BBQ bags. "Okay," I said. I'd never made out in a law enforcement establishment before. My toes curled in my flip-flops.

Luke brushed a row of bulldog buttons, making them sway. "Team spirit day?"

"Eloise went to UGA," I said, tipping up my face. My eyelids fluttered shut.

I felt Luke's lips hover over mine, then press firmly. Just as a small slip of his tongue teased out, my mouth went all haywire.

They slipped and cantered, and I kid you not, went in two different directions at once.

Luke jerked his head back, and my eyes popped open. He swiped at his mouth with the back of his hand.

"What has gotten into you?" he said.

A door banged open behind us and three officers spilled out, laughing.

"Did you forget the hallways are monitored, Harper?" hooted one uniform.

A tall, black officer I didn't know fluttered his eyelids and made kissing sounds. "How many lunches are you going to eat today, Deputy Harper?" he asked. "Lickety Pig's going to get cleaned out of pork just from feeding you."

"Shut up," said Luke and turned back to me. "Let's get you out of here."

"I'm going to visit Uncle Will," I said, sidling out from behind him. "Sounds like you already had lunch. Who's been bringing you barbecue?"

"Nobody important."

"Don't call admirers of the badge nobody important," hooted an officer behind us. "They're concerned citizens. Concerned you're not getting enough to eat."

"Good thing they brought you lunch," I said, "'cause looks like you're not getting any from me."

"Now, sugar..."

"I heard you, Jake Fells," I said to the deputy going back into the junior officers' room. "You're not getting any barbecue either."

I turned on my heel and marched to the sheriff's office, wafting barbecue aroma in my wake. I knocked and Uncle Will opened the door, casting his eyes to the scene in the hallway.

"Hello there, girl. Is that Lickety Pig I smell?" Will patted his capacious stomach, placed a firm hand on my shoulder, and steered me into his office. "Look at that getup you got on. Love to see you supporting my Dawgs. We're going to have a good season this year, I just know it. Come in and have a seat."

He shut the door while I scurried to his desk, plopping the paper bags on his blotter. I eyed the neat stack of files on his desk, but couldn't risk a peek with Will behind me. I took a quick glance around the wood-paneled room. Other than a crooked photo of Sheriff Will kneeling next to a K-Nine, order reigned in the office. The file cabinets were free of clutter, as was the credenza behind Will's desk.

I spied a small picture of Cody, Casey, and me. The photo had been taken at my graduation from SCAD—Savannah College of Art and Design—where the three of us, plied with celebratory libations, offered massive smiles for the camera. There weren't many photos of my family. We weren't much on snapshots. A small flash of guilt at tricking Will with barbecue licked my conscience and heated my cheeks.

"That was a happy day," Will remarked as he unrolled the paper bag sitting before him.

"I didn't know you had that photo here." I settled the frame back and fell into the armchair facing his desk.

"Doesn't surprise me. It is unusual for you to visit me at the office. I've only had it sitting there for, what? Five years or so?" He pulled out the paper-wrapped barbecue sandwich, a small tub of coleslaw, and the banana pudding. "I do love banana pudding. Thank you, Cherry, for this remarkable visit and spending the little cash you have on buying me lunch."

"Remarkable?"

He busied himself with topping his pulled pork with coleslaw before continuing. "My memory may not be perfect, but I like to think of myself as still pretty sharp. And as I can't remember you bringing me lunch at the office before, I would deem this visit remarkable."

My mouth opened to speak. I caught Will's look and snapped it shut.

He took a bite of barbecue and swabbed his face with a napkin before continuing. "When an event stands out as remarkable, my brain likes to jump to conclusions. As a man of the law, I don't act on conclusions. I've got to gather my facts. But my brain still takes a few hops to see just where this event might be headed."

"Can't I just be nice and bring you lunch because I was in the area?"

"Sure you could, but that wouldn't be in character for you. Which makes this wonderful lunch remarkable. Like it or not, part of my job is making character judgments. You wouldn't happen to have some lima beans in that other sack, now would you? I just love Lickety Pig's lima beans."

"No lima beans."

"Can't hurt to ask."

He took another bite of the sandwich, while I squirmed in my seat. I needed to grab control of the conversation.

"The Parkers deserve some information."

Will took a last bite of barbecue, rolled the paper into a neat ball, and threw it in the trashcan beside the desk. Leaning back in his green leather chair, he steepled his hands over his belly. He gave me a look he had used on his opponents while playing tackle for University of Georgia thirty years earlier.

"Seems to me," he said, "you're trying to tell me how to do my job. Is that really why you're here? To soften me up with pulled pork and then tell me how to do my job?"

The hairs on the back of my neck stood at attention.

"What's Deputy Harper saying about the death of your friend, Eloise?" he asked.

"Nothing."

"As he should. Because he knows interfering with police procedure can ruin an investigation. Not just in catching the perp, but later when the perp stands trial and his lawyer shows our investigation as a massive AFU. You know what that means?"

"Yes, sir."

"It means the perp goes free, and I look very bad. Not only could I lose my job next election, it also damages the trust I've built with the people of Forks County. Which hampers my ability to catch criminals."

"Yes, sir."

"Now," Will popped open the lid on the banana pudding, "what was it you wanted to talk about, honey?"

I crossed my arms and squished my mouth to the side.

"Don't pout, Cherrilyn. You haven't touched your lunch." He eyed the paper bag still sitting on his desk. "I know better than to ask if you're hungry, but since you're not eating, would that extra barbecue happen to be for Deputy Harper and not you?"

"It was," I admitted grudgingly.

"Was? So does that mean there is an extra sandwich available?"

I snatched the bag from the desk. "Now hold on, Uncle Will."

"Either that barbecue is for him or it isn't. You can't have it both ways, Cherry. You can't make a man think he can have barbecue and withhold it from him indefinitely. That would be extremely uncharitable. Wouldn't you agree?"

"Just what are you saying?"

"I'm saying, either give the man his barbecue or tell him he's not getting any. I know something about being hungry for barbecue and never being quite sure if I was going to eat it or just look at it."

"What?"

"A hungry man does not make a good officer. His mind constantly drifts to the problem of being hungry for barbecue. I have invested in Deputy Harper and so have the citizens of Forks County. Do not leave barbecue dangling before the man. I can't control other girls, but I do expect you to listen. Do not mess with my officers, Cherrilyn Tucker."

I tossed the bag onto his desk. "He can have the damn barbecue. God Almighty, Uncle Will, I don't know what you're getting all steamed about. I'm just bringing you lunch. So Luke and I had a little spat. I am not withholding barbecue to mess with your investigations."

"I am not talking about barbecue."

"I know what you're talking about. Luke's got crazy hours, and I know in his off times he wants some peace, but he never wants to do anything. He's too focused on his career. I'm young. I need to get out. I want a life that's more than waiting to see if he's coming over."

Will dropped his spoon back in the banana pudding. Tipping back his chair, he massaged his chin.

"Why do you look like that? Isn't that what you were alluding to with this whole barbecue thing?"

"You just sounded like someone I once knew. Gave me a shock is all." He shook his head. "Listen here, Cherry. You, Casey, and Cody don't usually play the victim to your childhood issues. I'm proud of y'all for that. But ugliness can seep in and manifest in other ways. You need to be careful and not push away what can truly make you happy. I've seen what can happen if you keep running away from people who care about you."

I pushed out of the chair to place my hands on his desk and lean over it. "Are you talking about my mother? Are you saying you know what's happened to her?"

"I'm not just talking about Christy. I see it all the time in my job." He shooed me away from the desk. "Go on now. I'll bring Luke his lunch. You think about what I said. My officers and I have a meeting in ten minutes, and I've got to prepare my notes."

I spun on my heel and stalked out of the office, keeping silent as Will buzzed me through the doors. Not only had I wasted the little cash I had on ineffective barbecue bribery, I now had a new worry. Christy Tucker's name was rarely mentioned. I wrote off the childhood fantasies of her living as a rock star or a famous artist. I had stopped thinking about her much at all except for the humiliating reminders of the legacy she left us. A penchant for falling for good looking men and a creative spark for making trouble.

The baffling words Will had spoken about barbecue and men fertilized a seed once planted by Casey. She had thought Will knew a lot more about our momma's whereabouts than he and Grandpa would admit. Maybe Casey, Cody, and I needed to lay that mystery to rest before we could willingly dish out barbecue to people like Luke. But that thought made my stomach queasy, and I pushed it aside. Anyway, Luke had enough family issues of his own that I wasn't so sure if he really wanted my barbecue. His parents didn't even know about me. And it sounded like he was getting other offers.

More importantly, I had two days before seeing the Parkers again and still no news to deliver. I should have known better than trying to outmaneuver Sheriff Will Thompson. That man hadn't held on to his seat of power by getting outsmarted by a little barbecue.

Even if it was brought by Cherry Tucker.

TWENTY

With a stomach yearning for barbecue, I pointed the bug-spattered grill of the Datsun north toward Halo and Grandpa's farm. The farm kitchen would abate the horrendous sounds of hunger bursting from my gut and a few words with my family might abate the worries niggling my mind.

With no giant goat sighting at the turn from the highway, I gunned the motor, reeled into the drive, and rocketed up the gravel lane. After all the trips to Sidewinder, the Datsun seemed to finally warm up in this last sprint. I squinted into the distance, searching for Tater and his gleaming white hide. He loved playing hide and seek even more than chicken. The stupid goat had an affinity for scaring the bejesus out of me.

No Tater.

Instead of Tater, a fawn colored goat pranced into the drive. We eyed each other for a long moment. She broke the look with a pawing motion, then burst into a gallop. I gaped while she barreled past the Bradford Pear, lowered her head, and aimed straight for the Datsun's front bumper.

"Holy crap," I said and jammed the gear into reverse. I tossed my arm over the seat and backed half-way down the drive before I realized I had allowed an unknown goat to chase me off my family farm. Jerking to a halt, I spun forward in my seat and watched the small dart brake at the fork in the lane. With her head lowered, she pawed the ground, and gave me the goat version of a stink-eye.

"What is your problem?" I yelled from the open window. "I'm hot, hungry, and have a heap of problems. I don't even know you."

She shook her head, turned around, and trotted back to the house. I inched along the lane until I reached the fork. The doe spun around and fixed me with a steely gaze.

"That does it." I parked and hopped out of the truck. "Who the hell are you to keep me from my own dang driveway?"

"Snickerdoodles," someone called from the house.

The little goat perked her ears and cranked her head toward the farm house.

"Snickerdoodle?" I said, plodding forward.

She whipped her head back around and dropped to butting position. I froze.

"Tater," I yelled. Where was the barnyard hellion when you needed him?

"Snickies! Nibblies!"

The goat turned and trotted toward the house. With my stomach pulsing at the word nibblies, I trotted after her.

Somehow my Grandpa's farm had been invaded by alien goats and people who used words like nibblies. As I suspected, Pearl stood on the porch steps, a bag of carrots in her hand. We watched Snickerdoodle trot around the back of the house with her muzzle full of carrot.

"Why, Cherry. Why are you walking around in this heat?"

I bit back a couple of choice remarks and forced a smile. "Is that your goat?"

"Did you meet Snickies?" Pearl pushed the carrot bag into the pocket of her capri pants. "Isn't she a pretty, little thing? A champion milker, too."

"What is she doing here? And by here, I mean freely wandering around the farm and blocking the driveway? And where is Tater?" I cast a glance behind me and hurried to the screened porch.

"He's around here somewhere. I brought Snickerdoodle over so they could get acquainted." She followed me onto the porch, slamming the screen door behind her.

"Well, take her back home after their meeting. The last thing we need around here is a bunch of baby goats clogging up the drive."

"I'm not mating her to that Saanen." Pearl stuck her calloused hands on her hips. Her aqua and fuchsia floral tank made a great showing of her blue boob tattoo. The ink that had once been a goat looked more like a giraffe.

I didn't want to know what Grandpa thought about boob giraffes. "Good to know. God only knows what kind of demon spawn Tater would produce."

"Phht." Pearl waved her hand in the air. "That goat is a big sissy. He's scared of little Snickies."

Maybe I could learn to like Snickerdoodle. Once she stopped trying to kill me with her evil goat eye.

We opened the front door and walked into the living room where Casey lay stretched on the couch, reading a magazine with the TV blaring in the background. She had abandoned the slutty biker outfit for a black halter top that showed off her shoulder tattoo and tramp stamp effectively. I hoped Pearl's goat-giraffe would deter Casey from any cleavage ink.

Casey gave me a nod, shot Pearl a slitty-eyed look, and returned her attention to the magazine.

"Hey, Case," I said. "We need to talk. Got anything to eat?"

Pearl pushed past me to bustle into the kitchen. "Let me make you a plate, honey."

Behind the magazine, Casey mimicked Pearl in a nasty drawl and flipped her the bird.

"How old are you?" I said, "I've seen eight-year-olds with better attitudes."

"What do you know? You haven't been here. She's taking over everything and is all up in my business."

"You're always complaining about having to cook for us. Why don't you just enjoy your time on the sofa?"

Casey popped up to sitting, scattering her long, brown hair around her shoulders. She pointed a recently varnished shamrock green nail at me. "You just wait. Pearl's all friendly now, but as soon as she's secured her place of power, there will be no more fixing plates for you."

"What?"

"She's talking about having her daughter's family over for Sunday dinner. Wants to make all their favorite foods. Keeps bragging about Amy's job and Amy's stupid husband's job and what hard workers they are."

"So?" I didn't press the issue, but Pearl might have a point. Casey and Cody took to hard work like a fish takes to a dock. Lots of gasping and ineffectual flopping.

"Don't you see? If Grandpa marries her, she's kicking me and Cody out for sure. It's all going to be about Amy."

Casey flounced on the couch, knocking the magazine to the floor. "Amy, Amy, Amy. I'm about sick to death of Amy and I've never met her."

"God Almighty, Casey. Would you grow up already?" However, if Casey and Cody were kicked out, that meant they might move in with me. I internalized my shudder.

"You're one to talk. What are you wearing anyway? You lost a button on your flip-flop, too. Looks uneven."

"I'm wearing this in support of Eloise and her love of Uga the dog. She was proud of her Georgia Bulldogs."

Casey frowned. "Sorry. I forgot about Eloise. Did Uncle Will figure out what happened yet?"

"No. Mr. Parker is beside himself. He's not getting any answers, so I thought I'd help him out."

"Just how are you doing that?"

"Asking around. I know a handful of people who got sick and a handful of people who didn't. I'm trying to see if it was the stew or Griffin's Genuine Juice which had arsenic in it." I tapped my head. "Deductive reasoning. Can't be that hard."

Casey squinted at me. "You think the police can't come up with that? What does Deputy Lover Boy think about you questioning folks?"

I chewed a nail and inspected the damage. "I am not going to tell him. He's not thrilled with me interfering in what he believes is police business."

I looked up. Casey had folded her arms, giving me her big sister stare down.

"Casey, you gotta understand. The Parkers don't have much except for their girls. Eloise was the only one in the history of their family who went to college, and although they don't know much about art, they know how talented she is. Was. And they were so proud she came back to Sidewinder to teach, when she really could have gone anywhere. It caused them so much pain to see her disease hurt and whittle her away to nothing. And then to lose her like this?"

"You know we're proud of you, too, for going to college and for your painting. We appreciate you coming back to Halo when you could've stayed in Savannah or moved to Atlanta or somewhere."

I rolled my eyes. "This isn't about me. This is about Eloise getting her life snuffed out early. It's not like her disease would have taken her. The Parkers want justice."

"Okay, there are no similarities between you and Eloise. This is about your need to right a wrong."

"Stop trying to make this about me. There is a chance that this poisoning was not an accident. Nor some psycho who wanted to see a bunch of people toss cookies at a festival and get his name in the paper."

"Eew." Casey curled her lip. "Thanks for that image. You think someone murdered Eloise?"

"Her musclehead boyfriend, Griffin Ward, thought he could cure her with his health drinks and it wasn't working. He was also a jealous sonofabitch who threatened to beat the tar out of me for interfering."

"Why would he kill her?"

"Maybe he didn't mean to kill her. Maybe he was just trying to make her feel sick so she would try his remedy in desperation."

"Wow. You came up with that on your own?"

With a grin, I blew on my fist and polished it on my button endowed tank top.

"So then how did everyone else get sick?"

"Dangit, Casey. It's one theory. I do have a few other thoughts I'm rolling around. I need to do a little more investigating before you start punching holes in all my notions."

Casey smirked. "What other bright ideas do you have?"

"I'm supposed to talk to this kid named Hunter Adams tonight. He has his own theory that his mom's boyfriend poisoned their stew and himself."

"That theory's even dumber than yours."

"I need to check it out anyway. The kid's got anger issues. You want to go with me to Sidewinder? I'm supposed to take Todd, but..."

"I've got to work at Red's tonight. We've been pretty busy. Tuesday is Ladies Night and last week a horde of grandmas descended on the County Line demanding Lambrusco wine and fried cheese sticks."

"That's odd."

"Tell me about it. And they're terrible tippers."

"About Todd..."

Before I could get Casey's advice on my Todd dilemma, my phone rang. I yanked it from my pocket and turned my back.

"Cherry, it's Dot from the Halo Herald. I was calling to see if you've learned anything else."

I scuttled toward the hallway leading off the living room. "Hey, Dot. I couldn't get anything from Sheriff Will, but the Parkers are upset. Because Eloise had that stomach condition, the officials aren't paying much attention to her death. The police are acting like someone pulled a prank or it was accidental."

"Poor things," said Dot. "When's the funeral?"

"Viewing is Thursday and funeral on Friday. In Sidewinder. I did talk to Marion Maynard at the hospital. And Hunter Adams. I tried to talk to the Gables, but that didn't work out so well."

"Did you now?" Dot's voice grew in excitement. "What did Marion and Hunter say?"

"Miss Marion thinks her neighbors, the Gables of High Cotton Farm, might have put something in her Brunswick Stew. I also saw Belinda Gable tagging after Max Avtaikin at church."

"Probably a bingo fan."

"She seems a tad young compared to the rest of his entourage. Anyway, Hunter is the son of Janine Adams who works for the Maynards. He thinks Lewis poisoned it himself. I'm going to talk to Hunter tonight. Hunter has sour grapes about Lewis's relationship with his mom. It wouldn't surprise me if Hunter did something to that stew, although I doubt he tried to kill anyone. Probably tossed something in it to make it taste bad and accidentally poisoned it."

"Interesting. Let me know what you learn from Hunter."

"I will. There's one more possibility and it has nothing to do with the cook-off."

"What?"

"I told you Eloise had a low-life boyfriend who threatened her. Griffin Ward. He's a health food nut and makes a veggie drink called Griffin's Genuine Juice. He thought he created some kind of elixir that would cure Eloise of Crohn's Disease. He passed out Genuine Juice at the festival and many of the people who ate the stew also drank his smoothie. Until the police know for sure where the arsenic came from, I'm still finding Griffin suspect."

"Hmmm." Dot seemed to drift off, but I wanted quid pro quo.

"What did you learn? Do they know what had the arsenic in it? I need something to tell Mr. Parker."

"No, they haven't found the source of the arsenic yet. However, I do have news, which was why I called you."

"What is it?" I spun around. Casey hung over the back of the couch, watching me.

"It's Lewis Maynard," said Dot. "He died. Arsenic poisoning."

"Holy sh—" I broke off one of my favorite expletives as Pearl walked into the living room, one hand on her hip and the other pointing a wooden spoon at my face.

"Hello?" asked Dot. "Did you hear me say Lewis Maynard is dead?"

"I'm on the phone, Miss Pearl." I turned my back on the spoon and stepped deeper into the hallway. "I heard you, Dot. Give me the details."

A hand snatched my phone and a spoon rapped the side of my head.

"Ow!" I yelled, rubbing my head. "Cut it out."

"It's time y'all started learning some manners," said Pearl, brandishing the wooden spoon.

"From somebody who lets goats run loose in the yard? Give me my phone."

She slapped it into my palm. "You better eat. And don't try that texting stuff."

"I can't afford texting." Pearl's antics had ended my phone connection. Realizing I would have to learn more about Lewis's suspicious death later, I stalked into the sunny kitchen and plopped into a rattan chair at the kitchen table. Before me set a plate laden with the bounty of Pearl's talents. I inhaled the southern goodness and took a tentative bite. She placed a glass of tea on the table.

"Casey, come in here will you?" I still needed her advice on the whole Todd predicament. She probably had a colorful opinion about Speedos that'd be worth hearing anyway.

Pearl took my holler as an invitation for a lunch chat and eased into a chair across from me. She placed a glass of tea before her and crossed her legs. I looked up with a questioning glance, which she ignored.

Casey plodded in and threw herself into the chair next to me. She pursed her lips and narrowed her brown eyes at Pearl.

"Just a minute." I held my hand up to stem the flow of Casey's ugly remarks. Todd's Speedo had led me down a new current of thought. A couple new currents, actually, but only one I could speak of. "Pearl, are you still going to Mr. Max's house for bingo?"

"I was, but he shut down for a few days. Something about his air conditioner."

"Did you ever see a tall, blond guy there?" I glanced at Casey. She drew her brows together, studying me.

"Real good looking. Likes to tap his hands all over the place?"

"Todd the drummer?" Pearl slapped the table. "I got a handful of that sweetness just the other day."

"Excuse me?"

"He sometimes calls the numbers and hands out the bingo cards. Some of the ladies get frisky with him and he backed into me. Accidentally parked that tight, little fanny right into my purse."

I moved the conversation away from Todd's tight, little fanny to prevent myself from taking another trip down Speedo lane. "So he's working for Mr. Max."

"I thought he drove a truck or something," said Casey.

"He must be moonlighting. Even Todd wouldn't be dumb enough to quit his job to deal bingo." Or would he? Todd had issues with poker and Max had once tried to entice him into his underground gambling ring. Todd came from a long line of gamblers. Most of the McIntosh clan had been created between rolls of dice and hands of cards.

"You ever see anyone playing cards or games other than bingo at Mr. Max's?" I asked Pearl.

"Can't say I have. He's careful to keep us in the Vegas room. That's what we call it, but it looks more like a Mississippi boat."

"I need to get into one of these bingo games."

Casey scrunched her mouth to the side. "Don't you have enough to worry about with Eloise's deal? And what about your screwball body painting thingy?"

"I can't focus on my art with all this poisoning and bingo nonsense," I said. "Besides I'm fixing to use Luke as a model. I'm going to have to hold out until I get my lips working again."

"I'll take you to bingo," said Pearl. "I usually go on Wednesdays. So tomorrow. Unless he still hasn't got his a/c fixed."

"Thank you, Miss Pearl. Maybe I should wear a disguise." My mind started picking through my wardrobe. "You think a wig and glasses would do it or would Todd and Mr. Max see through that?"

Casey buried her forehead in her hand. "Leave your Scooby Doo shenanigans at home."

"The ladies are fixing to see Todd's band play at the County Line Tap on Friday night," said Pearl. "Maybe you want to come with me to that, too?"

I pictured Todd on Red's small stage encircled by screaming blue-hairs holding lighters above their heads. "I'd be crazy to miss that Sticks performance," I snorted.

"You can snort all you want," said Pearl, "but some of us used to tear up the concert scenes pretty good. I've seen Johnny Cash, Conway Twitty, Waylon Jennings, and even Jimmie Hendricks."

"They're all dead," said Casey.

"What can I say? The good die young." Pearl shrugged. "You think I can get Ed to go to the concert with me?"

Casey and I looked at each other and whooped with laughter. I clamped a hand on the table to keep my buttons from shaking off.

"You can get Grandpa Ed to go fishing, but beyond that you're out of luck," I said. "Possibly the County Fair. To check out the livestock."

"Maybe a trip to the hardware store," said Casey, "or the feed store."

"But you'd have to drop him off so he can stand around the cash register and talk to the other old men who hang out there," I said. "He'll pretend like he doesn't know you if you go inside."

"We'll see," said Pearl. "He seems pretty content with having me over."

"Listen, Miss Pearl," I said. "Don't try too hard. Grandpa's a prickly thing, and I've never seen him wander out of his farm orbit, not even for my Grandma Jo. I'm sure he appreciates all your cooking."

"And goats," said Casey.

"But we don't want to see you get your heart fixed on him."

"Don't you worry about me," said Pearl. "I know something about old goats like Ed. They seem tough, but you just need to know how to soften them up."

"Well, it'll take a lot of butter to soften up that piece of gristle. But with my luck with men, I can't cast stones," I said. "And on that note, I'm fixing to go home to shower and change before I take Todd to the Viper. Although maybe a day's worth of sweat is what I need to keep some distance between us."

"If it's that hard maybe you're with the wrong guy," said Casey. "Maybe this is your subconscious telling you that you should have stayed married to Todd. Saw something like that on TV just an hour ago."

"Then my subconscious is stupid and not to be trusted."

Casey smirked. "That's not the only part of you that can't be trusted. Be careful with those lips, sister."

Dangit. I just hated when Casey was right.

TWENTY-ONE

I left Casey to worry about Pearl's conquest of Grandpa and pointed the Datsun back toward Halo and 211 Loblolly Avenue. Alone in my house, I couldn't settle into a project, although the Greek statues sketches called to me. If I couldn't get Luke to model, I'd need to find another victim. I couldn't outright copy the statues. Reconstituting Classicism meant a fresh take on the old subjects. Which meant a live body, preferably with an amazing V-cut, covered in Greek symbols and posed as the original subjects. That's my take on it, anyhow.

Lord help me, but if Eloise weren't already dead, she'd drag me to the grave. If I blew this gallery call, her professor would find me unreliable. And I wanted to see Eloise get her pottery show, even if it was posthumously.

I felt antsy to learn more about Lewis Maynard and any possible connection he might have to Eloise. What was protocol for the death of your mother's married boyfriend? Would Hunter still show at the Viper? And if Hunter did show, I didn't trust him.

I needed backup. A true wingman to fly with me into the Viper's pit and pull answers out of Hunter. Casey was working. Cody was undependable. I couldn't ask Leah to go to the Viper or her mother would kill me. Luke was out of the question. That left Todd, my usual wingman.

But Todd had been acting too peculiar with his working for Mr. Max, Speedos, and kissing. I had refused to return his cryptic messages. "Hey, baby, we need to talk" did not bode well. This girl needed to focus on her actual boyfriend before Luke started accepting other offers of barbecue.

If my lips didn't return to normal soon, I would have some serious explaining to do.

Just as I reluctantly pulled my phone from my pocket to dial Todd's number, I remembered I needed to call Dot. She probably thought I had been kidnapped and held hostage. Or worse: that I had flaked out on her.

"Halo Herald, Dot speaking," she warbled into the phone.

"Hey, it's Cherry. Sorry about earlier. I was attacked by a crazy woman with a spoon."

Dot took a minute to gather her thoughts. "What's going on?"

"I wanted to know more about Lewis Maynard's death. That and I was wondering if you liked to accompany me to Sidewinder tonight to talk to Hunter Adams, son of Lewis Maynard's side of fries."

"The medical examiner still needs to perform an autopsy, but while in his coma, Lewis had been tested and found to have high levels of arsenic in his system," she paused. "More even than Eloise. You want me to come to Sidewinder while you talk to Hunter?"

"Yep, to the Viper. It's a local bar, kind of seedy, but they've got a great menu. Any food you can think of that can be breaded and cooked in hot oil. The fried pickles are to die for."

"What with the poisoning in Sidewinder, I hope you're wrong," she cackled.

I grinned. Dot had the kind of morbid sense of humor I enjoyed. "I hoped that ignites a flame under the sheriff's office to do a little more poking than testing for arsenic in groundwater and dish soap. I hate to hear Lewis had died, even though he's a lowlife cheater, but the Parkers won't find peace in Eloise's death without answers. In my opinion, the sheriff's office needs to step it up."

"Really? Aren't you close to the sheriff?"

"Don't quote me now, Dot. I'm just speaking my mind and don't want any repercussions."

"Tell you what, I'll go with you to the Viper and I'll even buy dinner..."

I silently whooped for joy. If I had to pay for dinner, only one of us would eat.

"As long as you keep feeding me information about the poisoning," she continued. "I'd love to scoop the Line Creek Limited on this. We've got a local competition, and I want to rub their noses in a big story."

I had a vague recollection of Luke warning me not to talk to the press, but the thought of free dinner at the Viper overrode my memory receptacles. Call me a sellout, but the fried pickles were really worth another tussle with Luke. And as many times as we had fought lately, I looked forward to a great makeup session. Just as soon as I fixed my lips.

As the Datsun shuddered into the Viper parking lot, a chill washed over me. My last visit had been with Eloise. It felt eons ago, not a few months earlier. A row of angry looking Harleys, a half-dozen battered pickups, and two mud-splattered ATVs decorated the lot. My pickup fit right in. And even though I didn't have a proper gun rack, I had slipped my Remington Wingmaster shotgun box from under my bed to behind the seat of my truck. Not just to fit in with the locals, but the Remington gave me a bit of confidence in meeting Hunter.

Not that I'd shoot the kid. The Remington made me look taller.

Spying Dot waiting nearby, I hailed her, and left the shotgun in the truck. We walked into the cinderblock establishment with blacked out windows. It took a minute to adjust to the low lighting. Tuesday night seemed a popular time to grab a drink, judging by the tables of men with gnarled hands and sinewy biceps. Sweat stained their shirts and the sun had leathered their skin. They eyed me without moving their faces from their beers. The Viper made Red's look like Buckingham Palace.

I glanced at Dot standing next to me in brown capris and a cream print blouse. She looked like a bewildered bird that had flown into someone's old barn by accident. Nervous, but curious to see if there were any material for making a nest.

Toward the back of the dingy tavern, I spied Hunter slumped between a video hunting game and an old pinball machine. I sent Dot after him, and I maneuvered between tables toward the bar, squeezing between two men in John Deere caps and old cotton shirts with rolled up sleeves. A spit cup sat between them. Kind of sweet they'd share a cup for their chew. Behind the bar, a man with a snowy white beard and twinkling blue eyes smiled and chatted while fetching drinks.

"So this is where Santa hides during the summer," I said.

The man next to me set down his beer and grinned. "That's Sam," he said. "He owns the place."

"He's not what I expected."

"Don't let the bowl full of jelly act fool you. On Sundays he shuts down the Viper to ride his Harley with the other bikers." The farmer winked. "He'll let you sit on his lap if you want to give him your Christmas list, though."

The other farmer guffawed.

"He looks nice enough," I said.

"Hey Sam. There's a gal here who needs some service."

I tossed my ID at him and ordered two beers and a Coke.

Sam glanced at my license and shot me a hard look before his blue eyes mellowed. "You from Halo? I feel I've seen you before. We got a catfish special tonight."

"I'll take three plates," I said. "I've eaten here with my friend Eloise Parker."

"The art teacher?" Sam's face lit up.

"Do you know that kid, Hunter Adams, in the back, sitting with my friend?"

Sam looked over my shoulder and nodded. "Sure, he's from around here. Comes in to play games sometimes. Is he giving you trouble?"

"No, the Coke's for Hunter. I'm helping him, but I don't know much about his family. I just met his mom yesterday. Do you know her at all?"

"Janine? She's something else. She used to wait tables. Smart as a whip. Got her a rich boyfriend and now she thinks her you-know-what don't stink."

"That's the impression I got." I thought about telling Sam that Janine's boyfriend had passed but figured he'd find out soon enough. "Who is Hunter's daddy? Does he still live around here?"

"See that guy at the far end with his head near fallen into his whiskey? That would be Hunter's uncle, Keith Adams." Sam dropped his voice and leaned toward me. "His brother, Jerry, is Hunter's dad and a sorrier mess than Keith. Jerry Adams is serving time in prison for possession and distribution. He used to give Janine and the kid a hell of a wallop when he was drinking. Keith over there just drinks himself into a stupor. That's why I let the kid hang out in here. He likes to keep an eye on his uncle."

"That's a pretty sad story. Hunter's got a mean temper, but I guess that's why."

"You best watch yourself when you're with Hunter. He's gotten in trouble for fighting. He knows not to start anything in here." Sam pointed to a baseball bat behind the bar. "It's nice you're trying to help him, but he's like a feral cat. He'll just as soon bite you when you try to pet him."

"You think he would try to kill someone?"

"I would like to say no." Sam scratched his beard. "However, if I read it in the paper, I probably wouldn't be surprised."

Great. "Thanks."

"Anytime, honey. Just call on Sam for anything." He winked.

I sashayed with the drinks back to the table where Dot and Hunter waited in silence. Dot's gaze roamed the bar while Hunter stared sullenly at me. I slid in next to Dot and pushed the Coke toward Hunter.

"No beer?" he said. "You're not wearing one of your fancy outfits tonight."

My eyes dropped to my hot pink Myrtle Beach t-shirt. It ran long, so I had fringed and beaded the bottom with multicolored beads. "I thought I'd tone it down for the Viper. I got us all catfish."

"Catfish?" Dot chirped in excitement. "I love catfish."

"I heard Lewis died," I said to Hunter. "I'm sorry."

"I didn't do it," Hunter said. "But as far as I'm concerned, he deserved it."

Dot coughed into her beer and pushed it away.

"Your momma must be upset," I continued. "I'm surprised you came tonight."

"She didn't even notice me leaving. She's more upset Miss Marion has taken over the funeral stuff. Miss Marion's going to fire her, too."

"I guess you've been questioned by the Sheriff's Department?"

"This morning." Hunter sucked his Coke dry and slammed the plastic cup on the table. "Assholes. Brought up my juvie record. That's supposed to be sealed."

"What did they ask you concerning the day of the festival when everyone got sick?"

"Who was there, who cooked, who cleaned up. That kind of stuff." Hunter slumped back in his seat. "The cook-off rules are you have to make it on site. Lewis was the only cook. I didn't even show up until eleven when we started dishing out samples."

"What about the Gables?" I said. "I heard the two cotton farms like to go at it. Miss Marion said the Gables were messing around with your cook-off stuff."

He pulled back his lip and inserted a wad of chew without taking his eyes off me. Beside me, Dot slowly pulled a small notebook from her purse and left it in her lap.

"What?" I said. "What's with the attitude?"

"We don't talk about the Gables," he said.

"Who doesn't talk about the Gables?"

He spit into the empty cup and wiped his mouth off with the back of his hand.

I gave him an exasperated sigh. "You asked for my help, Hunter. I've got to ask questions."

"I don't know nothing about the Gables. That's my aunt and uncle, you know. Anyway, if they were messing around with our stuff, I wasn't there to see it."

"Fine." I glanced at Dot.

"You're a team, though, right?" Dot said. "Who else was on your cook-off team?"

"My mom, me, and Miss Marion."

"Why does Miss Marion participate in the contest when she knows Lewis and your mom are there together? Wouldn't she be uncomfortable, considering their relationship?"

"Lewis and Marion are still married. She sees my mom all the time since my mom works at Cotton Pickin'." Hunter spit into the cup as he considered Dot's question. "I don't know. It's like Marion don't notice. Or pretends like she don't. Maybe she's okay with it. Although she's into being proper and all."

"Then why does Lewis let Marion see him and your mom together?" Dot asked. "Why isn't he more discreet?"

"He don't give a rat's ass about Marion." Hunter folded his arms, staring through us. "That's why he poisoned himself."

"But that really makes no sense, Hunter," I said. "What would be the point?"

"To kill Marion, obviously. Look how sick she was. He just messed it up. She won't divorce him, won't even leave him. And he won't move off Cotton Pickin', either. Too much money."

"If he's such a jerk, why doesn't he kick Miss Marion out?" I said.

"I guess he could divorce her, but I don't know what would happen to the farm. He took her name so he can have rights to the land, but the land is really hers. Some old trust or something. She's the last Maynard. It's a big deal to Marion. Haven't you heard that story? It's kind of famous."

"I don't know much about Sidewinder history," I said. "I don't think many people do outside Sidewinder."

"Are you dissing Sidewinder?"

"It's not like you've impressed me with this little tale," I said. "You Sidewinder folks sound messed up."

"That's just Lewis and Marion," said Hunter.

"You're momma seems to put up with it pretty well. What did she tell the police?"

"Leave my mom out of this," Hunter said, curling his hands into fists. "She don't have nothing to do with this."

"Doesn't she want to get rid of Marion, too? And she seemed to avoid getting sick."

I saw the anger rising in Hunter and laid a hand over one of his fists. "I'm not saying she poisoned the stew, hon'. But would she have helped Lewis?"

TWENTY-TWO

Hunter jerked his hand away and narrowed his eyes, but relaxed at the approach of our food. A woman with a puff of auburn hair attached to a ponytail slid three plates of catfish onto the table. Delicately browned balls of hushpuppy dough rolled between a chromium oxide green mound of coleslaw and a pile of catfish fillets, golden and steaming. My stomach roared into life, like a primed outboard motor. At the sound, the waitress jerked back and dropped a fork on the floor.

"Look at that." I pointed to Dot. "That there's a beautiful plate, if I've ever seen one. That catfish is cooked perfectly. I bet it's as flaky as my Grandma Jo used to make her biscuits. And look at those hushpuppies." I pulled in a deep breath of fried goodness, reveling in the aroma of fresh oil and sweet browned butter.

"Hey, Mandy. These people are dissing Sidewinder," said Hunter to the waitress, "and they're from Halo."

Beside me, Dot shifted and slid her opened purse into her lap.

"What are they saying?" said Mandy. She rubbed the fork on her apron and stuck it in the pocket next to her order pad.

"She said we're messed up."

"What?" Mandy slapped a hand on her ample hip. "They're from Halo and they say we're messed up?"

"I didn't mean it like that," I explained. "I was talking about the Maynards. Anyway, you got another fork?"

Mandy's sharp eyes scanned me. "The Maynards are an old family. They are from good people."

"That may be, but sounds to me like the crazy train has stopped at this generation."

"You're one to talk, Miss Halo."

"Let's not escalate this, Cherry. We're all from Forks County," said Dot. "There's no reason to argue."

"What you don't understand, Dot, is that I've been hearing this kind of ugly talk about Halo all week," I said. "I'm a little tired of folks from Sidewinder making fun of Halo. Now, you got another fork or not?"

"I don't think I need to be serving uppity girls from Halo."

I straightened my back. "What's with y'all calling me uppity?"

"Are you deaf as well as uppity?"

"Cherry." Dot put a hand on my shoulder.

I shook her off. "Do I need to ask Sam for a fork, Mandy?"

"You do what you need to do, sugar. But you ain't getting a fork from me." Mandy flattened a hand on the table and leaned over me. "Sam ain't giving you one either, seeing as I'm Mrs. Sam."

"What's your problem?" I pushed forward, bringing my face just under hers without flinching.

"You people from Halo think you're so hoity toity, making fun of our town. You're no better than anyone else. Everyone knows about Halo's gambling and that murder a while back. We are good, self-respecting people here."

"Well, your good people murdered my friend, Eloise Parker, and made a bunch of other people sick at your festival. Including the Maynards."

She sucked in her breath. "You're friends with Miss Eloise?"

"Yes, ma'am. You can just back off your self-righteous Sidewinder bullcrap."

"You sure she was murdered? Miss Eloise was kind of sickly."

"She was poisoned. So was Lewis Maynard. He's dead, too."

"Lewis Maynard and Eloise Parker?" said Mandy. "Makes you look bad, don't it Hunter?"

Hunter glared at her. "Shut it, Mandy."

"Actually Mandy, what do you mean? Hunter here has some theories on Lewis's poisoning, but he never mentioned any ties to my friend, Eloise." I shot him a look. "However, he did give her a bunch of tickets exclusively for the Cotton Pickin' stew."

"I told you she was my teacher," Hunter whined. "We didn't get along."

"Hunter complained about Miss Parker enough to me," said Mandy. "He was in and out of detention and in-school suspension because she wouldn't put up with his crap. Now he's graduating late."

I eyed Hunter, and he stared at his catfish.

"I remember Eloise saying she was surprised to get all those tickets from you," I said, "Seeing as how you didn't do so well in her class."

"I know Sam can be soft on you, Hunter," continued Mandy, "but I believe in tough love, which means telling the truth. This girl here is friends with Miss Eloise. If you know something about what happened to your poor teacher, you better talk. If you don't, I'll let it be known. You'll have the police all over you again."

"You better not." Hunter gripped the table. A bright flush crept from his neck toward his face and a purple vein darkened the skin of his forehead.

"I know your momma. I'm not scared of you, Hunter Adams. You tell this Halo girl what you know." Mandy tossed the dirty fork on the table and whirled away.

"Good Lord, Cherry," Dot hissed. "You've got nerves of steel. I thought that waitress was going to gut you with a fork."

"That's nothing. Mandy's a good one. Although she didn't bring me a clean fork." I turned to Hunter. "Mandy's right. You fess up about Eloise, or I'm reporting you to the cops."

"I didn't do it."

"Didn't do what?" asked Dot. "Put something in the stew?"

Hunter glowered at us, grabbed his cup, and poured the remains of his chewed tobacco over our catfish. We watched in openmouthed astonishment as he dumped his plate onto the floor, slid out of the booth, and marched out the door.

"Well, there's the end of that conversation," I said.

"Do you think he poisoned the stew?" asked Dot.

"You know, I'm not sure. But he feels guilty about something. Either that or he's just a sociopath."

Dot shuddered. "You want to get out of here?" She opened her purse and laid a handful of bills on the table.

I looked sadly at my ruined dinner. "I guess. What a waste of some beautiful looking catfish." I grabbed Dot's fork and poked at a hushpuppy.

Dot laid a hand on my arm. "You've got to let it go."

"The catfish? It's nasty, but there might be a bite or two worth saving."

"Eloise's death. I'm going to report this incident to the sheriff. It may shed light on the mass poisoning for them. Hunter's got major issues."

"Don't you mention my name, Dot Cooper," I said. "Word gets out in the sheriff's office I was with Hunter Adams and I'll never hear the end of it. I'll probably be served with obstruction or something."

"I won't reveal my sources. But if Hunter really poisoned somebody, you could be in danger."

"Nah," I said. "I don't think Hunter did it. He did something, but I don't think he poisoned the stew. Did you do any checking into Griffin Ward and his Genuine Juice?"

"He's made a mess of licensing and getting patents. I heard he was trying to get the Parkers to endorse it as a testimonial to curing Eloise's Crohn's Disease."

"Guess that didn't work out too well."

"From what I heard, she refused to drink much of it, and he was working on her parents to convince her to use it."

"No wonder Mary Jane hates Griffin so much." I grabbed my beer and took a long sip to settle my nerves. "The Parkers didn't tell me. But they're such a mess right now, they probably didn't even think to mention it. And it sheds light on Griffin's ridiculous anger with Eloise. Guess he was frustrated with her blocking his scheme, too."

"You said he might have poisoned her on accident. Here's another idea. A little arsenic won't kill a person, but it obviously makes them very sick. The symptoms would be disguised by Eloise's Crohn's disease."

"You're thinking Griffin was slowly poisoning Eloise, then planned to cut the arsenic, and give her the Genuine Juice to show a miraculous recovery."

"You picked up on that quickly." Dot flashed me a smile of appreciation.

"Something similar crossed my mind. Only thing is, that takes some real evil genius. I doubt Griffin is capable of anything that creative or brilliant."

"Until the police can trace the arsenic, we won't know if Griffin was involved at all. Yesterday, they confiscated his cooler and his equipment."

"Did they?" I looked around the tavern and lowered my voice. "That's good news. They didn't find anything though?"

"I don't know. Maybe they're waiting on lab results. Sometimes those take a while."

"Their process is so slow," I complained. "What if he gets away in the meantime?"

"You don't know that he did it." Dot smiled. "You mentioned the Gables, obviously you aren't completely sold on Griffin."

"I drove out to their farm today. Kind of spooky. It looks like they're making an education center, just like the Maynard's, but no one was working on it. Lumber sitting around, but the place was like a detassler's ghost town. Corn as far as the eye can see, except for one small plot of cotton. I spoke briefly to Belinda Gable."

Dot's eyes rounded behind her glasses. "What did she have to say?"

"Didn't like me bringing up the Maynard's similar marketing plan. Said they were working on funding. Gave me the boot."

"Interesting." Dot tapped her cheek with a stubby finger. "So we have competing plantations. The girlfriend of Lewis Maynard is Belinda Gable's sister. Both have the same idea for reaping in money. Except it looks like the Cotton Pickin' team has pushed ahead of Team High Cotton in that game."

"Although Janine Adams will lose in the end. She did all the work for Cotton Pickin' plantation and her main squeeze is now dead. I can't imagine Miss Marion keeping Janine around any longer."

"True," said Dot, "Unless there's something in the will."

"The will? Won't everything go to Marion?"

"We'll have to see. The land has to stay in Maynard hands, but there was a lot of merchandising and other money. Also insurance money. Janine may have benefited somehow."

"You think Hunter is protecting his mom?"

Dot pursed her lips in thought. "Could be. Hard to tell now, isn't it? Looks like the list of suspects keeps growing."

"And there's still the nutjob theory."

"What's that theory?"

"Someone wanted to ruin the cook-off for kicks," I thought about Shawna. "Or ruin the cook-off for their own crazy notion of ambition."

I slid from the booth, said goodbye to Dot, and found the ladies' room before leaving. Hunter may have ruined our catfish, but our beer remained untainted and necessary after that brush with his temper. I wandered back to the bar and said my goodbyes to Sam and Mandy.

"You watch yourself now," said Sam. "When Hunter left tonight, it looked like he had worked himself up a full head of steam."

"He was pretty ticked we had suggested his mother might have something to do with Lewis dying," I admitted.

"You think that's true?" asked Mandy. "I never trusted that woman. She's a schemer. I felt bad for her because of that murdering husband of hers. Someone should have taken a shotgun to him long ago."

"Murdering husband?" I said. "I thought Hunter's dad was in jail for drugs."

"That, too." Mandy glanced down the bar at Hunter's uncle and lowered her voice. "Jerry Adams got busted during a deal that went bad. Another dealer got shot. But Keith over there tells a different story. Said Janine killed the guy and let her husband take the blame. Even if it's true, Jerry deserved it."

"But if Janine's killed someone before, that mean she's capable of murder."

"We don't know for sure," said Sam, "that's just what Keith says. You be careful around Janine and Hunter. They're as wily as a couple of barnyard foxes. She's made a nice nest from wrapping Lewis around her finger. And she done good making Cotton Pickin' place all fancy. I don't know where she gets her ideas, but they're making money hand over fist, the way I hear it."

"That Janine would leave nothing to chance," added Mandy. "She saw an opportunity and made use of it. Wouldn't even let something like marriage get in her way. Poor Miss Marion."

"Sounds like you've got no love for Janine Adams."

"I've got as much use for her as I do the stuff stuck to the bottom of my shoe." Mandy grabbed two bottles sitting on the bar. "Got to get back to my tables."

Sam watched his wife strut across the dingy floor. "My woman don't take guff from nobody. Janine got smart with her one time too many."

"You think Janine would have poisoned the stew to murder Lewis?"

"I can't rightly say. I would think that would be cutting off the hand that feeds her. But if Janine were done with Lewis for some reason and couldn't find another way out..."

"Or if Lewis left her a lot of money in a will or made her a beneficiary of his life insurance?"

"If there's money involved, I'd say Janine would have looked at all the angles. Her husband may have been the front guy of his weed business, but Janine kept track of his books and logistics and all that. She explained it to me once, trying to convince me to let her look at my books and do something with the Viper."

"You'd think she'd want to keep running a pot operation off her resume."

"Probably thought it would impress me. She was desperate back then," said Sam. "I best get back to my customers, too."

"Thanks, Sam." I fished a crumpled five from my wallet and laid it on the bar.

"Keep your money, hon'," Sam winked. "My advice is free today."

I grinned and scooted around the tables to the exit. From the corner of my eye, I saw someone slip from a booth on the far wall. Expecting Hunter, I spun around. A biker had shoved from his seat, calling out to Sam as he staggered to the bar. I watched his drunk weave and waited for my heart to stop pounding. I should have left with Dot. Didn't even think about walking her to her vehicle in case Hunter decided to do a reprise of the catfish incident. How could I be so foolhardy?

I shoved the heavy bar door open, but stood on the sill. Twilight had settled over middle Georgia. My eyes scanned the parking lot, searching the shadows. The parking lights flickered on. Dot's car was gone. Relieved, I stepped off the stoop and let the door swing close behind me. Knowing my Remington waited, I hurried toward my truck.

While I fished the key from my front pocket, I gazed at the vehicle next to mine. My mouth quirked at the ostentatious black and red rims and large spoiler, but my eyes stopped on the bumper, spying a red sticker. A Cadmium red sticker on a magenta car? I often wonder at the lack of thought people put into color choice.

Something about the sticker gave me an odd sense of deja vu. I unlocked the truck, feeling unsettled. Was it the color or the words I couldn't quite read on the bumper sticker that bugged me? I dumped my purse in the truck and turned back to the car. My fingers played with the beaded fringe on my shirt while I reexamined the vehicle. I left my driver's door hanging open and circled back.

The sticker appeared as a shadowy rectangle on the bumper. Dropping to a crouch, I squinted at the words covered in a film of dust and dirt. The logo for Squats, a popular Line Creek gym, hid beneath the grime. For the life of me, I couldn't think why a Squats bumper sticker would cause me so much unease. I grabbed the trunk handle to pull myself up.

Before I had straightened, a strong arm thrust me against the back of the car.

TWENTY-THREE

"Hey," I yelled. "What do you think you're doing?" I pushed off the car and attempted a pivot.

Griffin stood behind me, blocking my turn.

"I've got something to say to you." He shoved me against the trunk with the flat of his hand.

"Get your hands off me, asshole. You got something to say, say it. But lay a hand on me and I'm calling assault." I stepped hard on his foot as I turned to face him. It would have made more of an impression if I had been wearing boots instead of flip-flops.

"Shut up." Griffin's eyes narrowed. "I know it was you."

"You know what was me?" I stepped forward, but Griffin blocked my path. "Get out of my way."

"You're not going anywhere until you hear what I've got to say." He grabbed my Myrtle Beach shirt by the collar and fisted the material in his hand. "Listen. Stop squirming."

"Let go of me." I clawed at his hand and kicked in the few inches of space between him and the car.

He snatched my wrists in one meaty hand and tightened his grip on my t-shirt. "I know you told the cops I tried to poison the festival with my Genuine Juice. They took my cooler. Even took my last batch. I had to work all night making new stuff to get my deliveries out this afternoon. I barely slept."

"That's not my fault. The police have to test everything people ate or drank at the festival."

"You've been telling people I did it. That I tried to kill Eloise."

"I don't think you did it on purpose. What did you put in the Genuine Juice? Was it just enough to make her sick or an accident?"

The collar tightened on my shirt. Griffin yanked me higher, making my toes drag against the gravel.

"Don't be stupid. Put me down, Griffin."

His forward step pinned my legs against the car. Whiskey breath fanned my face. He held me close enough to see fire licking his eyes. "I heard you talking with that woman in the Viper. Y'all said I tried to poison Eloise. I want you to go to the police and take back all you said about me."

"I didn't tell the police anything." I licked my lips. "But you can bet your ass I'm telling them now."

With a frustrated cry, Griffin released his grip on me. My shirt tore as I dumped to the ground. Griffin stood over me, shaking with anger.

Too mad to be scared, I stared back with the meanest look I could muster. "You jerk. You owe me a new t-shirt."

"I've always hated you, you loud-mouth bitch," Griffin swore at me and swung his foot back.

I dodged his kick and scrambled crab-wise in the gravel.

"You've always had it in for me. Filled Eloise's head with BS about me." His shoe struck my chest, splaying me flat.

I grabbed a handful of gravel and threw it at his face. "And you're showing your true colors now. I knew you were smacking Eloise around."

He kicked again, but I rolled onto my stomach and hauled myself under his car.

"It was none of your damn business. Eloise had a mouth and she knew she deserved it. Someone should have taken a belt to your hide years ago." He stood over the trunk, kicking gravel after me. "Get out of there or I swear I'll run you over."

My cab light had gone out long ago, but by the dim parking light, I could just see the bottom of my truck door still hanging open. Hand over hand, I inched toward the door, but the exhaust blocked my forward movement. The car rocked as Griffin pushed on the trunk.

"Get the hell out from under my car," he screamed. "Or I'm going to really hurt you. Don't think I won't do it."

I heard him stomp to the driver's door, then realized the muffler and tail pipe would heat up when he started the car. What kind of idiot crawled underneath a psycho's car?

"Crap." I inched backward, feeling rocks scratch my thighs and catch in my t-shirt's beading. I pushed back with my toes, then felt hands grip my ankles. My shirt rode up and gravel grated my belly at Griffin's yank. My head cleared the tail pipe. I tried to flip over, but Griffin stepped on my back and held me firm.

"You gonna listen now?" he said.

I glared at the ground and set my mind to revenge.

"That's what I thought. You women need to stop fighting me when I know what's best." He pressed his foot harder and ground his toe into my back. "If you'd listen, I wouldn't have to take a hand to you."

I couldn't stay silent. I'll admit to calling his mother a few names and told him a few creative things he could do to himself. That got me a smack in the back of the head. My face bit the dirty gravel, and I swore I'd get even with the bullying sonofabitch.

"Tomorrow morning, you're going to the sheriff's office and clear up this problem. Then you're going to Chaney's garage and apologize to me in front of Chaney so he starts selling my Genuine Juice again."

I repeated my earlier offer for him to have relations with himself. And got punched in the head. This time the gravel tore a hole in my lip. Eloise might have feared his fist with her weakened body and strange ideas about love, but beating up women did not fly with this little, country girl.

"Is this what makes you feel good, Griffin? A fight with a girl half your size? What's the matter? Can't you get it up with the steroids you take? You fight girls because you're not a man anymore?"

The foot lifted from my back, and I flipped over. He waited until I pushed off the ground and stood. His eyes flickered over me and fixed on my torn shirt. I looked down and saw my neon pink bra peeking through the tear.

"I'm going to teach you a lesson you won't forget," he growled.

I didn't wait for his lunge, but pivoted and ran for my open truck door. I jumped in the truck, slammed the door shut, and pushed down the lock. He breathed on the closed window. I held up a single, middle finger and turned to the dash.

And realized there were no keys hanging from the ignition.

Griffin laughed, and I turned to look. He held up a finger, dangling the keys I had left in the door lock.

"Shit."

I dove over the backseat and yanked a long, narrow box to my lap. While Griffin fumbled with the rusty lock, my fingers fumbled with the tiny combination dials on my gun box. The lock on the door popped up. I glanced at the window.

Griffin grinned at me and hammered on the window. "Kiss your scrawny ass goodbye, Cherry Tucker."

I slid to the other side of the bench with the gun box on my lap. Griffin yanked on the door handle. The box lid flew up. I grabbed the shotgun inside. The driver's door wrenched open, and my gun box clattered to the floor. Griffin piled in, his hand reaching for me, then froze as I swung the Wingmaster to my shoulder.

"Hold it right there, you woman-beating S.O.B." I racked the pump and aimed the shotgun at his head, then lowered the gun slowly until my sight fixed his crotch.

"You bitch."

I slipped my finger to the trigger guard. "You want to try that again?" I scooted down the bench. "Give me my keys."

Griffin backed to his car and held the keys out. "Put the gun down and I'll give you your keys."

"I don't think so." I slid out the door and forced Griffin to back step around his Grand Prix.

An oversized truck roared into the parking lot and shined its lights on the two of us. "Hey," yelled a voice. "What the hell do you think you're doing? Stand down."

"Call the police," I hollered. "I'll put down this gun when they get here."

"Help me," screamed Griffin. "She's crazy. She's threatening to shoot me."

"Put down that gun."

"Get the sheriff here." I turned to squint into the glare of the truck lights. "This man tried to beat me up in the parking lot and he killed his girlfriend."

"I did not kill Eloise. She's crazy. Get her gun. She'll shoot me," yelled Griffin.

"I'm calling 911," said the man.

His truck door swung open and heavy boots hit the gravel. He walked into the headlights, holding a rifle.

"Drop your weapon," he said. "I'm holding you both here until the police arrive."

I lowered my gun to the ground. A second later, I was knocked into the gravel. I slammed my palm into Griffin's nose and bit his ear. Before his hand could grapple my throat, a blast burst the night air. The smoking barrel lowered between us, and we scurried to part.

"Y'all freeze or I'm not wasting my next shot on the sky. The po-po can sort y'all out."

In the parking lot of the Waffle House, I shrugged into Luke's t-shirt and attempted to comb my hair with my fingers. He watched me without comment with his arms crossed over his undershirt. His inscrutable eyes matched the color of slate. No dimples in sight.

"That's better," I said, tying the excess material into a knot at my waist. "Thank you."

"Everyone at the sheriff's office knows you're wearing a pink bra. I don't know why you feel so modest at the Waffle House."

"Come on, Luke." I followed him through the glass door and took an appreciative whiff of brewing coffee and bacon. "Are you going to stay mad at me all night? You should be proud of me."

He spun around and walked me backward through the door and onto the sidewalk. The door slammed shut behind us, announcing our absence with a ring of a bell.

"Proud of you?" he said. "For what? Almost getting raped in a parking lot of a biker bar?"

"How is that my fault? I told you Griffin was dangerous. I didn't know he was in the Viper."

"What the hell were you doing at the Viper anyway?" Luke scrubbed his hair, sending his dark curls into disarray. "God Almighty, Cherry. When I saw you all beat up with your shirt torn in half..."

"What?"

"I wanted to kill you."

"How about killing Griffin Ward instead?"

"Don't tempt me. Anyway, I don't know what you did to him, but he's puking his guts out in his holding cell." A smile hovered underneath Luke's stern features. "And he's going to sleep with that smell. We'll call the janitor in the morning."

"I wish I had shot him."

"No you don't." Luke snagged my shoulder and pulled me into his chest. His arms wrapped me tight, and I pressed my head against the soft cotton of his t-shirt. "Dammit, Cherry, you've got to stop scaring me like this. You're no bigger than a flea and you keep biting pit bulls. I told you to stay clear of this poisoning mess."

"It had nothing to do with the poisoning. Griffin and I have been enemies since day one. I couldn't watch my idiot friend go out with somebody like Griffin, even if she wouldn't listen to me. Somebody had to stand up for her."

"But there's just one little thing..."

"What?" I tipped my head back to see his face.

His smoldering gray eyes glared down at me. "Griffin Ward found you in the parking lot of the Viper. In Sidewinder. Don't tell me you needed to drive that scrapheap truck all the way to Side-winder to get a beer."

"The Viper makes really good catfish."

"Cherry," Luke's voice grew into a growl. "What were you doing at the Viper?"

"Eating dinner. Except I didn't get to eat my dinner, which is why I'm so hungry now. Thanks for taking me to the Waffle House. Let's go in and get you some sausage and gravy. I've got my mind on a pecan waffle."

His mouth drew into a tight line.

"Okay, I was with Dot Cooper. We were talking to Hunter Adams. He asked to meet me there, otherwise I never would have gone. And I took Dot so I wouldn't be alone. Aren't you glad I thought of that? Hunter wanted me to bring Todd and I didn't think that was a good idea." I bit my lip. Sometimes I just didn't know when to shut up. When Luke got that fierce look in his eye, I had a tendency to babble.

"I take issue with so much of that explanation, I don't even know where to start."

"Then don't." I smiled wide. "Let's eat."

His phone buzzed. He gave me one of those "we're not finished" looks and strode away. I banged through the door and received a surly look from the waitress at the cash register. She jerked her head toward the booths. I slid onto a red and gray seat. A moment later, two cups of coffee sat before me.

The bell rang above the door, and Luke slid into the booth. He blew off his coffee and took a deep slurp. His eyes had lost the recent pissed off look and appeared troubled and distant.

"What happened?" I asked.

The waitress slapped a plate of hash browns covered in cheese and onions on the table. She took her time arranging Luke's biscuits and gravy while he gave her a gracious smile for her trouble.

My frown deepened as she topped his coffee off and didn't bother to check my half-drunk cup.

Luke watched the waitress walk away and fixed his gaze on me. "Griffin's sick. They're taking him to the hospital."

"He was perfectly fine a couple hours ago. Didn't even cough when he hauled me out from under his car."

Luke scowled.

I changed my tone to humor him. "Do you have to go?"

"No. Billy Caruthers is on duty. I asked him to keep me informed of Griffin's condition. Do you know what he drank or ate in the Viper?"

"I have no idea what he had in the Viper." I tapped my carnation pink nails on the tabletop. "I didn't even know he was there, remember? But after that trucker broke up our fight, he let Griffin get his drink from his car."

Luke pulled his phone from his pocket. "What drink?"

"What else? Genuine Juice. But Griffin said he had made a fresh batch after y'all confiscated his stuff."

"Shit." Luke pushed off his seat and threw a twenty on the table. "Come on. Sounds like Griffin poisoned himself. Which means there might be more tainted Genuine Juice hanging around Sidewinder."

TWENTY-FOUR

Bar fights are good for creativity. That was my thinking when the day dawned with new ideas for the Greek painting and a puffiness to my lip. The scrapes on my belly could be hidden by bandages and clothing. But I used lip liner to make lemonade from the lemon of my fat lip. Casey told me it looked like a bad collagen job. I had hoped for a sexy pout. I ignored her comment out of a debt of gratitude. She had conceded to modeling for me, which made her grouchier than usual. As did the idea of joining Pearl for bingo.

I flipped a page on my sketchbook while examining Casey. The mid-day sun threw rays across my paint splattered living room floor. A few lovely beams glanced across Casey's bare shoulder and her surly expression. The lighting pleased me. I had dragged my vintage fainting couch to the middle of the room where Casey posed in a homemade toga. We had hot rolled her hair and swept it up with a band of leaves. More curls dripped down her back. A Victorian styled Aphrodite.

But a tad sluttier.

"I can't believe Griffin is dead," I said. "Why would he do himself in with his own Genuine Juice?"

"You think it was guilt?" Casey rearranged herself in a more comfortable position on my threadbare divan and pulled a magazine from under her thigh.

"He sure wasn't showing any guilt when he hauled me out from under his car. Maybe he forgot the Genuine Juice was poisoned. But maybe you're right. He knew he was facing some serious jail time for murder. By the time the police got him to the station he was too sick for a confession."

"Do the Parkers know?"

"I called them, but they had already spoken to the police. Took it real stoic. Mary Jane knew of Griffin's temper, but Eloise had hidden his abuse pretty well. But by taking his own medicine, that jerk denied them final words with their daughter's killer. At least they can put Eloise to rest at her funeral Friday."

Casey gave me a half-interested nod and leafed through the tabloid. I studied her from the side of my easel. "I need you to lean back more. And let those drapery folds fall to the floor. Stop bunching them up."

She darted me a look of supreme irritation, arched her back against the single arm rest, then threw the tabloid on the floor. "This is uncomfortable. And stupid. I'm wearing a sheet."

"I need classical Greek poses for this exhibition."

"You need a real job. Why don't you pick up shifts at Red's?"

"I'm going to make you look beautiful. And maybe a rich man will buy your portrait, hang it on his bedroom wall, and fall in love with you."

She snorted and rearranged the sheet so the neckline plunged dangerously low.

"I'm not painting porn, Casey."

"I'm trying to get the rich man interested. I'm going to leave my number on the back of your canvas. Besides, when you paint naked men, you don't call it porn."

"Forget it." I tossed my Berol number 3 pencil on the small table. "Togas are not working for me. I want to do a nude, but now I'm thinking about some rich perve getting off on you."

Casey stood and stretched. "You still haven't convinced Luke to pose, I guess?"

"He told me, 'over his dead body.' And then he said if I even thought about sketching him naked for a coffin portrait, he would come back and haunt me. Like I would do a nude coffin portrait."

"Anyway," Casey dismissed my artistic dilemma with a shrug, "if you want me to go to bingo, I need to get ready."

I glanced at the small clock sitting on my desk. "Go ahead. Pearl will be here any minute."

"I can't believe you talked me into hanging out with Pearl," Casey grumbled. "Just so you know, I'm only doing this to see Mr. Max's house. I heard he's got some fancy stuff besides that old Civil War crap he likes to collect. Why do you want to bust him so bad anyway?"

"It's not about busting him, so much as helping him learn how to be a better citizen. If I catch him I can use it as leverage."

"Some folks call that blackmail."

"A man like the Bear needs incentives to give up their illegal lifestyle." I thought about my recent exchanges with Max. "I also wanted to know why Belinda Gable was following him. Of course, that was before we knew Griffin had poisoned everyone."

"Everybody plays poker. I don't know why you make such a big deal about it."

"Did you forget that poker led to murder last spring?" I said. "I certainly can't."

"I think the man gets your panties in a wad and it makes you uncomfortable."

"I may be the only person in Halo who hasn't had the wool pulled over their eyes by a smooth talking, rich foreigner. Well, maybe not smooth talking, but you get what I'm saying."

"You got something against rich people. So you better chill when the rich man falls in love with my portrait." She stuck out her tongue, gathered the sheet around her body, and schlepped into the hallway.

While Casey changed, I poured over the quick sketches I had drawn. If I had spent more time in thoughtful consideration of my subject, I would have posed Casey in a forest thicket with bow and arrows. She'd make a better Athena than Aphrodite. Better yet, maybe a modern day Athena carrying a nine mm handgun and an Uzi. I hummed a happy tune at that thought and scribbled a note in my sketchbook. I'd just have to convince Casey to try some guerrilla poses. However, reclining came more naturally to her. And I was still stuck on my original idea.

I had four more days before sending digital images to the gallery for approval. And now that the poisoning outbreak seemed solved with the demise of Griffin, I'd have more time to convince Luke. Or find another model.

However, I only knew one man who'd willingly pose unrobed who wasn't already a degenerate or a flasher. Todd. Which meant a whole host of other problems.

While I pondered the intelligence of asking Todd to pose nude after he had caused my lips to desert ship, my front door popped open and Pearl stuck her head through.

"Yoo-hoo. Anybody home?" She walked into my living room wearing a t-shirt picturing a goat who had a white mustache and held a glass of milk. The bubble caption read "Got Lactose Intolerance?"

"Are you ready to win big money?" She stopped her progression across my pine flooring. "What happened to your face?"

"Ate some gravel. It's nothing." I ignored her raised brows. The quickening of excitement had coursed through my veins at her mention of big money. "Can you win big money at bingo?"

"Nothing over five dollars at a time. But if you play long enough, that adds up, particularly in Shorty's BBQ bucks and Tru-Buy dollars. You can play up to twenty-five games in three hours."

Twenty-five games of bingo sounded excruciating, but I let it pass. "There has to be a catch. Did you talk to the woman in charge of bingo at the Ladies Auxiliary?"

"Sue Rivers? She said Mr. Max offered us a great deal. He's paying her two hundred dollars a month for our bingo license. What a sweetie."

"I don't trust that sweetie. He's making money off y'all."

"Not Mr. Max. He keeps whatever's left from the two hundred, but how much could that be? He supplies us in tea and cookies after all."

"How many times does he have bingo a week and what does he charge?"

"We play for two or three hours, and he's been holding them most weekday afternoons. The ladies keep asking for more. I usually buy five dollar packages for each game. There are some crazy women who will hog a whole table with bigger packs. The odds are better at his place than at the Line Creek Rotary Hall."

"Well, the odds are against him today. I'm not letting a confidence man rip off old ladies."

"Who you calling old, missy?" Pearl barked.

Casey emerged from the hallway. "I'm going to distract Mr. Max and his posse while you look for whatever clues that will lead to your big bust."

I took a hard look at Casey. Her hair fell to her lower back in long, dark curls and she wore a shimmery, red halter that revealed more flesh than the toga. Her spiked heels only created a slight diversion from the length of leg ending at a black miniskirt my Grandma Jo would call genuinely unladylike.

"Holy crap, Casey."

She nodded. "Don't you worry about a thing. This is going to be fun."

I hesitated. She had a good point, but I feared dropping Casey's level of fierceness in the midst of women who teetered on the edge of strokes and heart attacks. Someone might break their hip.

Following a stream of cars, Casey turned her Firebird through the tall gates of Max's drive. "Would you look at that house?"

"It's just a big house," I said, eager to prove I was not awed by Max's riches. "And Pearl would you quit hollering out the window? You're drawing attention to our getaway car."

"I'm just calling to my friends," said Pearl. "Besides, it's kind of hard not to draw attention to a vehicle with a giant bird painted on the hood. Not exactly a bingo vehicle. If you're going to get ugly, I'm not going to help you."

"Actually you just made a good point. I see some other non-bingo vehicles."

Amid the Buick's and Chevy's, I noticed a Lexus and a Mercedes. When a BMW M6 sports car pulled in and followed us around the drive, my suspicion reflexes triggered. Casey parked before the genuine Civil War cannon in the middle of the circular drive. I watched the M6 maneuver around ladies tottering toward Max's veranda. The red sports car turned at a split in the drive and gunned its motor toward the basement garage in the back of the house.

No Halo senior citizen would drive an M6. If she did, I wanted to meet her.

We tumbled out of the Firebird and jogged after Pearl up to the house. While Pearl found her bingo buddies and Casey stared in wonderment at Max's estate, I took a stroll across the veranda. Clasping my hands behind my back, I feigned interest in the line of Boston ferns hanging from the rafters.

On the far side of the porch, I leaned on the railing and peered around the edge of the house. The five doors of the garage were closed.

Vehicles in a wide range of age, size, and horsepower were parked somewhere inside, another of Max's collections. Before the garage doors, the M6, a Lincoln MKZ, and a Ferrari were parked along with the Lexus and Mercedes I spotted earlier.

I smelled money. Middle-aged man money. Very different from the Avon and stale coffee scent of bingo money.

My attention swung toward the front drive as a white Cadillac pulled up before Max's house. Bruce Gable popped out the driver's side and ran around to get the passenger door. A moment later, Belinda Gable unfolded from the sedan. They kissed and he jogged to his door.

Belinda adjusted her giant sunglasses, glanced at the bevy of women on the veranda, and strutted toward the steps. I watched the Cadillac continue down the drive toward the garage where it parked behind the M6.

God help me, but I could not let that Sidewinder mare's nest alone. In the tiled foyer of Avtaikin's McMansion, I dragged Casey by her hand while she gaped open-mouthed at the staircase wrapping around the double storied space.

The chandelier above us spilled rainbows on the twenty foot white walls. Around us, groups of older women poked each other, whispered with an agitated fierceness, and stared at Casey. I caught the gist of their observations and felt an old shame lick my cheeks.

"Mercy, I think that's an honest-to-God hooker. I've never seen one before. You think Mr. Max hires out? I never would have thought."

"Naw. You think Mr. Max hired dancing girls? Maybe he's adding on a show."

"Isn't that the girl who works at the County Line Tap? She near about bit my head off when I asked for senior prices."

"That," announced the gray haired woman wielding the cane, "is Casey Tucker. Her momma is Christy Ballard, Ed and Josie's daughter, who up and disappeared on those kids twenty years ago. Obviously, the apple didn't fall far from that white trash tree."

I spun Casey toward the open door under the stairs leading to the basement. "Casey, you're drawing too much attention to yourself."

"I'm just getting started." Casey's eyes glittered and she offered me a sly smile. Casey and Trouble had a long acquaintance. I had a feeling they were about to renew their relationship. Hopefully they wouldn't have kids.

"You think this skirt deserves free bingo cards?" she announced to the crowd and strutted down the stairs to the basement.

The ladies followed, shoving me out of the way in their hurry to monitor Casey. I stumbled back a step in their crush and felt a strong hand grab my elbow. Max Avtaikin waited until I righted myself, then dropped my elbow to take my hand.

"Artist. Your lip color is quite interesting today." He pecked the back of my hand and let it drop. "Two visits in one week. Should I consider myself the lucky man?"

"I'm here with Miss Pearl and Casey so they can play bingo."

"Your interest with the bingo game continues. How grateful I am for your support of my insignificant endeavor for the ladies."

"We'll see about that."

"I hope you enjoy playing. Are you the sore loser if you don't win, Miss Tucker?" His mouth quirked. "Do you dismiss playing for fear of losing?"

"I don't fear much, Bear. And I always try to win."

"You are a worthy opponent, Artist. Enjoy your bingo."

I hesitated at the basement door. "Don't you come down to the game?"

He shook his head. "I leave it to my helpers. I have the other business to which I attend." His forehead creased, flexing the scar above his eye. "And the ladies seem excitable when I spend time with them. It is a distraction."

"For them or for you?" I chuckled and swung down the stairs. "See you around, Bear." As far as I was concerned, the Bear's cryptic comments gave me tacit permission to check out his dubious do-gooding. As long as I didn't get caught.

Sore loser, my butt.

I glanced over my shoulder to see him raise his eyebrow, a thoughtful expression on his face. He watched me descend the cherry stained stairs. A door remained open in the long, carpeted hallway at the bottom of the stairs. I knew from previous experience it led to Max's fancy Vegas themed game room.

Trailing my hand along the railing, I halted at the bottom step before the security monitor. The dark screen gave nothing away. I glanced up the stairs and caught Max's brawny figure strolling away. I pressed on the security monitor and a glowing keyboard appeared on the screen. The numbered buttons gave me no clue as to how to disable the system.

Giving up, I followed the hall to the open door and glanced inside. Multi-colored lights blinked from Vegas themed signs around the long room. The round poker table and leather chairs had been replaced with folding tables and chairs set up in rows.

They faced a bar once fully stocked but now laden with pitchers of sweet tea and plates of cookies. Women deposited more trays of baked goods on the bar and hurried to take their seats. Someone had slapped sticky notes over the lady parts of the reclining nude mural behind the bar. She now wore a Cubist styled bikini. At the brass barred cashier's booth, more women lined up to buy their cards. Some held packs of ten or more. Others arranged fuzzy topped bingo marker pens and stuffed animals next to their cards, fighting for space with their competitors on the cramped tables. Belinda Gable sat in the back, nine cards spread on the table in three precise rows. Each card had a different colored dauber. None were topped with fuzzy creatures or stuffed animals.

I grabbed Pearl and pulled her into a corner near the bar. "You know the brunette in the last row?"

"Not personally," said Pearl, flipping through her cards. "She's here all the time, though. Kind of stuck up. But she's a real Betty."

"Betty?"

"Addicted to bingo. She always plays a rainbow pack." At my dumbfounded expression, she added, "a pack of cards worth different prizes."

"What's her husband doing here? Does he play bingo, too?"

"Husband?" Pearl looked around. "We don't get many men in here. He must drop her off."

Knowing Bruce Gable had parked with the other luxury cars, I felt certain he played another kind of game for an even larger pot. Considering his competitive relationship with Lewis, I shouldn't have been surprised. I left Pearl to peruse the baked goods.

Near the door, Casey hauled a folding table to the side and plunked her one card on the table. "What's the plan?" she said to me.

"Something's going on in the back of the house," I said. "I'm going to see if I can check it out. Have you seen Todd by the way?"

"Nope. I didn't recognize the guy selling the cards. Maybe Todd's not working today. Or maybe Pearl was wrong."

My eyelids dropped to slits. "You keep an eye on the guy running the bingo. If anyone else comes by, keep them distracted. And if you see Todd, hold on to him. He wants to talk, and I'm only interested in an explanation of what he's doing for the Bear."

"Aye-aye." Casey saluted me. "I'm really hoping to meet Mr. Max. You can be sure I'm going to keep him busy."

That thought did not bring me comfort, but I had to attend to more important matters.

"Hey, you can't hog a table to yourself." A woman with a carrot-colored mane strode to Casey's table. A nicotine stick hung from her coral lips. She grabbed the table to drag it back in place.

Casey countered the move by sitting on the table. I took it as a good time to slip out the door. With a quick glance to the stairs, I kicked the door closed and walked down the hall trying all the doors, but found them locked. Jogging up the stairs, I thought about trying the front door and sneaking around the back but knew a tall fence encircled the pool and all exits into the house. I had a feeling a poker game took place somewhere in the vicinity of the garage.

I headed down the hallway leading off the foyer and through the gallery room. Before turning the corner toward the kitchen, I stood a beat and listened for Max. My eyes scanned the paintings and lighted on the modern Romantic of the woman in the burned out building. It burned my biscuits that his shady schemes involved Todd. At the time of our Vegas nuptials, I had rescued Todd from his gambling addiction. Or so I thought. Max obviously needed my help, too.

Hopefully I'd do a better job helping these boys than I did poor Eloise.

From the kitchen, I scuttled to the deck door and peered out. The chairs and table where Max and I had shared the delectable lemonade and cookies sat empty. I tried the handle, found it unlocked, and slid through the French door.

The pool water glittered in the late afternoon sun. I couldn't see the garage, but the pool house door stood open. Shadows moved in the open doorway. A tall, tanned, blond man in cargo shorts and a black t-shirt stepped onto the doorsill and grasped the door knob. Todd.

This kind of clandestine operation screamed illegal gambling. However, I needed to make certain my hunch was correct without scaring away the participants. My pocketed phone was ready for pictures. I would try to protect Todd, but perhaps he needed this wake up call. As for Max, I was pretty sure he wanted to be caught.

Well, maybe not pretty sure. But he should know me better than to think I'd let this kind of activity slide.

I looked over the railing at the fifteen foot drop to the patio below. I knew what I had to do. I just didn't know how I was going to do it.

TWENTY-FIVE

One nice thing about rich folks' homes are the well-maintained landscaping equipment. Which is why I trusted the trellis climbing the wall alongside the deck to carry my weight. The trellis appeared an arms-length away from a downspout, so I figured between the two, one of them would help me shimmy to the yard below. A rose climbed the trellis, dotting the wall with Carmine pink blooms and deep Prussian green leaves. The gardener had banked on that rose growing fairly high, for he had built the trellis for growth past the second story.

Between the deserted yard and the windowless pool house, I figured I could clamber down and dart over unseen. And then...well, I'd get creative.

I pulled the glass table to the side of the balcony and used it to step onto the high railing. I had been blessed with no fear of heights or other phobias many people held. Of course, those fears might counter foolish moves like climbing on trellises, but at the moment, I took my lack of inhibitions and put them to use.

Stepping from the table to the deck railing, I reached to grasp the edge of the wooden lattice and praised the gardener for nailing the thin wood into the side of the house.

I swung out and grabbed the trellis with the other hand. My flip-flops scrambled for a foothold. If only I had realized I'd spend my afternoon scaling walls, I would have worn my boots. Hindsight always dresses better than foresight.

I kicked the flip-flops to the bushes below, squeezed my toes between the crisscrossing slats, and hung there for a moment. My arms started to ache. I stared hard at my hands gripping the flimsy wood and ordered them to move.

Hand over hand, I inched down the trellis. When my foot brushed leaves, I smiled knowing I had achieved about five feet of progress. But when I tried to stuff my toes into the slatted hole, a sharp stab caused them to fly off the lattice.

I dangled, gripping the wood with my fingers, and forced my feet to find hold. Small barbs pricked and scratched my tender soles.

"Dangit," I muttered. "What breed of rose is this? Extra thorny?" I still had a good ten feet or so to go. The spiky leaves of the holly bushes looked sharper than normal. With my luck, Mr. Max had installed a fierce garden as an extra security measure.

Pulling my feet up, I hung with my rear hanging over the rose bush and decided to explore my other options. I examined the downspout to my left and realized my judgment had failed. The distance between the lattice and downspout was longer than an arm's length.

As my fingers began to cramp and turn white, I pondered the wisdom of throwing myself at the plastic rain pipe. I toed the rose bush, felt the jab of a dozen thorns, and retreated. My shoulders began to ache and a tingly sensation prickled my arms and deadened fingers.

"Come on, Cherry," I said, knowing how much I enjoyed pep talks. "Can't hang here all day. Someone will come out of that pool house and see you. I doubt they mistake me for a bird."

I inched to the edge of the lattice and stretched a hand toward the downspout, missing it by three feet. I snapped the hand back and attached it to the trellis.

My leg swung toward the downspout. My toes didn't even brush the plastic. I forced them into the roses, wincing at the pricks and jabs, but the lattice had disappeared beneath the looping vines and my toes couldn't find grip.

"Hellfire and damnation," I exclaimed and stopped my cursing at the sound of men's voices drifting in the air.

Someone had opened the pool house door.

I flattened myself the best I could. The voices quieted again as a door shut. I couldn't risk a glance behind me. The effort to turn my head would have pulled me off the wall.

My arms began to tremble and my toes slipped. I gripped the wood with my fingers, scrabbling with my feet.

The thin wood beneath one hand began to splinter, and I brought my feet up into a crouch. There was one option that didn't involve tearing myself up in the holly and roses. Fling myself backward and hope the lawn was softer than it looked. God willing, I could make like a ball and roll off the fall instead of cracking my noggin.

"Cherry," called a voice. "Just what are you doing?"

I felt like pounding my head against the wall, except the splintering trellis already threatened to break.

"Is that you, Todd?" I called. "I'm a little busy at the moment."

"Is this some new sport? Like free-running? I always wanted to try jumping from building to building like that."

"What kind of idiot jumps from building to building for a sport? I'm just trying to get to the ground. All the doors are locked."

"Oh."

While I stared at my white knuckles and felt a tremor set into my shoulders, Todd took a moment's consideration of that fact.

"That's on account of the ladies," he finally replied. "Sometimes they like to snoop through Mr. Max's things. He caught one in his bedroom checking out his undies once."

"Well, I've got no interest in Mr. Max's undergarments. I just plan on getting to the ground, thanks."

"That's good to hear. You want me to catch you?"

"Not especially," I said, although the thought of falling into Todd's arms sounded good. My entire body quivered and if my arms weren't already numb, they'd ache.

"You might want to think about getting down, though. I can see up your skirt."

"Stop looking," I yelled and quieted. I couldn't remember what panties I wore. Besides, it wouldn't do to have Mr. Max appear and discover my misfortunate lack of judgment. "I'm jumping. You better stand clear."

I squeezed my eyes shut and pushed off the wall, hurtling into space. I hit something hard and lumpy which felt more like Todd than a holly bush. We crashed to the ground in a tangle of limbs that were mostly Todd's cradling the ball of my body.

I popped my eyes open, found myself tightly encased in Todd's arms, and slammed my lids shut.

"That was cool," he panted. "You okay?"

"Fine. Thanks for breaking my fall. You can let me go now." I wiggled and felt his thick forearms tightening around me.

"Why are your eyes still closed? Are you sure you're okay?"

I attempted to push off the ground and my hands encountered something that felt like muscled thighs. They flew off the thighs. "What's with all the questions? Can't I just climb down a wall and out of your lap without looking?"

"Without looking at what?"

There was no way on God's Green Earth I would admit I didn't want to see Todd up close and personal, particularly in my position of sitting between his solid chest and thick arms. I feared my traitorous lips would do something rash at the sight of his blue eyes, square jaw, and long dimples framing those firm yet soft lips. To admit that would be akin to admitting some kind of defeat I had yet to understand. So I kept my eyes closed and stilled my body's struggles.

"It looks like you're eating your lips when you pull them into your mouth like that," he said. "But since I got you here, we need to talk."

"I can think of nothing we need to talk about, particularly in this position," I said. "But if you're going to hold me here, why don't you tell me what's going on in the pool house."

"Now hold on. You've been avoiding me for a week, then fell off a wall, and are sitting on my lap with your eyes closed. And you want to talk about the pool house?"

"That's right."

Keeping my eyes firmly shut, I turned to face him. His breath fanned my face, so I knew I had the right direction. Unfortunately, that breath reminded my lips of the air mixing we had shared some nights past. I ignored that memory and concentrated on the illegal doings in my vicinity.

"Is there a poker game going on?" I asked. "A big poker game with rich dudes? Hiding in a pool house in order to evade the law?"

"I don't know what you're talking about."

Knowing Todd, he could mean that statement literally. I squinted one eye open and met Todd's deep blue gaze. It was too hard to roll my eyes with one closed, so I opened them to give Todd the full extent of my serious aim. "Who is in the pool house? And what are they doing?"

"Nobody I know." He shrugged. "Nothing important."

"Then you won't care if I go check it out."

"Hold on." He squeezed me against his chest. "I want to talk about something else and this seems the only way I'm going to get to do it. You've been avoiding me."

"I've been busy. I'm still busy."

"You haven't called me back, and I've left messages. Every time I run by your house, you're not home. And I know you heard me when you were here the other day. Why did you run away?"

"You were in a Speedo! I can't talk to you when you're wearing a Speedo."

"Why not?"

"Because." I felt my cheeks heat. "That's ridiculous. And not the point. What were you doing in a Speedo in Mr. Max's house?"

"Swimming." He eyed me. "You have a problem with Speedos? I didn't bring my suit, so I borrowed one from Mr. Max."

The thought of Max wearing a Speedo brought me up short.

"Cherry, about the other day."

I snapped my focus back to the man within whose arms I was sitting. "I'm not talking about the other day."

"Are you still upset? Baby, I'm sorry."

"Sorry, my ass. You should never have done it."

"But you asked me to..."

"I never asked you to kiss me." I cocked my head at his astonished look. "Wait, what are you talking about?"

"Eloise. I've still got all her stuff from the festival. Your stuff, too. That's why I've been trying to get a hold of you."

"Oh." I closed my eyes again. The problem with rare bouts of stupidity is they generally catch you unaware. Maybe that kiss had meant nothing to Todd. I was the one with noncommittal lips.

"Did you want to talk about the kiss?" His hands slid across my back.

I snapped my eyes open.

"No." I checked my tone and bent the conversational track toward a more appropriate subject. "Thanks for holding on to Eloise's pottery. Actually, I told her parents I'd bring them to the visitation tomorrow. When can I pick them up?"

"I can bring them to your house."

We sat for a moment staring at each other.

"About that pool house..." I began.

"Todd McIntosh. Have you caught a prowler or are you using my garden for the rendezvous?"

We turned our heads to see the Bear striding across the lawn. I realized too late our conversation could be misconstrued as a cuddle, seeing as how Todd's hands had found their way to my waist and my hands had unintentionally settled upon his shoulders. I had been meaning to push myself out of his lap using those thick deltoids and seem to have forgotten my intent. I used them now and hopped off the ground with Todd following suit.

"Hey, Mr. Max," said Todd. "What's going on?"

"You are needed," said Max, jerking his head toward the pool house.

Todd trotted off with a wave to me.

Max turned to me with a scowl. "How have you found your way here, Artist?"

"Just admiring your yard." I gave him my best customer service smile. "Give your gardener my compliments. He's done a good job. You've got some mighty hardy roses."

Max gave me a customary eyebrow lift, waving his scar.

"So, what's going on in the pool house? And what's Todd doing here again? I heard he might be working for you, but there's another guy running the bingo."

"Did you come looking for Todd McIntosh?" He planted his large body before me, blocking my view of the pool house. "I held a belief that you had the sortir with the police officer?"

"No, I wasn't looking for Todd." Sometimes I liked Max's use of the French turn of phrase. Sometimes I wished he'd stick to his broken English. This was one of those times. "I remembered you had that pool house and just thought I would check it out."

"I see." He approached me, gathered my arm into the crook of his elbow, and ushered me toward his house. "Tell me, Miss Tucker, do you often explore a home without the owner?"

"Mostly yours. I was raised better, but curiosity got the best of me."

I cranked my head to watch Todd disappear into the pool house. I realized my flip-flops resided somewhere in a holly bush under the trellis, but my thoughts were on Todd and the mysterious pool house. I felt a regular Nancy Drew, and Nancy probably didn't stop for missing flip-flops. "Why does Todd get to go to the pool house? What is he doing for you?"

"Todd and I have become friends." Max patted my hand where it rested on his solid arm. "Sometimes he helps me."

"With what?"

We strolled to the patio door. Max kept my arm fitted against him, while he unlocked the door.

"Besides calling bingo numbers, what else does he do?" I continued. "You know he's got a good job driving a truck. I'd hate to see him lose it moonlighting."

The Bear jerked the door open and stepped through, dragging me with him. Turning to the keypad on the wall, he entered his security code, blocking my view with his large body. "Now then. We will begin the tour."

"Tour?" I said. "I didn't ask for a tour. I asked you about Todd and the pool house."

"I assume that with your curiosity about my house, you wanted the tour. This," he swept his hand before him, "is the recreational room. Which I do not use for the recreation."

I eyed the large room piled with boxes. "Actually I only wanted to see the pool house."

"There is sauna," he pointed to a door toward the left, "which I do enjoy. Someday I will make use of this space. Come, let us see the rest of the house."

I blew out a noisy sigh. "Fine. I can see you're not listening."

"I listen." Max cracked a thin-lipped smile. "I have excellent hearing, Cherry Tucker. You should remember that the next time you attempt to climb my walls."

TWENTY-SIX

Max whipped me through the rec-room door, past the raucous action in the bingo room, and up the stairs.

"Now listen, Bear," I said. "I don't need a tour. I am concerned about your sudden decision to host bingo in my town. You have a history of encouraging private gambling in your home—gambling that is illegal in the state of Georgia—and it's best if you just come clean."

"Come clean? Your idiomatic references confuse me."

"I also know you are entertaining a person of interest in the Sidewinder poisoning. Actually two, considering one's playing bingo and the other's in the pool house. Not a good idea, Bear."

"I had heard wrong that the poisoner had been caught? And died by his own hand?"

He examined my consternated look and before I could remark, pointed to the heavy wooden door on the opposite side of the foyer. "I believe you have seen my library with its Confederate States collection, no? Let me take you to parts of my home you haven't seen."

"I don't want a tour. Break up this party before you get in trouble with the law." I dug my bare toes into his tiled foyer as best I could. "I want you to fess up. They'll be easier on you that way."

"Fess up? Again Miss Tucker, please use the standard English with me." He pulled me across the tile to the winding staircase. "I have more collections upstairs. Come."

Curiosity got the better of me. I hopped up the stairs to match his long strides. "Can you at least relax your grip? My limbs haven't quite recovered from my, uh, climb."

He gave me one of those almost-scary smiles and drug me up the rest of the staircase. At the top, another hallway stretched before us. We shot past four closed doors to an end room.

Inside, Max released my arm and closed the door with his back. We had entered a kind of sitting room for what I suspected was a master bedroom.

I spun around to face him. "So what's all fired important in this room, Bear? Or are you just squirreling me away from the bingo crowd so they can't hear your confession?"

He folded his arms across his chest. "What confession would that be? The one where I have caught you trespassing on my grounds? You are trying my patience, Artist."

"Trying patience is my M.O. What are you getting out of this bingo deal?"

"Why do you doubt me so?" He sighed. "If you must know, I do receive the compensation for hosting. I have legitimately bought the license from the charity. The ladies appreciate my efforts. Why must you always look for the ulterior motive?"

"Because I caught you hosting big money poker once before. You got lucky the police were more interested in a murder at the time to pursue it. There is such a thing as bingo scams. I looked it up. Some guy made a million running bingo until he got busted. Do you know the punishment for illegal gambling charges?"

Max took a long step in my direction and stood over me. His girth and strength had never missed my notice, but his sudden proximity was unnerving.

Goosebumps broke across my arms. I took a small step back, but countered the move with my best redneck glare.

His lips twitched, and he took another step forward.

I planted my feet into his ridiculously plush carpet.

"Which worries you more, Artist?" he whispered. "That I'll be caught and punished? Or that I might get rich?"

He knew I didn't have an answer and took advantage of my pursed lip silence to whirl me around to face the opposite wall.

I gulped. In the center of the wall hung my commissioned portrait of Dustin Branson.

"This is what I wanted to show you," he said. "I have found a good place for the painting. I did not enjoy it with the rest of my collection as much as I do here. Beyond is my bedroom, but I do not think you need to see that room."

I took a deep breath and inhaled the spicy, exotic cologne he wore. The head rush left me dizzy.

"I have decided your talent may be worth something one day. I will be keeping the eye on you. I pay well, remember this." Max grasped my elbow and yanked me toward the door.

Once again we strode down the carpeted hall to the big staircase. I felt a bit dumbfounded, unusual for me, but it seemed to be a day for oddities. At the bottom of the staircase, Max walked me across the foyer, punched a few buttons on the security monitor, and opened the door.

"Wait," I said. "What about the bingo games? And your pool house? And Todd?"

"I have found in friendships, it is the slow revelation of self that is the most pleasurable." He leaned over my hand to kiss it. "Without an air of mystery, one becomes bored. Don't you agree, Artist?"

Before I could think out a smart reply, the front door shut. I found myself on his porch, Max inside, and the door locked.

"Hell," I said and sank onto the steps to wait for bingo to end.

TWeNTY-seVeN

By the time Pearl and Casey emerged from the Bear's bingo lair, I had worked up a fine sweat that had nothing to do with the weather. Neither Max nor Todd reappeared, and because I had been keeping a careful eye on Max's driveway, I knew Max's male visitors also remained. I had given up scaling walls, although attempting to climb a fence had crossed my mind, and used the porch time for introspection.

Todd could escape me at Max's House of Bingo Pleasure, but he promised to bring Eloise's pottery to my home. I would corner him there.

Max might slither out of my clutches, but Todd couldn't.

Casey tossed me my flip-flops with a grin. "Mr. Max said to give you these."

"Look at my winnings." Pearl waved her gift cards in my face. "You missed out on a good day and an appearance of that hunk of deliciousness."

I scrunched my face into a what-the-hey expression, which Casey caught.

"She means Mr. Max. He's a hunk of something," Casey mused, "although of what I don't know. I can see why you call him Bear. He's gigantic and kind of testy."

"Thank you," I said. "I don't know what's wrong with Pearl and her buddies. I'm not seeing their fascination."

"Yeah, right," said Casey. "But, he's rich."

"I need more than rich to find a guy a hunk of deliciousness. I don't understand him at all."

"I don't need more than rich," said Casey. "And I don't care about his accent. I'm not looking for conversation."

"I'm not talking about his language skills. I don't understand his motives. And you need to reexamine your values before you go looking for a sugar daddy."

"Your sister is right," said Pearl. "Money's not everything. You need common interests. Like your Grandpa Ed and me."

I suppressed a shudder at Pearl and Grandpa's common interests—which was goats as far as I could tell—and allowed my stomach to speak for the time.

"God Almighty, what was that noise?" asked Pearl, looking around Max's drive.

Most of the bingo ladies had left while we talked, so I couldn't blame my internal roaring on the backfire of a Buick.

"Cherry's gut," said Casey. "I've got to go to work now anyway. If you throw hot wings at her, the noise will back down to a low roar."

"I've got a County Line Tap gift certificate," exclaimed Pearl. "I was going to hold on to it until the Sticks performance on Friday night, but I guess I could spend it now."

Although my mood hadn't improved after cooling my hot heels on the Bear's porch, I decided a beer and hot wings might help. Usually it did.

That's what's great about wings and beer. Especially on someone else's gift certificate.

On the ride to Red's, I chose to not mention my tour of Max's bedroom in front of Pearl for fear it might cause her heart palpitations, but I did explain my theory on the fancy cars and inaccessible pool house. I hoped to put a damper on Pearl's enthusiasm about "sweet Mr. Max."

At the tavern, we followed Casey into the restaurant. She disappeared through the swinging kitchen doors to change into more practical clothes for waiting tables. Practical for Casey meant switching her stilettos for tennis shoes and putting on Daisy Duke shorts and an extra small County Line t-shirt.

"You want a table?" asked Pearl.

"Let's talk to Red," I said and steered her toward the bar. Red played the role of my personal bartender and therapist pretty well. I needed both after the confusion at Max Avtaikin's house.

Red's smile spread across his freckled face at our appearance. He snapped his bar rag with a flourish for Pearl. Red was sweet like that. Because of our long friendship, he liked to keep it real for me. I didn't get a lot of bar rag snapping.

"How you doing?" Red asked, handing me a beer. "I heard all about your friend Eloise. I'm sorry."

"Thanks, Red." I snatched the frosty mug with an eagerness that would have gotten me a smack on my hand by Grandma Jo. "Visitation is tomorrow. Funeral Friday."

"What happened to your face?"

"An abusive boyfriend." I touched the scrape under my lip.

Red's ruddy face deepened to a Perylene Maroon. "How?"

I waved my hand. "That's water under the bridge. I don't believe Griffin committed suicide. But whatever happened, three people are dead. I guess justice was served. But it throws a monkey wrench into Hunter Adams's theory. Maybe I should go talk to him again."

"Who's Hunter Adams?"

"This kid from one of the most dysfunctional family situations I've ever known. He thought his mom's boyfriend poisoned their Brunswick Stew in the Sidewinder cook-off. In order to kill his wife. But he died instead."

"Good heavens," said Pearl. "I had no idea you were running around with teenagers whose mother's had murdering boyfriends."

With my pinky, I drew a gun on my frosty mug. "If Griffin hadn't poisoned the Genuine Juice, I would have thought it might be Hunter's mom. She's murdered before."

"Good Lord, Cherry," said Red. "How do you get yourself in these situations?"

"I'm not in the situation," I said. "I'm just in the know. Because Eloise's family deserved to find out what happened. I guess instead of trying to figure out what Mr. Max and Todd are up to, I should be calling on the Sidewinder folks. I need to make a visit to Mrs. Maynard and express my sympathy. She's the one who lost the cheating husband who didn't poison the stew."

Pearl nodded. "Bring her a pie. I can whip you up a pecan if you want."

At the thought of pecan pie, my stomach ripped into overdrive.

Red hollered at Casey to bring hot wings.

"Well, I'm glad the police figured it out," said Red. "Sounds like an awful mess."

"They didn't exactly figure it out. I tried to tell them Griffin was dangerous and nobody listened to me. Just like this business with Mr. Max. I'm pretty sure he's ripping off the bingo community of Forks County. And running hot poker games again."

"You need to lay off Mr. Max," said Pearl. "He's a honey. I'm sure the men with the fancy cars were watching baseball or something."

"I don't think Mr. Max is the baseball type," I said. "He's the Monte Carlo-type you see in the 007 movies. Except the Bear's the guy holding a cat and playing with stolen money."

"What are you saying? Mr. Max is dangerous?" asked Red.

"There's no poker," said Pearl. "Just bingo. I was there all afternoon and didn't see any poker."

"That's because you were playing bingo and salivating over Mr. Max. They're doing it in the pool house and Todd's somehow involved. He's going to get fired from his job or worse. End up in jail for getting involved in an illegal gambling ring. And you know about his gambling addiction."

Red drew back. "You think? You want me to talk to Todd?"

"You can try," I said. "I'm going to see him later tonight when he drops off Eloise's stuff from the festival. I'm going to do my best to convince him to spill the beans."

"Speaking of spilling beans," said Red, "your buddy Shawna was in here the other night, trash talking you."

I slammed my empty beer mug on the bar. "What's she saying now?"

"After one too many appletinis—do you know I had to look that up? This is Halo, Georgia. Who drinks appletinis here? I don't know what she's trying to prove with an appletini."

I smirked and allowed Red's rant. He loved Shawna as much as I did.

"She wants me to create an art gallery on one of my walls to class up Halo." Red shook his head. "I told her I wasn't moving my softball trophies or my flat-screens. That's as classy as we get in here. Then she called me 'country'."

Pearl gasped at the insult and reached for a hot wing. Casey tossed us a bundle of napkins and stalked away before Red could yell about her poor service.

"But what did she say about me?" I persisted, pulling the wing plate down the bar. "She's on a roll. I don't know why she's acting so ugly now. I was flying low on her radar until the last couple months, when boom! I'm on Shawna's shit list."

"Well," said Red, repositioning the wing plate to force me to share with Pearl, "she had one too many appletinis, then went off on your mother and the quality of Bransons over Tuckers."

"Nothing new there," I said. "She thinks being a Branson is God's gift to the people of Forks County. And she's probably right about my mother, although I served her a couple fat lips in high school for saying it."

"It's childish," said Pearl. "Good breeding says you don't bring up a person's unfortunate circumstances, even with someone like your mother. God bless her."

As many times as Forks County citizens had my mother blessed, you'd think she'd be a saint by now.

"Shawna's just a hater," I said.

Red shook his head. "Be careful. She vowed to bring you down low."

"I do a pretty good job of that on my own," I sighed, thinking of my double-crossing lips. "Speaking of that, I've got to get home before Todd arrives. And I've got a Greek painting to attempt without a model. Red, would you pose for me?"

His cobalt green eyes burned with fear. "God Almighty. No. Don't you put me in one of those naked pictures. I will never serve you again."

"It's not a naked picture! It's called a life drawing. I am an artist not a pornographer. When are you Philistines going to get that?"

I hopped off my stool and stomped toward the door.

Casey caught my arm before I hit the foyer. "Just a minute, sister. Todd's coming over tonight?"

"Just to drop off some stuff, I need," I said. "Don't worry."

"Where's Luke?"

"Good question. I haven't heard from him today. But I assume Uncle Will's kept the deputies busy wrapping up the poisoning case." While waiting on Max's porch, I had called Dot. "They decorated Griffin's house with yellow tape and had his car impounded. The deputies are searching to bring in all available Genuine Juice."

"Maybe you should call him. You know, have Luke stop in while Todd's there."

"You think I'm going to cheat on Luke. Which I have no interest in doing."

She pulled me through the glass door into Red's vestibule. I leaned against a gum ball machine and glared while Casey searched for words that wouldn't cause me to kick her out of Great-Gam's house before she moved in.

"Listen, we both know we inherited a problem from Momma."

By problem, she referred to a mental issue we had around beautiful men. And by mental issue, I mean downright stupidity.

"I'm around Todd all the time and it's never been a problem before. Except for the Vegas fiasco."

"You let him talk you into marrying him. That's a pretty big fiasco."

"And when my thoughts cleared, I got it annulled. He didn't talk me into it. I think I was just lonely or something. Todd couldn't talk his way into a time share commitment."

"I'm not so sure about that. He knows how to push your buttons."

I smiled thinking about the buttons he was good at pressing.

"See what I mean," exclaimed Casey. "Look, just call Luke and have him come over. Then you don't need to worry."

I pushed off the gum ball machine and stalked to the outside door. "I can fight abusive men in parking lots and handle teenage boys with anger management issues. But around one simple, dumb guy, I suddenly need a babysitter."

"Yep," said Casey, swinging her hips in the direction of the restaurant.

I shoved open the door and slapped my flip-flops in the direction of home. "This is all your fault," I said to my lips. "If you'd just settle down and control yourselves, I wouldn't have these insane conversations."

TWENTY-EIGHT

That evening, Todd found me in my studio living room sketching scenes of mythological creatures with the heads of my friends and family. I'll admit, not my brightest artistic endeavor, but desperation had driven me to ridiculousness.

I still felt my portraits of famous Greek statue poses would gain me good feedback. I could rock a life drawing, and covering the model with tiny Greek letters? Edgy enough for the art crowd. But I still needed a model. And I felt desperate enough to search out the guy that liked to flash the audience at the Halo high school football games.

I was pretty sure he'd enjoy the exposure even covered in body paint.

"Why is Cody part goat?" asked Todd upon examining the sketches. "And why does Casey have drapery? If anyone should have a bare chest in this scene, it should be Casey."

At my look, he backed off the statement and ran to his car to retrieve the other boxes. I turned to the carton he had deposited on my paint-speckled hardwoods, peeled back the lid, and grimaced. Trash filled the cardboard container. Smelly trash.

It appeared Todd had boxed up everything from our festival booth including a half-drunk Genuine Juice bottle and a half-dozen empty Brunswick Stew cups. The Genuine Juice sludge looked moldy and the Brunswick Stew cups had a layer of grease that turned my stomach. However, as someone who had grown up around a county sheriff, I knew this disgusting box held valuable evidence.

I snatched my phone from my roll-top desk and dialed a number I had put off calling.

"Hey," said Luke's smooth baritone, "if you're looking for phone sex, I'll have to call you later."

"Never mind that." I bent over the box. "But if you're busy, I'll just call Uncle Will about the important evidence I have just collected. I thought I'd let you have a shot at looking important by hauling in this box of goods related to the death of Eloise Parker that now sits in my living room, but sounds like—"

"What are you talking about?"

"Todd just dropped off the stuff he boxed up from our festival booth. I had forgotten he had it."

"Todd?"

"Remember he helped me out when I went to the hospital with Eloise? He even boxed up the garbage, which I am looking at right now." I jerked my head up as Todd banged through my screen door with another load of cartons. "And that trash includes Eloise's leftovers from the festival. Including an empty Genuine Juice bottle. Thought y'all could use that."

"Hey, baby," Todd strode to the center of the room. "I've got one more box in the car. Where do you want these?"

I pointed and turned my attention to the phone.

"Todd's still there?" said Luke.

"I actually need to talk to him about some work he's doing for Mr. Max. That's something else you need to check into. There might be bingo fleecing and hot poker games going on at the Bear's lair."

"I'll mention it to Sheriff Thompson. Listen, I'm a little busy now. I'll grab that box later."

"Busy doing what? I thought your job came first. I have potentially given you the evidence that can close the case on your main suspect. A suspect brought into the light by me. Funny how when I need you to do something, your job comes first. Now I'm helping you with your job, and I just got bumped to third place."

"Now, sugar..."

I hopped up from my stoop and stalked into my kitchen. "Did you know whenever you begin a sentence with 'Now, sugar' I immediately get suspicious? What are you doing that's more important than confiscating evidence, Deputy Harper?"

He paused long enough for me to hear laughter in the background.

"Where are you?" I asked.

"Home. Mom's house."

"What's going on? It sounds like a party." I could hear someone questioning his etiquette for taking a call. "Was that Shawna? Are your parents having a family get-together?"

The background noise faded as a door slammed.

"Yes. It's JB's birthday," he said. "Believe me, I'd rather not be here. The house is crawling with Bransons. It's not a big deal."

"Oh." I snapped my voice from hurt to annoyance. "I guess that's why Shawna is there and not me? Because it's just family?"

"Sure." His voice betrayed his discomfort.

"Luke. Have you told your parents we're dating? Because I saw them in church and got the distinct impression they had no idea."

"Sugar, it's complicated. Let's not get into this on the phone."

"I'm putting the box of evidence in my car port. You can pick it up when you like." I hung up and turned around.

Todd leaned in the kitchen archway, his arms crossed. At my turn, he straightened and raised his brows. I caught the quick switch in his expression. He had looked contemplative. Which is odd, because Todd didn't spend much time with thoughts.

"You okay, baby? You sounded a little ticked."

"I'm fine." I brushed past him into the front room and surveyed the other boxes. "Thanks for bringing these. Even the garbage. You probably didn't realize this, but the trash could be important evidence proving Griffin poisoned Eloise."

"No way." Todd followed me into the living room and collapsed onto my ancient divan. "That's pretty cool. I thought about tossing out that box, but it's been sitting in my car and I hadn't gotten around to it yet. It was starting to smell bad, though."

"Well, your procrastination may serve justice. Nice job."

He beamed. I surveyed the six foot three tower of beauty. My lips quivered.

"You want a beer?" I scampered to the kitchen and returned with two longnecks. After handing his off, I sank onto the stool next to my easel and cooled off my lips with a long pull from the bottle. "So, what's going on with you and the Bear? I'm concerned."

"Why are you worried?" He took a sip of beer and eyed me over the bottle.

"Number one, you're moonlighting. Number two, Max likes to ignore details like legalities. Number three, you have issues with gambling."

"Shoot. Didn't I tell you they cut back my hours at work?"

"No. When did that happen?"

"A couple of weeks ago. You didn't notice. You've been a little wrapped-up in your own stuff."

"I apologize." I flinched. "And sorry about your job. But maybe you should look at legitimate work opportunities."

"Max is legitimate. He said he's got a green card."

"I mean a real job. What happens if the police raid his house and you get arrested?"

"Why would the police raid his house?"

"Maybe because I just tipped off a deputy that I suspect good ol' Mr. Max of running crooked poker and bingo."

Todd jumped from the couch. "Why would you do that? Mr. Max is a nice guy. I'm making more money working for him than I do driving the truck. And I just started figuring out his crazy English."

"I'm sorry, but wrong is wrong. All those ladies think he's hosting bingo out of the goodness of his heart. He's doing it to make money."

"So what?" Todd slapped the sketchbook on my easel. "Just because you don't mind driving a crappy pickup and sleeping in a shack, doesn't mean the rest of us want to live like that. You think being a starving artist makes you paint better?"

I felt more astonished by Todd's outburst than if he had turned into the mythical half-dog/half-man creature I had doodled. "You can't just make money any old way, Todd. Get your priorities straight."

"It's not any old way. I even filled out a W–4 thingy. I'm not the one with screwed-up priorities."

He stood over me, breathing hard, and shooting fire from his normally guileless blue eyes.

I rose to my full five foot and a half inches, then cranked my head so I could look him in his non-guileless eyes. "How are my priorities screwed up?"

He stared at me with an intensity of which I had not known him capable.

"What?" I finally exploded.

"Never mind." He spun around and stomped to the door. Thrusting open the screen door, he glanced over his shoulder. "Your foundation is crumbling. I've been meaning to point that out for weeks."

"Todd." I called, "I'm sorry."

I felt like someone had just shot my dog. And judging by Todd's final glance at me, I must have been the one holding the gun.

TWENTY-NINE

Although the men in my life had been replaced by aliens, since they sure acted like they had been subjected to anal probing, I sought out my blessings the morning of Eloise's visitation. For example, waking alone is preferable when you've pulled an all-nighter trying for brilliant creativity. And coming up with diddlysquat.

As you can probably guess, I woke grouchy as hell.

But dressing in my most conservative midnight blue sundress embroidered with tiny yellow sunflowers kept my perspective in check. Eloise would never have another argument with her boyfriend. She would never have a falling-out with a sort-of ex-husband (emphasis on the sort-of). And Eloise would never feel the stomach-squeezing pressure of important deadlines. God bless her, Eloise was in a better place, and I was going to miss her.

I put aside my own troubles for the poor people wiped out by the blight of Griffin's stupidity. After Eloise's services, I needed to do things proper. Visit Hunter and Miss Marion and express my condolences to that crazy-ass family as well as Eloise's.

After a day off from driving, the Datsun acted perkier, and I enjoyed the ride down to Sidewinder. Thunderclouds built up on the horizon and the air felt blessedly cooler. With the windows rolled down, the damp smell of hay and pine blew through the cab. I pulled into the First Baptist parking lot, spotted a sheriff's cruiser, and sought Luke out in the crowded vestibule of the church. He wore his deputy uniform, minus the walkie.

"Hey," he said, his eyes a somber pewter.

"Hey yourself. I wasn't sure you'd be here. I would have brought the evidence box to you."

"I actually picked it up last night. Everything's at the lab now." He shrugged off my look. "I grabbed it from your car port. Saw you through your front window at your easel. You looked like you were concentrating. Didn't want to interrupt you."

I scowled. "Wouldn't have made a difference. I still have nothing for that show. Are you sure you won't model for me? I really need a male model. With six-pack abs on the outside, not the inside."

"No way. Don't worry, you'll figure it out. You always do." He dropped his hand to the back of my neck. "You're looking real pretty in that dress. It's nice to see you in something normal-looking."

I punched him in the arm, but we were good. With a deep breath, I took Luke's hand, and we walked into the church.

An hour later, we walked out. Actually, I limped out on a broken flip-flop while holding my dress in place. Dark clouds rolled in, hovering over Sidewinder. The air had wrapped my hair in a warm towel of humidity and squeezed out all the smoothness. Wisps flew around my head like corn silk but I couldn't calm it with torn spaghetti straps.

Luke stalked me with hands shoved in his uniform pockets and a cross-section of lines burrowing across his brow.

I reached my Datsun, turned around to face him, and threw my hands in the air. Then slapped them back on my chest to hold my dress in place.

"Thanks for defending me in there," I said.

"You didn't look like you needed any help. Besides I didn't want to get caught in the cross-fire at a viewing." His last words drew from his lips in a hiss.

"Then why didn't you haul Shawna out of there? She's the one who started it."

"Shawna is not my responsibility. If she wants to make an ass of herself, that's her business."

"She attacked me, and I made an ass of myself?"

"You rose to her bait. She was waiting for you to make a crack about her attempts at bringing culture to Forks County. And, by the way, there is nothing wrong with encouraging culture in this country backwater. I would think you'd want to help her. It'd do good for your art business."

"The day I help Shawna Branson is the day my body is lowered in the ground." My remark brought us both up short, considering we had just attended a visitation. "She didn't have to take a swing at me."

"No, she didn't. And you didn't have to kick her."

"Considering I had to hold my dress in place because she tore it, I had no choice but kick her. And I broke my flip-flop. There is no point to kicking and climbing walls if you're going to wear flip-flops. I need to get my boots back out, no matter how sweaty my feet get."

Luke gave me one of those looks of extreme agitation. I was glad he didn't ask about the climbing walls remark.

"Maybe I let it go too far, but I got the worst of it. My dress and sandals are ruined. You let her attack me," I accused. "And I think it's because your parents were standing by."

Thunder rolled overhead, but lightening flashed in Luke's eyes.

"You're embarrassed to be dating me," I continued. "What happened? Did you drink the Branson Kool-Aid? Think you're better than the Tuckers, too?"

"That's Shawna's bullshit handed down to her by her mother and the rest of the Bransons."

"Well, it's mighty peculiar that you seem to show up at my Grandpa's farm for Sunday dinners, but I've never set foot inside the Big House of Branson."

"Look, I'm living at home and things are tenuous at best. JB and I have our own issues. Nobody's thrilled that I'm a cop. You're just another...complication." He dug his hands out of his pocket to reach for me. "Darling, I sure spend a hell of a lot of time in your rickety house. Doesn't that tell you something?"

"It tells me you only want to hide out when you're with me. So forget it."

"Cherry..."

I choked back what might have been a tear if I hadn't been so angry. "I'm more than a warm body you can find in bed at night, Luke Harper. If you're serious about the cow, you ain't getting the milk for free. And until you take me home and proclaim your love for me in front of JB and Wanda, this cow isn't for sale."

That didn't come out exactly the way I wanted, but I think he got the picture.

THIRTY

It seemed the perfect time to visit the Maynard farm. I had a lot of thoughts that I would rather not explore. And a couple gaping holes in my chest that felt like someone had taken a shotgun to me. I also had the convenience of already driving around Sidewinder. Luckily, the Feed Junction Grocery had duct tape to repair my shoe and dress. It's tricky to duct tape the inside of a dress, but I reattached the spaghetti strap without exposing myself too badly.

Although I might have given a man in the neighboring truck a cheap thrill.

After passing the Parkers' home to drop off the boxes of pots and to leave a note of apology for taking on a bitchy Amazon in the Baptist Church vestibule, I turned the Datsun in the direction of the Maynard residence. Handy signs sprinkled around town for Cotton Pickin' Good Plantation led me to a gorgeous wrought iron gate. Looping letters intertwined with cotton blossoms decorated the lintel.

The beautiful craftsmanship in an Art Nouveau style dated the gate to the turn of the past century. I longed for my sketchbook, a good pencil, and a minute to replicate the gorgeous work. I took a picture with my phone instead.

I turned onto the gravel lane and drove through the opening. Not a goat in sight, but several buildings rose in the distance, towering over the low shrubs of cotton filling the fields on either side of the lane. Groves of pecans grew amongst the buildings and a crumbling three story chimney exposed the remains of the old plantation house. I parked in front of a quad-pillared antebellum style house that made the Gable's modern, brick home look tawdry. Grabbing a box of Krispy Kreme's I had retrieved from the Feed Junction with my last dollars, I scooted out of the Datsun and dodged rain drops and the low rumble of thunder in the distance.

As I hopped the last step to the porch, Hunter walked around the side of the house, hunching his shoulders against the rain. I searched him for signs of hostility, but he seemed to have cooled from his previous mood at the Viper.

"Hey, Scarecrow," he said, ambling onto the porch. "What are you doing here?"

"Come to pay my sympathy. I met Miss Marion in the hospital." I waved my Krispy Kreme box at him.

He eyed the box with wanton covetousness. "She's in. My mom and I are moving."

"You live here?" I wrinkled my nose. Lewis Maynard was the dirtiest of old men, keeping his girlfriend in the same house as his wife. I didn't feel sorry for his death in the least.

"We live in an apartment above the museum. My mom's the manager, remember?"

"Sure. How's she doing?"

"Not so good." Hunter spit over the side of the porch. "She's pretty tore up over Lewis. Getting fired has pissed her off, too."

"I suppose so." I wasn't sure what good manners dictated in the case of the death of a home-wrecker's married boyfriend. "Where are you going to move? Are you staying in Sidewinder?"

"Dunno. I might go to my aunt and uncle's house for a while. But they won't take in my mom."

"Why's that?"

"There's always been bad blood between the farms. When Momma took up with Lewis, Uncle Bruce hit the roof. He didn't allow Aunt Belinda to consort with my mom after that. Besides, Momma and Aunt Belinda both think they stole each other's ideas about the cotton education center and whatnot."

"Your Aunt Belinda would let your mom go homeless?" Stories like this made me appreciate my messed-up family even more.

"Yep." Hunter leaned over to spit and drew up, his eyes on me. "Momma says Belinda's always thought she's too good, especially after catching Bruce. Didn't even help us after Daddy left."

He wiped his mouth with the back of his arm and strolled closer. "Pretty screwed up situation, ain't it? But don't worry about my mom. We just found out a couple hours ago that Lewis left her plenty. Which is probably why Marion fired her so quick."

"What about Miss Marion? Didn't he leave her anything? It looks like there's a lot of money sunk into this place."

"It's Marion's land. She keeps the Maynard stuff. But Lewis had my mom's name on the insurance policy and not Marion."

"Wow." Ka-ching, Miss Janine.

"I think that shows he loved my mom pretty good, don't you?"

I glanced at Hunter and felt another hole open in my heart. The boy was damaged goods, but he was still a boy.

"Sure, Hunter." I opened the box of Krispy Kreme and handed him one. "I guess Miss Marion doesn't need all six."

He spat the rest of his chew over the side, wiped his mouth, and took the donut. "Thanks, Scarecrow."

"Hey, you still think Lewis poisoned the stew? It looks like Griffin Ward's Genuine Juice did it. He was trying to make Miss Eloise sick so he could make everyone think his drink cured her. I guess it got out of hand or he didn't pay attention to which drinks he poisoned."

"Shit," said Hunter. "I know Griffin Ward. I heard he's dead, too. But I drink that stuff all the time and it never made me sick. He told me it would build muscle. You know, like he's got. Or had. What a bullshitter."

"You drank Genuine Juice all the time? Did you drink any at the festival? Griffin was handing out cups."

"I don't remember. Can I have another donut?" He reached for the box.

I whipped the carton away. "These are for Miss Marion." It's going to look bad that I already opened the box.

"Hunter. Did you or did you not drink Genuine Juice at the festival?" I used my best impression of a teacher's voice.

He used his best impression of a student who didn't give a crap about teachers. "I don't remember." He stared at the white and green box in my hands. "Maybe I'd have a better memory if I had something to eat."

"Well, get a job and buy a burger, because I'm not giving you any more donuts. These are sympathy donuts and they are not for you. Do you remember anyone on your cook-off team drinking Griffin's green stuff?"

"I don't see anyone bringing my mom sympathy donuts."

Probably because folks tend not to sympathize with white trash home-wreckers, I thought, but judiciously decided to keep that comment locked tight. "I don't know your mom. I know Miss Marion."

"You're just like everyone else, Scarecrow. But y'all will see. My mom doesn't need your freakin' Krispy Kremes after she collects Lewis's money. We'll be rolling in Krispy Kremes."

Leaving me with that interesting picture, he stomped off the porch and into the rain. I wondered if Krispy Kremes counted as blood money. Possibly, considering how good they tasted. Especially warm. My stomach jumped to attention, and I realized I had better hand off the box before I tore it apart.

I returned to my original mission, approached Miss Marion's front door, and knocked. She answered, wearing black, pearls, and lipstick. Appropriate, although I would find it hard to mourn in such fancy clothes. But that's me. Some people may find it hard to mourn in a t-shirt with the deceased's face outlined with Swarovski crystals. Because that's what I did when Grandma Jo died.

"Miss Tucker?" she said, fluttering a hand around her pearls.

"I'm here to offer my sympathies. I heard about Mr. Maynard." I handed her the Krispy Kreme box. "Sorry that it's open. I saw Hunter and offered him a donut. He looked hungry."

"Hunter is always hungry," said Miss Marion. "Do come in."

"Thank you. I will do."

I swept past her, hoping she couldn't tell my sundress straps were attached with duct tape.

We entered a sitting room that had probably been designed by Southern Living. The drapes, furniture, rug, and lampshades had coordinating colors. Fresh flowers in big bowls sat on tables. I sank onto the edge of a couch and held my knees together like Grandma Jo taught us.

"How are you holding up, Miss Marion?" I asked. "So sorry about your husband. And are you feeling better?"

"Much better, thank you." She took the silk armchair and placed the donuts on the coffee table between us.

I eyed the box and told my stomach to behave. "So I guess you heard about Griffin Ward? Sounds like the poison might have come from Genuine Juice."

"I am so glad the police figured that out. That man is deranged."

"Pretty much," I said. "So have the police told you anything? You think it's a closed case?"

"I certainly hope so. The fact that Griffin had a house full of poisoned drinks should settle things, I would think. I was so sure it was the Gables, getting back at us for our success with the Cotton Pickin' Plantation Educational Center and all."

"I'm not sure about the Gables. Although they do act peculiar. But, I did witness Griffin Ward drinking his own poison." I inched forward on my seat. "And I just discovered a box of trash from the festival. I guess the police can use that as evidence, too."

"How did you discover this box of trash?" Marion's hand drifted to the Krispy Kreme box and flipped the lid open. "Please help yourself."

"I might have told you Eloise Parker and I shared a craft booth at the festival. When she got sick, I went to the hospital and sent a friend to close up our booth. He just tossed everything in boxes and left them in his car."

"Goodness. So this evidence has been sitting in his car? I wonder if the police can detect arsenic if it's been sitting that long."

"I have no idea. Guess we'll find out," I said, reaching for a donut. I sank my mouth into a cloud of heaven so sweet my teeth itched. "You know to heat these up, right? Twenty seconds in the microwave and you'd think the Second Coming has arrived via your taste buds."

"Did Hunter tell you about his mother's inheritance?" Marion's hands stroked her pearls. "I imagine he did."

"Yes, ma'am. I'm sorry to hear about that."

"I suppose everyone will know soon," she sighed.

"I suppose." That was a fact of life in small towns. A relentless drive for gossip, churning up lives in its wake. "Are you going to be hurting for money?"

"Me?" She straightened in her chair and her hand dropped to her lap. "Gracious no. Lewis couldn't touch my daddy's money or the land. That remains in Maynard hands, thank the Lord. I wish I could have prevented that piece of trash from getting anything, though."

I kept my mouth busy chewing. Seemed safer.

"It's bad enough to live with this unfortunate situation even if she did improve my daddy's estate," Marion continued. "I guess that's why I tolerated her so long. It just galls me that gold-diggers like Janine still land on their feet. I hope she gets what she deserves."

"I guess she will eventually," I said. "Your situation is rather unusual, if you don't mind me saying so, ma'am. I hope you can hold on to some good memories of Lewis."

"Phwft." She swatted the air. "I certainly didn't marry him out of false ideas of love. Don't you worry about me, missy. Now tell me more about this new evidence. I'm very anxious to have this case closed so I can pick up the pieces of my life and move on."

"Not much more to tell, actually." I dipped into the donut box again. "They either find the arsenic in the remains of the Genuine Juice bottle and Brunswick Stew cups or not."

"Genuine Juice bottle and Brunswick Stew cups?"

I nodded and swallowed a hunk of donut. "The sheriff's team will confiscate any and all remains of food and drink when it's a poisoning case until they locate the source of the poison."

"But I thought they already located the source. Griffin."

"Yes, and it's solid evidence in Griffin's death. But because I have the remains of what Eloise ate, that would show what poisoned her. Hopefully."

"I see. Of course, our team had thrown everything away so the medical staff couldn't pinpoint what poisoned Lewis and me."

"Well, I wouldn't put it past the sheriff to have confiscated all the trash at the festival. It could turn up something, although to pinpoint Lewis's empties might be impossible. It would take a lot of time and effort to test all that trash. So finding Eloise's half-drunk bottle is a needle in a haystack."

"Didn't the police have other suspects?" she asked. "I mean before they discovered Griffin had poisoned his drinks?"

"They wouldn't tell me, although for a while they thought it could have been a lunatic who thought it might be fun to poison a festival. However, I'm sure they'd also look at folks in connection to Eloise and Lewis' death. Griffin, of course. And people in relation to your, uh, situation."

"Like the Gables."

"I suppose." I bit into another donut. "And Miss Janine and Hunter, too. I know the police questioned them. And now that Janine stands to inherit, she makes a good suspect. If it wasn't for Griffin, that is."

"If Lewis weren't already dead, I'd kill him for giving Janine all that money."

Wanting to laugh, I jammed the rest of the donut into my mouth and choked on sugar instead.

"You seem very knowledgeable about this evidence and all." She fiddled with her pearls. "Are you some kind of investigator?"

"No ma'am, I'm just an artist. But I've taken a keen interest in my buddy Eloise's death. I'd like to see justice served."

"I guess you've done what you can do. Turning in that box and all."

"To be honest, something is still gnawing at me. Probably the way Griffin died. I might do a little more nosing around." I hopped from the couch before I polished off the rest of the donuts. "I guess once I hear the lab results on that garbage, I'll feel better. I'll let you know if anything turns up."

"Well, thank you for stopping by." Marion rose and ushered me from the house. "Please come again. Folks drop off food, but nobody stays to chat. It's like death is catching or something."

"I'll stop in again, ma'am. I enjoyed it."

We strolled out to her porch, and she watched me hunker-dash through the rain to the Datsun. I gave her a final wave, pulled out, and skidded to a stop. Hunter jumped from the front of my truck. Rain coursed over the rangy boy. A baseball cap pulled low darkened his eyes and his mouth had pulled into a tighter grimace than his usual scowl.

I rolled down my window. "Hunter, what the hell are you doing? I almost hit you."

"I need a ride, Scarecrow. My momma took off to have it out with her sister. You got to take me to the High Cotton Farm before she kills somebody."

THIRTY-ONE

From the corner of my eye, I watched Hunter dripping water over my cloth seats. His usual "screw-you" expression had been replaced with an anxiousness that made me fretful.

"What's going on, Hunter?"

"Can't this P.O.S. go any faster?"

"No. That's the problem with P.O.S. trucks. That and not starting when you want them to. So, while you're enjoying the ride, tell me what the hell is going on."

"Mom called Aunt Belinda to find out when I can crash. Belinda told her I couldn't come. Miss Marion confiscated the Jeep Lewis had given Mom, so she took my truck to have it out with Aunt Belinda."

How had I entangled myself into this Sidewinder snarl? "Is she armed?"

"Who?"

"Your mother. Actually either sister. How dangerous is the situation? Are we talking run of the mill cat fight or am I going to need backup?"

"Don't you call the cops on my mom, Scarecrow."

I set my mouth into a hard line and focused on the drive. I still carried my Remington in the truck. After my tussle with Griffin, I didn't plan to go anywhere without it. At least until I could afford a smaller firearm, which would be never if I couldn't get my Greek paintings done. And what was I doing driving around Sidewinder with a teenager when I could be at home commencing to paint a masterpiece? I shot a sideways glance at my passenger, assessing him with a painterly eye and trying not to feel like a creeper.

"Hunter, have you thought about modeling? For a painting?"

The look he gave me combined with a judicious choice of expletives made me feel even creepier. We tooled along the blacktop. With Hunter pointing the way down county roads I didn't recognize, we arrived at the entrance of High Cotton Farm. I took the corn filled lane as fast as the Datsun could manage and careened around the gigantic lot. I pulled up alongside the brick house and parked.

"You think they're inside?" I said.

"I doubt Bruce let Momma into the house." Hunter peered out the window. Fat drops of rain slammed into the windshield. "Maybe they're around back. At the end of the day, Aunt Belinda and Uncle Bruce like to sit on their back porch, drink wine, and look out at the garden. Even though it ain't finished. They started building a pool but stopped. Since it's raining, maybe they started drinking early."

"So they've been drinking. And may be armed." I reached behind the seat to pull my shotgun box off the floor. "What about your momma? Has she been drinking or taking any happy pills today?"

"Both." Hunter hopped out of the truck and ran through the rain toward the side of the house.

"Shit." I snatched the Remington from the box, left my purse, and took after Hunter.

With my Remington Wingmaster in hand, I rounded the side of the house and skidded to a stop before a tall, wrought iron fence. Beyond the fence lay a massive hole and gigantic piles of weed embedded clay, like a Bobcat had taken liberties with the Gables yard. Near the giant hole, two women did their own version of bobcats—of the non-heavy equipment, feline type—hissing and growling with acrylic claws extended.

Hunter reached over the gate to unlock the fence. I stood watching the scene with the missile-like drops of the Georgia thundershower dousing my ruined dress and flip-flops. I had a feeling if I slipped through the fence, I'd end up in that backyard canyon.

"Hunter," I yelled through the fence. "Be careful of the pool."

He ignored me, edged past the hole, and slid forward in the wet clay. Bruce Gable stood on the patio under a pergola, watching the women. I wondered why he didn't try to stop the fight until I caught his voice under the rumble of thunder, encouraging his wife to take down "that slut who stole our money."

That "slut" being his wife's sister. Family dynamics are always so interesting.

"Momma," said Hunter, "stop it. We don't need them. Let's get out of here."

Janine slammed an open palm into her sister's chest. Belinda slipped and landed butt-first in the mud. She scrambled to standing, her silk capris covered in rust-colored clay.

"This is dry clean only," screamed Belinda.

"Serves you right," said Janine, "for turning your back on family."

"How can you call me family after ruining my life?"

Belinda shoved Janine with both hands. Janine tottered back a step, but regained her footing.

"We had to declare bankruptcy because of you," yelled Belinda. "Backstabbing, money-grubbing whore!"

"Stop it, Aunt Belinda," said Hunter. He grabbed his mother's arm, and she shook him off.

"I did not steal your fool ideas," said Janine. "Anyone could have come up with a cotton education center. It's not my fault you started building before your grant fell through. And don't tell me your bankruptcy was just for the history center. I know corn futures have taken a dive recently."

"Bull hockey," yelled Bruce. "We would have that grant if you hadn't swiped the idea and the money out from under us."

"I can't help it if some hick farmer doesn't know the first thing about business," said Janine. "I'm just smarter than y'all. You gotta make hay while the sun shines."

"You were making a lot more than hay," said Bruce. "Everyone knows you poisoned Lewis for his money."

Hunter gasped and turned toward Bruce. "That's a lie. I know she didn't do it. They caught Griffin Ward."

A large roll of thunder caused Belinda to skitter backwards. She spun and ran toward the patio, slipping and scrambling in her rhinestone sandals.

I darted a look at the dark clouds and thought about the brilliance of standing near metal fences in a thunderstorm. "Hunter. Let's get out of the rain before we get electrocuted. I'll take you home."

Janine glanced over her shoulder at me. "What's your girlfriend doing here?"

"I'm not his girlfriend," I said. "That's disgusting. I'm twenty-six-years-old, for heaven's sake. I gave him a ride."

"Well, ride yourself on out of here. This is a family matter. And mind your own business."

"My mom didn't poison Lewis," yelled Hunter. "Lewis poisoned the stew."

"You're deluding yourself, boy," called Bruce. "Calm yourself before someone gets hurt."

"You aren't my family, Janine," cried Belinda. "I wish you had eaten that poison. It should have been you. You deserved it. Lewis was just an idiot who couldn't keep it in his pants. And you weren't the first he cheated with."

Lightening ripped through the sky followed by another thunder burst. I bit my lip and stepped back from the fence.

"Hunter, get out of there," I yelled. Rain pelted my face, causing me to squint.

A flash of lightening cracked the sky, illuminating the figures in the yard. Hunter pushed his mother to the side and dashed toward the porch. Belinda scrambled toward the back door and ran into the house. Bruce darted toward the corner of the patio and returned with a baseball bat.

"Call your son off," I yelled. "He's going to get hurt."

Janine glanced at me, snarling. "Get out of here."

No one seemed to care Hunter charged at a grown man wielding a baseball bat. Bruce looked like he would do his best imitation of Chipper Jones with Hunter as the ball.

Bruce raised his bat. "Don't you do it, Hunter."

Hunter jumped onto the patio, his fists readied and head lowered. As Bruce swung, Hunter made a grab for the bat and missed. The bat slammed into Hunter.

I suddenly realized I still held my gun. I racked the pump and discharged a volley into the sky. Everyone froze but Hunter. He had taken a crack to his shoulder and continued his slump to his knees.

"Stop it," I yelled. "Hunter, get your butt out of there and come with me."

I stood on tiptoes and reached over the gate to pull up the lock. Marching through the wet grass and mud with as much dignity as I could, I passed the still snarling and now soaked Janine. I eyed Bruce Gable's bat, but continued on to the porch.

"Hunter's coming with me," I said, grabbing the boy's collar. "Next time just go in your house, Mr. Gable. There's no need to use a bat on this kid. He's just defending his mother."

"Then that low-class bitch should stop using her kid as a shield." Bruce looked at Janine and spit. "If I didn't have this bat, no telling what Hunter would do."

Hunter struggled to his feet, ready to lunge at Bruce.

I lowered the gun. "Hunter, it's not worth it. Let's go."

"You're making a big mistake," said Bruce. "That kid will break your heart. And his mother's likely to murder you."

My grip on the gun and the clamorous thunder kept Hunter heeled. He gave his mother a long look as we passed.

She stood with her arms crossed, staring at Bruce, seemingly oblivious to Hunter and I and even the rain.

Her blonde hair had unraveled from a twist and lay plastered against her head. The drenched and muddy clothes stuck to her body. Lightning tore through the clouds, and I realized I held a great conductor in my hand. Hunter and I ran for the truck and left the crazies to their own devices.

In the safety of the Datsun, I replaced my gun and then turned the key with a prayer. I felt pity for Hunter, who sat sullen and silent next to me. Not only did he have a messed up family situation, insanity seemed to run in his genes given what I had just witnessed between his mother and her sister.

"Where should I take you?" I asked. "You got some friends?"

Hunter stared out the side window, holding his shoulder and watching the rain bead and slick down the glass. Water dripped off his hat and down his shirt.

"You can't stay with me," I continued. "It wouldn't be appropriate. I'll take you home anyway so you can get your stuff."

"I ain't got no home," he mumbled.

I turned onto the county road, aiming for Cotton Pickin' Plantation. Maybe Miss Marion would take him in. She didn't seem to mind the boy even though she hated his mother. Hopefully she'd have some idea of what to do with him.

"Don't worry," I said. "We'll figure it out."

I cocked my head at the sound of a siren. Hunter jerked his head forward and then swiveled to check the rear windshield.

"Shit," he said. "Cops."

The wail magnified, and I squinted through the rain. "It's coming toward us."

Blue and red lights flashed in the distance as the road curved and banked.

"Let me out," said Hunter.

"Don't be stupid."

He grasped the handle of the door. "If you're not going to stop, slow down."

"What are you worried about. They're not after..."

Hunter popped open the door before I could finish. I hammered the brakes, fishtailed, and recovered. He held tight to the handle. Rain slashed the open door and his arm. As the truck steadied, Hunter pushed off the seat and jumped out the door. The truck skidded to a stop. He rolled onto the soft shoulder, hopped up, and limped into the corn field edging the road.

"Hunter," I yelled and slid across the bench. "Come back."

The siren scream halted. I glanced out my windshield. A brown and tan Crown Vic pumped its brakes and pulled to the left, stopping on the side of the road. As I pulled the passenger door shut, Luke donned his campaign hat and stepped out of the patrol car. Rain bounced off the brown felt brim covered in a plastic bonnet. He placed his hands on his hips and studied my truck for a moment before approaching.

I rolled down my driver's side window. "Hey there. What's up?"

"Didn't take long to find you," he said. "Lucky I was already in Sidewinder. Thank you for having the courtesy of stopping and not making me give chase. Not that it would have taken long in your P.O.S. truck."

I blinked.

"You want me to follow you to the Sheriff's Office?" he said. "If not, you're going to have to leave your truck and come in my vehicle."

"What for?"

"Did you happen to discharge a firearm on private property?"

"You mean at the Gables? You have got to be kidding me."

Luke drew his mouth into a tight scowl. "Do I look like I'm kidding?"

THIRTY-TWO

"Am I glad to see you," I said to Uncle Will. "I've been sitting in this interrogation room or whatever it's called for over an hour. And I'm still damp. My sundress and flip-flops are ruined. I'll catch my death."

I hopped up from my chair, crossed the small room in two steps, and reached to hug Will.

He blocked my hug with a crossed arm stance and steely look.

"You know what your deputy Luke Harper did to me?" I said. "He had the nerve to threaten to arrest me. After I came here peacefully to explain this whole ordeal. Someone had to stop him from putting me in a holding cell. Can you believe it?"

"Sit down," said Will.

I recognized that voice from the time I was ten, and he had caught Casey and I vandalizing a neighbor's corn crib with a can of paint. We had overheard the neighbor gossiping about Grandma Jo's poor parenting skills in controlling her trashy daughter and wildcat grandchildren. Of course, at the time, we didn't realize we supported the neighbor's opinion by vandalizing her barn. Even at ten, I had painted a pretty good likeness of the old biddy.

I scurried to my seat, and Will lowered himself into the chair across the table.

"I saw the complaint," said Will. "What kind of idiot shoots off her gun on the property of someone she doesn't even know?

They said you were trespassing and also accused you of appearing on their property two days before as a solicitor."

"I was not soliciting nor was I trespassing. Unless it's trespassing to give their nephew, Hunter, a ride. And then rescue the boy from having the tar beat out of him by Bruce Gable and a baseball bat. Did they mention that in their complaint?"

Will pushed out a long sigh. "What were you doing with Hunter Adams? You know he's a suspect in the poisoning case? And so are his mother and the Gables."

"I was paying my condolences to Marion Maynard and ran into Hunter. He asked me for a ride and I obliged. That's all."

"That's all, huh?"

"Pretty much."

He eyed me for what seemed an unnaturally long moment. "You didn't damage any property when you fired your shotgun. And you weren't criminally trespassing."

"I know that. And I'd do the same thing again. I'm glad I stopped Bruce Gable from hurting Hunter. Gable smashed Hunter's shoulder with a bat. If I'd done anything differently, I wouldn't have taken Hunter there in the first place."

"Maybe Gable wouldn't have hurt Hunter. Maybe he was just trying to incapacitate him. The boy was on the Gables property. And Hunter does have a history of violence. Did you think about that?"

"That's not what it looked like to me."

"You know Deputy Harper is ticked at you."

"I got that feeling when he hauled me in."

"I mean royally ticked," said Will. "Wanted to serve you with obstruction as well."

"He has issues."

"You have issues. I thought I told you to go easy on him."

"Are the badge bunnies going easy on him? Do you know they call him Luquified?"

"You know about them?" Will wiped off his astonished look and replaced it with a scowling squint.

"I know some women can't resist a man in uniform. I heard stories about them growing up, and I also heard I wasn't the only one bringing Luke barbecue."

"Doesn't mean he's taking their barbecue."

"He thinks I should learn to cook. And he never wants to do anything but watch TV or," I paused to catch my TMI, "other stuff."

Will wiped a hand over his face and peered at me through his fingers.

"His parents don't even know we're dating."

"This is none of my business." Will shoved out of his chair. "Give me a minute and then you can leave."

"Wait. Did anyone find Hunter?"

"We found him at the Maynard's. Mrs. Maynard is letting him stay in the apartment above the educational center. She said she'd keep an eye on him."

"At least that's good news. What about his mother?"

"Cherry," Will said and wagged a finger in my direction. "I'm ordering you to stay away from the Adams, Maynards, and the Gables. They are suspects in an ongoing investigation. I'm with Luke in serving you with obstruction if you spend any more time with Hunter Adams or even look cross-eyed at his relatives."

"How are they still suspects anyway? I thought Griffin Ward....wait, did you get the results back from the trash? What was in that Genuine Juice bottle Eloise drank?"

Will pinched his lips and fixed me with the sternest gaze he could muster.

"I gave you that evidence," I said. "Come on now. Was there anything in that Genuine Juice? I have been forthcoming with you."

"I'm the sheriff. You have to be forthcoming with me." He snorted at my look of exasperation. "All right, but keep your mouth shut. This is only because you brought me that evidence, but if I hear this story has been leaked..."

"I get it," I said. "What did you find out?"

"We got lucky with the lab. Of course they're concerned about our numbers. About fifty people were poisoned at the festival. Had to send some to neighboring counties to be treated once we found out it was arsenic."

"I know, I know." I waved my hand to hurry him along.

"Anyway, the lab processed all the food containers in that box of trash for arsenic. None in that Genuine Juice bottle."

"Damn," I said. "But the other juice did have arsenic in it."

"Was made after the festival. Griffin dated everything in keeping with health codes."

"So Griffin didn't do it?"

"Can't say since we did confiscate his property which had arsenic residue in it. But he didn't poison people with Genuine Juice at the festival. No evidence of that."

"But evidence of?"

"Arsenic in the Brunswick Stew cups," said Will. "From Team Cotton Pickin' Farm."

"Holy crap."

"Yep."

"I had them look for other toxins in that Genuine Juice bottle anyway. Guess what they found? Nicotine."

"Nicotine?" I paused for a long, meandering thought that brought me to a new conclusion. "Griffin knew cigarettes made Eloise feel better. That idiot put tobacco in her special remedy thinking it would cure her."

"Well, nicotine didn't kill her. Although it came pretty close. About fifty milligrams can paralyze internal muscles and she had plenty in her system. However, the arsenic did her in. Which means she was most likely poisoned by eating Brunswick Stew."

"A half dozen cups of Brunswick Stew. And Lewis was the cook. He probably tasted a lot of that stew."

"I assume so. And Eloise ate all that stew on an empty stomach with an already inflamed intestinal lining while taking an immune suppressor for her Crohn's." Uncle Will grabbed the door handle. "That's according to the M.E."

"So Griffin didn't kill her, but he did mess with her drinks." I stared at my hands, but snapped up at Uncle Will's sharp reply.

"We don't know who poisoned anything yet. So unless you want me to put a restraining order on you, you'll stay out of Sidewinder."

Will slammed the door, leaving my objection unheard. "Eloise's funeral tomorrow is in Sidewinder."

I reasoned that a funeral couldn't get me into trouble. It wasn't like I'd bring the Remington to church.

THIRTY-THREE

"I see you wore your funeral dress," I said to Leah upon exiting her mother's minivan.

We had arrived in Sidewinder for Eloise's funeral, held at the same church as her viewing. During the ride, I'd been too busy brooding over Luke's anger to notice Leah's god-awful dress in a kind of murky Mars Violet. I'd seen less ruffly dresses on those old china dolls with the spooky eyes and better rayon on my pre-deceased Grandma Jo.

"Those ruffles aren't hiding your chest. You just have ruffly boobs."

"Better than what you're wearing." She eyed my ultramarine-violet t-shirt dress.

I had spent the night gluing black and white sequins into a large, round pot on the back of my dress. "I ruined two church-worthy sundresses this week, so this is what I have left. Besides, I decorated this dress in Eloise's honor. It's a Raku pot."

"It looks like gigantic, sparkly butt cheeks."

"That's not a butt crack. The white sequins are supposed to represent dripping glaze."

"Everybody will think you're mooning the parishioners." Leah dipped into the minivan to lean over the seat. "Let me see if I have a sweater or something."

"Sweater? In this humidity?" The storm had passed, dropping the temperature a few degrees and replacing the blazing heat

with a sultry mugginess. My hair achieved a combination of limp-
ness and frizz that could only be saved with a ponytail. "Thanks for
driving again. My truck cannot handle this weather. It needs a new
starter and won't crank if it's overheated."

"And you don't want to be recognized in Sidewinder."

"That, too," I said and smiled.

"Which is why you wore a humongous butt on the back of
your dress."

"Not every idea of mine turns out perfectly."

"You think?" said Leah with a smirk.

We entered the church and exited an hour later, tears in our
eyes and noses running. We returned to Leah's minivan and followed the procession to the cemetery where they laid my good
friend to rest. I clung to Leah's hand and focused on the Parkers'
grief.

Back at the church, folks mingled in the hall while the church
ladies finished setting up for lunch. The scent of ham and casseroles hung in the air. We edged our way into the packed hall, seek-
ing out the drinks table for tea. Instead, I spied the dessert table
and steered Leah to check out the pies and cookies.

"It wasn't Griffin," I whispered to Leah.

"What wasn't Griffin?"

"The poisoner."

"Are they sure?" she said. "He was real threatening when we
visited him."

"Well, it wasn't the Genuine Juice that poisoned people at the
festival. I'm not supposed to be telling anybody this, by the way. It
was the Brunswick Stew."

"That's horrible."

"There might still be a killer walking amongst us," I said.
"Scary thought. And I just had another one. Out of the Cotton Pickin' Team, only two were poisoned. Lewis and Marion. Hunter and
his mother never got sick. Isn't that strange?"

Leah nodded and elbowed me to stop talking. Someone
called out to bless the food.

I waited for the prayer to finish, then leaned toward Leah. "That means Hunter and his mom never tasted the stew. Maybe because they knew not to taste it."

"I'm not going to eat here."

"Good idea." I scrunched my mouth to the side and bobbed my ponytail. "Except these pies look real good. I'm sure if we found out who made them, we'd be safe."

An onslaught of folks desperate for sweet potato casserole and pimento sandwiches jostled us. A man with a floppy comb-over shoved me out of his way in his reach for a slice of icebox pie. A hand caught me by the elbow, saved my stumble, and spun me near the wall. Luke released my elbow to cross his arms across his chest. He had exchanged his tan deputy uniform for a dark blue suit.

I wondered if he worked undercover or had taken time off to attend the funeral in consideration of my friendship with the Parkers. Then I caught his look. His charcoal eyes burned like double braziers, lit with an internal fire called "I've Had It Up To Here With You."

"What," he said in a voice better used for a slow-witted five-year-old, "are you doing here?"

I gave him my best "duh" look. "Attending my friend Eloise Parker's funeral. She was poisoned, remember?"

I watched a curl threaten to break free from his carefully groomed locks and bounce onto his forehead. I empathized with that curl. Luke shoved the curl in place.

"You aren't supposed to be in Sidewinder," he said.

"Kind of hard to make it to her funeral otherwise."

"Cherry, I warned you about interfering. And Sheriff Thompson also told you to stay away."

"Luke," I blew out a disgusted sigh. "I haven't been interfering with your job. I've paid some sympathy visits and helped a kid who comes from a family more screwed up than mine. He has a murdering mother."

"That kid has serious anger management issues. And we don't know if his mother is the perp."

"Oh, I know about Hunter's anger issues," I said. "He almost broke my arm at the hospital the other day. And his mother murdered the guy her ex-husband is convicted of killing. Everyone knows that."

Luke's lips disappeared. His shoulders tightened and fists clenched. I waited for his head to pop off his neck. A nerve throbbed in his forehead.

"I'll just be going whenever Leah is ready."

"Leah's ready now," said Luke.

"Let me go ask her. She had her eye on that lemonade pie."

"Go. Now."

"I don't know what you're so heated up about."

"You are giving me an ulcer."

"Maybe it's all the free barbecue that's hurting your stomach. Luquified."

The breath he pulled in made his nostrils flare.

I needed to stop. I didn't really want to give him an ulcer.

"Miss Cherry."

I peered around Luke. Miss Marion wormed her way through the crowd. She wore a straw hat, black sheath dress, and pearls like a proper griever. I seemed to be the only one at the funeral wearing tribute clothes.

Luke stepped to the side and sidled behind me. "You're friends with another suspect?"

"She's no suspect," I muttered. "That's Mrs. Maynard. She was poisoned herself."

"Anyone related to Cotton Pickin' Farm is a suspect."

"Hey, Miss Marion," I said in a voice loud enough to cover Luke's mention. "So nice of you to come in light of your situation."

"It's a small town, honey. If we didn't support each other at funerals and weddings, what else would we do?"

"Thank you for taking Hunter in," I said. "I know he's a handful, but he's still a kid. It's not his fault his mother is," I stopped myself from bringing up the home-wrecker to the home-wrecked, "his mother."

"Well, I've always had a soft spot for Hunter. And you're right. You can't pick your parents. That's why I appreciate my own daddy so much. The viewing and funeral for Lewis are on Saturday. Please visit me anytime. I'd appreciate the company."

I cranked my head to catch Luke's eye. "I would love to spend time with you at your home in Sidewinder..."

He glowered with a brief shake of his head.

"I'm not sure if I'll make it to the funeral," I finished.

"Oh, of course," she said. "Well, I guess I'll get to my dinner."

She turned, and we watched the crowd part to let her through. As she passed, folks nodded at one another. Some bent in whispered confidences. Marion held her petite head high as she paced through the congregation. She took a seat amid empty chairs. Folks stood with plates in hand, while Marion sat alone.

"Look at that poor woman," I said to Luke. "A social pariah in a town her family has lived in for generations. Because of her ass of a husband."

"Speaking of asses," said Luke, "why in God's name are you wearing one at a funeral?"

"It is not an ass. It's a Raku pot in memory of Eloise." Tears threatened and I rubbed my eyes with the back of my hand. "Don't you care Miss Marion sits alone? She asked me to spend time with her, and I can't because y'all don't want me in Sidewinder."

Luke shifted in place. "Visit her all you want after this crime is cleared up, but for now I don't want you in Sidewinder."

"Are you speaking as a cop or yourself?"

"Does it matter?"

"It matters if I'm going to get arrested."

"You are so frustrating." He shoved his hands in his pockets and stalked off.

At Luke's disappearance, Marion threaded through the crowd, holding a foil-covered plate.

"I almost forgot," Marion said and shoved the plate in my hands. "Watching you eat the donuts, you look like you enjoyed sweets. I made you brownies."

My heart crumpled into a beating mass of pity for lonely ladies with cheating dead husbands. "Thank you, Miss Marion. You know? I'm coming to your husband's funeral no matter what."

"Thank you, honey. You are such a dear. Don't you share those brownies. They are all for you."

My stomach sang, and Marion looked at me sharply.

"Did you hear that?" she asked. "Sounded like a broken generator? I wonder if I should tell the church."

Leah sauntered up behind me. "Good gracious, Cherry. Do we need to get you something to eat?"

"I'll just be going and leave you to your friends." Marion patted my arm and minced to her seat.

"Now there's a lady." Leah watched Marion slip to her still vacant table. "Poor thing, all alone. Hey, I just saw you with Luke. What happened? He doesn't look too happy with you, hon. What are you doing to that man?"

"I've no idea," I said. "Maybe if he'd tell me, I could do something about it. But that's part of the problem."

"What's the other part of the problem?"

"He wouldn't tell me that either."

We retraced our steps to the dessert table. Leah took a plate and eased aside for me. I held my brownies and eyed the red velvet cake covered in whipped cream cheese icing. A woman in a cow print dress pulled back the plate of cake she had held toward me.

"I know you," she said. "Where do I know you?"

"I'm Ed Ballard's granddaughter from Halo," I said, which generally served as explanation for the older community. "I'm also an artist. I'll just take a slice of that red velvet you've got there."

"I don't know the Ballards or any artists," she said, looking me up and down. "You were with Pearl Taylor at bingo. But you were bigger and had brown hair. And you didn't look like a lady."

"That'd be my sister, Casey."

"Your skirt distracted our bingo caller. Next time you need to dress properly."

"It wasn't me."

"Don't sass me. Maybe you're the reason the bingo was shut down. Maybe word got out girls with loose virtues been coming."

"Bingo was shut down?"

"You didn't know?" She set the cake on the table. "Mr. Max's bingo license was suspended. Sheriff's office is investigating."

"Really?"

"You think I'm telling stories?" She gave me a slow gander. "You're dressed more appropriately except for that doo-dad on your back. Is that supposed to be a peach? Why's it black and white?"

"It's a Raku pot. In honor of Eloise."

"Well, I never. Wearing drug paraphernalia on your dress to a funeral?" She whipped the cake away and handed it to the person behind me. "Get. We don't need that here."

"A Raku pot is the kind of pottery Eloise made..."

"Looks more like a picture of someone who lost their britches," said the familiar baritone behind me, "and bent over."

I turned and caught Luke's stern look.

"I warned you to leave." He forked a piece of red velvet cake in his mouth and walked away.

"Mercy," said cow print dress. "Of all things. Have you no respect?" She hollered behind her. "Jason. Dan. Help this girl to the door. Did you see what she's wearing to the poor Parkers funeral?"

"Don't listen to that Luke Harper," I said. "He just wants to get rid of me."

"Thank the good Lord for that. We don't need you and your provocative clothing disrespecting the dead and her family."

"What's more appropriate for Eloise's funeral? Cows or the very object of art the deceased made?" I said. "Do you even know anything about Eloise Parker? She would have loved this embellishment."

I halted my speech. Two beefy young men in clean overalls and neat checked shirts ambled forward.

"Momma?" They said to cow print dress.

"Get this druggie out of here," she said. "She's looking for food handouts and wearing pictures of derrieres on her dress. This kind of thing may fly in Atlanta but we have something called decency out here."

Jim and Dan grabbed my elbows. I gripped my brownies.

"Ask the Parkers who I am," I said. "I'm not a druggie. I'm Eloise's friend."

"One of her arty friends, I suppose, who spends her days doing drugs, vandalizing buildings, and calling it art," said cow print. "Get her out of here."

"I don't do graffiti. I'm a portraitist!"

Jim and Dan lurched forward, dragging me with them. Leah dropped her plate on the table and scurried after my escorts. The crowd parted, creating a path toward the hall's back door. Words flew about the drug-addled graffiti artist wearing X-rated clothing to a funeral. The church hall version of the telephone game.

As we passed Luke, he smiled with his teeth. "Told you to leave."

"Tell them who I am," I said. "I keep getting kicked out of Eloise's services."

"And whose fault is that?"

"I'll get you for this, Luke Harper," I hollered.

"Here's the thing," I said to Leah. "After that fight with Todd, I feel kind of bad about getting the Bear shut down. Pearl thinks the bingo was on the up-and-up, and Casey thinks I've got it in for Mr. Max because he's rich. That's not true. And to prove it, I'm going to apologize and give him these brownies."

We had sped out of Sidewinder for fear of pitchforks and torches. Now Leah's minivan idled in the drive of Max Avtaikin's reproduction of Tara. She stared at the cannon and bit her lip.

"I don't know if this is a good idea," said Leah. "Every time I go somewhere with you, we get kicked out or threatened."

"You're exaggerating. We've gone plenty of places without getting kicked out. I'm just apologizing to the Bear. Would I give up these delicious looking brownies if I didn't feel remorseful?"

"That's true. I'd never known you to re-gift food."

"Exactly. And I was the only one who didn't get cake at the funeral dinner. I'm starving, but I know Mr. Max enjoys baked goods, so I'm putting his needs before my own."

"That's very Christian of you," Leah said and smiled. "You want me to come with you?"

"Actually, he might be a teensy upset about losing the bingo, so you wait here. Just in case I'm threatened or kicked out."

Leah folded her arms over her ruffly bosom and frowned.

I hopped from the van, strolled onto Max's wide porch, and pressed the doorbell. A long minute later, Max opened the door and greeted me with a raised eyebrow.

"Hello, Bear," I said. "I've come to apologize."

Both eyebrows rose.

"I heard about your bingo getting shut down. And it might have been my fault. I wanted to give you these brownies."

"You ask the police to investigate my legitimate business and then you bring the cookies? This is your apology for killing my business? Cookies?"

"Brownies. Not cookies." I pressed the plate into his hands before he could curl them into fists. "And if your business is legitimate, the police will figure that out pretty quickly. No harm done."

"It is not how this bureaucracy works, Artist. It is not with the police I worry. There is threat of Internal Revenue Service and the state revenue service to investigate. Do you know how this will cost me?"

"Not really. But if everything is legit, then—"

The door slammed shut before I could finish my thought.

With hot cheeks, I ambled back to the minivan. I slid into the van, avoiding Leah's eyes, and slunk in my seat.

"Well, good news is I didn't get kicked out or threatened," I said.

"Bad news?"

"I have ticked off three guys in two days. And probably riled up a mob of grandmas by shutting down bingo for good."

"What now?'

"Guess I'll go to Red's. Sticks is playing anyway. If they're going to tar and feather me, I'd rather have a beer first."

THIRTY-FOUR

Friday night at Red's County Line found the bar ridiculously congested. The usual Friday patrons—Halo's twenty-somethings, lushes, and couples on dates—crowded the long, wooden bar and surrounding tables. However, middle-aged and elderly women thronged the far end of the room near the stage. Another factor pointing toward some misalignment in my universe.

I avoided that end of the room. Between Todd's stage presence and a mob of angry ex-bingo players, I knew to keep my bottom glued to my bar stool. Better yet, I would also try to keep my mouth glued shut. Which was much harder.

"Well, Red," I said, "Looks like I might be single again."

"Not surprised." Red deposited a long-neck before me. "You're a commitment-phobic, relationship self-sabotager. Which, oddly enough, attracts men like sugar ants to peanut butter."

"Don't give me your pop psychology tonight. It's not all my fault. Luke has issues, too. His family's defects are just hidden behind money and proper behavior."

"Listen to yourself." Red shook his head. "Just like with Todd. Nothing but excuses. You get your painting done?"

"No. I still need a model. Are you sure you won't do it? You don't even have to pose nude. Skivvies will work and of course, there's the body paint. I swear nobody from Halo will ever see it. I'm sending the paintings to a gallery in Athens if I can get them approved."

In answer, Red flipped his towel over his shoulder and strode to the other end of the bar.

I swiveled in my seat to observe the group of women gathered near the stage. Their purses and sweaters claimed all the tables circling the dance floor. Somewhere in the mob, Pearl waved a beer and clamored for "Hot Pants McIntosh." Chablis and mint juleps circulated amongst the rioters.

Leaving his table of mechanic and hardware clerk friends, Cody sauntered to the bar. Beer in hand, he eased between me and the next occupied stool.

"How you doing, sis?" he said.

"Not so good. I got kicked out of Eloise's funeral dinner."

"Huh. Don't let it bug you. What you want with some reheated casseroles anyway?"

"Love you, brother. I needed that."

His face reddened. Turning away from me, he leaned against the bar to scout the room for girls. "So you and Luke are on the skids?"

"Maybe," I said. "He's kind of mad at me for interfering in Eloise's murder case. So things between us are kind of muddy."

"Listen, I wanted to tell you about some pictures I found—" He cut off his statement as Luke and Shawna strode through Red's front door.

My heart sank to the ruby tips of my toenails. I swiveled back to face the bar and swigged my beer. I could feel Luke's fiery glower skimming over my cinnabar green halter and settling on my shoulders.

"Damn, he works fast," said Cody. "He's out with Shawna?"

"Shawna's his cousin," I said, noticing my voice lacked conviction.

"Everyone knows they're not related. She's more kin to us than Luke."

"You're really cheering me up here."

"Sorry." Cody scooted off his stool and tossed several bills on the bar.

"You're not staying to listen to Sticks? Todd'll be disappoint-ed." I said. "Where are you going?"

"Let's just say, you're not the only one who has issues with the Bransons. I stay here and I'm fixing to fight. Better I go."

My gaze followed him to the door, searching for clues as to why he wanted to fight Bransons. As a guy, Cody remained a mystery to me. I never looked for fights. They just happened out of the blue. And who was he planning to fight? I hoped it was Shawna, but I've never known him to belt a girl. I set aside the enigma that was my brother and returned to gazing in the bar mirror, scanning for Greek model prospects. And pretending not to watch Luke chat with a table full of Shawna's snobby friends.

Red sidled to Cody's abandoned spot, retrieved his empty glass, and scooped up the money. "Cody's not staying?"

"Guess not," I said. "He's been acting kind of strange. And he's mad at the Bransons."

"Why?"

"I have no idea. We've suffered from their ugly talk before. Don't know why it's bothering him now. Doesn't bother me much."

"The meek shall inherit." Red smiled.

"Then I'm pretty much screwed," I said. "Maybe you should tell me the line about the poor instead."

Red laughed and strolled off.

I waved Casey to the bar. Her plaid and pleated micro-mini skirt brushed the tops of her thighs as she walked. A breeze stirred her hair as men's heads turned to watch her approach the bar.

"What's going on with Cody?" I asked.

"Dunno," Casey shrugged. "Somebody's peed in his Wheat-ies, I guess. You know, he's been asking a lot of questions about Momma lately."

"Momma?" For twenty years, the family avoided mention of Christy Tucker. Now she popped into conversation like a Jack Russell on steroids.

"Momma and Daddy. It's different for Cody, you know. He never knew either one."

"Not like I got to know them much by age five," I said.

"It's still different. He was a baby. And Cody can do the math between his birthday and daddy's funeral. He's got questions."

"I agree with Grandpa. Those things are better left buried."

Casey shrugged, causing her cropped shirt to rise and expose her belly button ring. A whistle rose from the table behind me. She pretended to glare at the young men pursing their lips and left me to saunter to their table.

I ignored their flirting at the sight of Luke striding to the bar. He caught my gaze in the mirror. I held it, searching for the old Luke. The gray eyes looked as cool as wet slate.

"Thanks a lot for getting me thrown out of Eloise's funeral dinner," I said as he squeezed between me and the next stool.

"I told you I didn't want you in Sidewinder."

"How can you think I'd stay away from Eloise's funeral?"

"You could have asked me to take you instead of Leah."

"I didn't want a police escort. And I didn't get much support at Eloise's visitation when your step-cousin attacked me." I pivoted to glare toward Shawna. "By the way, are you out with Shawna?"

"I just got off work. Shawna was at Mom's house when I went home to change."

"Does Shawna know you're not on a date?"

"You and Shawna need to cut it out," he muttered. "You're both going to drive me to an early grave."

"Why would Shawna drive you to an early grave? I thought that was my role."

He leaned his elbows on the bar and watched Red fix a drink.

"She's hanging out with your parents an awful lot," I spoke to his back. "I don't remember seeing her in Halo much until you moved back home."

Luke swigged his beer and swept his gaze down the line of people crowding the bar.

"I knew it," I said. "Is she just stalking you or are you enjoying each other's company? Is she the one bringing you barbecue at work or are those just plain old badge bunnies?"

"I told you I didn't take anybody's barbecue but yours." He set his bottle on the bar and fiddled with a napkin. "Momma and JB like Shawna. They're hoping we'll get along."

I spun around and slammed my hand on the bar. "Why don't you tell me these things?"

"Because I know it'll piss you off. I don't want to date Shawna. She's not my type. You're my type. When you're not acting like a fool idiot by getting beat up in parking lots and hanging around a bunch of murder suspects."

"That's not the point, Luke. The point is your parents want you to date Shawna because you never told them you're going out with me."

"Can we do this somewhere else?" He said, yanking on my elbow. "I don't like my private life made public, especially in Red's."

"In case someone guesses we know each other?"

However, I also didn't want Red's public witnessing our fight, so I followed Luke outside and around the building.

We halted near a side entrance where we wouldn't be interrupted by incoming Sticks fans. I crossed my arms and leaned against the corrugated metal wall.

"I'm sick of all the secrecy," I said. "During our previous relationship, we were away at school. No big deal that I didn't meet your parents. But I'm an adult now. I said my piece at Eloise's visitation. You don't tell me anything. You don't tell your family anything. Normal relationships don't work like that. If you can't acknowledge me to your family, I don't see us having a future."

"You better be careful of what you say."

"At least I'm saying it. It's called communication."

"I was clear about how I felt about you interfering in my job. Communication also means listening."

"I admit it's not my best attribute," I said. "Todd implied the same thing. He's mad at me, too, for shutting down Max's operation."

"Get this through your thick head. You didn't shut down Avtaikin's operation. He shut himself down. According to the gambling laws of Georgia, anyone using a license for bingo is not supposed to make a profit of more than thirty dollars a day."

I gasped. "No wonder he's so angry. I'm real sure he was making more than thirty bucks."

"And thanks to you, your nosing around tipped him off. He poured all that money back into the Ladies Auxiliary coffers preceding our warrant to search his office and computer."

"Thanks to me? And he made me think I busted him."

"Cherry," Luke said and grasped my shoulders. "You need to cut this stuff out."

"I had lemonade and cookies with the man. Had a tour of his house." I skipped the part about scaling his wall to look for errant poker games. "I wonder if Max's air conditioning wasn't on to have a couple extra days to cook the books."

"This is what I'm talking about. Why are you even considering the hows and whens of Max Avtaikin's money laundering schemes?"

"Money laundering? You think?"

"Never mind what I think. Why can't you leave well enough alone?"

"I had to find out what Todd was doing at the Bear's house."

"Why? Why do you have to find out what Todd is doing at Avtaikin's house? Todd is a grown man. It's his business."

"He's my friend. That makes it my business. Just like with Eloise. I can't help that."

Luke released me to fold his arms over his chest. I noticed the twitch in his eye had returned with a vengeance. "You would interfere in a police investigation to help a friend."

"Of course," I said and then realized the stupidity of blurting out the truth. Me and my predilection for honesty.

The nerve above Luke's eye revved from twitch to hammer.

"I think I better go back inside," I said.

"I'm going home to think carefully about this conversation."

That didn't sound too promising for me. My lips bunched together into a trembling pout, but I had no sympathy for them. I blamed their ineffectiveness for some of this mess. Luke needed body heat my lips couldn't provide.

He gazed at my traitorous lips for a long moment and walked away.

If I hadn't broken us up earlier, I sure did a good job of it now.

THIRTY-FIVE

I hung outside of Red's and watched a server and cook steal out the side door to smoke. My stomach felt tight and queasy. I didn't feel like having a beer or dealing with Red's crowd. I also didn't feel like returning to my empty house. Alone. I could go to the farm, but even Pearl had abandoned Grandpa to watch Sticks perform. Watching fishing shows on a Friday night with Grandpa seemed too depressing to consider. I decided to go inside Red's.

And because the universe hated me, Shawna waited for me in the vestibule. I wouldn't say she looked trashy, but someone must have helped pour her into her zebra print sundress. That dress was a marvel of modern engineering.

"Where's Luke?" she demanded.

"The heck if I know." And because I wasn't feeling particularly friendly, I added a bit of helpful advice. "Did you know your boobs are supposed to go inside your dress? For future reference."

I didn't think Amazons like Shawna could get taller, but she stretched into a colossal tower of rage. Her fist swung and cracked my chin. I stumbled and fell into a rack of real estate ads. Above me, the Coors Lite sign blinked and cut off. Panting, Shawna rubbed her fist and stared at me. I tried to avert my gaze from her heaving chest, but the shock of getting cold-cocked had my eyes transfixed on the rise and fall of her double endowments. I was reminded of my Sidewinder nemesis and wondered if a difference in bra size could cause one to become a mortal enemy.

I shook my head out of my stupor, worked my jaw, and was hit with pain. "What the hell?" I cried. "I think you broke my jaw."

"If I broke your jaw, you couldn't talk," Shawna said. "And believe me, I wish I had broken your jaw. I would love to keep you from talking. Permanently."

"What is your problem? Since when do you punch me for making a remark about your clothes? Did you run out of comebacks?"

"You had that coming and you know why. And I've got more than that in me. I could beat the crap out of your puny self. Or worse. You remember that."

"I swear I don't know what I did. Is this about Luke?"

"Ha," she said, swinging the door open. With nary a glance back, she traipsed into the parking lot. A minute later, I heard the growl of her Mustang.

"Ha?" I repeated, rubbing my chin.

I hauled out of the mess of housing brochures and stumbled through the door into the bar. A new patron occupied my stool. I pouted a minute, then pushed through the crowd until I reached the bar. Red raised his head from washing glasses. His mouth dropped open. I should have checked my hair and makeup in the ladies before a public appearance.

"Who did that?" he said. "Luke?"

"Did what?" I said and attempted a smile. Which hurt. "You got some ice?"

"Go to the kitchen," he said. "I'll meet you there."

I sighed, pushed through the knots of drinkers, and into the kitchen. Red and Casey shoved me into a chair and pointed fingers at my face. I glared and threatened to bite.

"Look at her," he yelled to Casey. "That bastard. On my property!"

Heads popped up from behind the pass through at Red's exclamation. The kitchen staff abandoned their cooking and chopping to add to the huddle. Which did me no favors.

"I appreciate the concern, but ice?" I said. "Please?"

"Unbelievable," said Casey. She grabbed my chin, yanking my head up for examination. "It's huge."

"Let go," I said and reached for the baggie of ice handed to me by Red. "Is it already turning? That was fast."

"I never would have thought. When I saw your lip the other day," said Red, shaking his head. "I don't care if he is a cop."

"What happened?" said Todd, striding toward us. Leah, Sid, and Lewellyn, the Sticks bassist, paced after him.

Casey spun around and held her hands out. "Calm yourselves. She's fine. Just a little bruised." She turned to me. "You should have told us. Is this why you haven't been able to kiss Luke? And wanted to pretend to cook for him? Does he scare you?"

"Now hold on just a minute." I hopped up from the chair. "Call off the lynch mob. It wasn't Luke. I know we were fighting in the parking lot, but we were just arguing."

"You haven't been able to kiss Luke?" asked Todd.

"Focus, Todd," said Casey. "Now Cherry, don't try to deny it. Look what happened to Eloise. She hid the abuse and her boyfriend killed her."

"I am not Eloise," I said. "And it turns out Griffin didn't kill her. Probably. Unless he somehow poisoned the stew."

Casey shook her head and glanced at Red. He folded his brawny arms over his chest and pursed his lips. Then noticed the crowd in the kitchen. "Is anyone waiting on customers? Quit your gawking and get back to work."

"It wasn't Luke," I said. "It was Shawna. She caught me in the breezeway and socked me."

"Shawna? Are you sure?" said Red.

"Pretty sure. I had my eyes open until her fist met my jaw."

"Why would Shawna hit you?"

"I have no idea. I might have said something about the way she fit into her dress, but it didn't warrant a smackdown."

"Man, Cherry. You scared the crap out of me. You've gotta give it a rest sometime," said Red and slammed through the swinging doors into the bar.

"We're on in five," said Sid, annoyed I'd disrupted their Sticks huddle by getting slugged. "Let's get going."

"Honey, next time either keep your mouth shut or duck." Leah patted my head. "Come on, Todd."

Todd cast me an unreadable look—one I recognized from his serious poker games—and turned to traipse after his band members. I swung the ice to my chin and watched him swagger away. It should have been a comforting sight, but somehow Todd's butt in tight, faux-leather pants didn't have the magical effect it usually did.

"Shawna, huh?" said Casey. "Don't you worry. We'll get even."

"You have any idea why Shawna keeps trying to take me out?" I said. "Because I'm mystified."

Casey cracked her knuckles and swung her hair behind her shoulders. "Don't you worry about a thing. Cody and I will take care of this."

"That doesn't make me feel better. It actually makes me feel worse."

"That's just your pain talking."

I followed her into the bar. Pearl waited for us at the kitchen entrance. Tonight she had abandoned her goat t-shirt for a biker halter that showed off her blue goat-giraffe. Casey cast her a scathing glance and scurried away.

"Hey Pearl. Guess you're excited for Sticks' performance."

"I've got something to say to you, missy," she said. "I may have become a mother figure to you—"

"Not really," I said. "But go on ahead with the lecture. One more tonight won't kill me."

"What happened to your chin?"

"Ran into a fist," I said, keeping the ice over the spreading bruise. "You were saying?"

"We are very upset with you."

"Who's we?" I said, hoping she didn't mean Grandpa. I wasn't ready for that alignment.

"The Ladies Auxiliary. You had Mr. Max's bingo shut down."

"Not according to Deputy Luke Harper."

"Don't try to deny it. I told the ladies what you were doing during our last bingo meeting. Now we have no bingo because of you. And our sweet Mr. Max is guilty until proven innocent. He may be audited. The poor man."

"You told the bingo ladies I busted the Bear?" Fear helped me forget my pain. I lowered my ice-bag and focused on the Judas before me. "What have you done, Pearl?"

I flashed a look over Pearl's shoulder to the septuagenarian rabble who had turned their back on the stage and now glared at me. After their second round of drinks, the giant purse wielding mob didn't look eager to party. They looked eager to kick my ass.

"Oh, crap." I scrambled through the swinging kitchen doors and bumped into Sticks as they lined up to take the stage.

"Where are you going?" said Leah. "You're going to miss our performance."

"Believe me, you don't want me out there." I hugged her and backed up, careful to not step on her stilettoed toes. "Sing pretty and let me know how it goes."

"Come on," said Todd. "Your face doesn't look that bad. It won't disrupt the set."

"This is not about my face." I scowled at the blond beefcake. "Your admirers want to run me out of town."

"Admirers?" asked Sid. He smoothed his hair and tucked in his t-shirt.

"The bingo crowd," I said. "I don't think they even qualify as cougars. And they're furious with me for shutting down bingo."

"I'm mad at you, too," said Todd. "Now I've got to find another job."

"I'm sorry. Luke said it would have happened anyway. You can't make money off of bingo in Georgia."

"That Luke," said Todd. "What does he know?"

"The law? Because he's a cop?" said Leah. "Cherry's right. It's better this way, Todd. You don't want to get into trouble."

"That's what I've been trying to tell him," I said. "But I am sorry, Todd."

"Come on, y'all," said Sid. "Let's get this done. You can chit-chat with Cherry any old time. We have fans waiting."

He slung his guitar over his back and pushed through the swinging door. The clamor of the crowd swelled. A chant of "We want bingo" switched to "We want Hot Pants." Red would have his hands full tonight.

And I was sorry I couldn't enjoy the show. Not so much for Sticks, who I had heard numerous times, but watching Pearl peel off her twenty-four hour bra and throw it on the stage would have been worth the price of Shawna's wallop.

THIRTY-SIX

The walk to 211 Loblolly did me good. I successfully dodged bingo ambushers with a wary vigilance that kept me from ruminating on all the men who currently held grudges against me. Particularly one Luke Harper, whose lips I missed.

However, Grandma Jo's stories about men who try on shoes and take milk from cows without purchase lay heavy in my mind. How could we have a life together if Luke couldn't utter a few words about me to his mother, for heaven's sake? And let his stepfather think Shawna could have a chance of entwining her branch of the Branson tree around JB's trunk? That thought made my blood percolate.

As I approached Great-Gam's old cottage, I took heed to scout the area. The Datsun rested in the driveway, waiting for a new starter or a trade-in. I slipped past the sawhorse tables holding art supplies and thrift store junk. The glow from the kitchen fluorescents through the door's window gave me pause. I ran through the list of folks with access to the house. Most of that list could be found at Red's. Except Luke. And Cody.

I unlocked the back door and called out, expecting Cody to answer. Pausing in the doorway, I swept my gaze over the empty kitchen. I had no living room furniture to speak of other than the fainting couch. My bedroom TV was of the small and tube variety. If Cody would be anywhere in the house, it would be the kitchen, close to the beer cooler known as a refrigerator.

I retreated into the carport, spun toward the Datsun-turned-armory, and retrieved my Remington. Then proceeded to tiptoe through the house with a racked and loaded gun.

The front room and bathroom were also empty. I peeked in my unoccupied bedroom and relaxed my grip on the gun. A small twist of heartache stabbed my chest. I had half-hoped to find Luke sprawled on my bed asleep with the TV on, waiting for me. However, waking a cop while holding a shotgun was never a good idea, so probably best my wish didn't come true. I propped the Remington over my shoulder and kicked off my flip-flops. My gaze left the bedroom and fell upon the guest room door.

I flipped the shotgun around and approached the closed door. Grasping the pump with my left hand, I reached for the doorknob with my right. The door swung open. I slid my finger to the trigger guard and sidled into the doorway. A quick scan of the dark room revealed a lump lying on the bed. Squinting, I stepped into the room for a better look at my sleeping Goldilocks.

"Crap," I whispered and backed out of the doorway, shutting the door behind me.

Goldilocks was Hunter Adams.

THIRTY-SEVEN

With Hunter dead to the world (although considering the rash of poisonings, I should probably check my use of metaphors), I decided to let him sleep and deal with my angry boy stalker in the morning. I had had enough drama for the night and occupied my frustrations on a sketchpad with a box of pastels.

Early the next morning, I drank coffee and waited for Hunter to wake. It seemed the sleeping habits of teenagers were worse than adults with hangovers. Finally, I kicked open his door, carrying the Wingmaster over my shoulder for added affect.

"Hunter Adams," I said. "This house is not a hotel. Get your butt out of my bed and yourself together. Meet me in the kitchen in five. You've got some explaining to do."

I spun on my heel, slamming the door behind me. Seeing the kid shoot to the ceiling and fall on the floor almost made his unexpected visit worthwhile.

Ten minutes later, Hunter dragged his bedraggled form into my kitchen. He ran a hand through his hair and collapsed in a chair.

"What are you doing in my house?" I said. "And how did you get in? As a matter of fact, how do you know where I live?"

He rolled his eyes, folded his arms on the table, and buried his head in his hands. "You got anything to eat?"

"No," I said. "I never have anything to eat. So keep that in mind. Now, answer my questions."

"I couldn't think where else to go." He propped his chin on his arms. "I hitched a ride to Halo. My mom is missing."

I set aside the lecture on hitchhiking for another time. "I thought Miss Marion was putting you up. And maybe your mom is just finding a place to settle."

"Miss Marion is okay, but it's weird to be at Cotton Pickin' by myself. Mom doesn't answer her phone. She might be really pissed at me."

I handed him a cup of coffee and paced the kitchen. By helping Hunter, not only would I break that last straw held by Luke, I'd also defy Uncle Will.

"Why do you think she's mad at you?" I asked. "For almost getting the tar beat out of you by Bruce Gable?"

"No."

"You want to give me a clue?"

"You can't call the cops," he said and jerked to sitting. "Promise me."

I sank onto a chair next to him. "Hunter, what did you do?"

"I did it. I put something in Lewis and Miss Parker's stew."

"Oh," I said, while my brain screamed several obscenities. I hopped up and resumed pacing. "Okay. We'll find your momma and get this sorted out. It's better if you come clean."

"I don't want to go to jail," his voice cracked. "I didn't mean to kill them. It was just a prank. Miss Parker gave me a hard time at school. And I wanted to get back at Lewis for taking up with my mom. I hate him."

"I know you didn't mean it, honey. Don't worry. Just let me find your mom. You're going to need her. Have you called your Aunt Belinda? Has she seen Janine?"

"Aunt Belinda said she and Uncle Bruce decided to get out of town for a few days. They took off Thursday night, after calling the cops on you. They haven't seen her."

I narrowed my eyes. "Do the police know the Gables have left town? They were suspects. They should know better."

"Doesn't really matter, does it?"

"I'm calling the sheriff's office. I won't tell them about you, Hunter. But they can put an APB out on your truck and find your mom. They also need to know your aunt and uncle skedaddled. As far as the police are concerned, three of their suspects are missing. They'll find your mom fast. And then we'll figure out what to do."

I walked into the front room and snatched my phone from the charger. Hunter followed me and watched while I left a message on Uncle Will's voice mail.

"You're pissing me off, Scarecrow."

"Let's get you something to eat, Hunter." Hopefully food would placate the boy. "I'm taking you to the farm. You'll get a good breakfast, and we'll figure out what to do next."

The lane to the farm remained blessedly clear of goats and other creatures. I parked under the leafy oak and hopped out of the truck, suspicious of the unnatural calm.

Hunter banged his door shut, and I heard his grunt of surprise. I couldn't help a smirk.

"Don't worry, Hunter," I called. "They're relatively harmless. Which one is it?"

"Cool," said Hunter, circling the Datsun's front end. "They're just like dogs. I never had a pet."

"What?"

I scowled as two goats—one brown, one white—trotted behind Hunter in their very best goat behavior. I scrutinized the turncoats and caught Snickerdoodle's eye. Tater turned tail and shot toward the porch. Snickerdoodle stopped, lowered her head, and pawed the ground. I spun and ran for the house, leaving Hunter behind.

A few minutes later, Hunter sat at the table.

A plate of eggs, biscuits, and sausage and a steaming bowl of grits lay before him. Intent on their breakfast, Grandpa and Cody barely gave Hunter a glance. I eased into a seat across the table and began loading my plate.

Relieved that Pearl didn't grace the farm with her presence this early in the day, I chose not to bring up the events of the previous evening. No one remarked on the shiner on my chin. I figured Cody and Casey had already conferred, and as the offender was Shawna, they chose not to report the news to Grandpa.

Casey ambled forward, a pot and ladle in her hand. "Gravy," she yawned and dumped a pool over Hunter's biscuit.

He stared in open-mouthed wonder at the goddess before him. As Casey stumbled to the stove, his eyes did their best to peel off her boxer shorts and Braves t-shirt.

"Hey," I said. "That's my sister. Mind your manners."

Cody snickered, and Grandpa tipped his head up to acknowledge the newcomer. "Who's this now?"

"This here is Hunter Adams," I said. "I need to keep him at the farm for a little while. He didn't really murder anyone. I'm waiting to hear from Uncle Will on what to do."

Grandpa narrowed his eyes in thought. "Make sure he gets some milk, Casey. Boys need milk."

Casey glanced in our direction and schlepped toward the living room. "I'm done playing restaurant. He's Cherry's guest. She can get him milk."

"Hunter, I thought about calling Miss Marion," I said, ignoring the milk request. "But today's the viewing and funeral. Did you want to go?"

He wrinkled his nose while shoveling a bit of gravy drenched biscuit into his mouth. "No."

"Do you think your mom will go? Maybe I could pay my respects to Mrs. Maynard and look for Janine. If I could talk to your momma before the police find her, that'll help."

Grandpa squinted at me. "I thought Will said something about you keeping clear of this mess."

"It's a funeral, sir." I gave him my best salesman smile. "What could happen?"

THIRTY-EIGHT

Janine Adams did not show at the viewing. I paid my sympathy to Miss Marion, who seemed surprised at my bruised countenance and disturbed by my attire. My chin and scraped lip probably dropped me a couple notches down the social ladder onto the riff-raff rung. I made it worse by wearing the purple fringed sundress, but considering the state of my remaining dresses, it couldn't be helped. I certainly wasn't wearing the ass-pot dress again.

During the funeral, I hung out in the parking lot of the Episcopal Church, idling the Datsun so she wouldn't stall out. The church lot overflowed with vehicles from Sidewinder. Plenty of folks eager to pay their civic duty to the home-wrecked matriarch of the town. The sheriff's team had sent some representatives to the services as well. Luckily, I didn't recognize the officers and hoped they didn't know my yellow pickup.

By the time the funeral lunch began I had given up on Janine's attendance. My next destination would be the Maynards' farm. If Janine was too chicken to attend the funeral, she might use Marion's absence to pack up the apartment in privacy. Last stop would be the Gables' since their departure might also be a plus for Janine. After that, Hunter would have to trust the police to find her. Or I'd talk him into confessing to Uncle Will. And hoped he wouldn't be too hard on the boy.

I drove through the beautiful cotton blossom gate and followed the lane toward the Maynard place. At the education center and sales office, I left the Datsun's engine running and ran around to the side of the building. Stairs led to the second floor apartment. I scampered up the steps and beat on the door to no answer. After peering through the apartment window, I decided I was not beyond a breaking and entering. A key hiding at the top of the door jamb helped me to skip the breaking part. I took it as a good sign.

"Janine?" I called and stepped inside the apartment.

Someone had spent a lot of money for a place that should have been a glorified bonus room. Granite counters and stainless steel appliances graced a kitchen open to a living room with plush, modern furniture. I wrinkled my nose at the Richard Nagle knockoffs and detoured to the bedrooms.

The first revealed a mess of nudie magazines, tobacco cans, clothes, and video game equipment. I closed the door on the smell of Hunter's sweat-socks and moved on to the next bedroom. The headboard of the king size bed aligned with Hunter's bedroom wall. The thought of his mother and Lewis entertaining each other with the child next door made my stomach hurt. The mess of slick sheets and flattened pillows showed someone might have slept there, but I couldn't determine when. I glanced in the walk-in closet. Clothes packed the walls and covered the floor. I pawed through the mess and found suitcases.

With Janine's obvious lack of housekeeping, it was hard to tell if she still lived here or had taken off. She obviously hadn't heeded Marion's warning to pack up and get out. I left the bedroom and approached the master bath. If Janine had left, she would have taken her makeup and hair stuff. Women liked Janine wouldn't leave without their beauty kits.

The marble and granite tiled bath would have been impressive if Janine had cleaned it. Her makeup littered the counter. Still, the mess made it hard to know if she had run. But if she still lived at the apartment, Hunter wouldn't have thought her missing.

I left the apartment confused. The Datsun would run out of gas soon, and I needed enough to make it back to the farm. I hopped in the rusty truck and headed toward the fancy entrance gate. A quick perusal of the Gables' place before heading back to Halo, then let the police do their job. I felt I somehow let Hunter down, but he had to face his sins, accidental or not.

As I turned onto the county road, a black sedan approached and slowed, readying to turn through the Cotton Pickin' gates. The darkened windows didn't show the driver, but I guessed Marion. She didn't get many visitors.

Anxious to find Janine, I accelerated down the road instead of stopping for a neighborly chat. I hurried the truck, chewing my busted lip as the gas gauge dipped.

"Last stop," I said to the Datsun as we turned down the corn packed lane of High Cotton Farm. "Then we go back to Grandpa's, borrow some farm gas, and you can cool off under the oak."

Tall stalks and the long gravel lane extended along my horizon. A rush of wind pushed through the corn, and I shivered at the emerald wave of razor-tipped leaves. The lane emptied into the blacktopped clearing ready to handle parking for the nonexistent cotton education center. I drove past the framed shell of the museum and stopped before the red barn. A yawning gap stood between the large, rolling doors. No self-respecting farmer would leave his farm in July, let alone forget to close and lock his barn doors. He may as well have left his house unlocked. I kept the truck running and hopped out to glance into the barn.

Hunter's beater truck rested inside.

My hunch had been correct. Janine must have gotten wind of her sister leaving town and decided to squat for a few days. I stomped to the Datsun and drove across the parking area to the brick house. I had a few words to say to the woman whose son broke into my home so as not to sleep alone in his mother's den of iniquity. If Hunter poisoned these people, I hoped the defense would do some finger pointing at Janine.

With a glance at the gas gauge, I cut off the engine. Explaining Hunter's situation to Janine may take time, and I had better wait out an overheated engine than run out of gas in the middle of Children of the Corn country. I hopped from the truck and strode to the front door. I pressed the doorbell, then buzzed it twenty more times just to irritate the woman. After a few minutes wait, I cursed and stalked to the fence. The high latch gave me a struggle, but I opened the gate and propped it with a nearby rock. Skirting the crater for the swimming pool, I hiked across the churned earth to the patio. I peered through the sliding glass doors, yanked on the handle, and ripped a nail for my effort.

"Janine," I yelled, hammering on the glass, "I know you're in there. Hunter's in trouble. Open this door."

No response, which made me feel even less charitable toward the woman.

"Dammit." I turned to tramp back to the gate.

Picking my way through the yard, I tripped over a stake that marked a flower bed. I stood up, dusted my hands, and felt some pity for the Gables and the money pit of their garden. If they hadn't banked on grants for their cotton museum, they would have had a small piece of backyard paradise. The Gables took a big gamble and lost to Janine and the Cotton Pickin' Good Estate.

Maybe Belinda Gable was correct. Perhaps Janine was no promotion genius, but had stolen the marketing ideas from the Gables. And maybe Lewis had stolen the Gables' recipe for the Brunswick Stew cook-off. Janine and Lewis deserved each other as connivers and cheaters. They had certainly trampled on the innocent. The Gables, Miss Marion, and poor Hunter. A child turned serial poisoner.

My irritation with Janine led me away from the house to march across the steaming blacktop to the open barn. Now I had to wait for the Datsun to cool down. I would get the license plate number from Hunter's truck and report her location to the sheriff's office. Anonymously.

I slipped through the cracked barn door and stood before the old Chevy pickup. I noted the plates, then glanced in the back. A large, plastic jug, half-filled with liquid, sat in the bed. Having grown up on a farm, I recognized the size, square shape and label as a kind of chemical treatment for weeds or pests. Why Hunter would

have it in his truck gave me pause, unless this was the noxious sub-
stance slipped into the stew. He could have bought the stuff at a
farm store or stolen it from Cotton Pickin's supply. But why not
something easier to haul around? Something less complicated?

I hoisted myself into the bed to get a better look at the herbicide. Careful not to touch the jug itself, I peered at the sticker for a
moment. According to the caution label, the stuff would kill weeds
found in cotton fields and make a person real sick. Unless Hunter
was a total idiot, he would know the herbicide was lethal.

The poisoning couldn't be accidental.

"Holy crap. I left a killer at my Grandpa's farm." I needed to
call Uncle Will. I patted my dress, searching for the pocket that hid
my phone. And remembered the fringed dress had no pockets.

My phone was still in the truck. I shot to standing and the
truck rocked beneath me. I steadied myself with a hand to the back
of the cab and glanced in the rear window.

Slumped along the bench seat lay Janine Adams.

And she looked pretty dead.

THIRTY-NINE

My hands flew off the cab. I stepped backward, tripped over the herbicide jug, and fell on my rear. The truck's suspension jounced and the liquid sloshed in the bottle. I scrambled out of the truck and had a quick freak-out dance in the musty barn.

"Shit. Shit. Shit," I screamed, then crept to the window of the truck cab.

Janine lay face down on the bench seat, her blonde hair scattered and limbs askew. From my tip-toe view, there was no way to tell what killed her, and I wasn't about to open the door to find out. I spun on my toes to high-tail it out of the barn and stopped at the low rumble of a vehicle's slow approach.

I sped to the gap in the barn door and peeked. The dark sedan from Cotton Pickin' place circled the drive. My truck was parked near the house, about one hundred yards away. I needed my phone. But the Lexus's crawl around the drive jangled my nerves. Why would Miss Marion—if she did indeed drive that car—follow me here? I glanced back at Hunter's truck and shuddered.

The black car rolled to a stop before the barn. I back stepped into the shadows. Call me crazy, but I didn't want to get caught with a dead body. The large, dusty barn had walls full of tools and equipment, but no other door I could see. A tractor blocked my view of the far wall. I scurried toward the tractor hoping for a door hidden in the back. The barn door bumped at someone's push through, and I slid behind the tractor, hunching behind a big tire.

Miss Marion's shadowy figure stood between the heavy barn doors, lit by the sunshine falling through the gap.

"I know you're in here," she said and stepped into the shadow of the door.

Marion had changed from her black dress into what my Grandma Jo would call "weed-pulling attire." And she had swapped her pearls for a new accessory. The sunlight pouring through the door glinted off the barrel of a small handgun.

"Walk yourself over here, young lady," she called.

I stayed crouched and held my breath.

"You can't hide in here."

Unfortunately she was right. If only I hid in the machine shed, I could have secreted myself in a combine tire. I prepared to talk myself out of getting shot, but my body would not give up the crouch.

"Perhaps I'll just walk over and shoot you. I've got a pocketful of bullets," said Marion. "I can see the fringe of your ridiculous ensemble peeking from behind the tractor."

"I ruined three dresses this week," I said, rising from my stoop. "I'm sorry I didn't have anything more appropriate for the funeral."

"I don't believe fringe is ever appropriate. Unless you're attending a western function."

"Yes, ma'am," I said out of habit more than service. I treaded slowly toward her, my eyes on the derringer. "You don't need to point that at me."

"You didn't eat my brownies," Marion said.

"Sorry, no. I've been trying to help Hunter."

"You didn't let the boy eat them, did you?"

"The brownies? No." I stopped a few paces away.

"Where is Hunter? I'm worried about him. He didn't stay at Cotton Pickin' last night."

"He thinks he poisoned Mr. Maynard and Miss Parker," I said. "But he didn't, did he?"

"Obviously the Gables poisoned them."

"The Gables?"

"Why else would the truck be here? And the poison? You call yourself a detective? Can't you put two and two together?"

"I call myself an artist," I said and eyed the gun. "But I don't believe the Gables did this."

"You should have stuck to painting. Delivering evidence to the police, of all things." She waved the gun. "You should have eaten those brownies, too. The bowl and mix are in the Gables kitchen now. Clear evidence, don't you think? Now what am I going to do with you?"

Considering that was most likely a hypothetical question, I kept my mouth shut.

"I didn't mean for Miss Parker to die. I know she was your friend," said Marion, apologetically. "Since Miss Janine didn't care enough about Lewis to eat his stew, I thought she'd at least care about Hunter to leave town in disgrace. Miss Parker was an unfortunate side effect."

"What are you saying? You only intended for Lewis to die?"

"Lewis has been ingesting a little weed killer with his stew every Sunday for months. I knew he'd taste enough of the stew during the cook-off that it'd send him right over the edge. I forced myself to eat the festival stew, but Daddy always said hard effort returns great rewards."

"You poisoned yourself along with everyone else. Including Griffin?"

"Odious man, Griffin Ward. You gave me that idea. If everyone thought he had poisoned the drinks, it would have worked out just fine. Although then I couldn't implicate the Gables, which would have been unfortunate."

"You poisoned Griffin's new batch of Genuine Juice."

"I didn't know he was going to drink it all. And he should lock his doors to keep folks from tampering with that vile stuff." She glared at me. "I heard you fought with him before he died. In the Viper's parking lot. You are as trashy as Belinda Gable and Janine Adams."

"I'm not trashy," I said, "I'm colorful."

She raised her pencil thin brows. "Call it what you want, but in my book it's trashy. Sidewinder has become nothing but a cesspool of whoremongers, sluts, and gossipers. Daddy Maynard would roll over in his grave to see what's become of our town."

I expect her daddy was rolling in his grave at the thought of his princess on a murderous rampage, but I held back that remark as well.

"Now walk your skinny little hiney to the truck. I don't want to shoot you. That's too obvious. I'll have to make you drink the weed killer."

"Like that's not obvious," I said, then bit my lip for not cutting the sass.

She pointed the derringer at me, grabbing her bony wrist to hold it steady. "But I will shoot you if I need to. This is a .357 and the recoil isn't as bad as people say. Daddy made sure I could defend myself. He said it's important to be self-reliant."

"Self-reliant? You got married. You had Lewis take your name."

"I needed an heir. Lewis knew cotton farming."

"But he didn't love you."

"I didn't need Lewis to love me," she cried. "I had Daddy!"

My face must have betrayed my internal "Eew."

Marion's expression went cold. "Get in that truck," she said. "Janine's in there."

Marion rolled her eyes. "What does that matter? Just shove her over."

I shuffled to the cab and opened the truck door. My stomach rolled. The stench in the closed cab overpowered me. I backed up and bumped into Marion.

"Get in the truck," she said and struck my hip with the barrel of her gun. The rotting smell drifted past me. Marion gagged.

I spun around, rammed her with my shoulder, and took off.

I made it to the barn door when the gun exploded. I heard a metallic crack, but didn't slow to see where the bullet hit. I knew that derringer had a double barrel. My aunt Linda had a Texas Defender she kept in her pocketbook. The hollow point bullets would stop me in my tracks. And Marion had one more round before reloading.

If she were smart, she wouldn't waste her remaining bullet on a difficult target. If I were lucky, she was a bad aim.

I ran through the doorway gap into the sunshine, zigzagging toward my truck. The tarmac stretched before me, shimmering in the heat. I heard another blast and flinched. When the bullet failed to hit, I gathered a spurt of energy and urged my flip-flops to move faster. My chest burned and my hip ached where Marion clouted me, but I could see my beautiful, lemon yellow truck as I closed the distance between us. I had never loved my Datsun more than at that moment.

Another fire from the gun almost made me stumble, but I righted myself and continued forward. I could now see the shotgun holes on the side of the truck that I had never patched. Twenty yards to go. Pain radiated from my chest, up into my shoulders, and down my arms. I hated running.

I heard the sharp blast from the gun just as the bullet zinged past my arm. I felt searing heat, but didn't stop. I had a chance. Marion would have to reload again.

I grabbed the handle, yanked the door open, and slid onto the seat of the truck. With shaking hands, I turned the key.

And nothing.

FORTY

"No," I screamed. "No. No. No."

I glanced out the window. Marion stood in the middle of the parking lot, reloading. I flipped around and leaned over the seat to grab my Remington. And realized I had left the shotgun beside my bed after finding Hunter in my house.

My expletive scared the birds off a nearby pecan tree.

I grabbed the phone out of my purse and slid out the passenger door. My lungs protested another run. I pushed myself toward the patio and hoped Bruce had left his baseball bat, because I was planning on smashing that patio door. Then I'd lock myself in a room and call the police.

I rounded the side of the house, praying Marion wouldn't wing me with a hollow point. The pool gate remained open. I had forgotten to move the rock. I could have kissed myself if I wasn't so intent on outrunning the crazy woman with the gun. I stumbled over the staked bed again, tripped up the patio stairs, and did a quick standing search for the baseball bat. I spied it behind a grill, dropped my phone on the patio table, and grabbed the bat. Then I battered the door.

Which did not shatter. But it did send a mighty reverberation up my arm.

I scared more birds with my scream of frustration and took off running again, this time holding the bat. I quickly ascertained I had pinned myself in a cage with a tall fence I could not climb. My lungs, angry with the constant running, wouldn't let me breathe to curse, and my arm felt as if it had been sprayed with hot grease. I hurdled the stakes and aimed for the giant pile of orange dirt left from the swimming pool on the far side of the yawning hole. Maybe I would get lucky and Marion wouldn't know I was still in the back yard.

Panting and wheezing, I put my back against the small mountain of dirt and peered around the side. Marion stalked through the open gate and glanced at the unfinished landscaping.

"Where are you?" she called. Obviously Miss Marion didn't play hide-n-seek as a kid.

I reached for my phone. And remembered I still didn't have pockets. My phone remained somewhere on the patio.

Marion paced to the patio and tried the door without success. Placing a hand over her eyes, she surveyed the yard. I ducked behind the dirt, careful to gather my fringe. I held my breath. I couldn't risk a peek, but I could hear Marion mumbling to herself as she stumbled through the garden.

"The things I have to do," said Miss Marion. "And this clay will get all over my shoes."

I stood in a half-crouch, bat in hand. I'd go out swinging.

But I lost my nerve and swung the bat behind me as Marion followed the gun around the corner of the dirt pile.

She shook her head. "If you had just eaten the brownies, this business would be done. Come out of there."

She backed up, keeping the derringer trained on me.

I followed, holding the bat behind me. I fought my eyes to stay on Marion's face and not on the swimming pool hole we approached.

Just as she reached the edge of the pool, she stopped.

I silently cursed her good backing instincts.

"I don't think that bat will do you much good." She glanced at the crater beside us. "Maybe this will work. If I shot you and you fell in this hole, maybe they'll think the Gables did it. If there was only a loader or some such machinery to cover you up."

"You are something else," I said, hoping to distract her from the bat I still held. "No wonder you have no friends in this town. You do have good planning skills, though. I'll give you that."

"Any last words?"

"I wish I carried concealed," I said. "And I wish I didn't wear flip-flops so much. I can run better in boots."

"I meant a final prayer. Ladies shouldn't wear flip-flops in public. They're meant to be shower shoes. Although, the beach is acceptable."

"I also wear white before Memorial Day."

She narrowed her eyes and aimed the gun at my head.

"One last thing," I said. "If you could find some way to tell Deputy Luke Harper I'm sorry. I really do love him and didn't want to give him ulcers. And Max Avtaikin has your brownies, so you've got another poisoning on your hands. He thinks he's impervious to poison, but I'm carrying a load of guilt about accidentally killing him. It might hinder my heaven-bound status. Although I did go to church this week, which should help."

She tipped the gun away. "You gave my brownies to Mr. Max?"

"I didn't know you were trying to kill me with them!"

"How could you? Mr. Max is a dear. I don't believe in bingo. It's a form of gambling. A horrible vice practiced by people like the Gables. But Mr. Max's done much for the Ladies Auxiliary, which I support."

"Good Lord. I can't escape Max's minions, even at my own shooting."

"You are incorrigible."

"So I've been told," I said and held my breath, as she steadied the gun. I clutched the bat with my right hand and held my left hand before me. "You really don't have to do this."

She pushed the safety button with her thumb. On the patio table, my phone rang a shrill verse of "Do You Think My Tractor's Sexy." Marion glanced over her shoulder. I swung my bat. And she squeezed the trigger.

The gun's fire cracked the air. I felt my hair stir, but I stayed with the swing. The bat struck her arm, and the gun flew. I dove at Marion's knees. We fell into the dirt, and I held her legs while she kicked and shrieked. An arsenal of bullets rolled out of her pockets, scattering across the ground. I drew up to grab her arms, and she pulled her legs back and kicked me hard in the gut. I rolled over, clutching my stomach.

Marion scooted back, stopping just as her bottom touched air at the edge of the hole. Realizing her placement, she grabbed the crumbling ledge.

I slid forward and kicked her shins. As she swung her hands up to stop me, the ground beneath her gave away. Her arms wind-milled and caught air. She toppled backward with her legs kicking. One of her shoes landed on the orange earth next to me. I hopped up and looked over the edge. Marion lay on her side, breathing hard.

I spun and ran for the patio.

Snatching my phone from the table, I dialed 911, reported our location, and the fact that Marion Maynard had just tried to kill me. Which the dispatcher did not want to believe.

And as I jabbered on the phone like a gibbon on crack, the blast of the gun's remaining shot burst from the backyard pit.

I sat wrapped in a blanket on the Gables' patio and watched the EMTs and policemen pull the stretcher out of the giant hole. Uncle Will knelt before me with a hand on my knee, which he occasionally squeezed.

"Did you get a hold of Max?" I said for the hundredth time. My brain seemed to be stuck in a holding pattern.

"He didn't eat the brownies. Remember, he threw them away? Didn't trust you as a cook," Will forced a chuckle. "An officer's on their way to pick them up. Max said he doesn't want you to worry. Thought your concern was sweet."

"And Hunter," I repeated. "Is Hunter okay?"

"Sugar, I told you your Grandpa Ed is watching over him. We'll figure out Hunter's situation. It's time you get to the hospital and have that arm looked at."

"Did you find Janine?" I stopped, interrupted by a shouting match.

Will drew up and turned to check the argument by the gate. A deputy stood blocking the entrance while Luke hurled profanities at him. I shrank back in my chair. Leaving me with a pat on my shoulder, Will ambled toward the gate.

"Harper, we're processing the scene. You know the rules."

"Where is she?" Luke said, his voice grating against Will's calm.

"Cherry's in shock. And on her way to the hospital. You need to cool your jets, son."

"I told her to stay out of Sidewinder," he shouted.

"I told her the same thing," said Will, "but you know Cherry. She wanted to help Hunter. And she believed him when he said he poisoned the stew. She didn't think she'd be in danger."

"She could have been murdered," Luke's voice lowered, but the bite remained. "She doesn't think. And she doesn't listen to me."

"You are not helping, and I believe you are off duty," said Will. "Go home."

A tear dripped down my cheek. My arm hurt, so I let it continue its course rather than get rid of it.

"This was the last straw," Luke exploded. "One of these days she's going to get herself killed. That little fool-idiot."

That jerked me out of my stupor.

I hopped up and hollered back. "You take that back, Luke Harper. That's just plain ugly. And the next time I'm asked to give last words, they are certainly not going to be about you!"

FORTY-ONE

Sunlight poured through my picture window and danced across my sketchbook waiting for brilliance. Normally, I'd be inspired by the good light. But my creativity had as much vigor as a wounded snail. I ducked out of Sunday dinner at the farm to avoid my family's remarks about my encounter with crazy Marion and my guilt over Hunter's mom. It's a peculiar feeling hating someone who was murdered. I excused myself with my one day deadline to create a masterpiece for the classical exhibition.

Three canvases leaned against the wall behind me. Stretched, gessoed, and disappointingly blank. I seemed to be out of luck. I would disappoint Eloise. Her professor wouldn't respect me, and I wouldn't be able to convince him to give her a final show. That I really needed to place some art in that gallery call in order to pay my bills didn't bother me nearly as much as my failure in Eloise's final request.

I rubbed my arm below the bandage and thought about my meager remains from my last commission. I sold no paintings at the festival and wasted a lot of money the past week on sympathy donuts and bribery barbecue. Flipping a page on my sketchpad, I grabbed a B pencil and doodled a plate of waffles with a side of bacon. I wondered if they made Waffle House uniforms in my size.

A knock on my door brought me out of my absorption. I hopped from my stool, padded across my living room, and tugged open the front door. Todd stood on my porch.

"Hey," he said, studying the big bandage on my forearm. "Are you okay?"

"I'm okay. I didn't really get shot," I said. "And I'm taking ibuprofen by the bushel."

"I feel bad." He followed me into the house. "I got mad at you and left you alone. I should have stuck around."

"You know me." I shrugged. "I don't listen to anyone. I tick everyone off. And I made you lose your job at Mr. Max's."

"Aw, Cherry. I'm not chafing anymore. I'll get another job."

Todd's hug made my arm hurt, but I enjoyed his forgiveness. He kissed the top of my head and pulled away.

"I heard you need a model," he said.

My eyes widened. "Really? You'd do that for me?"

"You know I would."

"I won't body paint you right away. But you'll need to strip. The Greeks liked their men nude."

"No problem, baby."

"I'll get you a towel," I said and scampered to the bathroom. On the way back, I popped into my bedroom to grab my copy of Gardner's *Art Through the Ages* and flipped to the *Dying Gaul*. I could do a quick series of sketches and leave the Greek letters for later. Then I'd draw Todd as the *Discobolos* and the *Seated Boxer*. A triptych covering the Classical and Hellenistic periods. I would pull an all-nighter. Do an acrylic of each, using an oil stick for the letters, photograph them, and send the results to Eloise's professor in the morning.

My mind full of poses, color, and logistics, I stopped in the archway to my living room and gawked. Todd had kicked off his carpenter shorts and t-shirt and stood in all his lean, muscled glory.

"Gah," I said and dropped the book.

"Baby, you okay? Can you draw with your arm busted up?"

"Maybe you should step away from the window." I bent over to pick up the book. My lips throbbed, but they had learned their lesson. They had played with fire and been burned. I was now most definitely single. No question about it. Stupid lips.

I showed Todd the picture of the *Dying Gaul* statue, then turned my back while I readied my sketchbook and charcoal. I glanced over my shoulder and winced at Todd's elegant pose on the floor. He leaned on one arm with his head dipped in anguish, one leg bent, the other extended.

A perfect obtuse triangle. And, thankfully, with a strategically draped towel.

"So I heard Hunter is staying at the farm," said Todd with the nonchalance of a person accustomed to immodesty.

"Just temporarily," I said, doing my best not to look at the towel. "Poor kid. He spit tobacco in the stew and thought he poisoned everyone. He's grieving his mother and is in shock over Miss Marion. The Gables might take him in, though. They're working through their own pain."

"You did right to help him."

I nodded my thanks while the charcoal zipped over the bumpy surface of the paper. Composition filled my thoughts. I tried a front-view arrangement, flipped the page, and drew Todd from another angle.

"You still got that wallop on your chin," said Todd, after a few minutes. "Why did Shawna sock you in the jaw?"

"No idea." I turned to my tackle box for a bigger piece of charcoal. With an X-Acto knife, I sliced one round end into a point. "She's accused me of messing up her festival, and she wants to keep me from talking, of all things. I know I have a big mouth, but I guess she fears me talking about something specific. Maybe my thoughts on her becoming the pillar of the arts community."

I thought a minute about Shawna's manic behavior toward me of late and tapped my forehead with the charcoal. "I believe she's just plain crazy. And maybe jealous. Although she's got no reason for that now."

"What do you mean she's got no reason to be jealous?"

Leave it to Todd to take an entire pontification and ask about the one off-hand remark I didn't want to talk about. I screwed my lips tight.

"You have a funny habit of eating your lips when you don't want to tell me something." He stood to stretch. The towel dropped to the floor.

"Gah," I said.

"What's wrong?"

"I'm not ready for the discus pose." My cheeks flared. I looked at the broken charcoal I had squeezed into pieces and quickly changed the subject. "Good Lord, Todd. What's with the twenty questions?"

"I want to know why Casey said you couldn't kiss Luke anymore."

"And I want to know if you were playing poker in Mr. Max's pool house the other day."

I caught a flicker in his eye. Todd's eyes normally didn't flicker.

"Are you playing as a ringer?" I circled around the easel to face him. "You're duping Max's rich friends into thinking you're lucky at cards. And I bet you're splitting the winnings with the Bear. Lowdown, double-crossing, dirty-dealing..."

"Aww, Cherry." Todd strode forward, his hands held out in supplication. "You think I would do something like that?"

"Yes, I do. And Mr. Max would, too." I fixed my eyes on his face and not on other parts. "Don't give me that ol' shucks routine. You snooker people into thinking you're dumb, don't you? It's how you win. Is that what you're doing with me?"

At the creak of the screen door, we turned toward the sound.

"Cherry?" Luke called. He stepped over the threshold, cellophane-wrapped grocery store roses in his hand. His sharp gray eyes lighted on our scene.

Me in my wife-beater paint shirt that hid my cutoffs.

And Todd in his birthday suit, his arms open and hands stretching toward me.

I glanced at the towel on the ground and then up at the grin on Todd's face.

I really needed to consider switching to landscapes.

READER'S DISCUSSION GUIDE

1. Does Cherry have good reasons to get involved in the investigation? What about Luke's feelings about her interference?

2. Red called Cherry a "relationship self-sabotager" and said that her inability to commit "attracts men like sugar ants to peanut butter." Do you agree with his assessment? Why or why not?

3. Cherry chooses different friends or family to help with various missions. How does she match the person to the event?

4. In what ways has Cherry's mother still played a role in the lives of the siblings? What do you think they need to do to find closure?

5. What do you think of Uncle Will's role in the siblings' lives? What do you think he knows about Cherry's mother?

6. Do you think Cherry has a personal vendetta against Max Avtaikin? If not, what are her real feelings for him?

7. What role do you see Pearl playing in the Tuckers' future?

8. Have you ever known a Shawna? Can you suggest some reasons on why she hates Cherry?

9. Do you think Cherry is a vigilante? What kind of people does she seek to help and why?

10. What do you think will happen to Cherry's relationship with Luke? With Todd?

11. What predications can you make about Cherry's next adventure?

LARISSA REINHART

Larissa Reinhart loves small town characters, particularly sassy women with a penchant for trouble. *Still Life in Brunswick Stew* is the second in the Cherry Tucker Mystery Series. The first, *Portrait of a Dead Guy*, is a 2012 Daphne du Maurier finalist, a 2012 The Emily finalist, and a 2011 Dixie Kane Memorial winner.

She lives near Atlanta with her minions and Cairn Terrier, Biscuit. Visit her website, her expat blog, or find her chatting with the Little Read Hens on Facebook.

Don't miss the FIRST book in
The Cherry Tucker Mystery Series

PORTRAIT of a DEAD GUY
by LARISSA REINHART

In Halo, Georgia, folks know Cherry Tucker as big in mouth, small in stature, and able to sketch a portrait faster than buck-shot rips from a ten gauge -- but commissions are scarce. So when the well-heeled Branson family wants to memorialize their murdered son in a coffin portrait, Cherry scrambles to win their patronage from her small town rival.

As the clock ticks toward the deadline, Cherry faces more trouble than just a controversial subject. Between ex-boyfriends, her flaky family, an illegal gambling ring, and outwitting a killer on a spree, Cherry finds herself painted into a corner she'll be lucky to survive

Available Now
For more details, visit www.henerypress.com

IF YOU LIKED THIS HENERY PRESS MYSTERY,
YOU MIGHT ALSO LIKE THESE...

BOARD STIFF

by Kendel Lynn

As director of the Ballantyne Foundation on Sea Pine Island, SC, Elliott Lisbon scratches her detective itch by performing discreet inquiries for Foundation donors. Usually nothing more serious than retrieving a pilfered Pomeranian. Until Jane Hatting, Ballantyne board chair, is accused of murder. The Ballantyne's reputation tanks, Jane's headed to a jail cell, and Elliott's sexy ex is the new lieutenant in town.

Armed with moxie and her Mini Coop, Elliott uncovers a trail of blackmail schemes, gambling debts, illicit affairs, and investment scams. But the deeper she digs to clear Jane's name, the guiltier Jane looks. The closer she gets to the truth, the more treacherous her investigation becomes. With victims piling up faster than shells at a clambake, Elliott realizes she's next on the killer's list.

Available Now
For more details, visit www.henerypress.com

FRONT PAGE FATALITY
by LynDee Walker

Crime reporter Nichelle Clarke's days can flip from macabre to comical with a beep of her police scanner. Then an ordinary accident story turns extraordinary when evidence goes missing, a prosecutor vanishes, and a sexy Mafia boss shows up with the headline tip of a lifetime.

As Nichelle gets closer to the truth, her story gets more dangerous. Armed with a notebook, a hunch, and her favorite stilettos, Nichelle races to splash these shady dealings across the front page before this deadline becomes her last.

Available Now
For more details, visit www.henerypress.com

Diners, Dives & DEAD ENDS
by Terri L. Austin

As a struggling waitress and part-time college student, Rose Strick-land's life is stalled in the slow lane. But when her close friend, Axton, disappears, Rose suddenly finds herself serving up more than hot coffee and flapjacks. Now she's hashing it out with sexy bad guys and scrambling to find clues in a race to save Axton before his time runs out.

With her anime-loving bestie, her septuagenarian boss, and a pair of IT wise men along for the ride, Rose discovers political corruption, illegal gambling, and shady corporations. She's gone from zero to sixty and quickly learns when you're speed-ing down the fast lane, it's easy to crash and burn.

Available Now
For more details, visit www.henerypress.com

Lowcountry BOIL
by Susan M. Boyer

Private Investigator Liz Talbot is a modern Southern belle: she blesses hearts and takes names. She carries her Sig 9 in her Kate Spade handbag, and her golden retriever, Rhett, rides shotgun in her hybrid Escape. When her grandmother is murdered, Liz high-tails it back to her South Carolina island home to find the killer.

She's fit to be tied when her police-chief brother shuts her out of the investigation, so she opens her own. Then her long-dead best friend pops in and things really get complicated. When more folks start turning up dead in this small seaside town, Liz must use more than just her wits and charm to keep her family safe, chase down clues from the hereafter, and catch a psychopath before he catches her.

Available Now
For more details, visit www.henerypress.com

DOUBLEWHAMMY
by Gretchen Archer

Davis Way thinks she's hit the jackpot when she lands a job as the fifth wheel on an elite security team at the fabulous Bellissimo Resort and Casino in Biloxi, Mississippi. But once there, she runs straight into her ex-ex husband, a rigged slot machine, her evil twin, and a trail of dead bodies. Davis learns the truth and it does not set her free—in fact, it lands her in the pokey.

Buried under a mistaken identity, unable to seek help from her family, her hot streak runs cold until her landlord Bradley Cole steps in. Make that her landlord, lawyer, and love interest. With his help, Davis must win this high stakes game before her luck runs out.

THE AMBITIOUS CARD

BY JOHN GASPARD

The life of a magician isn't all kiddie shows and card tricks. Sometimes it's murder. Especially when magician Eli Marks very publicly debunks a famed psychic, and said psychic ends up dead. The evidence, including a bloody King of Diamonds playing card (one from Eli's own Ambitious Card routine), directs the police right to Eli.

As more psychics are slain, and more King cards rise to the top, Eli can't escape suspicion. Things get really complicated when romance blooms with a beautiful psychic, and Eli discovers she's the next target for murder, and he's scheduled to die with her. Now Eli must use every trick he knows to keep them both alive and reveal the true killer.

Available August 2013
For more details, visit www.henerypress.com

CROPPED to death

by CHRISTINA FREEBURN

Former US Army JAG specialist, Faith Hunter, returns to her West Virginia home to work in her grandmothers' scrapbooking store determined to lead an unassuming life after her adventure abroad turned disaster. But her quiet life unravels when her friend is charged with murder, and Faith inadvertently supplied the evidence.

So Faith decides to cut through the scrap and piece together what really happened. With a sexy prosecutor, a determined homicide detective, a handful of sticky suspects and a crop contest gone bad, Faith quickly realizes if she's not careful, she'll be the next one cropped.

Available Now
For more details, visit www.henerypress.com

CPSIA information can be obtained at www.ICGtesting.com
Printed in the USA
LVOW11s0014160816

500516LV00001B/50/P